PRAISE FO

"A breathtaking examination of women and science, Tea Cooper's *The Naturalist's Daughter* is a stunning entry on the roster of Australian historical fiction. With deftly crafted prose and a compelling cast of characters, this is a must-read for any fans of Marie Benedict or Tracy Enerson Wood. A true gem."

—Aimie K. Runyan, bestselling author of *Mademoiselle Eiffel* and *The Memory of Lavender and Sage*

"An exciting, moving and satisfying read."

—*Books+Publishing* for *The Naturalist's Daughter*

"An engrossing narrative... fabulous."

—Peter FitzSimons for *The Naturalist's Daughter*

"Cooper is a welcome inclusion to the rising ranks of female-centered historical Australian novels. The touch of Gothic romance adds to the fun."

—*The Herald Sun* for *The Naturalist's Daughter*

"I've loved all of this author's historical fiction novels, but must say this one is her best in my opinion. Highly recommended."

—Brenda Telford for *The Naturalist's Daughter*

"Cooper skillfully brings these settings to life. Verity flies around Sydney on her bicycle, trying to make a place for herself in a man's world. Clarrie and Sid struggle in Morpeth, living where they work, trying to be a family when their salaries aren't enough to support a single person. Through the excursions of Theodora and Redmond, the author brings to life the natural environment of the eastern coast of Australia: the birds, water, plants, and strange arrival of the Monarch butterfly . . . The several plot threads keep your attention and weave together into an exciting conclusion."

—*Historical Novel Society* for *The Butterfly Collector*

"The immersive latest from Cooper (*The Fossil Hunter*) interweaves two historical narratives linked by butterflies and family bonds . . . Cooper melds fictional lives, scientific history, and social issues into a compassionate story. This will please fans of historicals with smart women protagonists."

—*Publishers Weekly* for *The Butterfly Collector*

"Delightful and intriguing, this gentle story of love, loss and betrayal set in Australia's Hunter Valley is based on real events and characters including a major entomological discovery."

—Rhys Bowen, *New York Times* bestselling author of *The Venice Sketchbook*, for *The Butterfly Collector*

"An enthralling, unforgettable story of heartbreak and hope, featuring equally compelling dual timelines, dynamic heroines, and a twisty mystery spanning generations. Tea Cooper's latest historical stunner is not to be missed."

—Lee Kelly and Jennifer Thorne, authors of *The Antiquity Affair*, for *The Butterfly Collector*

"Beautiful writing makes way for a beautiful story in *The Fossil Hunter* by Tea Cooper. With the same care a paleontologist unearths a fossil, Cooper has crafted a historical mystery that reveals itself layer by layer, piece by piece, and secret by secret. Highly entertaining and much recommended!"

—Jenni L. Walsh, *USA Today*
bestselling author of *Unsinkable*

"Cooper paints a fascinating portrait of two women rebelling in their own ways against the expectations society and their family has for them. Historical-fiction fans will delight in this romantic tale of family and long-held secrets."

—*Booklist* for *The Cartographer's Secret*

"Cooper gets to the heart of a family's old wounds, puzzles, and obsessions, while providing a luscious historical rendering of the landscape. This layered family saga will keep readers turning the pages."

—*Publishers Weekly* for
The Cartographer's Secret

"Tea Cooper's meticulous prose and deft phrasing delight the reader. This fascinating novel informs the reader about Australia's storied past."

—*Historical Novel Society* for
The Cartographer's Secret

"*The Cartographer's Secret* is a galvanizing, immersive adventure following a family's entanglement with a vanished Australian explorer through the lush Hunter Valley at the turn of the twentieth century."

—Joy Callaway, bestselling author
of *What the Mountains Remember*

"In *The Cartographer's Secret*, Cooper invites readers into another sweeping tale full of her signature mix of mystery, history, romance, and family secrets."

—Katherine Reay, bestselling author of *The London House*

"Deeply researched. Emotional. Atmospheric and alive. Combining characters that are wonderfully complex with a story spanning decades of their lives, *The Girl in the Painting* is a triumph of family, faith, and long-awaited forgiveness."

—Kristy Cambron, bestselling author of *The Italian Ballerina*

"A stunning historical timepiece . . . With a touch of mystery and an air of romance, this new novel from one of Australia's leading historical fiction specialists will leave you amazed."

—*Mrs B's Book Reviews*, Australia, for *The Girl in the Painting*

"Cooper has fashioned a richly intriguing tale."

—*Booklist* for *The Woman in the Green Dress*

"Refreshing and unique, *The Woman in the Green Dress* sweeps you across the wild lands of Australia in a thrilling whirl of mystery, romance, and danger."

—J'nell Ciesielski, author of *The Brilliance of Stars*

"Readers of Kate Morton and Beatriz Williams will be dazzled. *The Woman in the Green Dress* spins readers into an evocative world of mystery and romance in this deeply researched book by Tea Cooper."

—Rachel McMillan, author of *The Mozart Code*

The Naturalist's Daughter

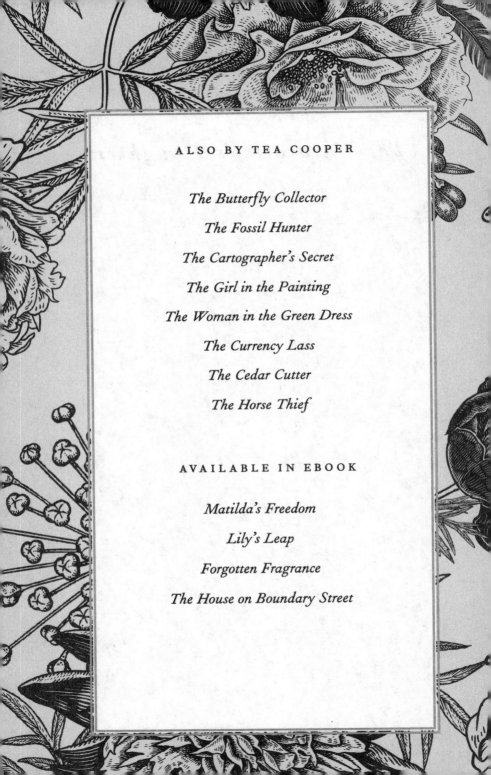

ALSO BY TEA COOPER

The Butterfly Collector

The Fossil Hunter

The Cartographer's Secret

The Girl in the Painting

The Woman in the Green Dress

The Currency Lass

The Cedar Cutter

The Horse Thief

AVAILABLE IN EBOOK

Matilda's Freedom

Lily's Leap

Forgotten Fragrance

The House on Boundary Street

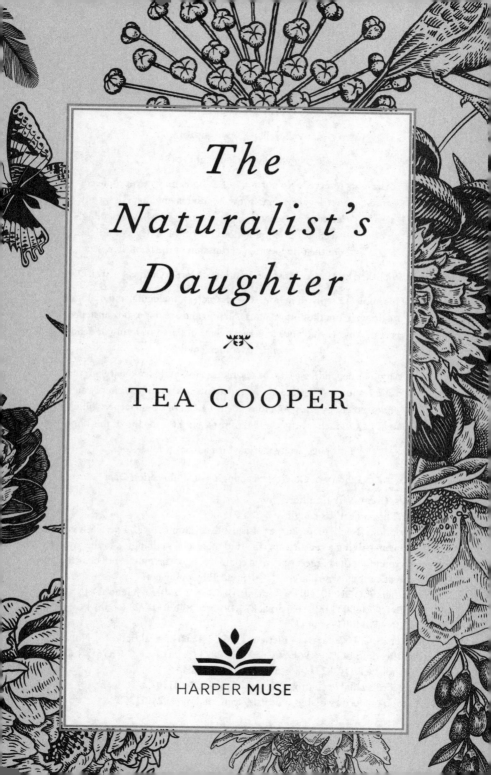

The Naturalist's Daughter

TEA COOPER

HARPER MUSE

The Naturalist's Daughter

First Australian Paperback Edition 2018

ISBN 9781489242426

Published by Harper Muse, an imprint of HarperCollins Focus LLC.

Title page art by marinavorona from Adobe Stock

Library of Congress Cataloging-in-Publication Data

Names: Cooper, Tea, author.
Title: The naturalist's daughter / Tea Cooper.
Description: [Nashville] : Harper Muse, 2024. | Summary: "Two fearless women—living a century apart—find themselves entangled in the mystery surrounding the biggest scientific controversy of the nineteenth century: the classification of the platypus"—Provided by publisher.
Identifiers: LCCN 2024011307 (print) | LCCN 2024011308 (ebook) | ISBN 9781400344710 (paperback) | ISBN 9781400344727 (epub) | ISBN 9781400344734
Subjects: LCSH: Platypus--Fiction. | LCGFT: Historical fiction. | Novels.
Classification: LCC PR9619.4.C659 N38 2024 (print) | LCC PR9619.4.C659 (ebook) | DDC 823/.92—dc23/eng/20240311
LC record available at https://lccn.loc.gov/2024011307
LC ebook record available at https://lccn.loc.gov/2024011308

Printed in the United States of America

24 25 26 27 28 LBC 5 4 3 2 1

For the storyteller's daughter, and Cooper

Nullius in verba.—*"Take no one's word for it."*

Author's Note

In a commitment to historical accuracy this novel employs the language of its era and historical setting, and in some instances reflects the prejudices and norms of that time. This commitment to accurately reflect the norms of the time period is in no way meant to offend nor to reflect the thoughts of the author.

Chapter 1

AGNES BANKS, NEW SOUTH WALES
1808

Rose loved Pa's dusty workroom filled to overflowing with notebooks and samples, paints and charcoals. A treasure chest of strange and wonderful objects. A charred boomerang; the tall, tall seed head from the shaggy grass tree; a huge *oh-don't-touch* emu's egg painted with careful patterns, more tiny dots than even she could count. Collected heads of banksia, their knotted faces leering; the beautiful curling tail feather of a bulln-bulln; and in the center of the worn table, her most favorite of all—the mallangong. Once it lived and breathed until Bunji's pa speared it out in the billabong. Now it sat, preserved for all eternity. That's what Pa said—*preserved*. She ran her hand over the dark brown fur and touched its funny little beak.

Pa rose from the chair, his brown face wrinkling as he smiled his special smile. "Shall we go down to the river, my heart?"

A trickle of excitement ran through her. She'd sat quietly waiting all afternoon for him to say those very words. "Yes, please, Pa."

"Put on your boots before you tell your mother we are off."

She rammed her feet into her clodhoppers, leaving the long laces trailing, and hoisted her knapsack carefully onto her back. Pa's supplies were precious. How she loved the wooden box with its tiny blocks of paint and brushes wrapped in fine linen. Pa promised she'd have her own paintbox when she was bigger, all her very own. Now she shared his and she had to be careful, so very careful not to break anything.

The box came from London a long time ago with Pa on the big ship when the colony was blackfellas' country. Now there were people everywhere—mostly convicts with their clattering, clanging chains and long, sad faces.

Some days Mam was sad too. She'd stare down the river and sigh as though she'd been waiting a long, long time, and every time Pa went to Sydney Town she asked him for a letter. When he shook his head, tears came to her eyes. One day she'd write her a letter so Pa could bring it back; maybe then Mam would smile.

"Mam, where are you? We're going to the river to see the mallangong."

Mam turned from her seat on the ground, her fingers dirty from scrabbling in the garden where she grew her medicine—herbs that made people well, helped birth their babies, fixed their fevers, and healed their cuts and bruises. That made Mam happy, but the letter sadness never left her eyes no matter how hard Rose tried to be a good girl.

"Tell your pa not to be late for tea. And don't forget to keep your hat and boots on. The sun's still strong."

"We can't come home too soon because the mallangong don't play until the sun goes down."

"You and your mallangong. I'm frightened one day I might lose you. You'll swim away and not come back to me, go and live with the mallangong."

She'd never do that, never leave Pa. Why would she do such a thing?

"Off you go now. That's your pa calling; he doesn't like to be kept waiting."

When Pa said he had two precious treasures brought to him by the piskies, it made Mam smile. A sad, faraway smile. Rose leaned over and brushed her lips against her mother's smooth cheek, wrinkling her nose when a curl of hair, black as black, tickled her face. "Bye, Mam."

Little puffs of dust rose at Rose's heels and her heart beat in time with her boots as she ran. The rain hadn't come, and it was hot and dry and dusty. Down by the river it would be cool, underneath the big gum where the fallen branch stretched its arms into the river. That's where the mallangong dug their burrows in the damp sand.

She skipped down the well-worn path. She was a big girl now and knew the way, but still Mam said never to go alone, not to go unless Pa was there. The blackfellas mightn't like it if she did. Mam was a silly fuss. Bunji and Yindi were her friends; they showed her all the secret paths up through the rocks where the grass trees grew and down to the swimming hole where it was never hot. Sometimes they laughed at her when she took off her hat and boots and tried to swim. Not her chemise; she never took off her chemise. Good girls didn't do that.

A jackass made her jump right off the path and almost fall into the long grass. She waved her fist at him. He didn't care. Just laughed and flew away.

She slowed and scuffed her feet. She hated her boots, hated them more than her pinny and her hat. Yindi didn't have to wear boots or a hat. She plonked down onto the ground and reefed off her boots, tying the strings together and hanging them over her shoulder, and tossed her hat into the scrub. Pa wouldn't notice. By the time she got to the river he'd have his easel set and his paints— Oh, his paints! No, he wouldn't. She had his paintbox in her pack.

Quick, quick. She must be quick. Her bare feet pattered on the dry earth as she leaped around the tough kangaroo grass. Not much grass now, only the bunches like tiny spearheads. The bulbs tasted delicious, soft and always juicy. Yindi's mam, Yukri, had shown her which ones to pull.

When she reached the big gum tree she skittered to a halt, her heart big and pattering hard. She loved Pa so much. His big, strong arms and rumbling voice made her safe. "I'm here, Pa." She waved and weaved along the track right to the edge of the billabong.

Pa raised his finger to his lips, then beckoned. He hadn't set up his easel yet; he stood staring across the gray-green water. "There's movement over there. Can you see it?" He took the pack from her back and settled it on the grass, then her boots. He didn't say anything about her bare feet, even though his lips made a funny shape as though he was eating his laugh. "Step lightly now. Shade your eyes with your hand, like this."

She peered across to the shadows beneath the roots of the big tree. Little ripples broke the top of the water. Then she saw it. A squeal jumped out of her mouth as the sleek, dark brown body dived and twisted.

"She's looking for food."

"Maybe she's got babies."

"Juveniles. Call them juveniles. See? Just above the waterline."

"Juveniles." She wrapped her tongue around the word, then squinted hard and moved her hand to and fro. "Yes, yes, there. I can see the hole into their burrow."

"Good girl. You watch carefully. Tell me what she does. I want to make a record."

"Can I make one too? Please, Pa, please."

He twisted one of her curls around his finger and tucked it behind her ear, not saying a word about her missing hat. Thank goodness.

Mam would be mad. Perhaps the jackass had made off with it by now.

"Sit down over there and I'll set you up. We must always record our evidence. It's the only way." He opened his paintbox and took out a little piece of charcoal. It was so precious and she mustn't waste it. Then he passed her little sketchbook to her from the pack. Squirming, she turned the pages past the first few drawings. They were baby drawings. Now she did better. She could make the mallangong's fur look wet or dry when she mixed the paint. Dark for wet and not so dark for dry, and she knew their fingers and their toes—webbed. She knew that word very well. And their bills, like a duck but not really; not hard and snappy like Mam's ducks but soft and bendy.

Pa sat down next to her, and his special smell of pipe and grass and scrunched-up leaves made her nose prickle. She turned her head to see his face, his deep brown skin almost like the blackfellas, with big creases around his eyes. He said they came when he was on the big ship and now they were even deeper, like the cracks in the sandstone rocks at the swimming hole. Maybe he was getting old. That made her goosey even though the sun was still shining. Bunji's grandfather was very old and he'd died. She'd snuck through the trees and seen the corroboree. Big bonfires, the dancing stomp of the feet making her chest bounce.

"So where is your drawing?"

Chewing her lip, she studied the empty page.

Hands laced, thumbs circling, Pa waited while she drew the outline and shaded it with a crosshatch of fine lines to bring the mallangong to life, just as he'd shown her.

"I think you've been dreaming. Here's my picture."

The riverbank, the tree, and there the little hole, the door to the burrow and the mallangong swimming through the water fast, so fast it left arrows on the surface. And then another diving deep.

"I didn't see two. Were there two?"

"No, my heart, just one. I wanted to show Sir Joseph one diving down. Why do you think they dive so deep?"

She knew the answer and Pa knew it too, but he liked to ask her questions just to make sure. "They push their bills along the sand at the bottom of the river, sucking up the fishes and"—she moved her lips and tongue into place—"crustaceans."

"Crustaceans, very good. And what are they?"

"Maybe prawns and other shellfish. If they're very hungry, mallangongs can eat half of themselves."

"I don't think they eat themselves." Pa's big, deep, rumbling laugh made her laugh too. But then it flew away and she frowned. He was teasing. She scowled back at him. "He eats half as much as he is heavy. There."

"That's right. You're such a clever girl. One day you will know all there is to know about these special creatures and I will take you to meet Sir Joseph. You can tell him and his fine friends all about *Ornithorhynchus paradoxus*. Would you like that?"

She rolled the words around in her mouth, her lips fighting the slippery rhythmical sounds. "*Ornithorhynchus paradoxus*. What's *paradoxus*?"

"It's an old word, from the Latin. Something that is contradictory, against common belief, differing from what people believe is true."

"But the mallangong is true. He's here. We see him almost every day."

"Indeed we do, indeed we do." Pa stared out across the water and tapped his charcoal stick against his teeth, the way he always did when he was thinking.

"Where does Sir Joseph live?"

"In London, in a very fine house."

London! That meant a ship, a ship with big white sails, not like the lighters that traveled up and down the river with their flapping square of ragged canvas. A voyage across the ocean. As long as Pa was with her, she might like that. "Can Mam come too?"

"No, Mam must stay here."

"Why? That's not fair. She'll be lonely if we leave her."

"Such a wise head on these young shoulders." He hugged her close, making his sketchbook fall to the ground. "You're right. She would be lonely. I was only dreaming."

"Mam says we mustn't be home too late or our tea will spoil." She bent over and picked up his open sketchbook, keeping her fingers right on the edge the way he'd told her, then blew across the paper so the charcoal wouldn't smudge.

He took it from her and gazed out across the river. The sun was setting and the mallangongs had gone home. "You're a good girl, and I love you and your mother very, very much. I will never leave her. Not after all she's lost."

What had Mam lost? Perhaps she could help find it. Then maybe Mam would smile. Everyone felt miserable when they lost something.

Chapter 2

SYDNEY, AUSTRALIA
1908

Dust, ink and old paper, binding leather and hushed tones cocooned Tamsin Alleyn in a familiar tranquility. Beneath the muted hum of the incandescent lights, she took a deep breath, her heart hammering and her fingers itching to unwrap the package from London.

"I thought I might find you in here. Why don't you come and have a cup of tea?"

"I just want to open this. I think it's more of the correspondence from London that I requested." She snipped the string securing the brown paper, rolled it into a ball, and deposited it in the desk drawer with a flick. Funding was tight at the Public Library of New South Wales now they were working on the Mitchell bequest, and every little bit helped.

"Come along, hurry up."

She'd spent months writing letters, sending requests to the Royal Society asking for the return of the letters sent to Sir Joseph Banks from the early Australian naturalists. Dear God, let her hard work be rewarded.

"Bring your lunch. I've got something I want to talk to you about." Edna Williams left with a spring in her seventy-year-old step that Tamsin envied.

Not game to ask what it was Mrs. Williams wanted to talk about, she reluctantly left the unopened package and made her way down the corridor and up the stairs. She'd been so pushy about the correspondence, determined the letters should be returned to Australia where they belonged. Besides, the display for the museum had gone some way in dragging her out of the morass she'd waded through ever since she'd sold Mother and Father's house. Not because of the memories, more because there weren't any. Try as she might, she couldn't feel any connection with the past.

She shouldered open the door to the tearoom.

"I've made you my favorite, a Grey's tea with some lemon." Mrs. Williams patted the chair next to her, her dark, beady eyes darting like fireflies around the room and her buttoned boots tapping. "Do hurry up." The no-nonsense woman rarely showed a glimmer of impatience, yet today her feet were jiggling around like a young girl promised a strawberry ice. She was up to something.

What had she forgotten? The two librarians from the cataloguing department threw closed-mouthed smiles at her, a cloud of bemused expectancy almost visible above their heads. Whatever was afoot wasn't a secret.

"Right. I'm ready." Tamsin picked up her cup and inhaled the aroma of bergamot. Quite what Mrs. Williams could have to complain about, she had no idea. Ever since Tamsin had managed to wheedle her way into the job, she'd given it her all. Coming at the lowest point in her life, as she faced the daunting prospect of having inherited a bundle of worthless shares and a house she couldn't maintain, a salary of ninety-six pounds a year was not to be sneezed at.

"Are you up for a trip? It's fairly short notice, I'm afraid."

"A trip?" A trickle of anticipation worked its way across her shoulders and she concentrated on the slice of lemon swimming on the surface of the tea while she tried to look calm, responsible, and professional. Of course she was. It was exactly what she needed. The last time she'd left Sydney she'd been wrapped in a shawl, clutched in her mother's arms.

"You're the obvious candidate, given all your hard work with the Royal Society."

Her heart took up an irregular patter. Surely Mrs. Williams wasn't going to suggest she take a trip to England. Highly unlikely. The Blue Mountains would do. Somewhere she could shrug off the lead boots that still made every step an effort despite the job of her dreams. She still couldn't believe it. When she'd filled in the application form, she'd simply been flying a kite, a badly balanced, hastily tacked together kite at that. And she'd landed here firmly on her feet, working in this prestigious establishment with a history dating back to the 1820s. "Of course I am."

If she was lucky, a trip might get her out of the celebration at the Missionary Society. Even after all these years, it still hurt too much. She hadn't managed to come up with anything to say that would be deemed appropriate. What could she say to commemorate her parents' deaths? She hadn't seen them since they'd handed her into the care of the Sydney Ladies Academy the moment she turned ten. She had nothing but bitterness to offer.

"It's not too far, and you're about the only person who has sufficient understanding of the matter. We can cover the transport and accommodation costs if you're willing to stay at one of the local establishments."

It must be something important if they'd managed to find the money for an overnight stay. "I'm all ears."

"I received a letter from a Mrs. Quinleaven; she lives just outside a small town in the Hunter. She has a book she'd like to donate to the

Library. She's getting on a bit and wants to make sure it's delivered before it's too late. She has no faith in the postal service, and transport to the area is a little patchy."

Tamsin pushed her empty cup away, tapping her fingernail on the table. "The Hunter's not too bad. The train goes to Maitland. I could do the trip in a couple of days."

"We might have to consider a traveling companion. Is there anyone you would like to invite?"

Tamsin shook her head. It didn't require much thinking; there was no one she could ask, except perhaps her housekeeper, but the thought of any kind of close contact with Mrs. Birkenhead didn't fire her with enthusiasm. "I'm quite able to travel alone. It's not far."

"You really should pay more attention to these things. It's hardly appropriate for a young lady to be seen traveling alone."

Tamsin lowered her lids, mostly to cover the rolling of her eyes. "I think at the ripe old age of twenty-five I hardly classify as young. Besides, this is the twentieth century, not Regency England."

"I know, I know. I'm sure you're quite capable of managing. Please don't start on the New Woman claptrap. I'm an advocate, remember?"

"I won't, I promise. Now what exactly is this donation?" A library full of books she could understand, but one book? It must be something quite special. She leaned forward, resting her elbows on the table, her chin cupped in her hands.

"A sketchbook. Detailed anatomical line drawings and watercolors." Mrs. Williams's dramatic pause signaled something more. She lowered her voice and leaned closer. "We think it belonged to Winton."

"Charles Winton?" Winton the naturalist, one of the first to send Sir Joseph Banks detailed information about the platypus. One of the very men whose correspondence she'd requested from London. "How thrilling. Where did the sketchbook come from?"

"The usual sort of thing. Been in Mrs. Quinleaven's possession for years and she never bothered to do anything about it." Mrs. Williams gave a disdainful sniff as though incapable of believing anyone could be uninterested in such a legacy.

"Winton's family?"

"No. No relation as far as we know. A promise she made, apparently. I've no idea how it came into her possession."

"I can go and have a look. If it's authentic, it would be a wonderful addition to the letters. As you know, I've requested Winton's correspondence in particular. I think that's what's in the parcel."

"The sketchbook will have to be appraised to certify its authenticity; perhaps the people at the Mitchell, although they have their work cut out preparing for the opening. I'd like you to check for signatures and dates, take a look at the paper type and construction, the illustrations, see if you can find any clues to previous ownership. You know the sort of thing. And while you're there, you might enjoy exploring the area. I believe there have been sightings of the platypus in the local waterways, although the exact location might be a bit difficult. A personal view would give you some insight into Winton's letters. Take a couple of extra days. It will make the display all the more relevant."

Tamsin pushed back her chair. "It would be an absolute pleasure, Mrs. Williams." She almost bent down and kissed the woman's peachy powdered cheek; instead, she grasped her hand and squeezed it, inhaling her dusty scent of rosewater. "Thank you so much for thinking of me. When would you like me to leave?"

"As soon as possible. Say tomorrow, and stay over the weekend, or longer if you need to. Make it a bit of a break. You could do with one. You've been looking a bit peaky lately. There's a hotel in the nearby town, Wollombi—the Family Hotel, I think it's called. They have rooms and it's very respectable. I've looked up the train times. The Brisbane Express leaves from Central Station. You'll be in Maitland in time for an early lunch, then pick up the branch line to Cessnock. After that you're on your own. It's about eighteen miles to Wollombi. There's a regular postal service every afternoon that takes passengers; if not, there's bound to be someone who can help if you ask at the station."

"Perfect."

"I understand it's very short notice. I wanted to give you first refusal. If you don't feel comfortable, Ernest and Harry are willing to go."

Tamsin shot a look across the room at the two cataloguers trying to look as though they weren't hanging on Mrs. Williams's every word by pretending to be deep in conversation.

And then she remembered and her shoulders slumped. "There's just one tiny hitch, but it can be resolved with a telephone call. May I use the office?" Not waiting for an answer, Tamsin headed for the door, barely managing to control her desire to dance across the room. If Mrs. Williams got wind of the fact she was supposed to be attending a function at the Missionary Society, Ernest and Harry would be off on the weekend of their dreams and she'd be sipping tea and making polite conversation with a group of starchy matrons who wanted to reminisce about Mother and Father.

She closed the door of the office behind her and picked up the handpiece. "One-two-five please." She stared out of the window over the rooftops at the palm trees fringing the entrance to the Botanic Gardens.

"This is Mrs. Benson."

Tamsin stood tall. "Tamsin Alleyn, Mrs. Benson. I'm afraid I will be unable to attend the function for Mother and Father. Please accept my apologies."

"Surely not. We have several people looking forward to meeting you. They feel they owe your parents so much."

Tamsin bit back a groan. "It's inescapable. I've been asked to go and assess a new exhibit for the Library. It's a great honor and if I refuse—"

"You do realize this is a charity event."

Tamsin rolled her eyes; no matter how hard she tried she couldn't summon any enthusiasm for the society. Everyone presumed she'd follow in Mother and Father's footsteps. She couldn't do it. Their shoes were far too big and uncomfortable. "I'm terribly sorry. There really is nothing I can do about it."

"In that case I shall be forced to make your excuses."

"I'm sorry to let you down. Perhaps we can organize another time." The receiver clattered into the cradle and she swallowed a whoop of excitement before belting back into the tearoom.

"All sorted, Mrs. Williams."

Chairs scraped as the cataloguers threw her looks that would have frozen the Hunter River and left the room.

Mrs. Williams rubbed her hands together and opened a file sitting on the table in front of her. "I know you are familiar with the story of Charles Winton."

"Absolutely. How does Mrs. Quinleaven know the sketchbook belonged to him?"

"Apparently some of the works are signed and dated. It's the dates we're very much interested in. According to the very limited information Mrs. Quinleaven provided, the drawings and notes predate the recognized timeline for the classification of the platypus. If that's the case, Winton should be credited for his discoveries."

"There's so much conflicting evidence. It took scientists three attempts before they came up with the scientific name we use today.

Although I have to admit I like *platypus*, from the original *Platypus anatinus*, even though they had to abandon it because it belonged to a beetle."

"That's not like you. You're usually a stickler for the correct terminology."

Tamsin didn't understand either. *Platypus* just felt right. "I didn't think any of Winton's sketchbooks and papers had survived. Wasn't there a fire or something?"

"You're thinking of the Garden Palace fire, well before you were born. It decimated our collection, and the few copies of his notebooks and drawings we held were lost, hence our desire to get hold of his correspondence. You've done a remarkable job, I might add."

An undercurrent of anticipation swirled in the confined air of the tearoom, working its way into her blood, burning away the lethargy and inertia that had plagued her for so long. "I can't wait." She wanted to go now. Now, this minute. "I'll make sure the parcel contains the letters and then collate them."

Mrs. Williams's lips twitched. "Just have a quick look to make sure there's nothing relevant before you go. I suggest first thing tomorrow morning. I'd value your opinion on the sketchbook's authenticity. There's no point in going through with this if it turns out to be some upper-class hobbyist's doodles."

"Surely Mrs. Quinleaven would have checked that out before she made her offer."

"Yes, well, time will tell. If you think it is worthwhile, bring it back and we'll get hold of someone in the Mitchell wing and ask their opinion. Ask all the questions you can think of, and remember the Royal Society motto—*Nullius in Verba*."

Take no one's word for it.

Tamsin entered the small town of Wollombi just in time for afternoon tea. She'd spent most of the journey trying to make sense of the notes she'd taken yesterday afternoon.

As soon as she'd left Mrs. Williams, she'd raced back to the package on her desk, and just as she'd expected, it contained several of Charles Winton's letters to Sir Joseph Banks.

There were twelve letters, which made twenty in all, counting those they'd already received. Written every year on the same date, July 3.

The pages were a mishmash of formality and afterthoughts. Notes crammed into the margins and small sketches littered between the words. They also made reference to enclosed illustrations, but either the Royal Society hadn't seen fit to return those or they'd been mislaid.

She'd discovered that in 1796, Winton had sent Sir Joseph Banks a platypus pelt. As a result he had seen fit to pay Winton a stipend, for which he was *eternally grateful*, and requested that he continue his research. But it was the last letter she found confusing. Dated July 3, 1818, it had gone into little detail, simply saying that with the aid of the natives he had unearthed a burrow and collected *irrevocable evidence on dissection* and that *Ornithorhynchus anatinus* were *oviparous* and possessed functioning *mammae*.

Which was where Charles Winton had suddenly become more than just one of the early Australian naturalists, in her view.

She'd had to double-check her memory and search through several books before she was certain that it wasn't until 1888 that Caldwell had sent his famous telegram—"*Monotreme Oviparous: ovum meroblastic*"—announcing to the world that the mystery of the platypus was finally resolved. The platypus laid an egg just like a bird.

Winton had reported this in 1818. Seventy years earlier!

Tamsin gazed out of the window at the passing countryside, no sign of platypus or even a billabong they might call home. How had Winton's sketchbook ended up in the Hunter Valley? Why hadn't he received credit for his discoveries? Why hadn't his name appeared in any of the reports of the Royal Society?

Eventually the postman deposited her outside the rather impressive Telegraph Office in Wollombi and pointed her in the direction of a two-story stone building down the road sporting a faded sign telling her she'd arrived at the Family Hotel. An old man sat outside, pipe stuck in the corner of his mouth, soaking up a dose of tobacco and afternoon sunshine. He lifted his head and studied her with a jaundiced eye.

"I wonder if you could help me." She threw him her sweetest smile.

The barrel-chested man lumbered to his feet and circled her, then finally came to rest almost nose to nose.

She took two steps back. Charming. If all the locals were this aggressive, she'd be heading back to Sydney empty-handed. "I'm looking for a property called Will-O-Wyck."

"The Kelly place?"

"No, well, maybe. I don't know. I'm looking for a Mrs. Quinleaven."

"Might be a bit late."

"I don't think so." The sun was still high and she'd left Sydney early. It couldn't be much past four. "Can you point me in the right direction?"

He frowned and shook his head from side to side, sending a cloud of pipe smoke into her face before slumping back down on his chair.

"Please," she added for good measure.

"Five hundred yards down the road here, over the bridge, and you'll see a track on your right. Down there apiece. House is on your left. Can't miss it. Three bloody great chimneys."

"Thank you." She picked up her bag, leaving the belligerent beery-breathed old man wreathed in smoke.

His directions were better than his reception, and in no time she'd crossed the timber bridge and found a gate marked Will-O-Wyck and a gravel road lined with flowering acacias. She made her way through the dappled shadows, the air redolent with the almond scent of wattle, and came to a halt at the end of the avenue. As she rounded the bend, she spotted a man leaning against the last tree looking somewhat bored. She dropped her bag at her feet and rubbed at her wrist, trying to ignore her dusty buttoned boots and the chafing of her skin from the high neck of her blouse. He'd think she'd come to stay for the weekend. If it hadn't been for the cantankerous old man outside the hotel, she would have thought to leave her bag instead of lugging it all this way.

He pushed his hands deeper into his jacket pockets and pursed his lips. With his smart black suit, pristine white shirt, and tie, he looked as though he belonged in a bank. Not at all what she expected. Everything Mrs. Williams said indicated that Mrs. Quinleaven was an older woman. This man was far too young to be her husband, but he could be her son, and if that was the case, why couldn't he have brought the sketchbook to Sydney?

She pulled off her hat and wiped at her damp forehead. "I'm looking for Mrs. Quinleaven."

A flicker of a frown crossed his face before he stepped forward and eased his hands out of his pockets. "I'm Shaw, Shaw Everdene. Mrs. Quinleaven, ah . . ." He combed his fingers through his hair, pushing it back from his high forehead. "She's unavailable. Are you a friend of the family?" Almost as an afterthought he stuck out his hand and raised his smoky gray-green eyes to meet hers.

She took his hand, feeling the strength in his fingers as he gave a brief squeeze. "I'm Tamsin Alleyn from the Public Library in Sydney. I'm here about a book. A sketchbook. I was hoping to speak with Mrs. Quinleaven about her donation."

"I'm afraid that's not possible. Mrs. Quinleaven was buried this morning."

Chapter 3

Wollombi, New South Wales
1908

Shaw grimaced. Too harsh. He'd made the poor girl flush the color of a tomato. "The funeral party has just returned from the cemetery. Perhaps now might not be the best time. Can you come back tomorrow? Alternatively, I could pass on a message."

"Oh!" She wiped her hand across her brow and sighed. "Do you mind if I rest here awhile?"

"Of course not. Have you motored up from Sydney?"

"I took the train to Cessnock, then a lift into Wollombi. I'm staying at the Family Hotel, so I walked from there."

That sent her up a couple of notches in his estimation. It was a good hike, especially carrying that heavy carpetbag. He shot a look down at her dusty booted feet; at least she had the sense to dress for a walk. He could imagine his sister tiptoeing a few yards and collapsing in a frilly bundle, refusing to go a step farther. "Why don't I tell Mrs. Quinleaven's daughter you're here and see what I can arrange?"

"That would be perfect. Thank you." A pang of disappointment shot through him when she manhandled her unruly curls back under her straw hat and clamped it down on her head. Her lack of pretense and enthusiasm was such a refreshing change.

She didn't look the slightest bit as though she belonged in the Public Library. The only librarians he'd ever met were male and as dusty as the vast collection of books and records they tended. How had they heard about the sketchbook? Mrs. Rushworth had only come across it when she'd arrived. She'd shown him the frontispiece, flicked through a few pages, then snapped it shut before he could get a decent look. He needed to have a chat with Miss Alleyn—there might be more to this book than Mrs. Rushworth had let on.

He glanced over at his motor car parked under the trees. Given the opportunity he would have liked to offer her a lift back to the Family Hotel and see if he could find out what she was up to, but he was here to do a job, and that had to come first. Maybe he could do both. "If you don't mind waiting, I could give you a lift back. There's a bench over there under the tree in the shade."

Her face broke into a delighted smile. "That would be perfect. I should have left my bag at the hotel. I was in such a rush to get here I didn't stop to think."

"Take a seat and I'll be back in a moment."

He made his way over to the lawn where a small group of people were standing under the trees balancing teacups in one hand and a plate of rather uninspired sandwiches in the other. All talking in hushed tones and nodding sagely at each other. He hadn't much time for religion of any flavor—it caused more problems than it solved—however, it was good to see Mrs. Quinleaven had sufficient friends to give her a decent send-off. She sounded like a charming old lady.

Mrs. Rushworth was standing to one side, her elegantly clad foot tapping as though she'd run out of patience and couldn't wait for them all to leave. He needed to catch her before she vanished into the house. "Mrs. Rushworth, could you spare a moment?"

"Ah, Shaw, yes, I really didn't expect so many of the locals to be interested in farewelling my mother. I suppose I should thank the woman from the telegraph office for organizing this. Let's go into the house."

She led him through the open front door and into the impressive library. It as good as made his mouth water. A few of the bookshelves were empty and the books were stacked in haphazard piles on the table and in wooden tea chests. On the top of the desk sat the old leather-bound sketchbook. Watermarks and the odd blob of ink stained the cover, all very worn and used and, heaven forbid, authentic. His fingers itched to open it and have a look, but once it had come to the crunch Mrs. Rushworth had become somewhat reticent. "You had a visitor, and I took it upon myself to tell her you weren't available. I thought now might not be the moment."

"A visitor?"

"A Tamsin Alleyn from the Public Library of New South Wales."

"What did she want?"

He gestured to the desk. "To talk to you about the sketchbook."

"How did the Library hear of it? I didn't even know it existed until this morning."

"It seems your mother contacted them." From what he understood from his father, Mrs. Rushworth hadn't spoken to her mother in many a long year, so it was hardly surprising. "Something about a donation."

"A donation! Did you tell her the book's not available?"

"No, I didn't. She's staying at the Family Hotel in Wollombi. I told her I'd speak with you and see if I could arrange a meeting."

She drew herself up to her full height. "Whyever did you do that?"

"Fate has played into your hands. What better way to get some inkling of the authenticity and value? The Library wouldn't be sending out someone who didn't have a fair amount of knowledge." If Mrs. Rushworth wanted to make the most out of her mother's estate, then this was the way to do it. And the fact that they'd found a couple of pairs of white gloves and an ivory rule inside the desk drawer indicated that someone thought the book held some value. He'd like to get a decent look at it.

With pursed lips, Mrs. Rushworth walked over to the desk, put down her teacup, and flicked through the pages. Shaw's insides crawled. She ought to have the gloves on; any grease on her fingers would transfer to the paper. The book needed to be kept in the best possible condition.

"Do you think it's worth anything?"

"Possibly. We'd have to establish its provenance." He peered over her shoulder, only managing to snatch a glimpse of some detailed line drawings and scribbled notes. The sketchbook certainly looked old. The paper was thick, surprisingly white and fresh, so no acid content, definitely rag pulp, not wood. That dated it prior to the 1850s. "The provenance will have a significant effect on the value."

"I'll leave it in your capable hands." As he expected, he'd hit her soft point. Money was her prime motivator, more than likely something to do with her husband's interest in the building boom in the suburbs. "However, I don't want the book to leave the premises. Tell her she can see it tomorrow at nine. But I'm certainly not donating anything."

"I'll do that. Until tomorrow, then."

He held out his hand, which Mrs. Rushworth ignored, then strolled back down the path. He'd have to find somewhere to stay for the night if he was going to bring Miss Alleyn back tomorrow, so he might as well see if there was a room at the Family Hotel.

Tamsin was sitting under the tree as he'd suggested, staring out at the brook, her booted feet propped on her bag and her hat on the seat beside her. Her hair had worked its way loose and cascaded down her back in a delicious array of shiny black corkscrew curls and swirls. She made a delightful picture. "You have an appointment to view the sketchbook at nine o'clock tomorrow morning."

"That's wonderful. You organized it very quickly—I was expecting to have to wait for a couple of days at least. Poor Mrs. Quinleaven. Her daughter must be devastated. I realize my timing is appalling, but it's important that I get the sketchbook to Sydney as soon as possible."

"Hold on a moment. I said you could view the sketchbook. It's not going anywhere. At least not without Mrs. Rushworth's agreement, and to be honest, I don't like your chances."

"What do you mean? Mrs. Quinleaven wrote and said she wanted to donate it to the Library. I'm simply here to collect it because she didn't trust the postal service. Everything has already been organized."

"Apparently Mrs. Rushworth, Mrs. Quinleaven's daughter, knew nothing about any donation."

"Why not?"

He shrugged his shoulders—it wasn't his place to question Mrs. Rushworth's relationship with her mother. He was just the messenger, and besides, if the donation went ahead, Mrs. Rushworth might be out of pocket to the tune of several hundred pounds, if his estimations were correct, and this very attractive little piece sitting in front of him might be able to confirm that. "I'll bring you back tomorrow to have a look at the sketchbook and you can take the matter up with Mrs. Rushworth when you see her."

"I don't seem to have much of an option." She let out a rather impatient sigh and stood up.

"Let's see what tomorrow brings." Putting her offside was the last thing he wanted to do, and if Mrs. Quinleaven had written a letter stipulating a donation, then it could well scupper Mrs. Rushworth's hopes. "My motor car's just over here." He pointed to his pride and joy: a Model T Ford, one of the first into the country. It had cost him almost as much as his tiny cottage and had eaten up the last of Grandfather's inheritance, but it was already proving to be worth every penny.

"Oh. I've never traveled in a motor car before." She positively glowed, snatched up her bag, and bounded across the grass.

He hotfooted after her and made it just in time to catch her running her hands over the shiny paintwork. "Is it difficult to drive?"

"No, not at all. It's very simple and perfect for Australian conditions." He offered his hand. "In you get. I'll take your bag and stow it."

Her face lit up like a child's as she climbed into the seat.

"I'm afraid it might be a bit dusty. Take my goggles, and if you have a scarf, you might want to cover your hair and your mouth."

"I'll be absolutely fine, I promise you." She pulled off her hat and slid the goggles down over her eyes, then he handed her his gloves and she shook her head. "You'll need them. Am I supposed to do anything?"

"Just sit tight while I crank the engine." Thankfully he'd got the routine down pat now, although it had taken him a while. If it hadn't been for the man who'd sold it to him, he doubted he'd have even taken it out of first gear. He gave the crank three turns to prime the engine and lifted his head.

She was standing up, peering at him over the windscreen, the goggles making her look like some sort of distorted butterfly. "Is it broken?"

"Just part of the routine. Now sit tight and I'll start the engine. One more crank in a clockwise direction and we'll be off. Ready?"

"Oh yes." She clapped her hands and sat back down, holding on as though she might blow away.

One half turn and the engine burst into life. He released the crank and jumped in beside her. Disengaging the handbrake, he put his foot on the pedal to engage first gear, and they were off.

"It looks very complicated to control."

"Not at all, once you get the hang of it."

"And so much quicker than a buggy, and more comfortable." She gave a rather delightful wriggle and dragged her hair back from her face.

"Certainly quicker. She's got a top speed of over forty miles an hour. Prepare yourself. I'm going to put it into top." He slipped it into high gear and they bumped out onto the road, the car's generous ground clearance making short work of the potholes.

By the time they arrived at the Family Hotel it was crowded with locals. He eased into a spot behind a wagon and climbed out of the car. "Could you stay here for a moment while I go and see if there's somewhere I can leave the motor car overnight?" He pointed to the bank of clouds billowing above the hills, threatening rain. "I'd rather leave it under cover."

"It does look like rain. I'll stay and do guard duty." She lifted her carpetbag onto her lap and sat hugging it tightly, staring straight ahead.

"I won't be a moment." He threaded his way through a group of gawking men toward the door of the hotel.

"Suppose you'd be looking for a room too, would you?" A grizzled old man pulled his pipe from his mouth.

"If you've got one, and somewhere I can park my motor car under cover overnight."

The fellow cleared his throat and hawked into the grass, then pointed around the corner. "There's an empty stable around the back; ain't got nothing to feed that contraption, though." He rocked back with a laugh. "I'd offer hay, but I don't reckon you'd be interested."

"That's not a problem." He gestured to the cans strapped behind the seat—he'd been caught out too many times before. Motor spirit was perhaps the biggest problem—scarce and expensive—but he'd found a pharmacist who carried it on the North Shore and he'd made sure he had enough for the round trip. "Got that all under control."

"Don't suppose you have much trouble catching it either."

Shaw refrained from answering and stuffed his leather gloves into his pocket and returned to help Tamsin out.

She untangled the goggles from her hair. "I'm fine."

"Let me take your bag."

Her wide mouth broke into the most engaging smile. "It's not necessary. I can look after myself." She handed the goggles back. "Thank you so much. That was such fun."

"It was my pleasure. I'll run you out tomorrow morning to see Mrs. Rushworth."

"Really, it's no trouble. I don't mind the walk. Please don't put yourself out."

Miss Alleyn was obviously one of those New Women who cherished their independence and right to vote above all else, although her looks were more in keeping with Charles Gibson's girls—statuesque, narrow-waisted, and totally at ease in her own skin. He might put it to the test; see if she was as avant-garde as she appeared. "Would you like to join me for dinner?"

"That would be very pleasant. Or was the invitation just to soften the blow about the sketchbook?" The smattering of freckles on the bridge of her nose danced, and he had an overwhelming desire to lean forward and touch them.

"No, not at all, but if there's a story behind the sketchbook, I'd love to hear it."

"Isn't there always a story behind everything?"

"It depends if you're interested in delving below the surface." Parry, thrust, parry, thrust. They might as well be fencing.

Her shoulders stiffened and she threw him a look, which told him he'd have to step more lightly, then disappeared into the crowd. Mrs. Rushworth would have her work cut out if she thought Miss Alleyn was going to give up without a fight.

The old bloke with the pipe ambled over and ran his hands along the paintwork. He sniffed. "How many horses has this one got, then?"

"Eight."

He whistled through the gap in his front teeth. "Ain't proper. These women gallivanting around the countryside on their own." He huffed, stuck his pipe back in his mouth, and rocked on his heels.

Miss Alleyn might be a lot of things, but he doubted proper was something she paid too much attention to.

"Here for the funeral, I suppose?" the old man asked.

"Did you know Mrs. Quinleaven?"

"Everyone did. Nice old woman, no matter what some people thought. And I'm happy to see her buried where she belongs. What's your connection?"

A good question, and not one he intended to elaborate on. "Can you give me a hand with this?" He pulled the cans off the back of the car and handed one to the old bloke before turning back for the other one. "I'll leave them outside the stable."

"There's talk of them selling this stuff up at the General Store before long. Lucky for you, you ain't got to wait." He winked, his eye disappearing into a bundle of wrinkles.

Shaw straightened up. "Who should I talk to about a room?"

"The wife. Better go and ask, especially if you've got someone to keep you company." The fool waggled his eyebrows suggestively. That wasn't what he was after. It was Tamsin's knowledge about books that fascinated him. For a day that had begun with a funeral, things were looking up.

Chapter 4

WOLLOMBI, NEW SOUTH WALES
1908

Tamsin swallowed the last of the tea and handed her cup and saucer to Mrs. Adcock. "A lovely breakfast, thank you."

"All part of the service. Enjoy your day. Dinner is at six tonight."

She found Shaw outside behind the steering wheel of his car, drumming his fingers on the wheel.

"I beg your pardon, Mr. Everdene. I didn't realize you were in a hurry."

"Call me Shaw." He threw her a cheeky grin. "I didn't think you'd want to be late."

"No, I don't." A kick of excitement caught her unawares and she tied a scarf around her hat to hold it down and pulled on the goggles Shaw had placed on the seat for her.

She wanted to know a bit more about Shaw Everdene; last evening he'd steered the conversation away from anything to do with the sketchbook or his relationship with Mrs. Quinleaven and Mrs. Rushworth. "So Mrs. Rushworth is a friend?"

"Of sorts. She's a client of my father's."

The silence hung while she waited for him to elaborate. Nothing happened so she tried a different tack. "Shaw's an unusual name."

"It is, isn't it? It was my grandfather's nickname. Tamsin's pretty unusual too."

"Not really."

"Any idea where it originates?"

"No. I think my mother just liked it." Or maybe hated it and that's why she'd been landed with it. Father called her his little gypsy. Her dark eyes and untamable hair didn't bother him, but Mother had never come to terms with her Romany looks. Then she'd discovered an old book of Cornish tales, all about a witch named Tamsin, and she'd convinced herself it was one of the reasons they'd sent her back to Sydney and deposited her at school with the Misses Green. They were ashamed to have her around. Missionaries and witches didn't sit well together.

"I would have thought you'd researched your name, and your family tree." He pushed his hair off his face and shot a look at her before returning his concentration to the potholes in the road. "Because of your job, your obvious interest in history. I'd expect you to be on it like a dog with a bone."

Did that mean he thought she was being too pushy about the sketchbook? Not a lot of point in tracking down family history when you'd always felt as though you'd been left like a suitcase at a railway station, a nuisance to your parents, whose interests lay in spreading the gospel, not raising a family. "As far as I know it's never been done. My parents were missionaries. Mother was a nurse and my father a doctor."

"But you didn't follow family tradition and go into medicine?"

"No. I couldn't bring myself to after they died."

"I'm sorry." He maneuvered the motor car around the bends in the driveway and made no other comment, thank heavens. She hated having to explain how horrifyingly little Mother and Father's passing had meant to her. Her feelings made no sense; surely everyone mourned. Yet all she had felt was a huge lethargy, as though she were wading through mud.

It wasn't until she'd started working at the Library that her life began to take shape. And then with the flurry of interest in Australian history surrounding the Mitchell bequest, she'd discovered the Royal Society held copies of the correspondence between Banks and the early Australian naturalists. That had led her to the rivalries and competition surrounding the platypus. The story reached out and tugged at her heartstrings—she felt an affinity with the shy little creatures that for so long had belonged to no family in the animal kingdom. Fanciful, but the platypus had become her totem.

Shaw pulled up in front of the house under the shade of a large tree and cut the engine. Her blood hummed with curiosity, and anticipation hammered away inside her skull. She could hardly contain herself.

"Just wait here a moment and I'll go and see if the time is right."

Shaw disappeared around the corner of the house, and she climbed out of the car and pulled off her hat and scarf and repinned her chignon. The weather was warm so she left her gloves and hat on the seat, smoothed her jacket, and made her way to the front door. It flew open before she had a chance to gather her senses, revealing Mr. Everdene and his broad grin.

"Miss Alleyn, come in."

"Thank you, Mr. Everdene."

"Shaw."

She'd rather expected a maid or even Mrs. Rushworth to open the door; however, Mr. Everdene—Shaw—looked very much at home. Perhaps he was a better friend of the family than she'd imagined.

"Is Mrs. Rushworth available?"

"She's busy. Told me to go ahead and show you the sketchbook. I want to have a closer look myself. Come with me."

She followed his broad back into the house and down a long corridor where the dust motes danced in the slashes of sunlight from the open doors.

"I expect you're looking forward to this."

Was she ever! Kicking her heels last night had driven her to distraction despite the diversion of Shaw's company over dinner. Before she fell asleep she'd read through her notes, committing the timeline of platypus research to mind. There was still so much debate about the reproduction, anatomy, and physiology of the platypus. They were the strangest of animals, and no one had managed to keep one alive in captivity for more than a few days—they either escaped or simply gave up and died. With luck she'd have time to explore the local waterways and see a platypus in its natural environment. She'd ask when she got back to the hotel. "Are you sure I shouldn't have a word with Mrs. Rushworth first?"

"Not necessary. As you can imagine, after the funeral yesterday she's not prepared for visitors." He regarded her with a lively curiosity. There was no doubt she perplexed him. Every time she told anyone she worked at the Public Library they raised an eyebrow, imagining old men, dusty tomes, and a surfeit of stifling conventionality.

"Follow me." Shaw led her into a smaller room dominated by an impressive oval table. He moved a brass work lamp to one side and threw open the heavy brocade curtains, changing the patina of the surface of the table to the rich hue of old cedar. "This is the dining room. Mrs. Rushworth is packing up the house. I moved the table closer to the window where the light's better."

Tamsin adjusted the curtain to let in more light and Shaw glanced up with a glint of amusement in his eyes. Swallowing her impatience, she sank down onto a padded chair and clasped her hands tightly in her lap in a vain attempt to look professional.

With a swish of a dustcloth he wiped the table and then handed her a pair of white cotton gloves and placed an ivory rule at her elbow. "I found these tucked at the back of the drawer with the book. Mrs. Quinleaven was obviously convinced of its authenticity."

She pulled them on, smoothing the creases from each finger, unable to contain the thrill that fizzled through her blood. Nothing in her life had ever produced this sense of anticipation and excitement.

Shaw turned to the sideboard, slipped on another pair of gloves, and opened the linen bag. Goose bumps prickled her arms and she pushed up in the chair, craning to get a clearer view. He took out the book, balancing it flat on his open palms. A cover of soft brown leather with well-worn edges was held together by a brass clip; a dangling piece of cotton that must surely have once held the pages in place protruded from the bottom. The book appeared to be in remarkable condition.

He placed it between them and sat down next to her. The cover was stained with ink and a few watermarks, and the brass corners were scratched and dented. It certainly looked as though it belonged to the early nineteenth century, if not earlier, and it was obviously well used.

Shaw drummed his fingers on the table, a strange reverence in his eyes. "I'll let you do the honors." She warmed to him; he was as fascinated by its possibilities as she was.

When she finally lifted the cover, a cloud of mildew and neglect billowed and the familiar blend of old paper and ink filled the air. A silverfish sneaked between the pages and scuttled away in search of freedom. Her heart pounded and her mouth dried.

"You've got the same look on your face I must have had. The sketchbook turned my innards upside down when I first saw it. I'm dying to get a decent look inside. Any idea how old it might be?"

"At least a hundred years going by the dates Charles Winton corresponded with Sir Joseph Banks."

"So you know the background of this man Winton."

Of course she knew the background. "Sir Joseph Banks dominated the scientific world, larger than life, although by the 1800s he was far too old to travel; nevertheless, his word was a command, and anyone with any desire to make a name jumped to fulfill his every wish.

"Charles Winton was an avid correspondent for over twenty years. He sent samples and sketches to Sir Joseph in London annually. Banks paid him a stipend after he sent a skin preserved in alcohol spirit. The animal had been speared by the Aboriginals. From what I can gather, their correspondence came to an end in 1818, which is strange because Sir Joseph maintained a serious scientific presence until his death in 1820 and research into the platypus continued." Perhaps the book would shed some light on Winton's disappearance from the world of science.

"So why did he drop out of sight?"

"It is unusual, especially for a naturalist, one right in the middle of the greatest debate of the century. Such a waste of talent." The paper rustled and her words dried in her mouth as she lifted the cover to reveal a line of copperplate:

DESCRIPTION OF THE ANATOMY AND HABITAT OF THE *ORNITHORHYNCHUS ANATINUS* BY CHARLES WINTON JULY 1817

"There's no concluding date." She turned the first page, the thin piece of waxed paper rustling with a thousand unanswered questions to reveal a detailed line drawing. And then another. Why hadn't these ever been sent to Sir Joseph Banks? And if they'd remained in

Australia, why weren't they destroyed in the Garden Palace fire with all his other notebooks? "There's no mention of a sketchbook in the correspondence I've seen, only a reference to some enclosed illustrations. Nothing of this nature."

She didn't need to look any further to know Mrs. Quinleaven was right; it belonged in the Library. "I'll get straight to the point. I would very much like the opportunity to have the sketchbook displayed in the Library, and perhaps in the Mitchell wing when it opens. It is of enormous historical and national significance . . ." Her words died on her lips. He must know the importance of the book, otherwise he wouldn't be treating it with such reverence. "It needs to be authenticated. A scientific notebook containing watercolors is most unusual. Presuming it's original, it must be displayed correctly for future generations."

"We haven't seen enough yet." Shaw turned another page. "These pen and ink drawings are signed. I expect because they are the scientific drawings. The others . . ."

The next page revealed a painstaking watercolor showing a platypus slipping from the bank into the golden-brown waters, every one of the dark hairs on its sleek body individually painted, the light catching the top of its leathery bill. "Beautiful." She let out a sigh. "He was very talented."

"It is definitely his work." He traced a gloved finger above the signature *C Winton*.

Her heart sank. "You thought it might not be Winton's work?" She leaned closer; he smelled fresh and woody, like a forest, with a touch of sweetness blending with the musty scent of the old paper and ink. The combination made her heart race.

She turned some more pages.

"Some are signed 'C Winton' and others aren't signed at all. I think it's safe to presume it is his work. After all, his name's on the frontispiece."

"What are you saying?" Creeping goose bumps flecked her arms. Were the works original or weren't they? Had someone else used the blank pages in the book for their own sketches? *"Some hobbyist's doodles."* Mrs. Williams's words quivered across her shoulders. If the book had been tampered with, it would lose much of its value.

"Let's go right through to the end. We can have a closer look afterward. I really value your opinion." He slid the ivory rule under the paper and gently turned to the next page. A line drawing; a close-up of a platypus's hind leg, male because the spur was clearly visible.

"Is there a date on that one? The idea the males were venomous was ridiculed until 1876, when a man named Spicer witnessed and documented a spurring."

"Ah, I knew there was a reason you came. This is the kind of knowledge we need."

Another watercolor; again, the same stretch of riverbank, this time a platypus, presumably female, shepherding two tiny juveniles down the bank to the water, their fur thinner yet their bodies rounded and plump. She could almost glimpse Winton's spirit hovering as they turned the pages, as though he was thankful to have his work acknowledged.

"You haven't—"

"Just a moment." She leaned in for a closer look, then gave up on vanity and grasped her spectacles from her top pocket and shoved them on her nose. A burrow. The mother lying curled, the two juveniles latched to her chest, the fur damp, and the tiniest drop of liquid visible on the juvenile's bill. "A mother feeding her young—that was disputed for years."

Shaw turned to the next page. Detailed anatomical drawings showing the internal organs of the male and the female, and on the facing page a cross section of a burrow showing two small platypus feeding and an unhatched egg and what appeared to be the remains of some eggshell.

"Stop. Stop right there. Is this dated?"

Shaw gestured to the scribbled signature at the bottom of the anatomical drawings—*C Winton*. "No date."

Tamsin's heart began to race. Here was Winton's *irrevocable evidence* he had written to Banks about. She itched to push Shaw's hands away and pull the book closer.

He must have sensed her frustration because he stood and began pacing.

"When was this drawn?" She scanned the page with the drawing of the burrow, searching for a signature, a date.

"I can't see one."

"And the style is slightly different from the pen and ink sketches and other watercolors, but there's no signature."

"I agree."

"So who drew it, and more importantly, when, because if it is correct, it predates all other references to the platypus being oviparous." Her mind was spiraling out of control, the implications bumping for space, crowding out other thoughts.

"I'm sorry. You've got me beaten. Oviparous?"

"It means they lay eggs like a bird. How did Mrs. Quinleaven get hold of the book? Do we know if it's original? And if it is Winton's, was he speculating or did he have proof?"

"Wait a moment." Shaw sat down in the chair opposite and placed his large hands over hers, stilling her drumming fingers. "Look at me."

She gazed into his gray-green eyes, the same color as the leaves framing the corner of the painting, then back to the page, blood throbbing in her right temple. She pushed her spectacles up, pulling her hair from her face. "I don't know what to think. I'm . . . This is . . ."

"Calm down. We'll go through each painting and every line drawing, but first let's get to the end of the book." He picked up the ivory rule and turned the pages rapidly past more line drawings and scribbled notes until he came to the back page.

Another scene on the bank of the river. Which river, for goodness' sake? A shaggy-haired, bearded man lounging against a tree trunk, one leg stretched out, a sketchbook resting on his thigh, and a twig, or maybe a stick of graphite, tucked behind his ear. It had to be Winton. There was no doubting the Australian landscape.

"Look, this one's dated." He pointed to the bottom right-hand corner of the page. "August 1819."

"Where's the signature? Do you think that's Winton? A self-portrait?" A nervous laugh bubbled between her lips. "It's not Winton's style."

"I don't believe it is a self-portrait; however, it's similar to the other unsigned watercolor."

"Wait, there's something written here right down at the bottom of the page." Tamsin squinted at the faded cursive script that wound its way along the base of a fallen trunk. *Resting.*

"So there is. A phantom contributor."

"Stop playing games with me." She pushed the chair back and leaped up. The frustrating man was toying with her, that sardonic grin tipping the corners of his lips again. "Do you know who painted it?"

"No idea." He sat back, folded his brown arms. "Maybe Winton had an accomplice."

She slammed her palms down onto the table. "Are you telling me that Charles Winton, a renowned scientist and naturalist, responsible for these meticulous drawings and notes, allowed someone else to scribble in his sketchbooks—books destined for his patron, Sir Joseph Banks?"

"Hardly scribble. This is a very well-executed watercolor. Look at the drape of his clothes, his face. You can touch every blade of grass and the hairs on his beard. Look at them."

She let out a sigh, her finger hovering over the painting. "I wonder how old he was. He arrived with the First Fleet. That would make him in his twenties in 1788, possibly older—so in his forties, more than likely. Not a young man."

Tamsin untangled her spectacles and pushed them up the bridge of her nose. Without a doubt the book belonged in Sydney, where its provenance could be explored in the hands of specialists. It was of national significance, and it needed to be authenticated by someone with far more scientific knowledge than she had. "I must take the sketchbook back to Sydney." She eased off the white gloves and laid them on the table.

"Not today." Shaw caressed the book with a protective gesture.

A stab of disappointment hit her, making her heart twist. "I'm booked into the Family Hotel for another night. I must see Mrs. Rushworth and discuss her mother's bequest."

He gave her a light, thoughtful frown before closing the book and sliding it back into the soft linen bag. "I expect she can fill you in with a few more details. Why don't you wait outside?"

With her mind racing, she turned to go and then stopped. "I don't suppose you know anything about the platypus down in the brook, do you?"

"Around here?"

"Yes. I've been doing a lot of work collating papers at the Library, reading about Winton, and I've never seen one in their natural surroundings. I was told there might be some around here."

"We could ask at the hotel. Would you like some company?"

"That would be lovely." The words were out of her mouth before she'd even thought about it. Now he'd probably think she was being forward. She offered a smile by way of apology. More excitement than anything else; her blood still thrummed with the implications of the sketchbook. "Thank you, I'd like that. Dusk is the best time to catch a sighting."

"Wonderful." He looked down at her feet. "I was going to say wear sturdy boots, but I see you've got that covered."

She wiped the scuffed toe of her boot on the back of her leg.

"You'll need a warm jacket too. It'll be chilly once the sun goes down."

"I think I can manage to dress myself. I'm not exactly a child." The haughty tone of her voice brought a flood of color to her face as she stomped across the old timber floorboards to the door. The man had wheedled his way under her skin with his nonchalant attitude, and she'd agreed to his company to see the platypus. She was completely at sixes and sevens. "Would you please go and find out if I can speak with Mrs. Rushworth?"

"I'll do that right now. Go and wait outside in the sunshine. There's a table and chairs on the verandah, to the right of the front door." And with that he left, taking the sketchbook with him and leaving her faintly disappointed. No matter what he or Mrs. Rushworth thought, the sketchbook had to go back to the Library. It had to be assessed.

After a quick glance around the dining room, bare of everything except the heavy cedar furniture and a brass lamp, she slipped out into the long corridor. The heels of her boots clicked on the wide timber boards as she passed the now closed doors. She rammed her hands in her pockets, trying to control the temptation to peer inside the rooms. The house felt as though no one had lived in it, as though it was crying out for love. Perhaps Mrs. Quinleaven had closed off a lot of the rooms. One woman living on her own would have rattled around in a house of this size.

The sunlight streamed through the front door, and it wasn't until she was about to step outside that she noticed the door on her right was ajar. Curiosity got the better of her. The brass doorknob was cold beneath her fingers when she eased the door open.

Everywhere bookshelves were crammed with row after row of wonderful leather-bound books. They ringed the room and the dusty scent of history filled the air. A large desk sat under the window overlooking the brook. A series of half-filled tea chests stood stacked in the center of the room. Mrs. Rushworth must have begun packing up. And overlying it all was the faint scent of something antiseptic. It reminded her of her father and his persistent demands that she wash her hands.

"What are you doing in here?"

She almost jumped out of her skin. "Oh! Hello."

A tall, thin woman with a canny look in her eye studied her from head to foot. "Miss Alleyn, I presume."

Caught in the act, and badly. She shouldn't have taken so long. She stepped forward, hand outstretched. "Yes. I'm sorry. My curiosity got the better of me, Mrs. Rushworth. It's a beautiful house." Mrs. Rushworth's cool hand touched hers for a brief moment.

"Come and sit outside."

Mrs. Rushworth ushered her out of the room and along a sandstone verandah to a small table and two chairs. The view over a paddock to the tree-lined brook seemed as far removed from Sydney as she could imagine. She inhaled the aroma of slashed grass and realized with surprise that her shoulders had dropped. In the distance where the trees met the brook, she could see an old woman wandering along, bending and picking the sundry flowers growing in the grass.

"You wanted to speak with me." Mrs. Rushworth flapped her hand in the air.

Her moment of relaxation disappeared with the words. The hint of impatience in Mrs. Rushworth's voice and her waving hand put Tamsin in mind of a persistent fly buzzing against a window. "I did. Thank you. Firstly, I would like to offer my sincere condolences, and those of all of the Library staff, for your loss. We greatly appreciated your mother's kind donation. It will not only benefit future generations but possibly address a series of unanswered questions about the life of Charles Winton." There, that had come out all right. She had practiced and refined the words over and over in her head last night in bed. She smiled into Mrs. Rushworth's eyes, expecting to see a softening from memories of her mother. Nothing, except a steely narrowed gaze and a charged silence.

"As I'm sure you know, Charles Winton was a renowned Australian naturalist. One of the first." Her words spluttered to a halt. She'd made a mess of that.

"Do you have any indication of the book's value?" Mrs. Rushworth placed a strand of hair behind her ear.

"I don't think anyone has considered it. It's highly unlikely it would ever come up for sale."

Mrs. Rushworth raised one perfectly manicured eyebrow and rested back in the chair, folding her arms.

"Your mother . . . Mrs. Quinleaven contacted the Library with regard to donating the book—"

"As my mother's only living relative, I am now the owner of the sketchbook."

"We have the correspondence from her." Why in heaven's name hadn't Mrs. Williams given her the letter to bring? "It was her wish the sketchbook should go to the Library."

"I don't want to discuss the matter any further, Miss Alleyn. I suggest you address all inquiries regarding the sketchbook to my solicitor,

Mr. Everdene. Good day to you." And with that Mrs. Rushworth tip-tapped her way down the flagstone verandah and back inside the house. The door banged shut behind her.

Tamsin closed her mouth with a snap. Solicitor. Shaw was her solicitor? He'd said Mrs. Rushworth was a client of his father's. Who was his father? What did it matter? She wanted to follow, hammer on the door. Didn't the woman understand the significance of the book? Or that her mother's last wish . . . She shook her hair back from her face and rested her elbows on the table and her chin in her hands. What a mess!

Chapter 5

AGNES BANKS, NEW SOUTH WALES
1819

Rose picked her way through the rough grass following the meandering path down to the river. She hefted the canvas bag onto her shoulder and tucked the easel tighter under her arm. She'd rushed through all her chores, determined to escape before Mam came in from her garden and she felt obliged to offer more help in some way or other. The light was perfect and she wanted to get the sweep of gold on the bend in the river before the winter sun sank too low.

Pa would be tucked away in the hide he'd built in his attempt to get closer to the opening of the mallangong's burrow. The slightest shadow on the water and the female would shepherd the juveniles inside. As a child she remembered far more animals than today. Maybe it was her imagination—those perfect days with no responsibilities and no boots. She scuffed her feet and wriggled her toes; maybe she'd take them off once she reached the riverbank. It made Mam livid when she took off her boots. She was getting so proper these days, insisting she should protect her complexion from the sun with a huge cabbage palm hat and, God forbid, wear gloves. How anyone could paint in gloves was beyond her comprehension.

Across the river lay the great green stretch of cleared land, which the natives burned every year to keep the grazing lands clear for the animals—their food bowl. One big old gum—a widow-maker—its dead branches hanging by a thread, waiting for a sudden gust of wind to bring them crashing down, threw a shadow across the grass. In deference to Pa's wishes, she tiptoed, as much as her clumping boots would allow, the last few feet along the path, then lowered her easel and the paintbox Pa had ordered from England for her eighteenth birthday to the ground. She slipped off her boots and hat.

It was only then she spotted Pa. Fast asleep, his back resting against the trunk of the old gum tree and his legs stretched out in front of him. She took a couple of steps closer, then stopped. Why disturb him? He looked so peaceful, his chest rising and falling in a soothing rhythm. His sketchbook must have slipped from his lap because it lay on the ground beside him, although his pencil still rested between his fingers and he had a graphite stick stuck behind his ear. She approached quietly and picked up his sketchbook, then reversed.

With the book propped on the easel, she flicked through the familiar images, Pa's bold signature at the bottom of his drawings. He had row upon row of books standing on the shelf in his workroom filled with drawings and notes and watercolors. Religiously, on July 3—his birthday—he carefully removed the best pictures with a knife to send in his annual package to Sir Joseph. Sir Joseph Banks, Pa's mentor. The one man above all others he revered, the greatest scientific mind in England. The man who paid Pa a twenty-pound stipend to allow him to continue his work. They'd corresponded ever since Pa had sent him the first mallangong skin, letters, and drawings. Despite their long association, he wouldn't even know what Pa looked like. He should. And she would remedy the situation, this very moment.

But what would Pa say if she painted a picture of him in the sketchbook? She'd recorded many of their findings over the years but never drawn or painted anything but the mallangongs. He could always remove her picture if he didn't like it. To ensure she didn't interrupt the sequence of drawings, she flicked to the very last page in the book, licked the stub of her pencil, and outlined the sweep of the river and the arc of the old tree trunk above the burrow. With a few swift strokes she sketched the curve of his back against the trunk, his hat pulled low shading his eyes, one leg bent at the knee, the other stretched out straight; the way he always worked. It took little or no imagination to place his sketchbook on his thigh and a piece of graphite between the fingers of his right hand.

That was enough to make her smile. Mam had tried so hard to make her draw with her right hand, and while she'd managed to train the devil from her writing hand, it refused to cooperate as far as sketching was concerned. Pa liked to pretend to Mam he'd never seen her use her left hand, for Mam had some superstitious dread of anything to do with the devil.

She stood back and squinted at the picture. It seemed unbalanced somehow. Dashing a look farther upstream to the fallen log that as good as spanned the river, she sketched it in. Perfect. She'd spend the evening with her watercolors filling in the brief outline.

Pa snuffled, pushing his hat back from his face and stretching his arms.

As quick as a wink she sneaked up behind him and leaned over his shoulder, placing his sketchbook back in his lap.

He jumped bolt upright, then tilted his weathered face to her. "Ah! Caught in the act. Sleeping away the afternoon. I must be getting old." He twisted the sketchbook and frowned at her attempt. "Not bad, not bad at all. I'm glad you didn't see fit to portray me sleeping."

"I couldn't do that. It's for you to send to Sir Joseph so he knows what you look like and how hard you work."

"He'll know what I look like soon enough." He closed the sketchbook with a snap and with a weary groan pushed to his feet.

"What do you mean?"

"I have been summoned to present my findings—our findings—to the Royal Society in London. Sir Joseph's patron is the King himself. I cannot refuse."

Bubbles of excitement whisked through her blood and she clapped her hands, sending the jackasses into a flurry of maniacal laughter . . . London. The King. Sir Joseph. Better still, the Royal Society. The focal point of the scientific world. And Pa's greatest dream would be realized. Charles Winton: Fellow of the Royal Society. "Can I come?"

"Would that you could, my heart. Would that you could."

"Why not?" For goodness' sake, she'd helped him with so many of the drawings, so much of his research and discoveries. Why, she'd been the one to find the entry to the burrow where they had found the juveniles feeding from their mother. Proof indeed that the mallangong should be classed *oviparous mammalia*. Given half a chance she would tell the Royal Society, London, and the rest of the world that their blank refusal to accept the truth was all stuff and nonsense.

She tilted her head back and gave him a warm smile. "It's all you deserve, and although I wish I could come with you, you are the one Sir Joseph Banks wants to see. You must go."

When Pa smiled, the years fell away, revealing the man he must once have been. The man Mam had fallen in love with, perhaps. His eyes sparkled and he threw his shoulders back; the stoop she'd always associated with too many hours over the easel vanished as she spoke those three words, *you must go*.

He was beside himself with excitement, almost dancing a jig in the leaf litter on the riverbank. "I have been summoned. Summoned to appear before the Royal Society. To take my drawings and show them the irrefutable evidence. I have waited more than twenty long years for this."

"When did you receive the letter, Pa?"

His smile turned to a sheepish shrug. "A while back. A few weeks, maybe a month or two. I've kept it hidden." With meticulous care he removed a folded letter from the back of the sketchbook, sighing. "I must have read it a thousand times. Look—the paper is so creased some of the words are obliterated."

"Read it to me, Pa."

"I know it by heart." He patted the folded letter.

"'Sir Joseph Banks requests the attendance of Charles Winton at the meeting of the Royal Society at Somerset House on the fourth day of June, 1820, to discuss *Ornithorhynchus anatinus* and further information gleaned from the direct observation of these ambiguous animals.'

"I suspect Sir Joseph has turned himself inside out in a frenzy at the thought of the French or the Italian scientists roaming the colony trying to solve the riddle of the mallangong. He couldn't bear it if the English were pipped at the post. I've booked passage aboard the *Minerva*. She sails at the beginning of December. The passage takes around a hundred and fifty days. It'll get me there with time to spare."

"What did Mam say?"

"That is the rub." He scuffed his hand over his eyes. "I haven't told her yet."

"Whyever not? She'll be thrilled to know your work has been recognized."

"I swore to your mother I would never leave her, and now by command of the Royal Society, I must break my oath. That is why you can't come with me. I need you to stay here with her."

Rose latched her fingers together and lay back, gazing up at the lattice pattern of the leaves above her head, the air warm and full of the hum of insects, against the cobalt blue of the sky. Yes! Cobalt blue—an exact match for the latest block of paint Pa had received along with the letter from Sir Joseph. A glorious color. She rolled over in the grass and propped her chin on her elbows, staring at Pa standing on the edge of the river peering across to the other side. He'd made no further mention of his trip and she had a sneaking suspicion he still hadn't told Mam, even though he'd been working long into the night on his drawings and notes. Leaving her spot below the trees, Rose crossed to his side. He lifted a finger to his lips, then pointed along the bank where a mallangong swam, lazily feeding in the shallow water, shuffling its beak through the mud. With a shake it lifted its head and crawled up onto a fallen log and rolled, scratching itself. "Watch, he's cleaning himself."

The mallangong combed first one and then the other of its hind claws through its fur, scratching and rolling in pleasure.

For long minutes, they stood silently side by side as the animal groomed its fur until it was as glossy and sleek as they'd ever seen, then it settled, a streamlined nut-brown bundle, atop the fallen log, relaxed as though napping in the sun. They took a step closer, then another, until both nostrils on the soft leather of its bill were clearly visible. The normally shy creature didn't move an inch.

They'd found dead mallangongs in the past; sometimes the black-fellas speared them for food, though Yindi always said they tasted like mud and she'd take baked lizard any day. A long time ago Pa found a specimen floating in the shallows and they'd taken it home and skinned it, then sewn the pelt back together, filling the innards with soft cloths—even an old chemise—and soaking the skin in rum to preserve it. Now it held pride of place on Pa's worktable under the dome of glass. Pa'd skinned one before she was born and sent the pelt to Sir Joseph.

Rose stretched up onto her toes and brought her mouth close to Pa's ear. "Is he resting? He can't be hurt."

Pa shrugged his shoulders and took a step closer. Still the mallangong didn't move. "I think perhaps he's basking in the sun; he doesn't look injured." He hunkered down and leaned in.

Rose held her breath as he reached out his hand and slid it under the mallangong's round belly to encourage it back into the water. The shock would stir it into action. If not, it would float in the shallows and they could retrieve it. She turned to check that the net was hanging in its usual place beside the easel.

Pa's hand disappeared beneath the dense brown fur and the mallangong uttered a low, soft growl, not unlike one of the dingo pups the blackfellas kept in their camp. "Did you hear that, Pa?"

His lips twisted in a smile and he raised his arm, the mallangong balanced like the doughy damper Mam made in the camp oven on his broad palm. Rose hardly dared look. This was the closest either of them had ever been to a live specimen.

Pa crouched and rested his arm on his knee to take a closer look, moving his hand from side to side to give her a better view.

Too many had died in the floods last year, their burrows swamped, the racing waters carrying the juveniles downstream to be buffeted and bruised, swept into unfamiliar territory where they drowned or, worse, became easy prey for water rats, snakes, and goannas.

Rose stepped closer, her hand outstretched, wanting to touch its leathery bill.

The animal coiled. Wrapped its hind legs around Pa's arm in some sort of weird embrace.

Pa's guttural scream pierced the silence. With a sickening thud he hit the ground, the mallangong now clamped to his thigh.

She grabbed at the broad, flat tail and flung the animal in an arc toward the river, where it landed with a splash and vanished beneath the surface.

Then she turned. A gasp of horror slipped between her lips.

Pa lay curled tight in a ball. He let out a monstrous bellow and his limbs thrashed. And then suddenly he was rigid, every one of his fingers splayed, his legs and arms outspread, flattened like one of the long-legged spiders Mam chased from the house.

The mournful cry of a bush curlew broke the silence, then Pa's agonized shrieks began again, assaulting her ears, sending a winter chill deep into her bones.

She knelt beside him. His breath shallow and rasping, he spluttered, "Blackfellas right," and rolled once more into a tight ball.

Rose's mind went blank. Why were they right?

A sheen of sweat covered Pa's gray face. Smoothing back his hair from his forehead, she leaned closer. "Venom." The word grated in his throat.

She unpeeled his fingers from his arm, revealing the puncture wound below his rolled sleeves and a small, clear, slightly sticky drop of liquid.

The mallangong had spurred him. The blackfellas said the venom could kill a dingo. Was it enough to kill a man?

Mam. Where was Mam? She'd know what to do. Rose wiped the wound clean with her petticoat, then tore a section from the hem. *Bind it, bind it tight*. Mam had done that for the snakebite little Freddie Barrows suffered and he was still running around telling the tale.

"Try and lie still, Pa."

She scuttled to the bank of the river and threw herself down, dangling the strip from her petticoat into the sluggish water. No sign of the wretched mallangong. There'd be another specimen sitting on Pa's table stuffed for all eternity if she got her hands on the animal. She wrung the water out of the strip of petticoat and crawled back up the bank.

"I'm going to bind your arm, Pa."

His eyes flickered open and his mouth twisted in a rictus smile.

Dear God, please. Her hands shook as she pushed his shirtsleeve high above his elbow and wound the strip of linen tight around his forearm.

For a moment it gave him some relief and his arm went limp, then the curling and rolling began again, punctuated by such agonizing cries they chilled her very blood. Pa's good arm flailed and fell across his thigh, his fingers pumping.

"Did he hit you here too, Pa?"

The spurs were razor-sharp; she'd seen them when they'd dissected a male specimen. Surely not sharp enough to pierce the thick moleskin of his trousers? There was no doubt in her mind now that the spurs were full of venom and the blackfellas were right. Unwrapping his clawed fingers, she reached into his back pocket and pulled out his Fullers knife. She flicked open the sharp blade, gritted her teeth, and sliced through the leg of his trousers.

Another puncture wound. Had the mallangong had time to inject more venom before she'd wrenched it free? With the knife in her hand she shredded the remains of her petticoat and wrapped it tightly around his leg.

Pa spluttered through the drool coating his lips. "Up. Up." His eyes fixed on her, unblinking, staring.

"No, Pa. Stay still." Mam said blood carried the snake venom around the body. She had to keep him still. "I'll get Mam. She'll know what to do."

"Up." He groaned and struggled to raise his body, then slumped in a quivering heap at her feet.

With her hands in his armpits, she dragged him back against the tree and propped him up, placing his hat on his sweat-soaked head. He toppled, almost fell, his muscles refusing to hold him steady.

"Try not to move. I'll fetch Mam." With one last look at the slouched figure, she thundered down the path, the sound of her pulse in her ears deafening her.

"Mam! Mam, come quickly." There must have been something in her tone because Mam appeared before she'd even reached the gate. "Pa's hurt." Her words caught, her chest heaved, and she bent over and vomited into the grass. "The mallangong spurred him." She wiped her mouth with the back of her hand.

"Not badly hurt. They're not venomous, not like the snakes." Mam eyed the dribble of yellow vomit staining her dress unsympathetically.

"Yes, badly hurt. The natives said the mallangongs can kill a dingo. We didn't believe them."

Mam's eyes widened and she shook her head, then she snapped into action. "Get the cotton sheet from your bed. Where's he injured?"

"His leg and his arm."

"We need to bind the wounds tight."

"I've done that with my petticoat." Rose staggered into the kitchen and reached for the pitcher, not wasting time to pour the water, gulping it direct.

Venomous like a snake. It couldn't be. Pa thought the males spurred their rivals during mating season and the blackfellas said they spurred their attackers, but to kill a man? A man who was more than ten times their size? She shook the thought away. That wasn't possible. Not Pa. Not anyone.

With the linen sheet tucked under her arm, she raced back down the path, Pa's screeches lacing the air, lending her feet wings. The linen sheet tangled around her feet and she stumbled, then plowed on down the path she knew better than anywhere on earth.

By the time she reached the riverbank, Mam had Pa clasped tight in her arms, trying to hold him still as he thrashed, rolled, and screamed, agony etching his haggard face.

"Hold him still. We must try to ease the pain."

How could Mam stay so calm? Pa's arm had swollen to nearly twice its size and his flesh bulged through the hole she had made in his trousers. She must have tied her petticoat too tight because the skin had turned blue and long red streaks spread like rays of the setting sun along the surface of his skin. She reached forward to loosen the bandage.

"Leave it!" Mam shouted.

Shouted. Mam never raised her voice. Rose's hands dropped to her sides, a sense of total helplessness swamping her. "Should we lance it to let the venom out?"

"We must bind his leg tighter and then carry him home."

"You said we shouldn't move him. The venom will spread."

"Not with the bandaging. Hurry."

Pa's groans grew louder and his writhing more feeble. Mam tipped his head back and slipped a piece of bark between his teeth. "Bite down on this. It might help." She ran a hand over his dripping hair, then dropped a kiss on the gray skin of his forehead.

"We must move him now before paralysis sets in, while he can still help. We'll bind his leg again. Tear the sheet, big long strips; it will stem the flow of the venom."

In a matter of moments Mam had tightly swaddled Pa's leg and arm, white like the picture of an Egyptian mummy in Pa's *Encyclopaedia Britannica*. Rose shuddered, pushing the thought of death away.

"Take his feet." Mam slipped her hands under Pa's armpits, and once she'd clasped his feet, Mam nodded her head and they lifted Pa's deadweight. No! Not dead. He couldn't die. Not Pa.

Time lost all meaning as they staggered along the path through the scrub. Pa groaned and rolled; every time his body convulsed, they all but dropped him. If the mallangong venom didn't kill him, he'd die of a cracked head. She clutched his ankles tighter, her muscles screaming with the unaccustomed weight. Sweat poured down her face, stinging her eyes—or was it tears?

When they finally lurched through the door, they laid Pa down on the bed he shared with Mam and Rose collapsed in a heap at the foot. The walls swirled and twisted in a horrid willy-willy as she tried to ease the cramping in her arms and the hammering in her heart.

Not so Mam. Yukri had appeared from goodness only knew where and scuttled around the kitchen filling the kettle, placing it on the hob, and stoking the fire. The smell of ti tree laced the air from Mam's tinctures littering the surface of the table as she mumbled, shook bottles, and squinted at labels. "Keep watch, Rose. Keep watch." Mam's voice echoed in the small room as she lifted the kettle from the fire.

Rose raised her head and licked at the salty tang of her dried tears. The trip back from the river had sapped Pa's strength as well as hers. Each breath was a labored gasp, and every few minutes his body writhed and he let out an agonizing shriek. He kept smacking his lips and chewing at his cheeks when the shafts of pain struck. Snatching back a useless sob, she wiped her hands over her face.

"How he looking?" Yukri's voice calling from the fire brought her back to her senses.

Swollen to a massive size, Pa's leg and right arm lay useless, great gnarled branches dangling over the side of the bed. Rose dragged herself to her feet and moved unsteadily into the big room. She couldn't sit and watch Pa die. "Yukri, what can I do?"

"Pour hot water slow over the leaves."

She tipped up the kettle and the smell intensified as the boiling water released the oil. "What will it do?"

"The infusion may help with the infection." Mam sounded like one of Pa's reference books.

"How will we know if the venom is spreading?"

"We watch. Big red lines from the bite. Him hurting real bad."

She'd seen the tracks on his skin, the red, radiating lines. Seen them down by the river. The venom spreading. She turned to look into the bedroom again. Mam . . . She almost dropped the kettle. Through the door she could see her hacking at Pa's breeches. She spliced them through and removed them, baring his legs. His shirt went the same way, and he lay pale and clammy like a speared fish on the bed he and Mam had shared all her life.

She'd never seen Pa's limbs, hadn't thought they'd be so white when his face was almost as brown as Yukri's. She shuddered and turned away, concentrated on refilling the kettle. How could a mallangong, the one animal above all others that Pa had dedicated his life to nurturing, have done this?

Chapter 6

AGNES BANKS, NEW SOUTH WALES
1819

As the afternoon turned to night and Pa's bellowing cries filled her head, the three small rooms of the wattle-and-daub shack became her world. Mam soothed and bathed him and at times simply sat, her head propped in her hands, her elbows on the bed, and waited. Waited for what?

"Is there nothing we can do?" Rose sat beside Pa, plucking the leaves off the ti tree branches. Waiting. Just waiting.

A long, heartfelt moan seeped from deep within Mam's misery. "The venom is spreading. I believe it will peak. We must wait and see."

"Can't we call the physician?"

"What can he do that I can't? By the time he gets here . . ." She shook her head, despair turning her face to an aged mask. "We must wait as we would for a snakebite. I never dreamed the mallangong was venomous."

Something skirted around Rose's mind, drifted in and out of her consciousness. Pa had never believed they were venomous, but Bunji said his grandfather told him to always pick them up by their tail.

Why their tail? Because of the spurs. Thank heavens she'd grabbed the wretched animal by the tail. What else did the blackfellas know that she didn't? Could they cure him?

"Yukri, do you know what else we can do for Pa?"

"Just waiting. Waiting to see. Mr. Charles, he bigger than them dingoes. Maybe he be good. Maybe not." She shrugged her shoulders, then pulled Rose into her arms and gave her the hug she needed.

"Mam, I'm going for a walk." Maybe if she could find Bunji, he might know, or he could ask one of his uncles.

"Stay here. I don't need to worry about you as well." Since when had Mam worried about her? She was always too busy with her eyes locked on the horizon, waiting for something that never arrived.

"I have to clear my head. I won't go far. Where's Bunji?"

"Dunno." Yukri followed her to the door.

Only yesterday she'd seen him. He'd waved as he set off with his friends, too manly now to care about the likes of her, a mere girl. Some days she longed for the freedom she'd enjoyed as a child. If she called him, would he come? Would he know what to do? He'd told her the story of the mallangong, shown her their burrows and the best places to find them, but nothing of how to treat the venom sweeping through Pa's body.

"I'm going back to the lagoon. Pa's sketchbook and paints are still there. I won't be long." She took off down the path, pulling the sweet clean air into her lungs. "Bunji! Bunji! Where are you?" What if Pa died? She couldn't bear it. "Bunji!"

She rounded the bend and there he was, squatting beneath the tree, his smooth, brown skin gleaming in the sunlight.

"Them big boss mallangong. Him, big trouble."

She nodded her head and sank down beside him. "We've tried everything. None of Mam's medicines work. Yukri's making the Geebung mixture."

"You wait. Wait long, long time."

But Pa didn't have a long, long time. The ship sailed to England in a few weeks and he had to go.

"You take this." Bunji reached behind him and pulled out Pa's sketchbook and box of paints. "You need it. You mallangong girl. Mallangong your totem."

She hadn't any answer, didn't want it to be her job. It was Pa's dream. With a sigh, she turned back to the house.

The days wore on and their vigil took its toll until finally she found Mam slumped across Pa's chest fast asleep. At least Pa's spasms had stopped, but he lay so still, only the irregular rise and fall of his chest convinced her he still lived. His arm and hand had swollen to two if not three times its usual size, and his leg was not much better. But he was calm. The lockjaw Mam had worried about hadn't eventuated, though he could take no more than a few drops of water, which they eased through his swollen lips with a spoon.

Rose scattered some dried chamomile flowers into a tin mug and poured boiling water over them, then set it to rest on the table. She tiptoed to the bed and reached for Mam's shoulder. "Come and rest. Pa is sleeping."

Mam jumped at her words, as though she had been caught slacking. "I'll stay here."

"Pa is quiet now. I've made you a cup of tea—go and drink it and eat some of the damper Yukri made. You've had nothing. I'll tend Pa. Sleep in my bed."

Mam offered a wan smile and made her way through the door, staggering as though she had taken the venom into her body. She'd given all her strength to Pa, willing him to heal.

Rose sat down beside the bed, pulled the three-legged stool closer. A fine sheen of sweat still peppered Pa's forehead, so she squeezed out the cloth. As the cool dampness touched his skin, his eyes flashed open. Clear and lucid. A great bubble of joy swam through her. "Pa?"

He licked his dry lips and she held the spoon to his mouth. He pushed it away, grimacing at the movement.

"Is it very painful?"

He closed his eyes for a moment and shook his head, shielding her from the truth, protecting her as he'd always done. If only she could make him well again. "Perhaps it's getting a little better."

"Rooossse." His thickened, chapped lips made her name sound odd, drawn out, almost pleading; a trickle of bloodstained spittle ran down his chin. She wiped it away, no longer panicking at the sight.

"What can I do? Anything?"

He lowered his head and his gaze slid to the door.

"You want Mam? She's resting."

He shook his head. "Clossse . . ." The snakelike hiss again as he tried to wrap his tongue around the word.

"You want me to close the door?"

His head lolled in a kind of agreement.

She lifted the wooden latch, securing it, then returned to the bedside, taking his uninjured hand in hers, soothing his burning skin with her fingertips. From the heat in his hand, she could tell the infection still raged, but without the same burning fury of the past days.

"England. Rose, England." His eyes pleaded with her, filling with tears with the effort of speech.

Sir Joseph's letter! It hit her like a stone. In the past days she'd forgotten all about it. "Have you told Mam?"

His head rolled to one side.

He still hadn't. "Sir Joseph will understand. There's plenty of time for you to recover." As she spoke the words, her heart sank. He could no more withstand the trip to England than he could fly to the moon. One hundred and fifty days aboard ship.

His eyes grew wide and his mouth opened and closed as he tried to form the words. What did he want to do?

"June." His raised his hand and held up four fingers, engorged like the sausages Mam made from pig entrails.

She ran the words of the letter he'd quoted through her mind: *on the fourth day of June, 1820.*

"Wait, Pa. Wait and see. There's still time." But there wasn't. A month at most. "Shall I write a letter? We can send it to Sir Joseph, tell him of your injury. Tell him we have indisputable evidence that the male mallangong is venomous. I can send sketches too. The ones from the dissected animal showing the spurs. There must be a ship leaving soon. I can be in Sydney in a day if I take the lighter, less if I borrow a horse or beg a ride along the Parramatta road."

He shook his head again from side to side on the pillow, the rocking movement sending spasms through his muscles as he tensed in frustration. What did he want?

"No letter, then."

"Go." The single word hung in the silence of the darkened room; even Pa's rasping gasps ceased.

He wanted to be left alone. "Sleep, Pa. I will come back in a while and see how you are." And in the meantime, she would go through his notes and his sketchbook, make sure the spurring was recorded, include some drawings and an explanation. Absolute proof that the blackfellas were right. The mallangong was venomous.

Maybe if Pa slept, he would be more lucid when he woke and he could help her frame the letter to Sir Joseph explaining why he couldn't go to England. And she'd pack up his sketchbook and take it to Sydney for shipment. She could arrange it as well as he could. She'd helped more times than she could remember.

His good hand clamped her arm and he shook his head again, his throat tensing as he swallowed. She reached for the water but he pushed her away, slopping it across the threadbare blanket. "You. Go."

She rose from the chair.

"To Sir Josssseph." The words slurred thick on his engorged tongue.

Her heart stuttered to a halt. To Sir Joseph? Was that what he meant? "To England?"

He nodded his head just once, slower this time. The tension in his body leached away and his hand lay gentle on her arm.

"You want *me* to travel to England?" Her mind raced as she chased the thought around. "To present your work to Sir Joseph?" The enormity of the thought filled her. How could she travel to England alone, a woman, hardly even a woman, not yet twenty? It was impossible. What would Mam think? She didn't even know he'd been summoned.

Rose turned Sir Joseph's letter over and over in her hands, trying to recall the exact words; she felt as though she shouldn't read it, as though she was being underhanded. The letter was to Pa, not her. But he'd told her of it. Asked for her help. With a sigh, she unfolded the thick paper and spread it on Pa's desk and read the words time and time again until she, too, knew them by heart.

He'd said he'd sworn to Mam he'd never leave her. Now he wouldn't have to break his oath. Would Mam understand, let her go in his stead? His life's ambition. Years of careful observation to pull together the body of knowledge represented in his latest sketchbook. Oh, how she wished she didn't have to take responsibility, but she did. Who else was there?

She sat down in the chair and rested her elbows on top of the worktable, scrutinizing the picture she'd painted of Pa under the tree. He looked so peaceful, the slight smile tipping the corner of his lips. Lips that now were swollen and cracked. What torment he must be in, not just the physical pain but also the agony of knowing he'd missed his chance, his opportunity to fulfill his heart's desire. She closed the sketchbook with a snap. She had to go. Pa was right, and she had to tell Mam.

Gritting her teeth, she picked up the letter. When Mam woke she'd show it to her, tell her that Pa had asked her to go. She'd know what to do. Better still, she'd read the letter to Mam at Pa's bedside and together they'd make the decision. That way Mam wouldn't think it was one of her far-fetched excuses to shirk her duties. She hugged herself tight. Pa would get better. He had to, and if she could ease his mental torment, then his physical recovery would be all the faster.

Yukri sat at the table stripping the berries from the Geebung, seeping them in the water to release the juice she said would heal infection. Pa had been taking it for days now; who knew if it helped.

"Is Mam still sleeping?"

"She tired. Too much waking and worrying."

Rose glanced across to the darkened corner of the room; the curtain covering her bed was drawn, closing it off to the main room. "And Pa?"

"He resting. Not sleeping. Not jumping no more. Arm still big. Real big. This here, this help when the goodness comes." She shook the jar and the small berries jumped and swirled in the water.

"I'll go and see him." She tapped the letter against her palm and gave a curt nod. She could do this. She'd even wanted to go to England with Pa when he'd first told her. But alone? It was nothing she'd imagined, not even in her most irrational flights of fancy.

Pa's eyes turned to the door the moment she stepped into the room. "How are you feeling?"

He twisted his head and tried for a smile, failed, and licked his cracked lips, his eyes pleading.

She reached for the water and held the spoon to his mouth. "I've been thinking about England."

The shadows lifted from his eyes and he turned his head away from the water.

"We have to tell Mam. Is there no one in England I can turn to?" Pa never mentioned any family, not that she'd ever asked. Pa was all the family she'd needed and she'd never questioned otherwise. And Mam? Mam never talked about her childhood, her life in England; said it was all in the past and best forgotten.

"Julian."

The word hung in the air. "Julian?"

As if summoned, Mam appeared by her side, her face blanched bone-white as she soothed Pa's brow with a shaking hand. "Hush now."

"Go to Julian." Pa sank back into his pillow, his face chalky and his chest laboring from the effort. "In London."

Mam sprang to her feet at Pa's words, her pale face turning redder than the cockerel's feathers. "You know where he is and you haven't seen fit to tell me?"

Every nerve in Rose's body stood on end. Who was Julian? "Rooossssse, go." A sigh leaked out between Pa's lips and his eyes closed.

A cold dread settled on her shoulders, heavy as a wet cloak but without the smell of the fresh-fallen rain. Was this why Pa hadn't wanted to tell Mam about the letter?

"Come, Rose. Come with me."

Torn between Pa's needs and Mam's demand, she stared from one to the other. Mam's face so drained, so shocked; Pa almost at peace for the first time since the spurring.

"Come now." Mam left the room without giving Pa another glance, her mouth pulled down at the corners, her jawbone rigid.

"Rest easy. I'll be back soon." She pulled the sheet up to his shoulders and cupped his cheek, then left the room. "Sit." Mam pointed to Pa's chair.

"I would rather . . ." She couldn't sit. Needed to move, needed the chance to dislodge the sense of foreboding lodged hard in her chest.

"Sit." Mam's hand came down on her shoulder and pushed her into the chair.

Mam settled onto her stool and stared at her across Pa's worktable.

"Listen and listen well. I thought not to share this with you, thought the past best buried. Now you must know. I came to these shores, not as a free woman with Charles, as you believe, but as a convict."

The words shrieked through Rose's brain like the windstorms that brought down the dead branches from the widow-makers. Whatever could Mam have done? She was the most honest person she knew, painfully honest, hurtful in her honesty. She tolerated no lies. Why, the only time Rose had been switched had been for lying.

"Listen, Rose, and look at me."

How could she look at her? She didn't know her. "What did you do?"

"I stole from my mistress. I came here on the *Lady Juliana* with two hundred other women."

The *Lady Juliana*. Everyone knew, everyone remembered. The Whore Ship. Her mother was a whore? Not just a whore, a thieving whore. It was rubbish, as surreal as Pa lying prostrate on the bed as good as killed by an animal no bigger than a half-baked damper.

"But Pa?"

"Charles is not your father."

It was as though someone had yanked away the ground beneath her and everything she had ever known was a lie. "Then who?" Mam a thieving whore and Pa—not Pa.

"A naval surgeon. A man named Richard Barrington."

She groaned aloud, felt the world tip and Yukri's warm hands rest on her shoulders. She clutched at Yukri's hand, a lifeline in a shifting dust storm.

"Sit quietly, then we'll talk some more." Mam's voice was harder than usual, not the gentle, vacant tone that soothed the sick and calmed the needy. Her other voice perhaps, the voice of a thief, a whore. "You need a moment to compose yourself."

A moment. She didn't need a moment. She needed a lifetime. "Yukri?"

"Listen hard, listen fast, little mallangong girl. It's best you know; then you can become the woman you meant to be."

Yukri pressed a cup into her lifeless hand and she wrapped her fingers around it, inhaling the smoky sweetness of the black tea.

None of the questions she wanted to ask would form. She closed her eyes and sipped while Yukri's fingers smoothed her arm. Yukri, who'd been there for as long as she could remember, longer perhaps than Pa. Her eyes flashed open. "Mam. Tell me."

"When the *Lady Juliana* arrived, the colony was crippled—few supplies, men and officers starving, rations cut, even the governor—"

"Mam!" She sat upright. She didn't want a history lesson; she'd heard this before. Selfish, perhaps, but she wanted to hear her story. How she came to be.

"I was assigned to a man named Richard Barrington as his housekeeper. He and Charles shared a tent next to the hospital in Sydney Cove." A hint of color stole across Mam's cheeks. "I mistakenly believed he could help me have my sentence rescinded so I could return home. I feared for my granfer." She lowered her lashes, wringing her hands. "I became Richard's wife, in all but name."

A hiss slipped between Yukri's lips rather as though she'd spotted a snake in the grass and warned of its approach.

"I gave birth to his son, Julian."

"I have a brother?"

"When Julian was five years old, Richard was recalled and he took him with him to England." Mam's voice hitched and she brushed aimlessly at the tears trickling down her cheeks. "To become a gentleman, his heir."

"And he didn't want me?" The plaintive note in her voice belonged to a petulant child. She ought to have a thought for Mam, but all she could think of was herself.

"He didn't know about you. It was only after he'd left I discovered I was with child. You were born eight months later."

And Pa, no, not Pa. She'd never get used to that. "Pa raised me. Did he want me?" Why would any man want another's child?

"You have always been and will always be Charles's daughter. The day you were born he told me that you were the daughter of his heart."

But not his loins, not his flesh and blood. Not one part of the man she'd loved all her life, believed to be her father. Loved more than Mam. "Where is he? This father?"

"He died at the Battle of Trafalgar when you were a child."

"I can't take this in." She knew she was being selfish; the pain on Mam's face was as bad as Pa's writhing agony. She stood, put down the cup. Mam reached out her hand to her, but Rose couldn't touch her. Had nothing to give to the woman who'd made her life a lie. She brushed past the table, threw a quick glance into the bedroom where Pa lay, his eyes fixed on some spot beyond the window, and stumbled around, blinded by tears of self-pity she could do nothing to stop.

Yukri propelled her outside into the sun, so bright it stung her eyes. How could the sun shine when her whole world had been turned upside down? "Not your mam's fault. Just like mallangong. That's why you mallangong girl."

Rose pushed Yukri away and walked down the path toward the river. She didn't want to hear any more about the wretched mallangong. Not from Yukri, not from anyone, and least of all did she want to be lumbered with another name. Wasn't it bad enough that the one she thought belonged to her was no more than a hideous fabrication, a lie? Her own mother had lied to her, had not only given her another's name but brought her up to believe that lie.

"That Barrington man, he one big rat. Not your mam's fault."

Rose spun on her heel, hands on hips, and glared at Yukri. "I don't want to hear any more stories. I'm sick of stories. My entire existence is a hoax."

"No, you listen here, girl, and you listen well. Yukri was here and Yukri knows. Now sit down here." She patted the spot of grass next to her. "Here!"

More from habit than anything else, Rose did as she was told and sank to the ground, hitching her knees up to her chin and wrapping her arms around her legs, rocking to and fro. Hot one minute, cold the next. She pulled her shawl tight around her shoulders and rubbed her cheek against the rough wool.

"You remember story."

Rose huffed out a big sigh and a little bit of the tension leached out of her muscles. "Remind me."

"My story says mallangong, she born after a beautiful female duck mated with a shifty water rat. The baby—she had her mam's bill and webbed feet and her pa's legs and brown fur. See now, that's you."

Rose wriggled her toes, digging her feet into the ground. "Yukri, this is not helping me one little bit."

"You not listening. Your mam was lonely. And miserable, and sad. She wanted to go home, back across the waters, but they not let her. That water rat, he a real crafty rat. He promised he help."

Everything went quiet; no noise from the river, no birds, no insects, just Yukri's words echoing in her head.

"You mean Mam was taken in by my father, persuaded to do something she didn't want to?" Heaven forbid. It didn't bear thinking about. "But Pa?" She shook her head. "Charles."

"Mr. Charles good man. He took care of her when that water rat stole your brother away. You go back there and you listen hard to your mam and you think what you can do. Your turn now. Your mam, she can't do nothing for your pa; she stuck here. You, you can give that man—he's your pa, the one who loves you—everything he's wanting."

Daughter of my heart.

Scratchy tears caught in her throat. Now the words held a different meaning. Yes, she could. She knew almost as much about the mallangong as he did and she owed him so much. But to travel alone to London? She'd spent time daydreaming about such a trip, only not by herself but with Pa.

She hitched up her skirts and ran back to the house, following the path she'd walked more times than she could remember with Pa, for no matter who had sired her, Charles was her pa. Mam couldn't leave; she couldn't present his work either. She knew all about plants and herbs and healing but nothing about the mysteries of the mallangong.

She threw open the door and slithered to a halt as the dark hit her after the brightness outside. And the quiet. So quiet. Had something happened to Pa? She couldn't be too late, surely. She tiptoed across the room. Pa lay on the bed, his face beaded with sweat and Mam holding his hand, her head resting on his chest, both of them asleep.

Leaving them, she crept into Pa's workroom where the light flooded in through the wide-open shutter. Pa's sketchbook lay where she'd left it, on his worktable.

She opened the heavy leather cover and flicked through the pages. Mostly Pa's and a few of hers, detailed drawings and notes covering each of the pages in his fine, clear writing covering each of the pages. Over a year's worth of research and discoveries; everything he'd intended to present to the Royal Society. Proof that mallangongs laid eggs and suckled their young. Enough to earn him a fellowship. Finally, to achieve his life's ambition, and now this.

Examining each page carefully, she added a few extra labels and headings, then thumbed through the pages until she reached the drawing of the spur. She added notes on the way the mallangong growled, curled, and reared, and the fact that it was safest to pick it up by the tail.

After she spoke with Pa and they decided what he wanted her to show Sir Joseph, she'd add some finer details. The thought brought her up short and she smiled at her reflection in the glass dome. Perhaps she'd take a mallangong too. Pa had only sent a pelt, never a full specimen to Sir Joseph, too annoyed that Governor Hunter had pipped him at the post and sent a specimen to England. Not that it had done much good; everyone believed the mallangong was native trickery.

Pa's spluttering cough broke her concentration and she stepped from the room. Mam stood at the table pouring boiling water, and the scent of lemon balm and aniseed filled the room. She lifted her tearstained face. "I'm sorry, Rose. I should have taken more care. Told you more gently. What must you think of me?"

"I think you did your best, Mam. I've had, thanks to Pa, the most perfect childhood anyone could wish for. Now it is my turn. I'll tell Pa that I will go to England."

"You can't, not alone. You're only a child."

But she wasn't, not now. She'd shed her childhood on the day Pa was spurred, like a red-bellied black snake leaving its skin. "I'm going. Pa trusts me with his work."

Mam clasped her in a hug and held her tight, tighter perhaps than she could ever remember. "I cannot come with you. I must stay with Charles. We'll write to Julian, send him a letter on the next ship. You can take Charles's passage on the *Minerva* and we will find someone for you to travel with. I shall speak with Mrs. Macarthur and ask her advice. She and her husband know everyone in the colony and he constantly travels to England. There will be some other families returning home"—her voice hitched on the word and she swallowed—"who you can travel with."

"Mam? Why haven't you written to Julian before?"

Mam screwed up her face and puckered her lips. "I made a promise to Richard that I wouldn't. Julian was to be brought up a gentleman by Richard's wife, free of the stain of the colonies. When he was old enough to understand, Richard said he would tell him about me and ask him to write."

"And he didn't?"

Mam shook her head, the familiar look of sadness that Rose knew so well clouding her eyes, and suddenly Rose understood. Even as a child she'd known Mam had lost something. "Oh, Mam." She reached out and touched her cold hand. "I'm sorry."

"You write the letter."

Rose picked up the nib and dipped it in the ink, then held it out.

"No, I can't break my promise. You write it; write it and explain about Charles. He was Richard's closest friend, until he left to return to England. He needs Julian's help. Julian might refuse me. If he'd wanted to contact me, he could have done so."

Rose flattened the paper, her heart squeezed tight with remorse. Such sadness, such misery, and to be able to do nothing about it. Well, she would. This trip to England would not only be for Pa; it would be for Mam too, because she would speak with this brother of hers and tell him that he had it in his power to mend his mother's broken heart. What son wouldn't want to do that?

> Agnes Banks, New South Wales
> October 27, 1819
>
> Dear Julian,
>
> I am writing to you on behalf of my father . . .

Her pen stalled and she scratched out the words *my father*. Not her father . . .

> Charles Winton, your father's closest friend. I should say our father's closest friend. I am your sister, Rose. I was born after you journeyed to England.
>
> I am traveling to London to present Charles Winton's work to Sir Joseph Banks and I would appreciate any assistance you can offer.
>
> My mother, your mother, sends her kindest regards and wishes to be remembered to you.

How ridiculous. That wouldn't work. She screwed up the paper and went to throw it in the fire.

"Try again. We mustn't fail Charles."

No, they mustn't. "Perhaps it would be better if we wrote the letter as if it came from Pa."

"We can't. That wouldn't be honest."

Nothing in this whole debacle seemed anywhere near honesty; why start now? "I think it would be better. Pa can't write the letter, but we can read it to him and, if he agrees, sign it on his behalf. It's not as though we are doing anything behind his back. It's what he wants."

She put aside the pen and picked up her favorite drawing pencil in her left hand; perhaps the familiarity would make the words flow as her drawings did. Ignoring Mam's raised eyebrow, she licked the stub.

> Agnes Banks, New South Wales
> October 27, 1819
>
> Dear Julian,
>
> I trust this letter finds you well. I am writing to request, in the name of your dear departed father and our long friendship, your indulgence and assistance.

"Mam, how do we know where to send this letter?"

"We send it to the Admiralty in London. They will know where to find Richard's son. They will have records." Mam's face crumpled and a tear oozed out of the corner of her reddened eyes. Mam knew how to find Julian and still she hadn't broken her vow of silence. How could she have allowed him to be taken away? What would make a woman do that? So much she didn't know or understand.

First the letter and then more questions.

Rose licked the stub of the pencil again.

> Sir Joseph Banks, my patron, has requested that I present a paper to the Royal Society in London on my findings regarding the mallangong . . .

No. She rubbed the word out with her thumb . . .

> *Ornithorhynchus anatinus*. Unfortunately, due to ill health I am unable to attend, and my daughter . . .

She scrubbed at the word, the pain ricocheting through her. Would she ever come to believe Pa was not her father?

> . . . your sister, Rose, is traveling in my stead. I would ask you to assist her on her arrival in London and secure appropriate accommodation for her. She will deliver my paper to the Royal Society on the fourth day of June, 1820.
>
> Passage aboard the *Minerva* has been booked. The ship leaves these shores on December 9. God willing and a fair wind will see her arrive in London in late May.
>
> I remain yours, most sincerely,
> Charles Winton

"What do you think, Mam?"

"I think we should take it in and read it to Charles. It is his letter, after all."

The enormity of the responsibility slipped slowly through her body, a strange mixture of elation and despair. This was to have been Pa's greatest moment and it had been snatched from him. However, the date was set and she hadn't a moment to waste.

Chapter 7

Wollombi, New South Wales
1908

Whyever would Mrs. Rushworth question her mother's dying wish? It would be a lovely memorial. Book donors are remembered forever."

"I have absolutely no idea." The lie tripped off Shaw's tongue with an ease that surprised him. When his father had asked him to drive Mrs. Rushworth down to Will-O-Wyck, he'd jumped at the idea—anything for a few days out of the office—but the longer he spent in her company, the more he'd come to realize that she was driven by one motive and one motive only. And that was money. Tamsin and the sketchbook had provided the perfect distraction. She'd occupied almost all of his time and his interest. He wasn't sure whether it was the expression of amazement on her face when she'd looked at the sketchbook or the fact that he was in awe of her expertise, but he enjoyed every moment he spent with her. Not only that, but it had occurred to him that Tamsin's knowledge would be invaluable when the time came to catalogue his grandfather's library, which had finally arrived from Oxford.

She'd been so quiet when he'd taken her back to the Family Hotel after seeing the sketchbook. She'd thanked him politely and disappeared to her room. When Mrs. Adcock had suggested taking a picnic to watch the platypus, he'd jumped at the opportunity to spend time with Tamsin.

Once she'd settled into the seat beside him, he gunned the car down the road.

"Is it very far?"

"No, about ten, fifteen minutes. We take the Paynes Crossing road out of the town, then there's a sheltered sandy spot just past the driveway to the house, according to Mrs. Adcock."

They took the dirt track over a narrow bridge that was nothing more than a series of timbers secured with rusted bolts. At least some of the planks were secure; others jumped and rocked as they clattered over, seesawing as the car bounced across. The dirt track became visible the moment they crossed the brook, and he veered to the right and came to a halt in front of a dilapidated gate.

"I'll get it." Tamsin swung open the door and climbed out. "I think the whole thing has seen better days." She heaved the gate up on its hinges and pushed it back, allowing him to drive through onto the scrubby track, then dusted her hands and slipped back into the car. "I don't think anyone has opened that for a while."

"We're on private property."

"Then how did you get permission?"

"Not much a few ales won't buy you." He eased the motor car to a halt. "I thought it would save carrying the picnic basket too."

"Picnic?" She shot him a look from under her dark lashes.

"Mrs. Adcock's idea. Got to eat something. I'll just get the basket out of the back. There's a blanket behind the seat if you can grab that."

A narrow path, maybe just a wallaby track, meandered down to the edge of the brook. It couldn't be called a creek—too picturesque with the overhanging trees and sandy banks. The locals all called it a brook. Platypus heaven. Heaven for anyone who needed a break.

"Here?"

"Looks good to me." Shaw put down the basket and spread out the blanket. "Have a seat. I've got some lemonade if you'd like a drink." He pulled out a couple of bottles, popped the lids, and handed her one.

"Do you realize the implication of this sketchbook?" Tamsin pulled her legs up and tucked them close to her body, shifting on the checkered blanket until she'd made a comfortable indentation. "It should be on public display, and Winton should be credited with his discoveries."

He shrugged. In many ways he agreed with her, if what she said was correct and the provenance of the book could be proven. "Private collectors would pay a fortune to get their hands on it." His grandfather would have walked across oceans for it.

"Private collectors? Don't you understand? This is a major discovery. It could turn the scientific world on it toes. The platypus was the obsession of the nineteenth century. It defied all the known classifications. If the dates in Winton's sketchbook are accurate, he was twenty, thirty years ahead of everyone else. If nothing else, he deserves recognition. It can't go into a private collection, no matter how much someone is prepared to pay. Please encourage Mrs. Rushworth to honor her mother's wishes and let me take it back to Sydney."

"It's not my decision."

"She said I should deal with you, that you were her solicitor."

"My father is." He shrugged his shoulders. His father wasn't the easiest man to get along with; however, he managed to maintain a civil relationship. "I work for him."

"You have some influence, then. What do you know about Mrs. Quinleaven?"

"Lived here for ages. From all accounts, she worked as a live-in housekeeper for Mr. Kelly for many years. He owned Will-O-Wyck. He was a local solicitor and took his wife's death very hard, and that's when Mrs. Quinleaven stepped in."

"What happened to Mrs. Rushworth's father?"

"Mr. Quinleaven? Disappeared, vanished. Never seen again. Some say he was a casualty of the African War, though I have a suspicion the marriage was over long before."

"And Mr. Kelly left everything to Mrs. Quinleaven when he died."

"So Mrs. Rushworth has led us to believe."

"Surely she knows."

"She was estranged from her mother. Hadn't spoken to her for many years."

"Why?"

"At a guess she didn't approve of her mother living under the same roof as Mr. Kelly."

"She was his housekeeper, for goodness' sake. And none of this helps us discover how the sketchbook got into Mrs. Quinleaven's hands."

"There's really very little that can be done. The decision will be made by the benefactors."

Tamsin let out a long sigh and stretched out her legs. "How do you know there isn't anything else significant in the house?"

"I don't."

She leaned across the rug, her dark eyes sparkling. "I'd give anything for a look around the rest of the house, especially the library.

There could be all sorts of interesting things hidden away. It seems strange there should be just this one sketchbook."

And so would he, but from what he'd gathered, the Rushworths would sell everything; they needed every penny they could raise. "The house and contents are to be sold."

"Oh, what a shame. Perhaps you could change Mrs. Rushworth's mind. There's so much interest in Australiana since Federation."

"I thought that was rather more in the line of household items. You know, all those ghastly jugs and cups and saucers with koalas clinging to the handles."

"Australia's answer to Art Nouveau. This is far more important, and once the Mitchell bequest is sorted out, there'll be a further surge in interest."

Which would increase the value of the sketchbook. "Maybe the Mitchell would buy it." That would solve the problem, the best outcome for everyone. Mrs. Rushworth would get her money and honor would be satisfied.

"No chance of that. The building alone is way over budget."

He stared out across the brook searching for any movement that might indicate the animals were about—and for something to change the conversation. He didn't want to keep saying no.

She was like a puppy with a shoe, and a bit of pleasure leached out of the day with the sinking sun. "Looking through the house and library might give us a clue as to how the sketchbook ended up there. All Winton's known work went up in flames in the Garden Palace fire. That's why I've been trying to get copies of his correspondence with Banks from the Royal Society. I can't imagine how one sketchbook ended up here in Wollombi."

He had to change the subject. Mrs. Rushworth's heart was set on making as much money out of the property as she could. There was no possibility she would let Tamsin go poking around the house, especially if she was advocating donations. "It's getting close to dusk, the perfect time."

"Adult males are most visible in late winter and early spring, so the season's right. They spend an increased amount of time on the water surface watching for rivals during the mating season." She let out a short, sharp laugh. "I sound like a textbook. I've become obsessed with the creatures since I discovered Winton."

"I'll be very surprised if we don't see one. The locals said they're around if the conditions are right."

The shadows stretched out toward evening and the bottles of lemonade Mrs. Adcock provided sat in a puddle of late afternoon sun. Tamsin hadn't touched a drop.

She brought it to her lips and grimaced. "I'm sorry."

"Toss it out. I've got tea in the flask."

She flicked the lemonade in a high arc, sending it toward the bank of the brook, catching the last rays of the sun as it dipped behind the surrounding hills and disturbing the water skippers hovering on the calm water surrounding the reeds.

"Try this."

She took the cup and clasped it between her two hands and looked directly at him with a gaze of such intensity it disconcerted him. "I have every intention of convincing Mrs. Rushworth the book needs to be assessed and displayed in Sydney. Perhaps she'd be prepared to leave it at the Library on view for a period and still retain ownership; maybe it has some special personal significance."

Shaw leaned back on his elbows and stretched out his legs. She could try, but he didn't like her chances, not unless a payment was involved.

Tamsin swirled the tea and inhaled the steam.

"Is the tea to your liking?"

She took a sip. "Yes, thank you. The water is incredibly calm; there's not a breath of wind."

"The best kind of weather for platypus spotting, I'm told." He stood and held out a hand to her. "Bring your tea. We'll sit down over there, closer to the water. I was told the burrow is in that sandy part of the bank on the other side."

He pulled her upright and she swung close to his chest, her scent filling his nostrils. Linen and lavender and a tiny dab of something citrusy—lemon, unless he was mistaken. Her dark hair brushed against his hand as he steadied her and he felt a stab of lust.

She must have noticed his reaction because she raised her hands and stepped back, a ghost of a smile crossing her face. "I've never seen a platypus before."

"Move over a bit closer to this tree." Shaw patted the smooth trunk of the gum. "It'll mask our outline." He'd dropped his voice to a whisper, forcing her to lean closer to catch his words. "They don't like sharp noises or sudden movements. I'm told we have to look for telltale bumps in the water."

Tamsin kept her eyes riveted on the bank on the other side of the brook. "Everything I've read indicates they're shy and secretive creatures. In this light they'll have a silvery shine, not the usual chocolate brown."

He scanned the shallow water. "One of the locals said he spotted one feeding the other evening." He pointed to the right of the bank. "He was diving and coming up, then just floating around treading water while he chewed his dinner. The man said to watch for a bull's-eye pattern on the top of the water." He closed his hand around her arm and inclined his head.

A flash of response flickered in her eyes, from either the prospect of seeing the platypus or maybe his proximity. The latter, he hoped. She was gorgeous and totally natural; not a flicker of pretense or flirtatiousness.

The slightest splash echoed in the sheltered hollow and she drew in a gentle sigh, undoubtedly for the platypus, whose glistening shape glided through the water before it arched its back and launched downward.

Counting the seconds in a whisper, she chewed on her lip, eyes glued to the water, waiting for the creature to resurface, and sure enough, it reappeared about twenty feet downstream.

"Watch the pattern on the water."

The concentric circles spread outward and he envisaged the webbed feet paddling below the surface; then a hind foot appeared almost on the surface and the platypus gave a leisurely scratch before diving again, its path marked by a stream of small bubbles as the air squeezed from its fur. The ripples on the surface of the water spread wider until they reached the bank.

"Magical, just magical." Tamsin whispered the words, her eyes filling with tears. "I've read so much about them and yet this is the first time I've seen one. Here in the twilight I can imagine how Winton must have felt when he first discovered the creatures."

They stood, shoulders almost touching, in companionable silence while the platypus frolicked in the crystal-clear water and the light dimmed.

"The show's over for tonight." Her voice broke the silence, making him feel strangely disappointed, and they picked their way carefully back up the bank to collect the remains of the picnic.

"Can you imagine how many hours Winton must have spent watching them to collect so much knowledge? His drawings are so detailed. That's what makes the sketchbook so valuable, not just its antiquity but the body of work it represents."

After tonight he wasn't very sure selling the book was such a good idea; perhaps she was right, but any chance of Mrs. Rushworth giving it up would vanish once she realized its true value.

He stowed the picnic hamper in the back of the car and helped Tamsin inside, placing the rug on her lap. "It might be cold now the sun's gone down."

They clattered back down the track and he leaped out at the gate before she had the chance to offer. She looked so contented, warm and snug with the blanket tucked around her, he didn't want her to move.

Once they turned back onto the road, she sat up a little straighter and loosened the blanket. "I believe Winton relied very heavily on the blackfellas' knowledge, and in those days, no one took the natives seriously. They thought they made it all up, were just saying what the white man wanted to hear, that they couldn't be trusted to observe correctly. I don't understand why he didn't go to England to champion his discoveries. His knowledge would have brought science so much further."

"Perhaps he harbored some sort of grudge because someone stole his work, made their name from it, and he stayed bitter and angry."

"That can't be right. And I can't for the life of me work out how the sketchbook ended up here. He lived at a place called Agnes Banks, outside Parramatta. I wonder if there are still platypus there."

"You said they were shy creatures. Agnes Banks is a thriving rural community now." The kind of area his father and Mrs. Rushworth's husband would have their sights set on before too long—cheap land offering the opportunity to develop and make an excellent return. "That's the advantage of this area. It is as though time has stood still."

"Which is why I'd really like to see inside the house." She didn't let the opportunity slip. "Will you put a word in for me with Mrs. Rushworth? I must ensure the donation goes ahead."

"I'll see what I can do." What else could he say?

Shaw cruised to a halt outside the hotel, and before he could get out and open the door, she shrugged off the blanket and stood beside the car. "Thank you for a wonderful evening. I really feel closer to Winton now I've seen the platypus in its natural habitat."

"It doesn't have to end now. It's still early. Let me treat you to a nightcap. I'd like to hear a bit more about the Library and your job." And her thoughts on Winton's book. He had a sense she wasn't sharing everything, and any little extra bit of knowledge would help him decide what he should do.

"Perhaps another cup of tea."

"I was thinking of something a little stronger. Can I tempt you?"

"Tea will be fine."

He pushed open the door and stood back while she walked through into the dining room.

"You sit down here and I'll go and have a word with Mrs. Adcock. You're quite happy if I leave you for a moment?"

She gave him a look from under her heavy brows that stopped him from saying anything else, and he sauntered off to the bar.

"Mrs. Adcock, could I trouble you for a pot of tea and some whisky?"

"Strange combination."

"The tea is for Miss Alleyn and the whisky for me."

"And did she enjoy her picnic?"

The delights of a small town. He let out a huff of annoyance. Everyone believed it was his or her right to know everything. He was sick and tired of people poking and prodding into his affairs. "She did. I'll bring the hamper in once we've had our nightcap."

He slid into the seat opposite Tamsin and she lifted her head and studied him, a slight frown marring the skin of her forehead. She was nothing like the girls his sister brought home, with their rouged cheeks, coiffed hair, and high-pitched giggles. Her no-nonsense dark brown eyes appraised him and she rested her chin in her hands.

"So tell me the story of the donation."

"There's not much to tell. I'm surprised Mrs. Rushworth didn't mention it."

"She knew nothing of it. Came as quite a shock. Didn't even know the sketchbook existed until we arrived the morning of the funeral. It's been a difficult time for her."

"I can imagine. Losing parents is never easy."

Perhaps that accounted for the lingering sadness in her eyes. But more importantly, he wanted to shout, *Tell me about the sketchbook!* All this polite conversation was getting him nowhere. "The sketchbook?"

"Right, yes. The Library received a letter from Mrs. Quinleaven saying she had a sketchbook dating back to the beginning of the last century and she believed it might be of national significance. She wished to make a donation. She'd made a promise."

"What kind of a promise? To whom?"

She shrugged her shoulders. "I don't know."

"Nothing more?"

"Only that she wasn't prepared to trust it to the postal system, which is where I came in. I had some background knowledge because I'd requested the correspondence of the early Australian naturalists from the Royal Society. It's been my responsibility to coordinate the project to tie in with the opening of the Mitchell wing." A blush tinged her cheeks as though she was very proud of the fact but didn't want to brag. She must hold down a significant position at the Library, unusual for a woman.

"How long have you worked at the Library?"

"Coming up for five years."

Most unusual. "How did you get the job?"

She let out a peal of laughter. "You mean, what's a woman doing with a job like that?"

In a nutshell. "Yes." There was no pulling the wool over her eyes. She could read him like a book. He groaned inwardly. Probably spent her time reading between the lines.

"I answered an advertisement."

"They advertised for a woman?"

"Not specifically. But then, they didn't advertise specifically for a man. My credentials were accepted and I was asked to sit an examination. Along with forty-three others. When I turned up, they realized I was a woman."

That certainly wouldn't be hard to miss. Her eyes sparkled, almost as though she was laughing at him.

"And you sat the examination and passed it."

"Topped it, actually, and since they hadn't blocked the position to women, there was nothing very much anyone could do. They were opposed, but Mrs. Williams championed my cause. Her husband was the Principal Librarian until he died and she'd worked in a voluntary capacity for years."

When Mrs. Adcock placed a teapot and cup and saucer in front of her, she stopped speaking.

"Sugar and milk?"

"Yes, please."

"And here's your whisky." Mrs. Adcock put it down with a bang and winked at him. "Don't you keep the young lady up too late."

"Thank you, Mrs. Adcock." The wretched woman hovered for a few more minutes and then, when neither of them resumed the conversation, she flounced off.

"So you know my story." She lifted the cup to her lips and peered over the rim at him. "Will Mrs. Rushworth definitely be selling everything?"

He took another sip of his whisky. "Ultimately. Once the will is finalized."

She gazed out of the window into the darkness. "I really would like the opportunity to speak to her again about the sketchbook. I feel certain once she appreciates the national significance, she will agree to let the donation go ahead."

He wasn't going to manage to put her off. So be it. "I'll drive you out in the morning."

"Thank you, that would be lovely." She gave him a self-satisfied smile, downed the remains of her tea, and stood before lifting her hand in a brief wave and slipping through the door.

Shaw sat for a few more moments. He couldn't help feeling a little guilty. He should be encouraging Mrs. Rushworth to donate the book, not prolonging the entire exercise, but Tamsin fascinated him. She was unlike any woman he'd come across before. Independent and a tad feisty. The kind of girl who would give his mother a fit of the vapors and his father a run for his money.

Chapter 8

Wollombi, New South Wales
1908

When Mrs. Rushworth's icy blue gaze lodged firmly on her practical skirt and boots with the same disdain as yesterday, Tamsin wished she'd given a little more thought to her appearance.

"You'd better come in, Miss Alleyn." She swept down the hallway and took a sharp turn into the library where she'd caught Tamsin yesterday.

The stack of tea chests had multiplied overnight and most of the shelves were empty. Tamsin's stomach took a dive along with last night's dream about stumbling on some hidden treasure that would explain how the sketchbook arrived in Wollombi and solve the whole conundrum of Winton's life.

Shaw must have had a similar thought because he smoothed his hands over the bare surface of the desk until his eyes lit up at the sight of a pile of leather-bound volumes. He picked up one and turned it over, running his long fingers over the embossed leather cover. The man seemed to have an insatiable curiosity where old books were concerned.

"I'd appreciate it if you would have a closer look at those, Shaw, and see if they are of any interest. They seem to be in very good condition."

The external condition of the books came a very poor second to the contents—surely Mrs. Rushworth was aware of that. "Can you spare me a moment to discuss the sketchbook?"

Mrs. Rushworth jumped and turned almost as though she had forgotten Tamsin was in the room. "Such a fuss about an old book. I could understand if it belonged to da Vinci or someone renowned, but the jottings of some unknown convict . . . Nevertheless, it should remain in the family."

"Winton was not a convict; he was a freeman and quite well known in his field. He was one of the colony's early naturalists. And Mrs. Quinleaven obviously thought the sketchbook of some value and that it should be donated."

"For whatever strange reason she omitted to disclose."

Tamsin clamped her lips tight, capturing her irrational spark of temper. The woman infuriated her. She seemed not to show any sadness for the loss of her mother or any interest in fulfilling her wishes or recognizing the national significance of such a work. If she could just get her to agree to her taking the sketchbook to Sydney, she might change her mind. "I'd like your permission to take the sketchbook to Sydney to have it assessed."

"Of course."

The air sucked from Tamsin's lungs. That was too easy, far too easy.

"I have absolutely no problem with that. I'd like to know what it is worth." Only yesterday she'd refused to discuss the matter. "Providing Mr. Everdene agrees to take responsibility."

Shaw's face broke into a grin highlighting a dimple in his cheek she hadn't noticed before, and an inkling of a smile creased Mrs. Rushworth's pampered skin, obviously satisfied she could trust Shaw to follow her instructions.

"Is there any possibility we might have a look at the other books?" Shaw's voice wavered, his fingers compulsively stroking the leather coverings. Her comments last night must have sparked some idea in his head. If the sketchbook had been among these books, then there was the chance that others might have been missed.

"It is highly unlikely anything has been overlooked. They are being packed for removal tomorrow morning. Anything you unpack must be replaced."

"Can you tell us how your mother came by the sketchbook, Mrs. Rushworth?" Tamsin asked.

"How should I know? She had the reputation of being a recluse." Her face colored a little and she turned to the window. "After my father died, my mother and I lost touch . . ." She shook her head. "To be honest, I don't think she set foot outside the property for nigh on twenty years. *Testy* might be a better word to describe her."

Another wave of melancholy swept over Tamsin. Poor Mrs. Quinleaven. Her estranged daughter, someone who didn't give two hoots about her or her possessions, stood to inherit everything. There was something intrinsically sad about the entire situation. "Did you grow up here?"

"No, I did not. My mother took it into her head to up sticks and move here without a moment's consideration for my situation." She gave a disdainful sniff. "My husband holds a very important position in the city, sits on a number of boards, and is very involved in the demand for new housing. Our lives revolve around Sydney. This little backwater is of no concern to us. I simply want the property sold. Now, is that all? I think I've been more than forthcoming with my time."

What a repulsive, money-grabbing woman. No wonder Mrs. Quinleaven had attempted to make arrangements for the sketchbook before she died.

"Tell me when you're leaving. The sketchbook is in the dining room." She walked out of the room, leaving nothing but the cloying scent of jasmine. Shaw moved to the window and drew back the thick velvet curtains, letting the morning sun flood in. The light revealed a pile of magazines and pamphlets in a corner behind the door and two half-packed tea chests.

"If Mrs. Quinleaven lived by herself, as a recluse, she certainly hadn't lost contact with the world."

"I don't think she was the kind of recluse Mrs. Rushworth portrays—more to do with her own guilty conscience inheriting a tidy sum from an estranged parent. The old man at the hotel reckons Mrs. Quinleaven volunteered in the Court House once a fortnight. She catalogued all the old newspapers and frequently wrote articles for the *Maitland Mercury*. She was keen on family history."

"She sounds like a fascinating woman. This must have been a beautiful house once."

"I expect Mrs. Rushworth will be able to sell the property without too much of a problem."

People could be funny about the past, frightened to take on buildings with a history. Perhaps that was the reason Mrs. Rushworth wanted to sell—she simply didn't want to be reminded of the past. That she could understand. It had been one of her reasons for selling her parents' house and not taking up medicine as Mother and Father had always intended she should. "Hopefully the money from the house will satisfy her."

The library was the most beautiful room, with its floor-to-ceiling shelving and soft filtered light; she could imagine sitting in the leather chair reading or perhaps simply daydreaming an afternoon away. She turned to take in the view from the window and caught sight of some old newspapers and magazines tucked against the skirting board.

She bent down and collected the newspapers up in her arms. "How are we going for time?"

"What's this lot?"

"They were on the floor." She heaved them up onto the table and started flicking through them. A collection of copies of the *Maitland Mercury* and *Bell's Life in Sydney and Sporting Chronicle* and some copies of the *Penny Magazine of the Society for the Diffusion of Useful Knowledge from England*, one featuring a front-page article on "The *Ornithorhynchus Paradoxus* or Water-Mole" dated June 1835. "I'd love the opportunity to read this."

"Stick it inside one of those books." Shaw gestured to the heavy leather-bound volumes he'd put to one side and winked at her.

She tucked the pamphlet inside the cover and returned to the pile. There was a huge collection of the *Dawn*. "I think our Mrs. Quinleaven might have been something of a suffragette."

"What makes you say that?"

"These." She flicked the pile of magazines. "Louisa Lawson's publication. If it hadn't been for her, I doubt women would have the vote in New South Wales. They ought to be kept too." She stacked them neatly. "Perhaps Mrs. Rushworth would let these go."

"We'll have to ask her."

Tamsin reached down for the remains of the papers. "Oh!" A pain shot up her leg as her ankle twisted, and she bent down to rub it and spotted the culprit. A tin.

"Are you all right?"

Shaw was at her side, hands on her arms, helping her to her feet.

"Yes. I'm fine." She shrugged him off and stood up. "This must have been underneath." Tamsin shook the tin and it rattled. She latched her fingers around the lid and tugged. The rust caught in her fingernails but the lid held tight. "Any idea what might be in here?" She held up the rectangular tin.

"Peek Frean biscuits. Reckon they'd be well and truly stale by now."

"I can't get the lid off."

"Give it to me. I'll have a go." Shaw rummaged in the pocket of his trousers and pulled out a handful of coins, then selected a shiny new sixpence and pushed the rest back. He lodged the tin against the table and wedged the coin between the lid and the base and twisted. "It's stuck fast." He shook the tin. "It's got something in it, not sure what. Doesn't sound like biscuits."

"Have you finished in there?" Mrs. Rushworth's voice rang down the hallway.

Tamsin gritted her teeth. She wasn't ready to leave yet. She grabbed the tin from Shaw and tucked it under her arm. "I want to take it with us as well as the copies of the *Dawn* and the *Penny Magazine*."

The door swung open to reveal Mrs. Rushworth with the linen bag containing the sketchbook dangling precariously from the drawstring. "I'll have to ask you to leave now. Shaw, don't forget we have an appointment this afternoon." She studied the last remaining bits and pieces on the table, handed Shaw the sketchbook, then leaned in to scoop up the papers on the table. "These can be burned. There's no point in keeping old newspapers."

"I'd like to keep some, if I may." The words leaped out of Tamsin's mouth. "The copies of the *Dawn*—it's almost a full collection."

"For goodness' sake, take them. You're turning the place into a bazaar."

"And this." Something about the tin drew her. "I collect old tins." She gave a wan smile. She had no idea which part of her mind the lie sprang from, but she wanted it. Surely Mrs. Rushworth wouldn't refuse.

A knock sounded on the door. "That'll be the furniture dealer. I must ask you to leave."

They dutifully filed down the hallway, Tamsin clutching the tin and the copies of the *Dawn*, Shaw the linen bag with the sketchbook inside and the four leather-bound volumes.

"Thank you very much for your help, Mrs. Rushworth. I'll let you know the result of the Library's appraisal of the sketchbook, and thank you for the tin."

"For Miss Alleyn's collection." Shaw shot her one of his cheeky grins and they stepped out and left Mrs. Rushworth to deal with the poor cloth-capped furniture dealer.

Tamsin didn't envy him. Insufferable woman. They shot down the path with their treasures like a couple of kids raiding a lolly shop and it wasn't until they'd collapsed into his car that they burst out laughing.

"That was strange, really strange. The woman gives me the shivers."

"And tins."

If nothing else, he broke the tension, made her laugh. "I know it was a whopping lie. I have no idea what made me say it. I just wanted the tin. Had to have it. Probably because I couldn't open it."

"Come on, Miss Alleyn, let's go back to the hotel and I'll see if I can get the lid off your consolation prize. Can you nurse these books on your lap?"

She settled the four volumes with the papers and the sketchbook, then balanced the tin on top. "I think you'd better call me Tamsin. Miss Alleyn sounds far too formal for a coconspirator."

The moment they pulled up outside the hotel, the barrel-chested man sauntered out to the car.

"Any chance of using your workshop?" Shaw asked him.

"That newfangled machine of yours broken?"

"No, but I need a vise and a screwdriver or two. I have a tin I need to open." Shaw lifted the tin from her lap and rattled it.

"Be my guest, but leave the car out here. I'd like to have a look at it."

"That's fine. Tamsin has some things to take care of in the back." Shaw took the sketchbook and got out from behind the wheel. "Why don't you sit here and try it for size."

The man didn't have to be asked twice and levered himself in, hands resting on the wheel, eyes riveted straight ahead.

"Keep an eye on him. I won't be long," Shaw murmured before disappearing around the back with the tin while she stacked the four books and the papers neatly behind the passenger seat, covering them with the blanket they'd used for the picnic. When she straightened up, the man had taken to turning the wheel and making a series of strange noises that sounded nothing like a motor car.

"Give me a horse any day." He yanked down on the wheel, making the tires groan. "Got a really hard mouth, this thing."

Tamsin could hardly wait to get away from him. The noises coming from the workshop behind her had her mind whirling. She'd definitely heard a long-drawn-out sigh and then silence. Had Shaw managed to get the lid off the tin? The wait was driving her to distraction. The contents had become almost more important than the sketchbook. She had no idea what could be inside or where her strange affiliation with an old biscuit tin had come from. She didn't even eat biscuits!

With a series of grunts and groans the cantankerous man heaved himself out. "I don't reckon these things'll ever replace a horse." He kicked at the tire, then ambled into the hotel.

The moment he'd gone Tamsin barreled through the door of the shed. Shaw raised his head and raked his fingers through his hair, his eyes wide with curiosity.

The hint of fresh sweat, motor oil, and warm leather, so delightfully male, almost intimate, made her toes curl.

"Success?"

He pushed his sleeves farther up above his elbows, exposing the bunched muscles of his forearms, and wiped the back of his hand across his forehead, leaving a trace of the rust clinging to his damp skin. Then with a flourish he eased off the lid of the tin.

"You got it off. What's in it?"

"I thought you'd like the first look. It's your tin, after all."

Her fingers itched to touch it, though she had no idea what she might find. She peered over Shaw's shoulder at a pile of crumpled yellowed paper. "I wonder if we missed anything particularly important back at the house."

"Like what?" He slid the tin across the top of the workbench and waggled his eyebrows. "Another sketchbook? A moth-eaten nineteenth-century platypus pelt?"

"Don't be silly." She peered into the tin and plucked at the layer of paper, releasing a dusty sweetness that made her nose twitch. A small package lay underneath three handmade envelopes tied with a faded pale blue ribbon.

"Letters?" Shaw moved closer, leaning over her shoulder, his warm, manly scent combining with the whispered secrets of the tin.

Her heart skipped a beat and she wiped her hair back from her face. "We should get some gloves."

Tamsin toyed with the tin while Shaw delved into the linen bag containing the sketchbook. He retied the bag and made room on the workbench. "Here you are. Put these on." A ribbon of excitement laced his voice as he handed her the gloves.

She shot a look at him from under her lashes, the sense of camaraderie filling her with a warm glow. As much as she wanted to know what was in the tin, this was the moment she treasured. The anticipation.

Those brief few minutes when she simply didn't know what the future held. She'd felt the same way when the first of Winton's letters had arrived from England, and when she'd first seen the sketchbook. She pushed the gloves on and interlaced her fingers, making them fit tight. "Ready?"

Shaw nodded. "Come on. I can't wait any longer."

Picking up the faded ribbon she lifted the envelopes, releasing a more intense whiff of the sweetness belonging to the biscuits that once inhabited the tin, and lowered them to the table. She plucked at the bow. The ribbon fell free and she unfolded the thick piece of cartridge paper and scanned the beautiful swirling script, an artwork in itself.

JENIFER TREVAN, LOVING GRANDDAUGHTER
OF GRANFER TOMAS TREVAN,
MAY 24, 1772—FEBRUARY 2, 1788

"Is that all?"

She turned the piece of paper over and back. "That's all."

"I was hoping for something more exciting." Shaw's hand reached for the package and something snatched at Tamsin's throat. She didn't want him to touch it. It belonged to her. What nonsense! He had as much right as she did, more in fact. He'd introduced her to Mrs. Rushworth. She dropped her hand and gave an apologetic smile. "Sorry. For some reason I feel possessive about the tin and its contents."

He chuckled. "It's because you found it, and now you know how I felt about the sketchbook once I'd seen it."

She hadn't thought about that. Perhaps it wasn't only Mrs. Rushworth who was hesitant about allowing her to take it to Sydney; with his interest in old books, Shaw might feel the same way. "I'm sorry, it hadn't occurred to me."

He shrugged his shoulders and took a step back from the table. "Come on, let's see what else is in there. Try to keep everything in order."

She lifted the next envelope and placed it face down on the table. It was thicker than the last. She ran her gloved hand over it. "It feels like it's padded." She lifted the flap of the envelope and her fingers closed over a piece of material. "I think it's a handkerchief. It's old. Look at the lace. Eighteenth, maybe early nineteenth century. Beautiful." She lifted it to her nose and inhaled the faint scent of lavender. "I wonder who it belonged to. Jenifer Trevan, perhaps?" She unfolded the frail linen. "No, not Jenifer Trevan." She ran her fingers over the embroidered corner. "A rose and the initials *CM*."

"Keep going. Let's see what else is there."

She slid the handkerchief back into the envelope and picked up the package, thicker than the envelope. She let the paper fall open. Wrapped in a piece of tissue paper was a daguerreotype, framed in dull red cardboard. "Look." The perfect Victorian portrait, not staged, taken outside and not an aspidistra in sight like most of the others she'd seen before: a man and a woman, and standing beside them two young women, their arms linked. She wiped the finger of her glove over the glass, so scratched and tarnished it was as though a group of ghosts peered back at her.

With a frustrated sigh, she put down the daguerreotype and foraged in her skirt pocket for her spectacles.

Shaw reached for the picture.

"No, wait, please. I can't see it clearly." The color rushed to her cheeks. Bad enough wearing spectacles, but admitting to her shortsightedness was right out of character. She turned the daguerreotype over: *George Goodman, George Street, Sydney*. "That doesn't make sense. Goodman opened his Sydney studio in 1845. It can't be Jenifer. Look at her dates: 1772 to 1788. Her children, perhaps? No, she died when she was sixteen. This woman is much older." She squinted at their features, obscured by the scratched tangle of light and dark.

"The advantages of dealing with someone who knows their stuff."

"I was reading about the history of photography not long ago and . . ."

"And you remembered?"

She lowered her head from his intense gaze in a vain attempt to hide the flush blooming on her cheeks. "Just a mind that retains silly bits of information." An obscure failing, an embarrassment more often than not. As a child she'd hated the ease with which she could remember dates as just one more thing that marked her as different from all the other girls at school.

"Very handy. What's next?"

Tamsin's shoulders dropped and she blew a strand of hair from her face. Perhaps she wasn't the only one with a freakish interest in history. She squinted at the picture of the woman in a floppy hat—a bit like the cabbage palm hats they wore in the early days. The man was in shirtsleeves rolled up to his elbows, an unbuttoned, homespun waistcoat over the top. Both of the young women had dark hair, pinned back from their faces. "I wonder if they were sisters." She passed the daguerreotype to Shaw, who carried it to the door and let the sunlight fall on the glass.

"Interesting. They look as though they are wearing identical dresses." He wrapped it back up in the tissue paper.

"I don't think it has been in the tin for long. It must have been in the light to deteriorate so much."

"Can't win 'em all." He winked, the laughter lines crinkling around his eyes. "Anything else?"

"Maybe it's Mrs. Quinleaven."

Tamsin turned the last envelope over; it was slightly bigger and much thicker. Her fingers shook as she opened it. And then her heart dropped.

The lined paper looked as though it had come from a solicitor's notepad, each page covered in a confusion of scribbles and arrows—some sort of list—and worse, it was all written in faded pencil. "It's nothing. Just someone's notes. And quite recent. Maybe it has to do with the daguerreotype."

"Is there a signature or any indication who wrote it?"

Tamsin squinted down at the faded writing. "I can't make head or tail of it."

"Let me have a look." Shaw reached out and took the sheet of paper. His face creased in a frown and he tilted the paper under the light and then gave up. "I can't either."

Tamsin looked down at the paper in his hand. The spidery writing was all but illegible, and much of it had been crossed out, the frustration oozing from the page. One large circle in the middle remained. The name *Jenifer Trevan* in block letters and long arrows that went nowhere.

Happy enough to go along with Tamsin's biscuit tin hunt, Shaw hadn't realized how the time had flown. He wanted to get back to Sydney and see if they could find out anything more about the sketchbook. He was totally fascinated.

While Tamsin carefully wrapped and folded the bits and pieces and placed them back in the tin with a huge degree of reverence, he slipped the sketchbook from the linen bag to take another look.

There were a number of private collectors in Sydney who might be able to date the book. To his eye, the paper looked very much as though it was rag and not wood, but it could easily be a forgery, especially if Tamsin was right about the fact that a scientific notebook containing watercolors was unusual. Perhaps there was someone at the Library who could date those, or better still, recognize the style and fill in the details.

"Shaw?"

Startled from his reverie, he looked up at Tamsin, standing in the doorway with the sun behind her, dressed today in a severe skirt and blouse with her hair caught in softly at the nape of her neck. She could have been the woman in the daguerreotype. For goodness' sake, his imagination was running away with him.

"I'll be heading back to Sydney tomorrow." A wave of regret washed through him. He'd enjoyed the last few days in her company; didn't want them to be over.

"I will be too. I can't wait to get Mrs. Williams's opinion on the sketchbook. She has an amazing grasp on early Australian history."

"I have to go back to Will-O-Wyck this afternoon to see Mrs. Rushworth." Not strictly true—the local solicitor was expected for the reading of Mrs. Quinleaven's will and Mrs. Rushworth wanted him to attend, but it wasn't his place to discuss that with Tamsin. And he had to find out how and when Mrs. Rushworth intended to go back to Sydney. He harbored some sort of foolish idea about offering Tamsin a lift back, but he was duty bound to make sure Mrs. Rushworth had made plans. "Why don't we have dinner here tonight?" It was a shame there wasn't room in the car for two passengers and Mrs. Rushworth's luggage. Tamsin's presence might ease the tedium of Mrs. Rushworth's incessant prattle.

Tamsin chewed on her lip as if weighing up the alternatives. "I want to have a walk around the town. Get a feel for the place in case there is a connection between Winton and Wollombi. Perhaps we could have dinner after that. I'll be taking the train tomorrow morning."

"Right. I'll meet you in the dining room at, say, six thirty."

"And you'll bring the sketchbook to the Library?"

"I'll be on the doorstep bright and early the day after tomorrow." He wouldn't be missing that opportunity. "I'll give the copy of the *Penny Magazine* to you at dinner; it's still in the car. *Ornithorhynchus paradoxus*. What a mouthful."

"That's why I prefer *platypus*." She bestowed a radiant smile on him and left.

He stood in the door of the workshop watching the sway of her hips when she lifted her hand in some kind of a wave without turning back.

With a sigh, he tucked the sketchbook under his arm, just in case Mrs. Rushworth decided to change her mind, and headed back to the car.

He didn't pass another soul on the road and pulled into the driveway only a few minutes later. If luck was on his side, Mrs. Rushworth would have taken matters into her own hands and made her own arrangements to return to Sydney.

When he parked outside the house, the front door was wide open and Mrs. Rushworth was pacing the verandah as though in training for an Olympic marathon.

"And about time too. I expected you back here earlier. Your father led me to believe that you would deal with the solicitors. For what other reason did you accompany me? A little holiday? The opportunity to chase a bit of skirt?"

He closed his eyes and counted to ten before he answered. He'd picked her as demanding and somewhat short-tempered, but her complaint was totally inappropriate. Tamsin's interest lay in the sketchbook. What business was it of Mrs. Rushworth's what he was doing as long as he fulfilled his obligations? He'd returned at the appointed hour. He bit back a retort, strolled down the verandah, and dropped into a chair without an invitation. "What time are you expecting the solicitor?"

"*Was* might be more appropriate. Mr. Lovedale of Kelly, Baker, and Lovedale has already called." She huffed and rolled her eyes.

"And?" For goodness' sake, the woman drove him mad. Now he wished he'd arrived earlier, not spent the time playing with Tamsin's tin and missing Lovedale's visit.

"It would appear I have been led up the garden path. The property did not belong to my mother."

"The house?"

"Not even that. It's totally outrageous after all she did for that Kelly man. According to Lovedale, when Kelly died he bequeathed her a life interest. It gave her the right to live in the house until she died, and she received an annual income of two hundred pounds."

Nothing wrong with that. He wouldn't mind two hundred pounds a year. He could do a lot with that and stop having to dance to his father's tune. Make a start on cataloguing Grandfather's library; give away his father's dream and pursue his own.

"On her death the bequest ended and the house, contents, and income from his not inconsiderable investments passed to his next of kin."

"Fair enough." Except of course it wouldn't appear fair to Mrs. Rushworth. She'd had her heart set on selling the place to finance her husband's adventures in suburbia. "Who's his next of kin?"

"His daughter, apparently. They haven't had much luck tracking her down and are placing advertisements in the *Maitland Mercury* and Sydney papers."

"I'm afraid there's not much we can do, then." He stood up and brushed his hands down his trousers.

"I want the sketchbook sold immediately."

"Until the estate is sorted out, you're not in a position to do that."

"I am entitled to my mother's personal possessions. I specifically checked with Lovedale."

"I really suggest you wait. These things take time."

"Time is something I don't have."

"I fail to see why. Even if the sketchbook did belong to your mother and is yours to sell, if you want a decent price, you will have to show a degree of patience." If his guess was correct, the sketchbook might fetch a very tidy sum on the open market.

"Sit down, Shaw, and let me explain. The book must be valuable. Why else would they have sent that girl out here? I need to raise some money to tide us over. Selling the book would solve our immediate problems."

"And after that?"

She pursed her lips. "For an up-and-coming solicitor, you can sometimes be a little slow on the uptake. I intend to challenge Kelly's will. My mother must have some rights. She lived in the house for over twenty years; that would have to give her some claim. When you return to Sydney, discuss the matter with your father. She as good as prostituted herself for that man, and what does she get? Nothing. Simply nothing."

It sounded as though Mr. Kelly had seen to it that Mrs. Quinleaven was more than adequately provided for; he simply hadn't seen fit to continue his largesse in perpetuity.

"I shan't be returning to Sydney immediately. I shall stay here and make sure there's nothing I've overlooked. There is no official record of the sketchbook; there can't be, otherwise Lovedale would have mentioned it. We must act immediately. Contact me when you have a buyer."

"You want *me* to sell the sketchbook?" It was as though she'd handed him a golden key—the opportunity to make his name in the closed and hallowed world of antiquarian book collectors.

Chapter 9

LONDON, ENGLAND
1820

"Bad night at the gaming tables?"

Julian's face resembled the winter sky over Bodmin Moor and he looked as though someone had dragged him feetfirst through the marshes. He snorted, raked his hands through his overlong hair, and lifted a set of bloodshot eyes. Definitely a long night, and judging by his missing cravat and stained shirt, he hadn't looked in a mirror—an unusual occurrence. An empty decanter stood at his elbow and a cut-glass tumbler emitted the pungent remains of brandy.

"As odd as it may sound, no. I've only just arrived back from Wyck Hall. Been home all evening."

That made a pleasant change. Perhaps his refusal to bail Julian out of his last round of gambling debts had finally hit the mark. "Last evening, old chap. It's morning." Finneas gestured at the lightening sky.

His brother rubbed at his face and gazed vacantly out of the window. "So it is."

Quite out of character. At nine o'clock on a winter's morning, Julian would usually be found abed, sleeping off the previous night's revelries.

"Is everything all right?"

"In a nutshell, no." Julian held out a folded piece of paper.

The thick sheet was folded twice and appeared to be slightly water-stained. It as good as sprang open in his hand. So Julian's sins had caught up with him. No doubt a letter from some irate father demanding his darling daughter's reputation be restored. There had to be a string of disappointed girls across London and the Home Counties. No one could accuse Julian of being parsimonious with his favors. "Got yourself in a spot of bother, have you?"

"Not me this time. Seems I am to pay for my father's sins. I'd rather hoped he'd taken them to his watery grave."

Hardly any way to speak of a member of the Royal Navy who'd given his all at the Battle of Trafalgar, but then, Julian had a reputation for talking as his gut guided him and trampling roughshod over any and all niceties. Finneas plucked the paper from his hand and gazed down at the sprawling signature. Barely a signature, more a feminine flourish at the end of the letter. "Who's it from?"

"Someone by the name of Charles Winton."

Not feminine, then. "It would appear I have a sister." Julian lifted his shoulders, spread his hands wide, then let them fall with a disgruntled slap onto the table.

"And you don't remember her?"

"Never met her. Just read it. Read it."

"'I am writing to request, in the name of your dear departed father and our long friendship, your indulgence and assistance.'"

"Not out loud, man. I've committed it to memory. The contents are etched on my very soul, believe me."

The likelihood of Julian having a soul was a matter he would one day like to debate. Not today, however.

"For once in my life I'm asking your advice."

Finneas's eyes raced down the page. *Sir Joseph Banks. The Royal Society. Ornithorhynchus anatinus.* None of it made any sense. He folded the paper and placed it down on the table. "Man, that's phenomenal news. What I wouldn't give for a sister."

Julian blew out his cheeks and reached for the empty tumbler, brought it to his lips, wrinkled his nose, and tossed the glass aside. "Some convict spawn."

Convict spawn or not, Finneas would give an arm and a leg to have someone who shared his blood. To remember his mother or father would be an added bonus.

"My father's indiscretion coming to roost firmly on my doorstep. We are siblings only in blood. We have never met."

"Wait a moment, I don't understand. Your birth mother or Richard Barrington's wife . . ."

"I've spent twenty years trying to put this behind me. And now it has come back to haunt me."

"I think you'd better explain."

"My father, the esteemed naval surgeon Richard Barrington, took his convict housekeeper to his bed and I was the result. When I was five, we returned to England. He intended I should be brought up as his heir. His wife, quite understandably in my book, refused, and so Caroline took me in. Least she could do for her brother."

"His housekeeper was a convict?"

"Happens all the time. Morals of alley cats."

The pot calling the kettle black, without a doubt. "What was she transported for?"

"Life. Sentenced to death for theft apparently and then reprieved at the last moment."

"She must have stolen something worth having if she was sentenced to death." Finneas clapped Julian on the shoulder. "Chin up. It'll do Caroline good to have someone else to think about."

Julian picked up the letter and tore it in half, tossing the pieces over his shoulder. "Written in pencil. Can't even manage to run to pen and ink."

Finneas grabbed the pieces as they hit the floor. "Stop."

"I want nothing to do with the entire debacle. Can you imagine my reputation if I am seen in London with the daughter of some convict trollop?"

Not something that had bothered Julian before, though the convict element was original. Finneas pieced together the two parts of the letter and sat down in the chair in front of the fire and scanned the words. All in all, it sounded quite interesting—what was this *Ornithorhynchus anatinus*? Beak-nosed? Duck-like? It sparked some strange memory, a bit of a fuss because someone argued about its authenticity. Never mind Julian's attitude. How could this woman deliver a paper to the Royal Society? "Women aren't permitted in the hallowed halls of Somerset House." He turned to find Julian slumped at the table, head resting in his arms. Snoring.

This wouldn't do at all. Perhaps finish the letter, then ask the questions. He read the rest in a matter of moments—more about traveling arrangements. Good God, when was the letter written? *October 27, 1819*. Six months ago. It had taken an age to get here and she was arriving when? *On the* Minerva, *due to dock in London late May* . . . It was late May already. The matter must be dealt with forthwith. The poor girl couldn't arrive in London expecting her brother's assistance and find him slumped over a brandy bottle spewing vitriol about his dubious heritage.

Finneas walked across to the door and yanked on the bell pull. Hughes toppled in through the door, obviously waiting right outside, his curiosity aroused. "Bring coffee. Lots of it, and something to eat. Breakfast. Eggs, ham, kidneys. Something hearty. Mr. Julian is in need of sustenance." And so was he. A thrill of excitement coursed through him. He might not have any living relatives, but he and Julian were as good as brothers. What would that make Rose? Lovely name. His stepsister?

He'd regarded Julian as his older brother ever since the Methenwycks had taken him in. Julian was the heir and, in all honesty, he knew he'd never be more than the spare. It didn't matter one iota. Caroline had pulled Finneas flea-ridden and starving from the Poor House and he'd be thankful forevermore. Without her backing, he'd never have had the opportunity to attend the Hunterian School of Medicine or gain his diploma in medicine at the Royal College of Surgeons. Caroline had championed his cause and installed him in the house at Grosvenor Square. Though he'd sometimes wondered if it hadn't been to keep an eye on Julian, whose preference lay in the gaming clubs, Brooks's specifically, and some other "gentlemen's clubs," as he dubiously referred to them.

With a discreet knock on the door Hughes appeared with a tray. "Put it over . . . Just one moment." He shook Julian's shoulder.

"Come on, man, sit up. Something to eat. It'll do you good."

Julian lifted his head, groaning as though it weighed more than he could manage, and slumped back in the chair, rubbing at his eyes.

"Right here, Hughes, and perhaps you'd be good enough to take this."

"Yes, sir." The butler set the tray on the table, then cleared away last night's debris.

"Leave it with me, thank you."

With a look of disappointment on his face, Hughes made his way out of the room and closed the door behind him.

"Right now, drink this." Finneas poured the coffee and pushed a cup in front of Julian. "No point in trying to hide from this one. You have a responsibility."

"Responsibility to my standing. I am to inherit the Methenwyck fortune and all that entails. I cannot be seen to have a convict sister. The gossip will be all over town in a moment. I shall be drummed out of any and all respectable establishments."

"Not if we handle it correctly. When Rose arrives, we shall offer her accommodation as this man requests. By the way, who is this Winton chap? Do you remember him?"

Julian shook his head. "Not really, vaguely perhaps. Uncle Charles maybe. I was only five. How much do you remember that far back?"

More than he'd like to admit. Some things didn't fade, and the horror of the Poor House and the griping pangs of hunger and misery would always remain etched in his memory. He blessed the day Caroline had brought him to Wyck Hall and given him a family. "And you don't remember a sister? A baby?"

"Not at all. Just vague recollections of long, dark curling hair falling across my face and the smell of something sharp, medicinal, lemon perhaps. My birth mother, I suppose."

"*Eucalyptus obliqua*—the genus dominates the tree flora of New South Wales."

"Speak English, man! For heaven's sake, my head's thumping fit to bust."

"What else do you remember?"

"The voyage. The ship was a Noah's ark full of animal and plant specimens. Black swans . . . I remember black swans. Most of them died along the way. Then not much until Caroline and Cornwall. Not something I like to dwell on. Put it all firmly in the past. Damn it. It is the past. I won't have it impinging on my future."

"Sadly, it's not an option, and you must make the best of it."

"We'll send her down to Cornwall, to Caroline."

"That's probably the best idea you've had. However, we can hardly bundle her into a carriage for a two-hundred-and-fifty-mile journey the moment she steps off the ship. And there's the small matter of the Royal Society. Sir Joseph might be getting a bit long in the tooth, but you wouldn't want to cross him. He has the King's ear and if, as the letter said, this Winton chap is a friend of his . . . well . . ."

"Oh, you're right. I'll be going down for Midsummer. She can come with me then." His face brightened and he drummed two fingers on the table. Such a strange habit, the index finger and the small finger like some misshapen pitchfork. "I want no further reference to my birth mother. Caroline is my mother, and yours too, I might add."

"Here, eat this." Finneas pushed the plate of eggs in front of Julian. The coffee had brought the color back to his face a little, softened the god-awful chalky hue, although his eyes still resembled a bloodhound. "My suggestion is this. I'll go and find out when they expect the *Minerva* to dock. We'll meet the girl, bring her back here, and then we'll know what we're up against, what she needs, and exactly what this Royal Society business is all about."

"That's more up your alley than mine."

Rose was almost disappointed as the ship edged its way into the mooring. As much as she longed for news of home and missed Pa, she'd enjoyed the freedom and excitement of the voyage—the wind in her hair, the unbelievable sights and terrific explosions of color and life she'd witnessed at the ports they'd visited.

She'd set sail for London one hundred and sixty-eight days ago, and from the moment she'd walked aboard her imagination had stirred. Decked out in their dashing uniforms, the various detachments had lent an air of romance to the trip, the soldiers snapping smartly to attention and escorting her hither and yon at every given opportunity.

With the cargoes of sealskins, wool, and coconut oil, an exotic aroma permeated the ship for the entire trip. Then there was the day they'd rescued whalers stranded after their ship was rammed and sank. No one had offered any explanation about the poor whale, but the three crew members seemed hale and hearty.

And here she was about to step onto the streets of London. Pa hadn't been able to tell her anything about the city he'd left over twenty years ago and Mam, as always, hadn't offered very much—just said the biggest city she'd seen was Plymouth when she'd boarded the *Lady Juliana*. Rose pushed her shoulders back and stared at the crowds lining the docks, feeling quite the adventurer.

The ship nudged into the quay and men scrambled like monkeys as the gangplanks were lowered.

"Now, my dear. We're going ashore."

"Mrs. Metcalf, I want to thank you for looking after me on the voyage."

"Tut, tut. Nonsense. You did more for us than we did for you. Amelia will perpetually be reminded of your instruction. I believe one day she might make something of her watercolors, and her reading has improved a thousandfold. Why, she's even retained a few words of Latin. I can't wrap my tongue around all those botanical names. If you find yourself in any difficulties, don't hesitate to contact us."

"Thank you, Mrs. Metcalf; however, I—"

"I know, I know. Your father's research; but life can change on the toss of a penny. Should you be in any kind of trouble, our door will always be open and Mr. Metcalf would be more than happy to offer you a position as governess. Amelia will be at home with me while the boys are away at school. It would put his mind at ease when he returns to the antipodes to know I have a companion."

Heaven forbid! As much as she'd enjoyed little Amelia's company, she could no more see herself as a governess than fly to the moon. Truth be told, she'd like to travel some more. Take time to visit some of the other ports they'd called into. The world had so much to offer and now her curiosity was aroused. No. First and foremost Pa's research. She had a job to do, and after her initial hesitation—nothing more than cold feet, really—she'd decided she would do her very best to make sure Sir Joseph got a full report. What she wouldn't give to return home with his recognition for Pa's work; perhaps they even presented fellows of the Royal Society with a medal. Now the time had come, she couldn't wait. Her feet itched to step onto dry land and get matters rolling.

"Miss Winton."

She turned to the lieutenant standing at her shoulder looking very smart in his blue uniform. "The captain requests your company. Follow me."

"There you are, my dear." Mrs. Metcalf gave her shoulder a small squeeze. "I expect your brother has arrived to meet you. Your trunk has gone ashore with ours. Don't forget to collect it." She clutched her hands to her ample bosom. "Family reunions. Just lovely."

Rose swallowed the surge of excitement and trepidation and hugged Amelia, then offered Mrs. Metcalf her hand. It was pushed aside and she was clasped in a breath-snatching embrace. "Just remember what I said. You know where to find us if necessary."

She bent down and picked up her dilapidated carpetbag containing Pa's sketchbook and the mallangong specimen, which she hadn't let out of her sight for the entire voyage.

And now she was to meet her brother.

What did you say to a brother you'd never met? A brother who'd always known who his father was while she'd believed Pa was hers. He was. Nothing would change that. No matter what science might say, on that she was firm. Pa said she was the daughter of his heart. Well, he was the father of hers.

With a brief wave to Mrs. Metcalf and Amelia, she followed the starchy back of the lieutenant along the deck until he came to a sudden halt and saluted the captain.

"Miss Winton. I have received word from a Lord Julian. You are to be escorted to his carriage and will be taken to Grosvenor Square."

Her excitement curled a little. Lord Julian? Did that make her Lady Rose? She sniggered. Highly unlikely. Not even desirable. Mam hadn't said anything about Richard Barrington to indicate he had a title. Simply that he was a naval surgeon.

"Lieutenant Goulding, see to the lady's baggage and escort her to the carriage." The captain waved a hand somewhere in the direction of the wharf. "Good day to you."

So now she was a lady. Whether it was with a capital or just an improvement on *girl,* which was the way he'd referred to her throughout the trip, she had no idea.

Although the ship no longer rolled, the moment her feet hit dry land her head swam and her legs turned to rubber. A surge of nausea swamped her. She hadn't suffered one minute of seasickness on the voyage, and now she'd left the ship, the world as good as tilted, making her stagger. Her carpetbag fell to the cobblestones with a thud.

A hand clasped her arm and steadied her. "Miss Barrington."

She blinked and looked up into a pair of nut-brown eyes so close to the color of a platypus pelt she might have been dreaming. "Winton, not Barrington. Rose Winton." The shadow of a beard stubbled the smooth skin stretched taut over his high cheekbones.

"I beg your pardon, Miss Winton. Finneas Methenwyck, at your service." He sketched a bow, still holding tightly to her arm. "Allow me to help you to the carriage. You'll get your land legs soon enough.

After all that time aboard ship, the liquid in the inner ear tends to be disrupted and causes the dizziness you are feeling. It will pass fairly quickly."

She pulled herself upright and turned to thank the lieutenant, but he had vanished. "I'm looking for my brother, Julian. Lord Julian." Goodness, that sounded pompous.

"Fear not, I have no intention of abducting you. Julian is my brother. He's somewhat tied up at the moment. The hour is early."

Her head swirled, nothing to do with her inner ear. "Your brother? But he is *my* brother." She shook her head. "I'm sorry, I don't understand. Perhaps we have the wrong . . ."

He let out a rumble of laughter. "I should have said adopted brother. We share no blood." Rich brown hair flopped over one eye, his gaze so piercing it made her heart hitch.

"Let me take your bag." He handed her up into the carriage and she sank down onto the plush seat with a sigh. Perhaps she should be more careful climbing into a carriage with a man she'd never heard of? "Where is my brother?"

"As I was saying, he is at home, Grosvenor Square. Rest here a moment and I will go and make sure we have your baggage. How many pieces?"

Now that she was sitting down and the earth had stopped tilting, his words were beginning to make sense.

"I have just one trunk, and my carpetbag." She pulled it closer to her feet. Goodness, how paltry that sounded. "My trunk was taken ashore with the Metcalfs' luggage. You must think I am your country cousin and a dreadful nuisance."

"On the contrary, I am more than happy to meet you. I've always wanted a sister."

She'd never wanted a brother, never needed one, and now it appeared she had two.

Finneas disappeared into the crowd and she sat staring at the rushing flood of people and the conglomeration of streets cutting a swath through the cramped buildings like a blazing fire. The chaos of the carriages with liveried men balanced atop and the constant cries of street vendors made her blood race and her heart pound. Nothing she'd seen before had prepared her for this.

Through the throng Finneas returned with a portly man carrying her trunk on his muscled shoulder. When it was strapped firmly to the back of the carriage, Finneas sprang inside, bringing with him a sharp blast of freezing air that she hadn't noticed earlier. She pulled up the collar of her pelisse against the biting wind. Pa said the seasons were upside down, but she hadn't imagined it would be this cold; aboard ship she'd always managed to find a spot out of the wind. The other side of the world . . . it made perfect sense, yet she hadn't been quite prepared for it. She clung to this little piece of knowledge, enjoying the security of an inescapable scientific fact.

"How was your trip? Not tedious, I hope."

"No, not at all—I enjoyed every moment of it." They veered down another cobbled street, a far cry from the dusty tracks winding through Parramatta. "So many different sights and sounds, such an explosion of color."

"And now you've landed in London Town in the middle of spring."

Spring! "It is a little colder than I imagined. I thought once we docked it would be warmer."

"And you had company on the trip?"

"Oh yes. Before I left, my mother arranged for me to travel with the Metcalf family. Free settlers returning to England to see their sons established in school. I acted as governess for their daughter, Amelia, on the trip. She became quite proficient in Latin."

"Latin?"

"Well, yes. Because I worked with my father . . ." It was so difficult to remember Pa wasn't her father. ". . . Charles Winton, it became almost a second language to me, third maybe, if you count the blackfellas'."

"You speak the native tongue?"

"I only know a few of the words the local blackfellas use. They have many different languages. We live in a place called Agnes Banks. A long, narrow freshwater billabong runs parallel with the Deerubbin River. Pa first sighted a mallangong there when one of the natives speared it." She snapped her mouth closed, swallowing her babble of words. She couldn't believe how easy it was to talk to this man. He didn't feel like a stranger. His eyes didn't stray from her face. She ought to have felt embarrassed, but instead she was comfortable, at ease. There was a light woody scent about him too, an aroma she couldn't quite place. It tweaked some distant memory, something that reminded her of the lemon-scented ti trees Mam cultivated. "I'm sorry. I'm talking too much."

"Not at all, I am fascinated. This mallangong is . . ."

Dear, oh dear. If she was going to speak to Sir Joseph Banks, she must sound more knowledgeable, more informed and scientific. "Platypus, water mole, duckbill, *Ornithorhynchus anatinus* or *paradoxus*. *Mallangong* is one of the native words I used as a child because it was easier to get my tongue around."

"Three languages all in one sentence. I'm very impressed."

That didn't sound quite right. What had Mrs. Metcalf said? She mustn't put herself forward; be reserved and quiet. She turned to stare out at the passing streets.

"We are almost there now. I expect you are looking forward to meeting Julian."

"To be honest, I am finding it a little bit difficult to understand I have a brother. I thought myself an only child."

"Were you not lonely?" he asked with a crooked, self-effacing smile, as though he had suffered from a similar complaint, though she couldn't imagine how such a friendly man could ever feel lonely.

She'd rather expected him to question why she didn't know of her brother; perhaps Julian had explained when the letter had arrived. She tossed the thought away. It was just one more thing she would deal with when the time came. "Not at all. I look upon Bunji and Yindi as my siblings." She smiled into his eyes. The irises were the most unexpected color; gold flecks appeared depending on the light. He raised one eyebrow, caught her studying him. A frantic heat rose to her cheeks as the blood surged beneath her skin, sending her heart into the most unusual rhythm.

"Bunji and Yindi? Blackfellas? Natives? I was under the impression they could be dangerous. You mentioned spears."

"We've never had any trouble with them. My mother has a long friendship with one particular group. They exchange knowledge, work together, and without the blackfellas, Pa's research never would have progressed this far."

"And Charles Winton is a naturalist."

Before she had a chance to answer, the carriage slowed and turned right into a square, a large grassed area set out with geometric precision. It looked like nothing she'd ever seen before. Paths intersecting and in the center low trees and a neat gated fence encompassing the area, the entire carriageway illuminated by oil lamps with watchmen walking up and down the perimeter of the garden as though they were on guard.

"Almost there."

"Is this where the King lives? Are these government buildings? The King's residence?"

"No. This is Grosvenor Square."

"And you live here?" There must be some mistake. Towering buildings surrounded the square—not two stories like Government House in Parramatta that Governor Macquarie had only just extended, but three, in some cases four. She craned out of the window, trying to see through the heavy twilight. Some had rooms buried partially underground. Four stories. And made entirely of brick, not a scrap of wattle and daub in sight.

Finneas let out a bark of laughter, making the color flood back into her cheeks. What had she said?

"No, private houses. There are about fifty surrounding the square; a very pleasant place to take the air, though the garden behind the house might be more to your liking. A little more private, perhaps."

"Private houses!" Who on earth would live in buildings that size? She and Mam and Pa managed quite well in their three-room cottage, though as she'd grown she'd longed for a little more privacy than the threadbare curtain around her bed provided. One of these buildings would house half the population of Agnes Banks.

"Town houses, mostly. The occupants tend to use them when they are in London from their country estates, usually for the Season, the period when Parliament sits. It begins around January and runs into July."

"And you live here, then? Julian lives here? You must be very wealthy." She clamped her hand over her mouth. Every single thing Mrs. Metcalf had instructed her not to discuss; already she was making herself sound like a ninny.

"More by good fortune than our own endeavors. Here we are, 44 Grosvenor Square. Commit that to memory and there will be no chance of you getting lost if you wander too far from home."

Before the coachman even had the opportunity to leave the box, Finneas threw open the door and leaped out. In an attempt to still the cramp of fear almost paralyzing her, she grabbed her precious carpetbag before taking the hand he offered. Stepping carefully, loath to disrupt the stones carpeting the pristine carriageway that made the newly constructed Parramatta road look like a forgotten wallaby track, she approached the front door.

Chapter 10

LONDON, ENGLAND
1820

Rose fascinated Finneas. All he wanted to do was ply her with questions, but when the carriage rolled to a halt it became perfectly obvious that the poor girl was thoroughly nervous and overcome. The tremor in her fingers had transferred to his palm as he'd handed her down from the carriage, and a pinched look bracketed her full, wide mouth.

Hardly surprising if reports of New South Wales were to be believed. Grosvenor Square would contain some of the most imposing buildings she'd ever set eyes on. A matter he intended to rectify. Nothing would delight him more than to help Rose discover all London had to offer, and perhaps in return she could appease his insatiable curiosity about all things antipodean.

Hughes threw the door open before he had the opportunity to prepare her for the grandeur of the Methenwyck town house. "Good afternoon, sir. Miss Rose." He bowed low and reversed to allow them to enter. "I shall serve afternoon tea in the blue sitting room if that is to your liking."

Rose's eyes widened and the pink of her cheeks faded.

"Thank you, Hughes. And would you please see Miss Winton's bags are taken to her room?"

"Am I to stay here?" Her fingers tightened around the disreputable carpetbag that she refused to let out of her grasp.

"That is what Julian intended. I'm certain the room will be to your liking, and there is a small sitting room set aside for your private use. Would you prefer to take tea there? Perhaps you are tired."

"I would like a moment to . . ." Her words trailed away and her eyes widened even farther as she stared up the stone staircase to the fresco. Something he'd never been terribly partial to: a classical figurative scene redolent of some unearthly paradise where nymphs frolicked beneath the kind of cloudless sky London rarely offered.

"Not a lot has been done to the house since Lord Methenwyck lived here as a young man, before he married. He no longer visits London, nor does Caroline, my mother. My suspicion is she enjoys being in town; however, Lord Methenwyck can't do without her. He suffers from a weak heart and some disability after an apoplexy."

Swaying, she set her bag down on the stairs and reached for the balustrade. She needed sustenance, a cup of tea or maybe chocolate with a good dollop of sugar to bring back the color to those lovely cheeks. "Hughes, see that Miss Rose's luggage is taken up to her room. And bring some tea and hot chocolate. She needs to rest."

"No, I'm not tired at all. Just a little overcome. This is not quite what I anticipated. We live much more simply."

"Would you prefer we arrange alternative accommodation for you?"

"I'm concerned you have already gone to too much trouble. I don't want to be a nuisance."

How to explain that neither he nor Julian had lifted a hand, had left it all to the servants? "Julian and I rattle around here like two old codgers. There are at least ten or twelve vacant bedchambers." And on that subject, where was Julian? It was hardly past four; he couldn't have gone to Brooks's yet. Surely he would wait to greet his sister.

"Ten or twelve. Oh my goodness." She swayed again and he reached for her elbow.

"Come and take some refreshment." The poor thing was quite beside herself. He couldn't wait to hear about her life. He'd heard rumors that many were choosing to make a new start in the colony, buying land or better still being granted land and making a good living. Only last week he'd read about John Macarthur's grandiose plans, not just sheep but now racehorses and grapes. "And then your luggage will be unpacked and you can rest."

"Unpacked? I can do that."

"The servants will see to it."

"Not my carpetbag. Where is it?" Her voice became slightly higher pitched as though in panic.

"Come and sit down." He led her into the sitting room. "I'll make sure your bag is brought to you." Whatever the bag contained, it was obviously more precious than the contents of her trunk.

Hughes had done what Hughes did best and two chairs were drawn up in front of a roaring log fire and a pleasant heat permeated the room.

"Let me take your coat."

"Thank you." She shrugged off the appalling brown pelisse, disclosing a pretty if somewhat outdated day dress covered in some tiny flower pattern, and settled in the chair, her feet neatly crossed at the ankles, revealing a pair of substantial boots. Caroline would have a field day. He could see her calling her dressmaker and lavishing hours on the task of turning this little colonial miss into a fashion plate.

A discreet knock on the door heralded Hughes with his trolley laid with enough cakes and sandwiches to feed a regiment and a steaming pot of hot chocolate. After Rose was settled, he'd head down to the kitchen before he made his calls at the paupers hospital; a sweet treat or two cured myriad illnesses if applied at the correct time. "Hughes, could you make sure Miss Rose's carpetbag is brought in here? It is not to be unpacked."

One of the butler's eyebrows as good as disappeared up his forehead and he opened his mouth, no doubt to point out that he had everything under control.

"Now, Hughes. And is Mr. Julian home?"

"No, sir, he hasn't arrived yet. I believe he had pressing business at his club."

Damn the man. *Pressing business.* At the gaming tables, no doubt. He could quite easily have accompanied him to collect Rose.

A pulse visibly pounded in Rose's temple and her eyes darted from side to side until Hughes reappeared with her tattered bag and the tension seeped from her shoulders.

"Thank you. I'd like it just here." She indicated the spot beside her equally tattered boots. "I'm sorry to cause such a fuss, but it contains my father's research, and while I could live without the contents of my trunk, the contents of this bag are irreplaceable."

Fascinating. His fingers itched to open the bag; instead, he poured her a cup of chocolate and placed it on the table next to her. "Would you like something to eat?"

"Not at the moment, no, thank you." She lifted the cup to her lips and grimaced slightly as she swallowed, then smiled.

"It's not to your liking."

"No, it's lovely. What is it?"

"Hot chocolate. Have you not . . ."

"No. It's delicious. We usually drink tea at home, or water." The tip of her pink tongue traced her lips before she took another sip with a quiet sigh of satisfaction.

"You must tell me all about home and in return I shall delight in showing you London."

"When will Julian be home?"

"I was expecting him to be here when we arrived." His non-appearance was something of an embarrassment. Finneas was sick and tired of making excuses for the man's appalling behavior and bailing him out of the ridiculous situations he managed to become embroiled in. "While we're waiting, tell me something of Winton's research."

With a delightful blush she rose from her chair and squatted down next to the carpetbag. Her dress pulled tight across her shoulders, showing a well-defined and somewhat muscled torso. Her life to date had without doubt been an active one.

Clutching a dilapidated leather sketchbook, the cover splattered with water stains, and a burlap sack, she settled back into the chair. The reek of something vaguely dusty, with overtones of what he thought might be a mixture of alcohol and arsenical soap, permeated the space between them.

She settled the sketchbook on the table and clutched the sack in her lap.

"What have you got in there?"

"A specimen. Originally named *Platypus anatinus* but the German anatomist Blumenbach independently named it *Ornithorhynchus paradoxus* in 1800. Sadly, *platypus* had already been bestowed upon a poor unsuspecting beetle, so Blumenbach's *Ornithorhynchus* was combined with the earlier species name, *anatinus*, to give the scientific name *Ornithorhynchus anatinus*."

"*A specimen.*" Uttered without a moment's hesitation, where he'd expect a fit of the vapors from any other female of his acquaintance. He sat upright and leaned forward. And as before, the Latin rolled off her tongue as though she'd conversed in the language daily.

She slipped her hand inside the bag. "*Duckbill* is the less scientific name that we colonials prefer, from *Ornithorhynchus*, meaning bird-nosed, although I like *mallangong*. The word I used as a child. Others refer to it as a water mole, but it is in no way related to the mole. Would you like to see? Some people find it a little unnerving."

She was telling him, warning him, a physician, who spent more time in the basement of St. Bartholomew's Hospital dissecting cadavers than he was prepared to admit in polite society. Oh, this girl was a delight.

She cradled the cat-sized specimen on her lap. "Pa and I prepared it. They're not very good eating, rank and fishy, really. It's the pelts that are the attraction; they make excellent blankets. Pa sent a pelt to Sir Joseph over twenty years ago. That's when their correspondence began. Numerous people cast doubts on its authenticity, said so quite emphatically in several descriptions that were published. That fueled Pa's desire to prove otherwise. Sir Joseph requested direct observations. That's what I have here."

He could see why people doubted its authenticity. Its sleek body was covered in fur the color of an otter. He ran his fingers over its back down to the broad flattened tail, then returned to the head. Instead of terminating in a snout, as he would have expected, it had a beak. A beak like a duck, broad and compressed, round at the lip and covered with some kind of cartilaginous, leathery membrane. A total paradox. However would it be classified? Half *mammalia*, half *pisces*, with a serious dollop of *aves*. How did it procreate? Perhaps not the question to ask at this moment, though he had no doubt Rose would take it in stride.

"This animal was washed downstream during the floods and we managed to retrieve it. We tanned it, then Pa was able to procure some arsenical soap and we stuffed it with a hotchpotch of old . . . rags." She gave a rather embarrassed laugh. "Mostly old nightdresses and a chemise because finer material is more suited, helping to retain the true shape."

Taxidermy: the art of collecting, preparing, and mounting objects of natural history recommended for the use of museums and travelers. He'd read in one of the journals only recently of a newer method using some other chemical.

"And this . . ." She turned the specimen onto its back and lifted the back foot. "This is the venomous spur. That is why Pa cannot be in London. He was spurred."

"Surely not. The animal's barely two foot long. It couldn't contain sufficient venom to harm a man."

She looked down her aquiline nose at him, nostrils flaring slightly. "Believe me, it does. I witnessed the spurring and helped my mother nurse Pa until I left."

"What symptoms?" His voice sounded sharp, as though he was denying the truth of her statement. It wasn't what he intended; her words held him captive.

She didn't miss it, and raised a skeptical eyebrow, quite prepared to accept his challenge. "The pain was intense. Paralyzing. Pa drifted in and out of consciousness. Within half an hour his entire arm was swollen to the shoulder and quite useless, and his leg was not much better."

"And his pulse rate?" He snapped the question.

"Very low. Suffering from shock without a doubt."

An adequate diagnosis. "And his vision and speech were impaired?"

"Yes. And vomiting persisted for days. Mam was concerned for lockjaw, but it didn't eventuate."

"Most intriguing."

"Made worse by the fact he was spurred twice, once in his arm and once in his leg."

"And he has made a full recovery?" Whatever made him say that? Her face collapsed and tears filled her big brown eyes.

"I don't know. I left four weeks after the attack. Pa already had passage booked and was determined his work should reach Sir Joseph."

Which was why Julian received such short notice of her arrival. His mind darted back to the letter, the flowery female hand in total contrast to the contents of the letter. "And you wrote the letter to Julian on your father's behalf."

With a look of excruciating guilt she nodded her head. "With my mother's assistance. Yes." She lifted her chin as if daring him to call her to task for her misdemeanor.

"Admirable." Like everything else about this girl. Admirable.

Before he had a chance to form his next sentence, the door flew open and Julian lurched in. One look was enough to ascertain his state. Drunk, as drunk as the lord he believed he'd one day become, and from his scowl and disheveled appearance, in no mood to meet his sister.

"So the doxy's landed."

There was no doubt Rose understood his words. She reared back in her chair, her eyes wide and her face bone-white as she stuffed the creature back into the burlap sack.

An overwhelming desire to put himself between Rose and Julian shot Finneas to his feet. "May I introduce Miss Winton, Rose, your sister."

The drunken sot ignored him, strolled across the room, and stood warming his hands above the fire, then turned very slowly. His gaze raked Rose from the top of her glossy curls to the toes of the particularly disreputable pair of boots peeking from beneath the hem of her dress.

After an agonizing minute he sauntered across the floor until he stood right in front of her. "My pleasure." He gave a bow that skirted the edge of civility and sat down at the chair nearest the window, his index and little fingers beating the familiar irritating tattoo he favored. "I have a question, about the antipodes."

She lifted her chin and stared right back at him in challenge. "What might that be?"

In that brief second their likeness became apparent. What was arrogance in Julian was strength of character and determination in Rose. She would hold her own, and if she didn't, Finneas would make damn certain the cad was called to question.

"I have a fascination with the place."

She inclined her head. "As I would expect. It must be difficult knowing nothing of the land of your birth, your heritage."

Oh, very nicely done. That put the boot on the other foot.

"A relief, I can assure you. A place populated by criminals, the dregs of humanity."

"And your birth mother."

"Unfortunately, yes."

Finneas cleared his throat, threw back his shoulders, and offered what he hoped was an intimidating scowl. How dare Julian patronize his sister in this way. The insufferable bastard was as much convict stock as Rose and nowhere near as graceful. When he got him alone he might remind him of that. It would go down a treat at Brooks's if a word was slipped into the wrong ear. He'd be hounded out of the place.

"Present company excepted, of course," Julian offered with a smirk and picked up the two-fingered tattoo again.

He had to stop this now, everything to do with the ridiculous notion that the colony was nothing more than a dumping ground for England's outcasts. Next Julian would be telling her that her chains were rattling.

"So you've spent your childhood on the land, outside Sydney."

"I did. We moved to a place called Agnes Banks when I was three." A gritted smile. "About forty miles from the center of Sydney Town, close to Parramatta."

"There is a gaol there?" Julian produced a rapid succession of blinks and a snort of cynicism from the back of his throat.

"My mother has served her sentence and my father, Charles Winton, is a freeman. He was never a convict."

"Charles Winton." His voice carried something of a sneer and she lifted her chin.

"Yes, my father."

"And Charles Winton, this eminent man of science . . . Why have I never heard of him?"

An out-and-out lie. He'd said he remembered Uncle Charles. Nevertheless, Julian had as little interest in science as he had in the plight of the homeless who swarmed the London streets.

"It is for that very reason I have come to England in my father's stead. This research breaks new boundaries. We have evidence that the female platypus lays eggs and suckles its young. It is an animal *sui generis*. A species all of its own, unique."

Julian peered down his long nose in the most unpleasant fashion, his nostrils flaring, then pinching.

The sweet young thing didn't appear to be in the slightest concerned. Her nervousness when she'd first arrived at the house appeared to have dissipated now she was on familiar ground. She glanced up at Julian and then delved into the burlap sack and revealed the creature, her hands running across the perfectly preserved thick brown pelt. "*Ornithorhynchus anatinus* is something of a paradox. It appears to possess a threefold nature: that of a fish, a bird, and a quadruped, and is related to nothing hitherto seen."

Julian snorted and poured himself a shot of brandy, not bothering to offer the decanter. He took a long slug, then peered more closely at the specimen. "Is it an amphibious animal?"

"Oh yes. It lives in a burrow in the riverbank and seeks its food from the crustaceans living in the mud and sand of the waterways." She ran her fine finger along the beak of the animal. "It can eat up to half its own weight daily."

"And you intend to present this creature to the Royal Society?"

"With my father's extensive notes and drawings, yes. As I said, they break new ground." She inclined her head to the sketchbook on the table. "Research from direct observations requested by Sir Joseph Banks," she added, throwing down her trump card.

Finneas stood and picked up the leather-bound sketchbook and flicked through the first few pages. "These illustrations are remarkable. Mr. Winton is responsible for them?"

A rather pretty blush stained her cheeks. "A few of them are my own."

Not only did she have an excellent command of the facts; she also appeared to have a certain skill in representing them on paper.

"For goodness' sake." Julian turned to him with a snide leer. "Will you put the poor child out of her misery or will I?" He rocked back on his heels and folded his arms. The supercilious look on Julian's face made him want to knock the bastard to the other side of the room.

It was something he had hoped to introduce more gently into the conversation, rather than hitting her with the horrible truth within only moments of her arrival. "A woman will never tread the hallowed floors of Somerset House."

"More succinctly, they will not permit you to present these . . . these"—Julian circled his hand—"doodles," he finished in a derogatory tone.

Her face crumpled, then she lifted her shoulders. "Sir Joseph Banks himself set the appointed time."

"A private appointment?"

"No. A firm date to present this body of work to the Royal Society." She placed the animal on the floor beside the chair where it sat looking somewhat healthier than Julian, eyeing the proceedings. "May I have Pa's sketchbook, please?"

Finneas handed it to her and she sat down again, turned to the back, and produced a well-thumbed piece of paper, which she unfolded with care and spread on one of the open pages. She cleared her throat. "'Sir Joseph Banks requests the attendance of Charles Winton at the meeting of the Royal Society at Somerset House on the fourth day of June, 1820, to discuss *Ornithorhynchus anatinus* and further information gleaned from the direct observation of these ambiguous animals.'"

She closed the book with a snap, folded her pretty little hands in her lap, and looked up at Julian with an expression that said nothing more and nothing less than *I told you so.*

Finneas muffled a laugh. No one could accuse Rose of lacking courage, or anything else, for that matter. She was delightful. He plunged his hands into his pockets in an attempt to control his overwhelming desire to applaud her.

Julian sniffed. "An invitation issued to Winton, not you."

"But I am here as my father's representative." She drilled the point as if to ensure she could distance herself from any familial association with Julian, something he'd often wished he could do.

"I rest my case, though none of this is significant. The invitation was not issued to you because as a woman you cannot address the Royal Society. Mouths would gape. It simply isn't done."

The poor girl. She had traveled thousands of miles, weathered God only knew what conditions to arrive here, only to be told she couldn't achieve her aim because of the hidebound nature of the arrogant men who held science as their personal domain. It was ridiculous, and she certainly wouldn't make a fool of herself. She was articulate and, he'd hazard a guess, possessed with a greater scientific grasp on the matter than anyone else other than Winton. "Julian, I feel sure we could arrange something, perhaps a special dispensation, under the circumstances."

"They will not allow a woman into the meeting room." Julian turned to the window, his arms folded, ending the conversation. "I have already made inquiries."

If Julian had bothered to inquire, no doubt he'd been blunt and ill-mannered.

"Leave it with me and I shall see what I can arrange." There had to be a way to get Winton's work in front of the Royal Society.

"I wouldn't hold your breath."

Finneas's mind started to race, taking his heartbeat with it. "I believe there is an alternative. Unless I am very much mistaken, there is a precedent."

With a dismissive shrug, Julian concentrated on the heavy rain trickling down the window.

"William Herschel, the astronomer, presented a paper on the comets that his sister, Caroline, had written, some years ago."

With a bound Rose was on her feet, her mouth a perfect O and her eyes bright once more. She took a step toward him, her hands outstretched, and for a moment he swore she thought to hug him tight; instead, she clasped both hands firmly in front of her.

"And of what relevance is that?" Julian continued to consider the windowpane, his thick black brows drawn into a deep arrow above his large nose.

As usual Julian was a little slow. Not so Rose. "It occurs to me that perhaps *you* could offer the same assistance to *your* sister."

At that point Julian turned and fixed his steely and somewhat intimidating glare on Rose.

She lifted her chin and the corners of her mouth tilted in the beginning of a smile. "Why, it's the perfect solution. Would you, Julian, please? For our father's sake."

"A father you denied not five minutes ago."

"For the friendship that once existed between your father and . . ."

She was going to say *mine*. He knew it and that would be the end of it. Julian's short temper was legendary.

"Charles Winton."

Julian emitted some sort of harrumph and stuck his hands into his pockets.

The man was a self-centered cad. He could at least make some effort. Finneas placed himself between Rose and Julian. "If you don't feel you are capable, let me."

"And have the whole of London know that I refused my sister assistance?"

A masterstroke. "In that case let me call at Somerset House and see what can be arranged." That way Julian wouldn't be able to renege on the meeting or twist the truth.

His efforts were rewarded with a brilliant smile, which turned Rose's walnut eyes almost black. He and Miss Winton made quite a team.

Chapter 11

WOLLOMBI, NEW SOUTH WALES
1908

Tamsin walked across to the small desk in the corner of the parlor. "Mrs. Adcock, are you busy?"

"No more than usual. Be here for dinner, will you? I've got a nice chicken pie in the oven."

"Yes, please, and Mr. Everdene will be joining me."

Mrs. Adcock gave her a wink. "Nice young man, that. Lucky he was here and he could drive you around in that motor car of his. It's a long walk out to Mrs. Quinleaven's."

Tamsin swallowed a reply that said she was more than capable of walking and that she didn't want or need a motor car, because it wasn't strictly true; she had enjoyed Shaw's company. It had made her realize just how lonely her life was. Sometimes independence wasn't all it was cracked up to be. "I was wondering if you could help me out."

The woman's eyes lit up, no doubt smelling the possibility of a juicy bit of scuttlebutt to entertain her customers. "Do what I can. Are you in a spot of bother?"

"It's about Mrs. Quinleaven."

"Why don't we have a nice cup of tea and some of my fruitcake. You sit yourself down. I'll be back in two ticks. Tea's brewed."

Tamsin sat down at the table overlooking the brook. She had the feeling she was missing a part of the jigsaw puzzle, but she had no idea what. She should make the most of Mrs. Adcock's local knowledge.

"Here we are. Tea and fruitcake. Can't beat it."

"Thank you." She pulled the cup and saucer closer. "Before Mrs. Quinleaven died she donated a book to the Public Library in Sydney, and we're trying to establish the provenance."

"The providence?"

"Provenance. Where the book came from and its original author and subsequent owners."

"Oh! You think Mrs. Quinleaven flogged it? Nah, she wouldn't do a thing like that. Bit of a character, not light-fingered, though."

"She was Mr. Kelly's housekeeper, wasn't she?"

"Among other things." She cleared her throat and shot a glance over her shoulder. "They had a bit of a thing going, you know, after his wife went." Her cheeks pinked and she licked her lips. "Poor Mr. Kelly. Heartbroken he was when his wife died. Spent his whole time blaming himself, did poor Mr. Kelly. Mrs. Quinleaven as good as brought him back from the grave. Mind you, he never left the property after that. Never went to that solicitor's office of his. Just stayed at home. The funeral put paid to the rumors, I can tell you. He'd bought two plots side by side, special like. One for 'im and one for Mrs. Quinleaven. You don't get buried alongside someone for all eternity if you don't like 'em, do you? Often wondered what his poor wife would be thinking, if she knew."

Tamsin stared out of the window at the church opposite. St. John's. She didn't remember seeing any gravestones, and buying a plot made it sound as though space was in high demand.

"Are they buried over the road?"

"Nah. No one's buried there; a couple of plaques, not much more. Cemetery's been up the road since the 1840s—full of pioneers, free settlers, and convicts. No difference once you end up in there unless you're a Catholic; then you have to go on the left-hand side. Catholics and Anglicans got their own patch, one on either side." She laughed uproariously. "Reckon it's so they don't get muddled up on their way through the pearly gates. You know—Catholics to the left of me, Protties to the right."

"Where exactly is the cemetery?"

Mrs. Adcock threw out her right hand. "On the edge of town, opposite the school, before you get to the millpond. Can't miss the millpond, where the old flour mill was. Burned down a few months back."

Which would make it difficult to use as a landmark. Tamsin bit back a smile.

"Just a couple hundred yards on your left, past the Catholic church, St. Michael's."

Swallowing the last mouthful of fruitcake, Tamsin washed it down with the remains of her tea. The sun hadn't set and a walk would do her good, especially after being driven around like royalty.

"Thank you. I'll just get my hat." She lifted the tin from the table and wrapped her hands around it protectively. She'd leave it in her room.

"What've you got there?"

"Just an old tin. I collect them." The words rolled over her tongue with surprising ease. She turned the tin so the lid was showing. "Peek Frean biscuits."

"Them specially made things. Can't see why anyone'd buy biscuits in a tin. I like 'em straight from the oven. That Mrs. Quinleaven, she was one for those tinned biscuits. Such a sweet tooth."

Tamsin schooled the twist in her lips. The tin almost certainly belonged to Mrs. Quinleaven and contained some treasures she'd decided were important. Thank goodness the odious Mrs. Rushworth hadn't thrown it out with the rubbish. "What time for dinner?"

"Six, six thirty. The pie'll keep till you're ready."

She raced up the stairs and buried the tin in the bottom of her bag, grabbed her hat, and took off down the stairs at a gallop. First stop, the cemetery. She felt she owed it to Mrs. Quinleaven to pay her respects. Then she'd wander around the rest of the town and work up an appetite.

"Thank you for the lovely tea, Mrs. Adcock. I'll take a stroll down to the cemetery before the light goes and walk off the fruitcake, delicious as it was." She patted her stomach.

"You could do with a bit of meat on your bones. Make sure you're back before too long. Don't hold with hanging around cemeteries once it gets dark. Never know who you might bump into." She let out a ghostly warble and stacked up the plates.

With a laugh Tamsin wandered outside. The tiny church, St. Michael's, was on her right and she crossed the road to take a closer look. Built out of hand-carved sandstone blocks, it looked as though it had stood solid and firm since the little town was first gazetted. It was a perfect match for the Court House on the other corner and the Telegraph Office next door.

Bearing in mind Mrs. Adcock's advice about cemeteries after dark, she continued up the road at a quick pace, past the General Store and another fine two-story sandstone building and what looked like a storehouse or a hall. The flagstone pavers turned to crushed stones as she walked along the footpath.

There were no streetlights as there were in Sydney, and when the shadows began to lengthen, she was pleased she'd left straightaway and hadn't wasted time. As she rounded the bend, the cemetery came into view. She hadn't noticed it when she'd arrived, probably in too much of a hurry. A post and rail fence enclosed the rows of headstones, and as Mrs. Adcock said there were two signs—Catholics on the left and Anglicans on the right. Foolishly she'd forgotten to ask on which side Mrs. Quinleaven was buried.

She slipped through the double gate and latched it firmly behind her, a flutter of anticipation dusting her skin as she wandered between the headstones. Most of the graves belonged to children. The mortality rate in the early days of the colony must have been agonizing. The joy and anticipation of having a child, and then the brutal truth as they were snatched away.

She worked her way along the rows, and when she reached the back fence, she rested her elbows and looked out across the millpond, the setting sun sparkling on the calm water; no sign of the old flour mill, though. She turned and leaned back against the fence. She'd covered every row except the one closest to the town. As she ambled along, soaking up the sense of tranquility, a woman appeared between the graves, head down and a bunch of wildflowers dangling loosely in one hand. Tamsin picked up her pace. "Hello."

The old woman lifted her head, looked around, then offered a tentative smile.

"I was wondering if you can help me. I'm looking for Mrs. Quinleaven. She was buried the day before yesterday."

She gestured with the flowers to a mound of dirt close to an older grave. "Buried alongside each other, they are. As it should be." She bent a little, one hand resting in the small of her back, and dropped the posy of wildflowers onto the freshly turned earth. "Knees ain't what they were."

"Let me." Tamsin squatted down and straightened the posy until it lay neatly across the top of the dirt mound.

"Won't be able to do this much more."

"I'm sorry."

"Then there'll be no one left to keep 'em neat and tidy."

Tamsin certainly couldn't imagine Mrs. Rushworth making a visit to tend the grave of her mother. To the left of Mrs. Quinleaven's grave a plain headstone read *Michael Kelly 1822–1888.*

"Heartbroken, he was. Heartbroken." The old woman sniffed and tried for a smile.

"Why's that?"

"The flood took her, poor Jane." A large tear rolled down her weathered cheek and she batted it away with her overlong sleeve. "Just swept her away."

Not Mrs. Quinleaven. Who was she talking about? "How dreadful. A flood?"

"Happens all the time. Mind you, that wasn't the big one. That was"—her gaze shifted to some spot beyond the millpond—"March, nigh on fifteen years ago, it was. Fifteen years. That's when they moved the church."

"Moved the church?"

"Yep, picked it up stone by stone and carried it up the hill. She did her best, looked after him until he was ready to go. Be nice them all being together."

"All being together?"

"His housekeeper, she was." She flicked her thumb in the direction of Mrs. Quinleaven's grave. "When my Jane went, she took care of him, chased his sorrows away."

Mrs. Quinleaven sounded like a lovely woman despite her daughter's disapproval, and now Mrs. Rushworth stood to inherit everything, including the sketchbook. Mr. Kelly might not be too happy about that.

"Time I was getting along."

Tamsin stretched out her hand and rested it on the woman's arm. She felt a strange bond with her—perhaps the fact that she had known

Mrs. Quinleaven and cared enough to put flowers on her grave after Mrs. Rushworth's dismissive remarks. "Thank you. It was lovely to meet you. My name's Tamsin, Tamsin Alleyn." She grasped the woman's brown hand, the thin, dry skin like tissue over the pronounced bones.

"I'm Gayadin." She shuffled off down the path and out of the gate, then turned toward the millpond and disappeared into the mist.

Tamsin shivered; someone walking over her grave, no doubt. Perhaps Mrs. Adcock was right and cemeteries weren't a good place to be once the light began to fade.

She rearranged the posy on Mrs. Quinleaven's grave and ran her hand over Kelly's headstone before making her way back to the village. When she reached St. Michael's, she wandered up the path. Set in the wall she found two foundation stones: *Sunday, October 22, 1893, laid by the Rt. Reverend James Murray, Bishop of Maitland* and around the corner a much older one. She couldn't make heads or tails of the Latin but for the date, *MDCCCXL*. Stopping for a moment to sit on the stone wall, she worked it out: 1840. The church had weathered floods for fifty-odd years and then it had all become too much, so they'd moved it. A labor of love, without a doubt.

Making her way around to the front of the church, she tried the handle on the pair of doors; one swung open and she slipped inside. Row after row of timber pews sat like teeth amidst the Gothic style of the church, presided over by a beautiful stained glass window behind the altar. The shaped sandstone surround enclosed an image of the church's namesake, the warrior archangel Michael, and an ornate stenciled frieze ran around the nave walls and the sanctuary.

With a sigh, she closed the doors and made her way through the gathering twilight back to the hotel. The trip to the cemetery and the church had left her feeling oddly at peace.

Shaw's car was parked outside the hotel, and the moment she entered the dining room he was on his feet helping her with her coat. "Come and sit down. I was wondering if you'd like a ride back to Sydney tomorrow, instead of taking the train." He held her chair while she settled at the table.

"I'm not sure . . ." Oh, for goodness' sake, she'd love to ride back to Sydney in his motor car. She might never have the chance again. "Yes, please."

"All settled, then." He propped his elbows on the table and gazed at her, his eyes crinkling at the corners. "Mrs. Adcock said you'd gone for a walk."

It was almost as though he was laughing at her. Why? "Have you still got the sketchbook?" The man would think she had no other topic of conversation. No matter how hard she tried, she couldn't shake the feeling that it might never make it to the Library, obsessed with the thought that Mrs. Rushworth might change her mind.

He nodded. "It's in my room, all safe and sound."

"Oh, that's wonderful. I'm sure Mrs. Quinleaven would be thrilled. I hope everything will work out perfectly."

Shaw leaned back in his chair, fiddling with his knife, making patterns on the tablecloth. "Where did you walk to?"

"Just down to the cemetery to see Mrs. Quinleaven's grave. Did you know there was a flood in 1893 and they moved the church?"

"Here you are." Mrs. Adcock plonked down two chicken pies, steam rising from the top, and a beautiful bowl of vegetables. "Bloody awful that flood was. Can remember it as clear as day."

"Where was the church originally?"

"On the Paynes Crossing road, just before Cunneen's Bridge. You would have driven over it in that machine of yours." Mrs. Adcock threw Shaw a wink.

"The water must really flow when it floods."

"Sure enough it does. Wollombi—meeting place of the waters, the locals call it. You'd be sitting up to your neck in it right now in a bad flood. How was the cemetery?"

"Fascinating, and I ended up at St. Michael's. I can't imagine moving a church stone by stone."

"And who told you about that?"

"There was an old woman putting flowers on Mrs. Quinleaven's grave."

Shaw's head lifted and he raised an eyebrow.

"Ah, that'd be Gayadin."

"Yes, that's what she said her name was."

"Been around here for donkey's years. Must be eighty if she's a day. Lives down by the brook, where the old church used to be. Sees it as her job to tend the graves. Her mother did it before her, apparently. Lives in a bit of a half-world, she does. Not one of the natives and not one of us. Still, she gets along all right. Enjoy your meal." Mrs. Adcock bumbled off.

"Good cooks always are great gossips. Should have thought to ask for a bit more of the local color." Shaw popped a forkful of the steaming chicken pie into his mouth. "Excellent!"

"I like it here. There's something about the town. Homely."

"You sound wistful."

"No, not really. Just so many hidden stories waiting to be told, and to be honest, Mrs. Rushworth annoyed me. I'm so glad you managed to sort everything out."

Shaw cleared his throat and delved back into his meal.

She probably shouldn't have said that. After all, Shaw had a job to do and he'd helped her no end. He'd convinced Mrs. Rushworth to allow the sketchbook to go to Sydney, and once they established the authenticity, she was certain Mrs. Rushworth would honor her mother's donation.

They set off early the next morning for Sydney, Tamsin's bag strapped to the back of the car and the sketchbook and her tin resting at her feet. The climb out of the Wollombi Valley exercised pretty much every one of the driving skills the bloke had taught him; he changed gears more times in the space of an hour than he'd done during the entire trip down. Still, it was too late to backtrack and take the route through Cessnock to the coast.

Finally, they hit a stretch of clear road and he put his foot down and managed to get the car up to thirty-five miles an hour. Tamsin let out a little cry of pleasure and clamped her straw hat down on her head.

"Not too fast?"

"No, I love it. You are so lucky to have a motor car." The wind whipped her words away, saving him having to respond. The car, his pride and joy, was something he might well have to forgo once he told his father he intended to leave the business. A few days out of Sydney only served to reinforce how happy he'd be never to return. If he owned a house like Mrs. Quinleaven's place, he wouldn't be selling it—the library would make a perfect home for the bequest from his grandfather.

By lunchtime they'd reached St. Albans and he pulled into the forecourt of the Settler's Arms. "I thought we'd grab a bite of lunch and that you might like to have a look around. It used to be the stop-off point for Cobb and Co stagecoaches running between Sydney and Newcastle."

Tamsin's eyes lit up and she climbed out of the car and headed around the corner, her fingers trailing along the hand-cut sandstone blocks. When he returned about fifteen minutes later with a pile of ham sandwiches and a jug of lemonade, she was sitting at a table under an enormous white cedar tree looking as pretty as a picture. The usual group of admirers stood around the car nodding sagely to each other and pointing out its various attributes.

Keeping half an eye on them, he put down the plate. "Lunch. Simple but looks pretty tasty. The bloke inside wanted to know if we were here for the dance tonight."

"Dance?"

"Apparently this is the place to be and people come from as far afield as Wollombi and Windsor. They start at eight o'clock in the evening and go until midnight, when there's a supper break, then it all begins again and keeps going until morning."

"I think I might give it a miss." She threw him a radiant smile above the huge doorstep sandwich, took a bite, and chewed thoughtfully. "I'm not sure the Library will be too happy if I stay away from work any longer."

"The sketchbook will keep you out of trouble. They'll enjoy looking at it." He couldn't wait to hear what they had to say about it. And to get a decent look at the pictures under a magnifying glass.

"Where to after this? The train line ran up the coast, so this is a real adventure."

"We head for Wisemans. There's a new vehicular ferry that'll take us across the Hawkesbury, then into Windsor and on to Sydney."

"Goodness, it sounds like a long trip."

"We'll make better time once we cross the river. The condition of the roads on the other side is far superior. You might want to dispense with your hat; just use a scarf because I should be able to get the speed up to about forty miles an hour."

"So back to Sydney before dark."

"Not long afterward."

As they reached Milsons Point, he slowed the car. "Where would you like me to drop you?" She'd said the North Shore but nothing else; the area was a bustling metropolis now, professional and commercial businesses mixed in with skilled tradesmen and laborers. That was what he liked about it; that and the fact he'd been able to afford one of the smaller cottages, something he wouldn't have been able to do on the south side.

"Twelve Lavender Street."

"Perfect. Not out of my way at all. In fact, we're almost neighbors."

Tamsin's head came up with a jerk. "That's a coincidence."

"I've just acquired a little house in Blues Point Road, number 121, more of a workman's cottage than anything else. Lavender Street's handy for the ferry. Is that how you get to work?"

"Yes. I love it. It's a little irregular. Can't always guarantee what time I'll arrive, but the Library has become used to that and I rarely leave on time, so they don't complain about my hours."

"One day we'll have a bridge spanning the cove and then the ferries will be out of business."

"I can't see that happening. Francis Greenway proposed building a bridge from the northern to the southern shore of the harbor at the beginning of the nineteenth century and nothing has ever come of it. There was a new flurry of interest not long ago, but the design submissions were considered unsuitable."

He slowed down and pulled up in front of a very solid terrace that made his recent acquisition look like a kennel. "Your family home?"

"No. The family home in Miller Street was simply too large so I sold it. I rattle around in this one as it is."

He killed the engine with a strange reluctance. The wistful note was back in her voice. He didn't want to say goodbye. He'd enjoyed her company, and it sounded as though there was quite a story in the sale of the house. She hadn't said *we*; she'd said *I*. Most unusual. "Let me unstrap your bag and I'll bring it and the copies of the *Dawn* in. You've got your tin and the *Penny Magazine*, haven't you?"

"Yes. Thank you." She walked up the path and slipped the key into the lock. He couldn't help but wonder whether she lived alone. Highly unlikely, yet she seemed so independent. There'd be some housekeeper or companion, maybe an aged aunt. Most women who could afford to live in a place like this wouldn't be bothering with a job. It was surprising some bloke with his eye on the best chance hadn't snatched her up.

"Just put them down here. I can manage."

He tucked the bag and the pile of papers inside the door.

"If you can bring the sketchbook to the Library tomorrow, I'll arrange for the use of the large magnifying glasses and we can take a closer look at the signatures. That's the first thing we need to do, and then I can cross-reference the handwriting with the letters. It will go some way toward establishing the authenticity, and there are other books from that era so we can compare the binding, paper, and ink."

"I'll look forward to it. Nine o'clock?"

"Make it ten. As I said, the ferries can be a bit erratic and I'll need time to fill in Mrs. Williams on all the details. She'll be beside herself with curiosity. Goodbye, Shaw, and thank you for the ride." She held out her gloved hand and he took it in both of his. A bit presumptuous, but he couldn't help himself.

"Thank you for your company. I've very much enjoyed the last few days."

A flush of color tinted her cheeks. "And so have I." She extracted her hand and closed the door behind her, leaving him standing on the step.

It took less than five minutes to pull the car into the shed next door to his little cottage. Tucking the sketchbook under his arm, he let himself in and eased into the narrow hallway, edging past the piles of boxes stacked against the wall. It would take him months to unpack them all, had taken him months already, but he wasn't giving up.

He put the bag containing the sketchbook down on the kitchen table, filled the kettle, and stuck it on the hob. He wanted another look before he took it to the Library tomorrow.

A coil of excitement twisted in his belly. Apart from the sketchbook, Tamsin would be such a wonderful contact once he began cataloguing Grandfather's books. Not only was she a mine of information; she had all the tools at her fingertips. He hoped she wouldn't be too disappointed if Mrs. Rushworth decided to sell the sketchbook, hoped she wouldn't see him as the villain in the piece.

With the gloves on he turned the pages, hunting the mixture of the neat copperplate and irregular slanted scrawl for signatures and dates, but the thought of how disappointed Tamsin would be if she knew Mrs. Rushworth's plan had taken the edge off his pleasure. He was going to have to tell her, and soon, but there was little point until they knew for certain it was authentic.

He tucked the sketchbook back into its bag and wandered into the front room. He'd started to unpack some of the boxes, and stacks of books lined the walls three and four deep.

From the very first moment he'd walked into Grandfather's library as a raw thirteen-year-old and inhaled the scent of candle wax and polished wood, ink and old paper, dusty books and binding leather, he'd known where his future lay.

He'd spent every school holiday visiting old bookshops, helping to restore and catalogue Grandfather's latest finds and dreaming of setting up his own business in Oxford, until Father had summoned him back to Australia, saying he needed him in the family business. He hated it. Planned to return one day.

It still made his blood boil to think that Father had kept Grandfather's death from him, and then he'd received his inheritance. Piles of antiquarian tomes jammed into crates and shipped across the globe arrived just in time and saved his sanity. Not much money, but enough to buy his tiny cottage and his car, allowing him to move out of the family home and make the first steps toward the dream he'd cherished for so long.

When he'd been collared by his father and sent to deal with Mrs. Rushworth, he hadn't imagined it would lead to such an opportunity. Selling the sketchbook would be his first step toward establishing a name for himself in the world of antiquarian books. The picture of Tamsin with her air of innocence and determination and her enthusiasm for Winton—his work and its national significance—flashed before his eyes. He could understand her commitment; they shared the same ideals, but could he let this opportunity slip through his fingers? She would see it as a betrayal unless . . .

The whistling of the kettle broke his reverie and he rushed back into the kitchen and turned off the heat, then sat down, running his hands over the linen bag.

If he could sell the sketchbook to the Mitchell, honor would be satisfied. The book would be in the public domain, the Rushworths would have sufficient money to stave off the creditors, and he would broker the deal. Everyone would benefit.

One way or another he had to get to the bottom of the story behind the sketchbook. There was no point in entertaining the thought of a sale until the provenance and authenticity were established.

Chapter 12

Sydney, Australia
1908

Tamsin walked from the Quay through the Botanic Gardens to the Library, her feet barely touching the ground. Just as she'd predicted, the ferries had run late and she only had a few minutes before Shaw was due to arrive. She wanted to fill in Mrs. Williams on the details of her trip, and the odious Mrs. Rushworth, before Mr. Everdene got there. It was impossible to believe that the wretched woman wouldn't honor her mother's dying wish.

The moment Tamsin pushed open the big brass doors, Mrs. Williams rushed across the foyer, her face alight with curiosity. "I was expecting you earlier. Have you got it?" She took one look at Tamsin's satchel hanging on her shoulder and her face fell. "It's smaller than I anticipated."

"It's not in here."

"Where is it? Don't tell me . . ."

"I've got it; however, it's a long story." She glanced up at the clock. "And I only have ten minutes to fill you in. Can we go to the tearoom?"

"Yes, come with me." Mrs. Williams took off at a gallop, and the minute the door was closed she stuck her hands on her hips and said, "Well?"

"This has to be fast, so please excuse me if I sound a little brutal. When I got there Mrs. Quinleaven was dead."

"Oh!" Her eyes widened in horror. "And the sketchbook?"

"Her daughter was at the house and she had a man with her, a solicitor named Shaw Everdene."

"Everdene? The name rings a bell."

"Everdene, Roach, and Smythe."

"Of course, of course. They have offices in George Street."

"That's right. Shaw is Mr. Everdene's son; he works for him. He lives in Blues Point Road."

"Ah! Shaw." Mrs. Williams's beady eyes appraised her and Tamsin turned to the window to hide the flush on her cheeks.

The coincidence of it all still flummoxed her. It hadn't occurred to her to wonder where he lived while they were in Wollombi. "Mrs. Quinleaven's daughter refused to hand over the sketchbook to me; however, she entrusted it to Shaw. He'll be here at ten."

"I see, hence the hurry. But tell me, is it authentic?"

"I believe it is, although there are some discrepancies that need clarification." She wouldn't go into the whole business. Wait until she'd had a better look. "There are notes, line drawings, and some watercolors."

"And they're signed and dated?"

"Some, not all. The frontispiece has his signature and the date 1817. I want to compare the signatures with those on Winton's letters, have a closer look at the paper, see if I can date it. I'm almost certain it is early nineteenth century."

"Very good, very good. I've set up the big magnifying glasses."

A knock sounded on the door and Harry's head appeared. "There's a Mr. Everdene here, Mrs. Williams." His eyebrows wiggled suggestively. "He's looking for Tamsin."

"Thank you, Harry, that will be all."

The door shut with a disappointed click.

"Your Mr. Everdene has obviously aroused some interest. Take him downstairs. I've got a few things to do. I'll come down later and you can introduce me, and of course I'd like to have a look at the book."

Tamsin slipped through the door back into the foyer. She couldn't wait to get downstairs.

Shaw's face broke into his trademark grin, which did nothing to slow her already galloping heart rate. He had the linen bag tucked under his arm and she had to fist her hands tight to prevent herself from snatching it from him. "I'm sorry if I kept you waiting."

"Don't apologize. I'm a little early. I couldn't wait—" He bit off the remainder of his sentence and smiled down at her, his eyes twinkling.

She had the distinct impression he was going to say he couldn't wait to see her, but it might have just been her own foolish wishful thinking. She'd spent half the night tossing and turning, replaying parts of their conversation and the strange sense of companionship she felt.

"Follow me." Shaking her thoughts away, she led him through the foyer and into the basement of the building. "It's a bit of a labyrinth, I'm afraid."

"It's fascinating." Shaw's head flicked from side to side as they eased past old display cases, boxes, and crates. "This is far more interesting than some of the exhibits upstairs." He gave a sigh of wonder and stopped to look inside a glass-fronted cabinet housing some old maps. "There must be untold treasures here. What a wonderful place to work."

It was. Today, at this moment with Shaw standing next to her, although like any other job, it had its downside. The drudgery of the day-to-day routine and cataloguing and the interminable grind of preparation for the Mitchell wing sometimes got her down, but right now excitement bubbled and swirled inside her. "I can't tell you how thrilled I am about this sketchbook. I feel as though we're unraveling some kind of a mystery."

Shaw chuckled. "You sound as though you've taken up with Sherlock Holmes. Lead the way. It's having the same effect on me."

She pushed open the door and stood back to let him walk into the cubbyhole of an office. There were no windows, and once inside every thought and action was accompanied by the hum of the erratic incandescent lights. "The brass glass on the stand, the one with the variety of lenses, has the best magnification."

He strolled across to the map cabinet, his gaze riveted on the box on top. "That's a beautiful piece of work. Can I touch?"

"You can do more than that. Open it." She was so proud of the early-nineteenth-century collector's chest made from red cedar and Australian rosewood she'd managed to unearth. It had a series of drawers and a green leather writing surface. All of the correspondence the Royal Society had sent was stored in there, and the writing surface beneath the lid would be the perfect spot to display the sketchbook.

Shaw lifted the top and his eyes lit up. He pulled out the drawers and lifted the lids on the various compartments. "This is wonderful, space for ink and nibs and paper and correspondence. The perfect way to showcase these old letters."

Her face flushed at his praise, and she picked a pair of gloves and busied herself putting them on. "And perhaps the sketchbook."

"Mind if I take my jacket off and sit down?"

"Of course not."

He hung his jacket on the back of a chair and rolled up the sleeves of his white shirt, then sat down and eased the sketchbook from its bag and placed it on the desk.

She pulled up another stool and sat down, so close to him she could feel the warmth radiating from his skin. A prickle of awareness ran through her as his long fingers picked up the magnifying glass and wiped it clean with the cloth before putting on a pair of gloves.

Shaw turned straight to the back of the book, his fingers grasping the magnifying glass tightly as he peered at the portrait of Winton, moving the glass until the fallen log was center of the lens.

"Interesting. You have a look." He stood and she slipped onto the stool, angling the magnifying glass. The image blurred, then returned to focus, and she lifted her head, the hairs on the back of her neck prickling.

No, surely not.

She pulled her spectacles from her pocket and hooked them over her ears. With her gloved finger she traced the faded writing along the tree trunk, and where they thought there had been no signature, she spotted *R Winton* written in pencil along the fallen branch of the tree.

R Winton. Who was R Winton? Right from the beginning she'd thought the style of the painting was different, that someone other than Charles Winton had painted it.

She traced the *W* on Winton, then turned back to the previous page. Nothing like it. Charles Winton's signature was an impatient scrawl, no fanciful scrolls and swirls. She turned back to the painting. The foot of the *R* curled down under *Winton*, making an almost flowery, feminine line to the signature. She turned to the title page.

There was no doubt about it. Two different Wintons had contributed to the sketchbook. Not just Charles. But who was R Winton? His son? His brother? No, it couldn't be. That was a feminine hand if ever she'd seen one.

With her mind churning she turned back to the painting. His wife. He didn't have a wife. He wasn't married, unless it had happened after he arrived in the colony. She'd checked the First Fleet records; they listed him as a single man. The early letters he'd sent to Sir Joseph Banks corroborated that, made him sound a solitary sort of chap buried in his work.

She leaned forward and pointed out the faded writing running along the fallen tree trunk. "It doesn't say 'Resting'; it says 'Pa Resting,' then 'R Winton.'"

"No doubt about it. Hang on." His fingers grazed her arm.

She froze as his touch sent a flurry of goose bumps across her skin.

"Sorry, I can't see." He rested on his elbows and moved the magnifying glass. "It definitely says 'Pa Resting.'"

She rammed her spectacles farther up her nose, then leaned closer into the warm cloud of sandalwood soap surrounding him. "'Pa Resting' . . . Then R Winton is Charles Winton's daughter."

"Or son."

"She can't be a son. No boy would have writing as flowery as that."

"I wouldn't have thought a daughter would be encouraged to record anatomical drawings such as the ones earlier in the book."

"Whyever not?"

Shaw pushed back his chair and sighed. "Because we know the dates. The earliest is June 1817 and the watercolor is at the end of the book; the latest date is October 1819. Girls didn't make anatomical drawings in those days. It wasn't appropriate. Not even today. And look at the detail and the dissections." His finger hovered over an intricate line drawing and the annotation *a common cloaca for reproduction and excretion*. The male platypus must have been dissected, all its organs clearly marked, including the spurs on its back legs and the venom gland. And below the drawing notes, in that feminine hand, a description of the effects of the venom.

"Oh, rubbish. If he was her father, it would be totally acceptable." She huffed. For some reason she wanted R Winton to be a female.

Deep in her heart of hearts, more than that. She knew R Winton was Charles's daughter.

Shaw raised an eyebrow and turned a few more pages. "These ones, for example." He pointed to the detailed line drawings of the female suckling its young. "No woman would draw something like this with or without her father's permission, not in the early nineteenth century. It was the era when girls were hothoused and chaperoned to death."

Tamsin studied the picture of the platypus in the burrow, the two juveniles clamped to her body. Maybe he was right. She couldn't imagine Father discussing such things, and he was a physician.

"More to the point, it wasn't until 1832 the evidence of mammary glands, the distinguishing feature of mammals, was accepted. This one is dated 1819."

She bit her lip and tugged the book under the magnifying glass. "Can you see a signature on this one?"

Shaw's big warm hand covered hers and he edged the glass to the right. "Yes. Right there. See? 'Winton.'"

She extracted her hand and pushed her spectacles farther up her nose. "Where's the *C*?"

"There," Shaw said with an air of triumph.

She leaned so close to the glass her nose almost touched the surface. She was right, she knew she was. "That"—she traced the top curve of the letter—"is the top of the *R*. Look more carefully." She skidded her stool back and stood up, stretching the cramped muscles in her back.

Shaw leaned forward, arms resting on the desktop so the material of his waistcoat strained across his shoulders. "Maybe."

If only she'd had Shaw's help when she was organizing the correspondence. Truth was, she liked working with him, liked him a lot. She snuck a glance at him from under her lashes. He really was quite handsome. "No maybe about it. I need to record this." She reached for a pencil and paper. "Can you go back to the beginning? I'll write down the page numbers and we'll go through all the drawings and see if we can find a signature on each one."

"Okay. Page one: Watercolor—Platypus on bank. C Winton, June 1818. Is it all right if I name the drawings?"

"Fine. It'll make it easier, in fact. So long as you don't annotate the book."

"Of course not. This is just for us."

Us—she rather liked that. *Us*. It was so nice to have a work colleague, especially one who made her feel the way Shaw did. The thought took her by surprise. Always a loner, she'd relished the opportunity of working by herself and believed she'd enjoyed it. Now she wasn't so sure.

"Page two: Line drawing—Dissected male platypus. C Winton, July 1818. This is strange." He peered down at the facing page. "The drawing is signed 'C Winton' but the notes are written in the other handwriting."

"R Winton's writing, you mean?"

"Yes, and they're dated October 1819. They explain the symptoms of toxicity." His gloved fingers hovered over the words. "Goodness, it sounds dreadful: 'writhing, intense pain, lockjaw.'"

"Wait a minute. What was the date?"

"October 1819."

It couldn't be. Tamsin's heart started to thump and she turned to the pile of papers on the shelf behind her desk. She had to find it. Somewhere she'd made a timeline to try to plot the history of platypus research. "Here it is. 'The pain was intense and almost paralyzing . . . The arm was swollen to the shoulder, and quite useless, and the pain in the hand very severe . . .' That was written in 1876. There were some earlier references to the spur, but nothing about toxicity." She ran her finger down the column of dates. "That picture of the female suckling its young."

"Hang on a minute . . . Here we are, page ten. You can see the eggs too. And there's a dissected female on the next page."

She peered over his shoulder. "See there . . . an egg in the uterus." She stabbed at the drawing. "Jamison's observation that females laid eggs was disregarded in 1816. It wasn't until 1884 that it was proved that platypus were oviparous. Someone shot a female that had laid one egg, and when they dissected the poor creature they found another in the uterus, finally ending the eighty-year-old argument."

"So what you're saying is that no one knew of Winton's research—no one could have?"

"That would seem to be the case."

"Maybe it's all imagination. Supposition."

A flash of anger streaked through Tamsin. "Don't be ridiculous; the man was a scientist."

"And allowed someone else to annotate his notebook. How do we know R Winton didn't add her drawings and notes years later and just forged the dates?"

She bit back a sigh. "Let's look at the rest of the pictures and then we have to find out who this R Winton is."

By the time they'd reached the end of the sketchbook, Tamsin had a three-page list with each drawing named and the artist identified; a little over half were signed by Charles Winton and several by R Winton, including a series that had no signature, just additional notes and the same date, October 1819.

"Look at this." Shaw straightened up and caught her eye. A quick frown crossed his forehead, then he waved a sheet of cartridge paper in his hand and laid it carefully on the tabletop and unfolded it. "It was tucked in the back of the book under the endpaper that had come loose. I hadn't noticed it before."

A line drawing, a pencil sketch that almost sprang off the page, a lake and a bleak moor, unlike anything she'd ever seen. "That doesn't look like Australia."

"I don't think it is. What do you think?"

"I have no idea, but it isn't Australian. Look at the clouds; they're hanging so low and they're so threatening. And it has a title, 'Dozmary Pool.' Where's that?"

Tamsin tucked in the loose ends of her hair, then pushed back her stool. Her mind whirled. "Let's have a break; we deserve it. I'll go and get us a drink. Tea? Water? No coffee, I'm afraid."

"Water will be fine."

"What time is it?"

He pulled his watch from his fob pocket. "Lunchtime. Time I was making a move."

"I'd better check and make sure we haven't been locked in. Mrs. Williams always closes up down here before she goes to lunch."

"Maybe we're trapped."

"Don't! It sounds like a horror story."

"I wouldn't mind. I've enjoyed every moment." Shaw threw her a smile.

Her face flushed the color of a beet. "It's a shame I can't take the sketchbook home and work on it tonight." Anything to change the subject.

"No chance. I promised Mrs. Rushworth I'd take full responsibility and see it was kept locked up. To be honest, I was worried about it last night. It should be kept under lock and key."

"So you must be convinced it is authentic."

He rubbed his hands together. "I wonder what it would be worth on the open market. We need to discover who this R Winton is. If we had her dates, birth and death, we could at least rule out tampering. It seems that more than half the drawings might be hers."

Hers. "So you agree with my thesis that R Winton was a woman, Charles Winton's daughter?"

"Perhaps. Or his wife. Granddaughter even. It needs some more investigation. I cannot understand why Winton handed over control of his research."

"Plenty of women were capable artists, even in those days. And anyway, if Winton had sent it to Sir Joseph Banks, the book wouldn't be tucked in some house in the back of beyond. It would have been lodged with the Royal Society in London and the whole question of the platypus would have been resolved long before 1884."

And Charles Winton would have received credit for his discoveries instead of being consigned to some forgotten shelf in a dusty old study in the Hunter. "It would be nice to give him credit for his years of research, even if it is posthumously."

Shaw closed the sketchbook and slipped it back into its linen bag. "I've got to go now. I'll be back tomorrow and we can take a closer look. Is there somewhere safe we can keep this while we're appraising it?"

"Of course there is." The idea of the sketchbook remaining at the Library filled Tamsin with a huge sense of achievement. Not only was it the first step to it remaining; it meant that Shaw trusted her. She swung open the door of the safe under the bench. "Put it in here."

He slipped the bag inside and she took the key from the hook above her desk and locked the door. "Quite secure." She patted her pocket where she'd put the key.

"Good. The responsibility was getting me down, and now we know a little more, I'm convinced it is more valuable than I anticipated."

"I'll go back over the paperwork from England and see if I missed anything. My curiosity is killing me. I need to know who R Winton is, and I want to make certain Winton's signatures match with the correspondence."

"Are you two still in here?" Mrs. Williams stood in the open doorway. "Hello, Mr. Everdene." She held out her hand. "Nice to meet you. I'm Mrs. Williams. I was rather hoping I could take a look at the sketchbook."

"Tamsin's just locked it in the safe. I'm afraid I have to leave, but I'm happy for her to show you." He shrugged into his jacket and picked up his hat. "Don't forget to tell Mrs. Williams about the Peek Frean family too."

"Peek Frean? As in biscuits?" Mrs. Williams tipped her head to one side.

"Hasn't Tamsin told you about her little discovery?" He stood with the same cheeky grin on his face that he'd had when they'd first asked Mrs. Rushworth for the tin. It made her feel as though they had a special bond.

"No, she hasn't."

"Then you have lots to catch up on. I'll call in tomorrow."

She didn't want him to go. Wanted him to stay and help her find out more about R Winton. "Goodbye." Her voice held a disgustingly plaintive note, which she doubted Mrs. Williams would miss. The door closed behind Shaw and she stood for a moment relishing the last hint of sandalwood soap.

"Now show me your sketchbook." Mrs. Williams rubbed her hands together, sounding very much as though she were trying to cheer up a child whose attention needed diverting. Was she that transparent?

"Tamsin?"

She brought her eyes back into focus.

"The sketchbook." Mrs. Williams sat down on the stool. "My curiosity is killing me."

She pulled the key out and unlocked the safe. "I didn't think Shaw would leave the sketchbook here."

"Whyever not?"

"He promised Mrs. Rushworth, Mrs. Quinleaven's daughter, he wouldn't let it out of his sight."

"However, he's happy if it's here under lock and key. He obviously thinks you can be trusted." She let out a laugh. "It's ridiculous. This woman sounds like a nightmare."

Tamsin loosened the drawstring on the bag and placed the sketchbook back onto the workbench, then passed Mrs. Williams a pair of gloves.

"Mrs. Quinleaven must have had an idea of its value, otherwise she wouldn't have contacted us. It's in remarkable condition."

"A silverfish scuttled out when we first opened it, but I don't think it's done very much damage. There's a thread loose in the binding. I'm presuming the water and ink stains on the cover are simply from use."

A strange set of expressions worked their way across Mrs. Williams's face as she turned the pages, interspersed with the odd sigh and gasp. Tamsin sat waiting with her hands clasped in her lap. There was no doubt about the authenticity of the book in her mind, but why would Winton let someone else add to it? It made no sense at all, even if it was his daughter. Or son.

As much as she hated to admit it, Shaw was right. In those days girls spent their time on embroidery and taking tea, not dissection and anatomical drawings. According to Mrs. Benson at the Missionary Society, Mother had caused enough of a fuss when she'd signed on as a nurse at twenty-one, and all she was doing was bandaging wounds and changing bedpans.

Mrs. Williams moved the magnifying glass aside and rubbed her eyes. "If you want my opinion, it's authentic. Certainly early 1800s. The paper, the binding, even the ink. The thing that confuses me is the two totally different styles, yet the title on the cover makes no reference to anyone other than Charles Winton. I wonder if we can get any sort of time frame on the images that aren't dated."

"I thought of that, but they are interspersed through the whole book. It's not as though the last pages of the book were filled with watercolors. Under the glass we picked up another signature."

Mrs. Williams closed the book and folded her arms. "Come on, tell me."

"The work in the sketchbook isn't entirely Charles Winton's."

"If they were completed over a period of years, the different styles would also be understandable. He may have changed his approach. The watercolors remind me of an exhibition I saw at the Gallery a few months back. Impressionists."

"I'm talking specifically about the picture of Winton. The portrait."

Mrs. Williams's eyes darkened and a slight frown puckered the skin of her forehead and she held her body very still. "What makes you say that?"

She turned to the last page. "Under the magnifying glass you can see the pencil lines beneath the tree trunk. They weren't part of the original sketch, before the watercolors were added as I first supposed; they were a signature. R Winton, not C Winton." She raised her eyebrows and sat back in the chair.

Mrs. Williams huffed loudly. "What makes you so certain?"

"The flourish. The *R* has a flourish and it's matched in the *W* of *Winton*." She swallowed back the excitement in her voice; she must be calm and rational, analytical, before she dropped the next bombshell. Folding her arms, she leaned back in her chair. "I'm certain it's a woman's writing."

"A woman? Don't be ridiculous. Why would Charles Winton allow a woman to record his findings?" Mrs. Williams reacted just as Tamsin had expected.

"Perhaps his wife?"

"You found nothing in the correspondence to indicate he married, did you?"

"He's hardly likely to have discussed personal issues with Sir Joseph. He was his patron. He as good as employed him. What about the other watercolors and the line drawings? A lot of the drawings, especially those dated October 1819, aren't signed."

"So what's your premise?"

She didn't know what she was thinking, just that she felt as though she were standing on the edge of a precipice looking down, all jittery and weak-kneed.

"You can't go jumping to conclusions. Surely you've learned that by now."

Tamsin pulled the index across the table toward her. "Here are the page numbers and the signatures. As you can see, quite a lot are unsigned. The watercolor says 'Pa Resting' and it is signed 'R Winton.' I think R Winton is Winton's daughter."

"A baseless guess. Most unlike you. A little bit more work is required before I'll agree with that. The sketchbook itself looks genuine enough. I hope it hasn't been sullied. You've a lot more work ahead of you, my girl. You can't even suppose that the watercolor is of Charles Winton—it could have been added years later. It could be anyone."

Trust Mrs. Williams to put a damper on things. She was as bad as Shaw, refusing to acknowledge the fact that a woman could have done the drawings. It made her blood boil.

"Now tell me all about these biscuit people."

Feeling an irrational spurt of anger, she let out a sigh. She'd prove it one way or another. R Winton was a woman. She was right; she knew it with every fiber of her being. Pushing the thought aside because she could do nothing until she went back to Banks's letters, she turned back to Mrs. Williams. "Shaw took me to meet Mrs. Rushworth the day after the funeral. She was sorting out the contents of the house, throwing pretty much everything out."

"Nothing we'd be interested in, I hope. This modern disregard for our heritage is a disgrace." Mrs. Williams gave a dramatic shudder.

"That's why I took a chance and snuck into the library. The majority of the books were packed, but there was a pile of newspapers and pamphlets from ten, fifteen, twenty years ago and a set of the *Dawn*. She said I could have them; they're at home."

"I love that paper. That woman is an absolute gem."

Maybe, but her beliefs hadn't influenced Mrs. Williams enough to entertain the thought that R Winton was female. Perhaps it was time they discussed some of Louisa Lawson's ideas in greater depth.

"I also found a copy of the *Penny Magazine* from June 1835 with an article about the water mole. I thought perhaps I could include it with the letters, and this old Peek Frean tin fell out when I was picking up the papers. I couldn't get the lid off so I asked Mrs. Rushworth if I could have it. Shaw said it was for my collection." Her mind darted back to his naughty grin; it still made her want to giggle like a schoolgirl involved in a prank.

"I didn't know you collected old tins. I must show you some I have. They belonged to my mother."

Tamsin pulled the tin from her satchel and her heart rate picked up just the way it had when Shaw finally removed the lid. "A handkerchief with the initials *CM*, some illegible penciled notes, and a daguerreotype, a family, from 1845."

"Oh, very early. Australian? One of George Goodman's?"

"Yes, it must be . . ." Her voice fizzled out as a series of goose bumps flecked her skin.

"Yes. And?" Mrs. Williams drummed her fingers on the table. "Tamsin?"

She took a sip of water, her throat suddenly dry. "Sorry. Someone walked over my grave. It happened the other day. I might be coming down with a cold or something."

"I want to know about the biscuit tin. You young things with your butterfly brains."

"There was also a name and some dates, almost an epitaph."

"An epitaph? What are you talking about?"

"It said 'Jenifer Trevan, loving granddaughter of Granfer Tomas Trevan, May 24, 1772–February 2, 1788.' I feel as though it's all intertwined; I just haven't sorted everything out in my mind." She lifted the cool glass of water to her lips more for something to do than the need to drink.

"Tamsin?" Mrs. Williams's calm voice cut through the swirling confusion in her brain and she blinked away the image of the old woman in the graveyard.

"I might be wrong." Her entire reaction to the sketchbook and the tin annoyed her. She'd never felt this invested or connected with any of her parents' possessions or anything at the Library in all the time she'd worked there. The biscuit tin. Something skirted the edge of her mind just out of reach.

"Well? Come along."

"The tin was obviously some sort of record; the handkerchief and daguerreotype were tied up with a blue ribbon. Someone had gone to great lengths to preserve them."

Mrs. Williams tilted her head. "Was the daguerreotype annotated? Was there any indication who the people were?"

"I hoped, but nothing. The only name in the tin was Jenifer Trevan." And the nagging thought in her mind that somehow the contents of the tin and the sketchbook were connected.

Mrs. Williams didn't miss a beat. "You think the people in the daguerreotype might have something to do with Winton?"

Tamsin nodded. It was ridiculously far-fetched.

Chapter 13

London, England
1820

Rose paced the floor incessantly, peering out of the window at the driving rain, the gray sky, and the low clouds that shrouded everything in gloom. What she would give for the cobalt sky of home instead of this soaking, soggy weather that passed for spring. Every time she set foot outside the house, the cold ate into her bones; her two dresses and muddy brown pelisse did nothing to keep out the wind's chilly blast. She traced her finger over the condensation on the window, scrawled her signature—*R Winton*. She'd never be a Barrington, didn't want to belong to a man she'd never met, and in all honesty, she wasn't too sure she wanted Julian for a brother. She'd rather have Finneas. She sighed and rubbed her name away with the heel of her hand. It wouldn't do to labor the point.

Julian's reception had terrified her; he seemed so aggressive. Whereas Finneas appeared to be prepared to go to great lengths to make the meeting at the Royal Society eventuate. They'd talked about science and nature and politics and family; everything under the sun. Nothing seemed taboo. Of course, the fact that he had such an interest in the mallangong had immediately endeared him to her.

And his offer to go and speak to the gentlemen of the Royal Society. Truth be told, she had the distinct feeling Julian would rather she'd fallen overboard somewhere around Cape Horn.

What if the Royal Society refused to accept Pa's work? She simply couldn't fail, couldn't entertain the possibility. She should be allowed to present his research. All this ridiculous nonsense about women being some sort of inferior species. She'd like to think at least the great minds of science would accept there was no difference between a man's and a woman's brain.

A little over an hour later a carriage stopped outside the house and Finneas leaped out, physician's bag in hand, his rich brown hair tousled from the rain, and took the steps to the front door two at a time. The very sight of him made her heart lift. He had to have good news; why else would he be so exuberant? She left the window and smoothed the front of her dress, wiping away the dampness remaining on her hand.

The door flew open and he bounded into the room, eyes sparkling and a wide smile lighting his handsome face.

She couldn't contain herself. "Well?"

"Well, I have failed."

The air swept out of her lungs. She was so sure he'd succeed; he didn't look as though he'd ever failed at anything in his life. It didn't appear to worry him very much. In fact, he looked thoroughly pleased with himself.

"I couldn't speak to Sir Joseph. It appears he is suffering dreadfully from the gout and has been confined to his bed on his physician's orders, not receiving visitors or attending to correspondence." Finneas threw himself into a chair, drumming his fingers on his knee and chewing his lip as though he was trying to find the best way to deliver the final calamitous piece of news. "However, I did manage to speak to the gentleman who will be chairing the meeting tomorrow evening."

"And?"

"He wouldn't budge. You cannot make a presentation and you cannot attend."

"Oh, Finneas." Tears sprang to her eyes. Was she to be thwarted at every turn? And why did he still have that ridiculous smile on his face? She'd imagined he would be more sympathetic to her plight. "What about Julian?"

"No. Unlike Herschel, he is not a fellow and therefore cannot present your paper." He pulled back his shoulders, his eyes positively sparkling with delight.

The wretched man. And she'd thought Julian was the stumbling block.

"However, the secretary is prepared to make the presentation on your behalf, providing the president and the fellows present grant permission."

She sank down into a chair. He hadn't failed. "Will they agree? Will you be there?"

"The secretary was optimistic. I shall be in the audience. I've been lucky enough to attend meetings in the past because of my interest in the sciences, and they have agreed you may sit in the anteroom. The door will be left ajar. It will enable you to hear the entire speech and the response of the audience. There now. That has made you smile. I intend to ensure you do that more often."

He gazed across at her and for one foolish moment she thought to throw herself into his arms. A heady warmth washed her cheeks. "Thank you, from the bottom of my heart. I cannot convey to you how happy you have made me. I will be eternally in your debt."

"Something I wouldn't mind in the least." He stood and stepped closer, his now familiar woody scent enveloping her.

Without a second thought she stood and clasped his warm hand between both of hers. "While I was aboard ship I wrote what I hope is a suitable presentation. I hope the secretary deems it worthwhile."

"I have no doubt he will. I have never met a girl with such a lively intellect and knowledge of the sciences."

His praise made her face flush again and her heart skipped a beat.

"Shall we go in to dinner? I believe Julian has taken himself out tonight, so I shall have you all to myself."

She was in London, not in New South Wales where life was much simpler. She thought back to Mrs. Metcalf's etiquette lessons. "Would that be appropriate?"

"Entirely! I am your relative, well, close family friend, since we share no blood. This house belongs to my mother and your brother lives here. And I promise you will be perfectly chaperoned by Hughes and Mrs. James. It is entirely acceptable."

Rose gazed around the door of the anteroom at the assembled crowd. Her chest tingled and her palms grew damp as she waited. It was one thing to present Pa's research herself, quite another to leave it in the hands of a man whom she had never even spoken to, but what alternative did she have?

She peered at the interesting mix of people filing into the room. Judging from the assortment of clothes and styles, these men were from all walks of life. Some would be more than comfortable at court while others had the disheveled look of scholars or poets. And there wasn't another female in sight.

There was an interminable wait while the secretary brought the meeting to order, read the previous minutes, and attended to the correspondence. Finneas had explained that the meetings ended promptly at nine regardless of whether the business had been concluded, and already the clock on the mantel indicated eight thirty.

The secretary walked to the lectern. The buzz of conversation ceased. "With the agreement of our president, who unfortunately is too ill to attend tonight's meeting, I have been asked to . . ." He cleared his throat.

Rose leaned forward in her chair, trying to interpret his sudden pause. Was there some sort of a problem? Perhaps he found her handwriting difficult to decipher. To the best of her knowledge he hadn't even glanced at the paper when they arrived, merely tucked it beneath a pile of others.

"I have been asked to present Charles Winton's direct observations of the internal structure of the *Ornithorhynchus anatinus*."

She exhaled slowly and drew her shoulders back, as though she was on the podium, preparing to speak.

"More commonly known as the water mole, this native of the Great South Land is one of the many species of flora and fauna that would appear to be unique to that fascinating country.

"Charles Winton has spent the last twenty years compiling a full case study. Evidence of his recent, groundbreaking research is thoroughly documented in this book." He held up the sketchbook for all to see.

A grumble drifted across the tightly packed seats and the secretary cast a quick look over his shoulder at the anteroom, then lowered his head. "According to Mr. Winton's research, *Ornithorhynchus anatinus* is a taxonomic riddle. It does indeed nourish its young with milk. However, that is where the similarity to other *mammalia* ends. Apparently the female of the species lays eggs, or so Mr. Winton contends."

She hadn't written that. He hadn't even mentioned the fact that they had dissected the specimens.

"Lays eggs. What a nonsense."

"An affront to our intelligence."

"Employ a scientist, not a half-baked colonial dabbler to acquire some reputable information."

All the blood rushed from Rose's head and she dropped her face into her hands. She was going to be sick. She dragged in a deep breath and lifted her head when the secretary cleared his throat and waded once more into the sea of discontent lapping the walls of the room.

"The water mole is aquatic in its habits, frequenting rivers, small streams, and lagoons or, as the natives refer to them, billabongs. They are more often found in heavily wooded areas, being shy animals happier in the dappled shade. The natives often hunt the water mole for its pelt, but it has the ability to defend itself as it has a strong, sharp, venomous spur on each of its hind legs that can inflict dangerous, if not fatal, wounds." He gestured to Pa's specimen, which he'd placed on the table beside him, and indicated the spurs on the back legs.

"The animal's no bigger than a cat."

"Venomous spur. What nonsense."

"Where's your proof?"

The secretary could certainly answer that question: he only had to look at her notes where she'd detailed Pa's spurring. He did nothing, just stood, then raised his hand. "Gentlemen. Gentlemen. A degree of skepticism is not only pardonable but laudable . . . I, too, doubt the testimony."

Peering down at her set of notes, the secretary ran his hand over his forehead; even from this distance she could see the beads of sweat peppering his domed brow as he skipped back up to the previous paragraph. "With the aid of the natives Winton captured several water moles and dissected them."

Rose wriggled her toes in her boots in impatience. Why was he using the name water mole? She hadn't written that.

"The female digs a more extensive burrow than the male. The eggs develop in the female's body and one to three are laid in this burrow. After ten days they hatch. The female then feeds her young on a milky secretion which seeps from the skin."

"Absolute poppycock."

She squirmed in her seat. If only Pa could be here. He wouldn't have remained silent. He'd be right at the front challenging the men whose questions and incredulity merged into a disparaging rumble.

That was it. She couldn't stand it a moment longer. With her heart hammering so hard she could feel it beneath the cotton of her dress, she shot to her feet and stepped from behind the door and up onto the podium. A long, loud combined gasp silenced the incessant rumblings. At least she had achieved something.

Julian reached her side in a moment. "Rose, you can't. Leave at once." He hissed the words into her left ear and a whiff of brandy made her nose wrinkle.

"I will not." She shook off his restraining hand.

"Good evening, gentlemen." Stunned silence greeted her words and the audience sank back into their seats. Making the most of the lull, she plowed on. "My name is Rose Winton. I am Charles Winton's daughter."

Julian drew himself up to his full height, opened his mouth, then sank into the nearest empty chair.

"I grew up in a place called Agnes Banks, west of Sydney, where my father has a house and a small parcel of land alongside the lagoon on the traditional lands belonging to the Darug people. Much of the flora and fauna you find so fascinating is as natural to me as the lilac and larkspur your wives grow. I was present when the native retrieved this animal." Her voice seemed unnaturally squeaky in the high-ceilinged room as she gestured to the mallangong sitting next to the lectern.

"Native." A raucous guffaw of laughter replaced the silence. "Notoriously disreputable."

"Perhaps the case has been somewhat overstated." The secretary's piercing gaze scrutinized her like some scientific oddity. How dare he! She met his look with a defiant lift of her chin and moved forward. "I am able to provide an eyewitness account of *Ornithorhynchus anatinus* and settle once and for all the conjecture and disbelief that have been rife concerning this poor creature."

She gave the stuffed specimen an affectionate pat as the grumbling reached fever pitch.

"Rose, leave now!" Julian's voice cut through the furor.

"I will not." Was there nothing she could say that would sway them? "My father was unable to attend this meeting. He was spurred." That got them. The murmurings and mumblings settled again. She held the creature high in the air, indicating the spur on its back leg. "The venom causes intense pain and the affected limb swells to twice its size."

"A poisonous duck now."

"A mere trick of taxidermy. A fraud. A beaver and a duck combined. The Chinese are masters at it."

Surely there was someone in the room who was interested in what she had to say. For the first time since the beginning of the long voyage, she was pleased Pa wasn't here to witness such a debacle.

She would not let them ridicule his work, her work. There was nothing she hadn't witnessed with her own eyes. She stood tall. "*Ornithorhynchus anatinus* is an egg-laying mammal, and its offspring are born live. It is one of only two we are aware of—*Tachyglossus aculeatus,* the echidna, another indigenous animal akin to an anteater, being the other.

"We have dissected an animal and proved this. I have a drawing here . . ." She opened the sketchbook and held it aloft.

"It is a hoax."

"Hoax. Hoax." The cry was taken up.

She caught Julian's eye and he shook his head. She would not give up. "Despite the great deal of debate, I assure you that this is no hoax.

Ornithorhynchus anatinus does lay eggs and feed its young. Your disbelief is the hoax, not the animal itself."

"Some fool took a chance with a dissection knife and then passed the pieces onto a seamstress."

The thirty-strong crowd roared its approval.

"Gentlemen, if you would resume your seats." The secretary's heavy hand came down on her arm. "I must ask you to leave, Miss Winton."

Finneas strode down the aisle between the rows of outraged men surging toward Rose. She stood clutching the sketchbook to her as a kind of talisman in the maelstrom of madness that surrounded her. He'd let her down by suggesting the secretary should speak for her. He should have offered to do it himself; he should have protected her, should have insisted.

Rose took two steps back and opened her mouth again.

Finneas reached her side before she could utter a sound. "We have to leave now."

Rose huffed, holding on to the sketchbook as though her life depended on it. "They are nothing more than a bunch of lily-livered, addle-headed, self-opinionated jackasses."

"Come on." Swallowing the urge to applaud her assessment of the assembled crowd, he tugged at her arm.

She wriggled from his grasp. "Not without my mallangong."

"I'll get that." Julian sprang to life with more enthusiasm and dedication than he'd displayed since Rose had arrived and snatched the animal from the table, tucking it under his arm.

"This way." Finneas grabbed Rose's hand and towed her through the door into the anteroom, where he opened another door leading to the street and they eased out, closing it behind them.

Julian stood for a moment looking up and down. "This way around the corner and down toward the river."

With Rose's warm hand firmly clasped in his, Finneas led her into the courtyard and through the gates. As they rounded the corner, the door opened and the members poured out of the meeting room laughing and carrying on. The word *hoax* floated in the night air and he tugged Rose in the opposite direction. She didn't need to hear their insults again.

An unruly mob of bystanders lurking beside the river took up the cry like hunting dogs picking up the scent.

"Come on. Give me the sketchbook. We'll have to run." Finneas snatched it from her and thrust it under his arm and took off. Casting a look over his shoulder, he caught Rose's enigmatic glance, and before he was aware, she had sprinted into the lead, her skirt lifted high, revealing her clodhopping boots.

"We're going to have to split up. They're onto us." Julian's voice came in broken gasps, the mallangong still tucked under his arm. "I'll see you at Grosvenor Square."

Finneas grabbed Rose's arm and dragged her into one of the narrow cobbled alleyways running behind the houses. "We'll go the other way. Put them off, make it more difficult."

The drumming of feet gradually subsided and Finneas came to a halt, bending double, hands on his knees.

Rose turned back to him. "Where are we?"

"The mews—the stables and carriages. They run behind most of the houses." He rested his back against the wall, his chest heaving. "You're hardly even panting." Whereas he was bent double.

"The advantage of never having owned a carriage. I've probably run more miles than you've had hot dinners."

He grasped her wrist. "Your pulse is barely elevated."

"Let's go, then. Can you manage?"

Could *he* manage? "Slower this time, I think. We'll stick to the mews."

They walked at a rapid rate past rows of stables, stopping only to cross the main street before entering another narrow cobbled alleyway.

"Not much farther. This is the back of 44. We'll slip in through the basement."

He pushed open the door to the servants' quarters and with a groan of relief collapsed into one of the chairs at the kitchen table. "Sit down and catch your breath."

"Are we home?"

"Indeed we are."

"Where's Julian?" She pulled the door ajar and peered out, almost as though she were playing, and enjoying, some sort of game of hide-and-seek. "I hope he hasn't dropped the mallangong." As did he. No knowing what Julian would do to save his own skin, although he had plenty of experience avoiding debtors, so perhaps it would stand him in good stead. "He knows his way around. Close the door. He'll come in the front, I expect."

She closed the door and hoisted herself up onto tiptoes and turned on the tap, taking a long drink from the stream of water cascading into the sink.

Hughes's burly figure appeared in the doorway and he cleared his throat loudly. Rose wiped her mouth on the back of her hand and turned to face him, not looking the slightest bit perturbed that the butler had seen her with her head stuck under the kitchen tap.

"Ah! Mr. Finneas. I wasn't expecting to find you down here. May I get you something, Miss Rose?" He raised a quizzical eyebrow. It wasn't the first time Hughes had found him roaming the servants' quarters late at night, but with a young lady in tow it was no doubt more than a challenge to his sense of propriety.

"Hughes, can you bring us some brandy up to the blue sitting room, please? Mr. Julian should be home very soon."

"I think you'll find he's a little ahead of you. He came through the front door not long ago and I have left the brandy with him. Miss Rose, can I get you a cup of chocolate?"

"Thank you, that would be lovely." She turned to the door and Hughes emitted a rather loud harrumph. "Perhaps I can get you some slippers, miss."

Rose looked down at her boots and lifted her foot. The sole was coated in horseshit and clods of something he'd rather not dwell on. His boots were an equally disgusting mess. He toed them off and leaned forward to unlace hers.

"What are you doing?" She reared away from him.

"We don't want to walk up the stairs and muddy the carpets. Our boots are covered in horse manure."

She shook her head. "I'll go outside and clean them."

"You will do no such thing. The crowd could be waiting. Just take them off and Hughes will fetch you some slippers."

She shook her head and folded her arms, determination and some sort of strange embarrassment flickering across her face. He couldn't make her take off her boots and he certainly wasn't going to let her go outside.

Hughes's eyes widened and he puffed out his chest. "Please don't concern yourself, Miss Rose." He eyed her boots with a barely concealed distaste. "I'll send one of the maids to clean up later."

"Isn't there a boot scraper in the scullery?" Rose let out a disgruntled huff, totally at odds with her usual sunny nature.

"Indeed there is, miss. Follow me."

She stomped through the door muttering an indecipherable string of words that sounded very much as though she'd learned them aboard ship.

A few moments later she reappeared, her boots somewhat cleaner. She raised her eyebrow at him, then dusted her hands and disappeared through the door.

Finneas could do no more than follow.

In the blue sitting room Julian stood peering out of the window, a glass of brandy in his hand. "I thought I was outrunning a pack of hellhounds baying for my blood."

Strangely he almost seemed to be enjoying himself, and he couldn't take his eyes off Rose's flushed face and bright eyes. A licentious leer crossed his face, sending a spark of jealousy shooting through Finneas. For heaven's sake, had the man no decorum? The girl was his *sister*.

Chapter 14

London, England
1820

The poor mallangong lay tossed on the floor, one of its back legs dangling from a thread and its fur dark and damp from the rain. Rose bent to pick it up and the fumes of the brandy Julian was slopping into a glass brought tears to her eyes. Not for the first time tonight did she regret Pa's absence. He wouldn't have run; he'd have stood and fought for his research. The truth. Not a hoax. She'd witnessed everything with her own eyes. How could they dispute the facts?

"Sit down, Rose. Stop pacing. There's nothing we can do tonight." Finneas led her to a chair and with his hands on her shoulders nudged her down and handed her his glass. The acrid stench seared her throat.

"Take a sip. You're suffering from shock."

She wasn't suffering from shock—she knew exactly what that looked like after watching Pa. She was suffering from a very plain and ordinary case of anger. Fury at her inability to stand and fight and rage at the stupid, narrow-minded men who wouldn't believe the evidence if it was shoved right under their noses.

It was the first time she'd acted as an adult. The first time she'd taken matters into her own hands, done what Pa couldn't do.

And she'd failed.

She sipped at the brandy. It made her lips burn, and when she swallowed it caught, making her splutter. Julian threw his long, lanky body out of the chair and flounced off without a backward glance.

She thumped the glass down on the small table. "I'm not giving up. Pa trusted me with his life's ambition and I have failed him." She let out a frustrated sigh. "It's ridiculous, ridiculous." What right had the secretary to make such judgments? *"Perhaps the case has been somewhat overstated."* He knew nothing of Pa's work. Knew nothing of the hours of labor it had taken to present this evidence.

She stroked the creature's fur, hoping her anger would dissipate. In the background she could hear a perpetual hum of voices, the clatter of carriage wheels, and the constant growl of the city. For the first time since she'd arrived, she longed for the wide-open spaces of home and the friendly smiles of Yukri, Bunji, and Yindi, and most of all Pa.

By the following morning Rose had made her decision.

"I would really like to give it one more try. I know Sir Joseph is unwell, but I wondered if he might grant me a private audience when he is recovered." She sipped a cup of hot chocolate, which had fast become her favorite beverage.

"I took matters into my own hands and wrote asking the very same thing last night."

Finneas was so handsome standing there smiling down at her. The day began to brighten, the sun appearing through a break in the pewter sky, giving the clouds a silver rim.

The door swung open and Julian fell into the room, his face suffused with blood, looking like one of the bunyips Bunji described when he spun his far-fetched yarns of mythical creatures. "This is the final straw." He threw a crumpled piece of paper down on the table.

"The streets are as good as papered with the wretched things. The presses must have run all night."

Finneas picked it up and as his face fell, so did her stomach. "What is it?"

He stuffed the crumpled paper into his pocket. "Nothing you need worry yourself about."

"And everything I need worry about." Julian scowled at her. "I hold you entirely responsible for this debacle. I will be the laughing-stock of Brooks's."

Rose put down her chocolate and stared into her brother's furious face. "I'm sorry, I don't understand. Finneas?"

"For heaven's sake, show her."

Finneas pulled the paper from his pocket and smoothed out the wrinkles. "Perhaps it is for the best."

Rose jumped to her feet and stared down at the drawing. A very well-executed drawing, but not in a style she was familiar with. It portrayed a man, long black legs flying as he ran down the street. Tucked under one arm was something that looked remarkably like a mermaid. Flowing black curly hair trailing to the ground and a face uncannily similar to her own above the fishlike tail that curved around his upper leg and dangled from the fingers of his right hand . . .

Her heart almost ceased beating as she picked up the paper, carrying it to the window where the light was better. It was a mallangong. There was no doubt about it, just as there was no doubt who the man portrayed in the picture was. She cast a look under her lashes at Julian. The artist had captured him perfectly. Hooked nose, the arrogant tilt of his head as he peered over his shoulder at the band of men chasing him down the darkened street. Even his overlong hair, so like her own, curling on his collar. She ran her hand over her head and shuddered. "Who is responsible for this? Why have they drawn it?"

"It's a satirical print, a lampoon; a very popular way of making social comment."

She unrolled the remainder of the sheet and her eyes fell to the caption at the bottom: *Nullius in Verba*. It summed up the bunch of narrow-minded men of the Royal Society perfectly. No one believed Pa. She screwed up the paper and threw it into the grate. "Get rid of it!"

"Would it were that easy. Not only will every member of Brooks's have perused it, but there are crowds gawking at the thing, spending their hard-earned pennies on a copy. They'll be hammering on the door next seeking a brush with fame."

"Don't be ridiculous." Finneas glared at Julian.

Rose's knees gave way and she collapsed into a chair. "I see. I'm so very sorry, Julian." Thank heavens Pa wasn't here to see this. He'd be devastated. And then the full implication settled. What would Sir Joseph say? Would he refuse to see her? "Would you excuse me, please? I need to take some air."

"I'll come with you."

"No, please, Finneas. I'll just take a walk across the square. Clear my head." She had to get out of the room, out of the house. The rage, or perhaps it was humiliation, rolling off Julian in an almost visible cloud frightened her. She needed to think.

Without further ado she closed the door behind her and went upstairs to find her pelisse, hat, and gloves—such a palaver just to get a whiff of air. What she wouldn't give to be at home where even in the middle of winter the sun shone and she rarely needed anything more than a shawl to keep her warm. Far better than this horrible damp that never seemed to lift.

Suitably attired so even Mrs. Metcalf wouldn't be able to complain, she let herself quietly out of the house. She didn't want to have to explain to Hughes where she was going or be told she needed to be accompanied. She was only halfway across the street toward the square when a loud cry made her turn.

A group of people led by a large man bellowing, "Hoax! Hoax!" raced toward her.

She spun around, intent on returning to the house, but her path was blocked. Seeking only to escape, she lifted her skirts high and ran across the square. The shouting man was so big, his legs so long, that for every one of her strides he gained on her.

His hand landed on her shoulder, fingers digging deep beneath the bones. He turned her to face him. She flew back and landed on the ground with an agonizing thud that sent the air rushing from her lungs.

"Play possum. Play possum." Bunji's words echoed in her head and she lay limp, trying to deceive him.

It didn't work.

He grunted in triumph, hovering above her.

Suddenly he stiffened, reared back, and flew away from her. A fist slammed into his face, and with a long-drawn-out sigh he crumpled to the ground beside her.

Watery-kneed with fear, she stared up into Finneas's face as he dusted his hands together as though he'd completed a well-done job. He sketched a bow, which brought a hysterical gurgle of laughter to her throat.

"Next time I will come with you when you want to take the air." Finneas swept her up into his arms and marched across the square while the onlookers dispersed, ushered away by the watch she'd seen on the first day.

Hughes stood by the front door, a look of total despair on his face. "I beg your pardon, Master Finneas. I had no idea Miss Rose had left the house."

"Just bring my bag, a blanket, and some brandy." Finneas deposited her like a precious package into the chair by the fire.

And she promptly burst into tears.

"I hold myself entirely responsible. I didn't realize the print would have caused such a commotion. I should have known better." Finneas hovered over her like some guardian angel.

Rose's lips puckered. "I'm perfectly all right. I have no idea why I burst into tears like that. It's not my usual behavior. What a disaster. I'm beginning to regret coming to London. Pa will be so disappointed. Maybe I should go home." Which was the last thing she wanted to do—give up and crawl away. But she had brought so much disruption to Finneas's and Julian's lives.

"I've received a reply to my note. Sir Joseph wasn't in a position to respond, but his personal secretary has agreed to an appointment at eleven o'clock on June 30. He is anticipating Sir Joseph will have recovered by then."

The weight lifted from her shoulders. "Once again I'm in your debt. I really don't want to make your life a misery."

"You aren't and you haven't. Let me tell you the rest of my plan. While you wait to see Sir Joseph, I propose a trip to get you out of London. A way to escape this harassment. It is time you met your aunt."

"My aunt?"

"Indeed, Lady Methenwyck is your aunt. Your father's sister."

"Pa has no sisters . . . Oh!" The ramification of his words settled slowly. She'd forgotten all about Lady Methenwyck, hadn't thought beyond Julian, whom she wasn't even sure she cared for very much at all.

What was the alternative—run back to Agnes Banks with her tail between her legs and spend the rest of her life wondering?

"While we're away the furor in the scandal sheets will die down and Julian will regain his good humor. When we return you will have your opportunity to speak to Sir Joseph. I have no doubt he'll be up and about in no time. Wyck Hall is between Bodmin Moor and the north coast of Cornwall. It is a delightful escape, and I'm certain you would enjoy the opportunity to see more of the English countryside."

"How far is it?"

"About two hundred and fifty miles."

"What about Julian? He needs to get out of London too."

"Julian travels back and forth several times a year and will, I'm sure, make his own decision. I go less frequently—a trip is well overdue. What do you say?" His boyish face broke into an all-encompassing smile, his eyes pleading with her. "Please say yes."

What had she to lose? Almost a month until she could see Sir Joseph, and there was a distinct possibility that she would go mad if she had to stay inside this house. And as difficult as it was to see anyone but Pa as her father, perhaps she owed it to Mr. Barrington to make this trip, meet her aunt.

"It sounds like a marvelous idea. But don't you have responsibilities at the hospital?"

"I have made arrangements for my rounds to be covered and I have no other pressing engagements."

He brought her hand to his lips and brushed a kiss over her knuckles. Tears sprang to her eyes again. She loved his look of concern, as though her needs were the most important thing in the world to him.

"We'll take the mail coach. It leaves London most days for the West Country."

"A mail coach? Do people write that many letters?" Goodness, he was going to think her such a simpleton. At home a man carrying the post rode from Sydney to Parramatta twice, maybe three times a week. Letters were handed over and any new ones passed to the next rider. The system was less than perfect. Bushrangers often got the better of the riders and the delivery was always late. She knew that well enough because Pa's packages for Sir Joseph went that way. At every turn something else she didn't know or understand.

"It's the fastest way to travel. Coaches make a good twelve miles an hour, with four coaches per route, two going in each direction with two spare coaches in case of a breakdown. Four horses, and far faster because there are no tolls. We'll break the journey at Exeter. The New London Inn is quite adequate." He rubbed his hands together, excitement flashing in his eyes. "And then from Exeter to Bodmin. At the Jamaica Inn we'll pick up horses and ride to Wyck Hall." His eyes widened and he took both her hands in his. "You are able to handle a horse?"

That she did know and understand. "Of course."

"Then it is all sorted out. I shall go and organize tickets and at the same time call at Soho Square and see how Sir Joseph fares, tell his secretary we will be away until the end of the month. If by any chance there has been an improvement and Sir Joseph is receiving, we can return earlier."

"Shouldn't I come with you, in case . . ." She shuddered, cowardice perhaps, but the thought of stepping out into the streets and risking ridicule after her ignominious treatment at the hands of the lampooners was more than she could bear. "Thank you. I'd like that, and while you are gone I shall go and pack my belongings."

"Excellent. Don't forget to call on Mrs. James if you have any difficulties." With a wave of his hand, Finneas picked up his hat and bag and left.

Rose watched from the window as his long-legged frame strode down the road. Finneas was so much nicer than her brother, with his open-faced honesty and delight in life. Such a contrast to Julian's scowling black looks and the discontent that seemed to ooze from every pore.

When he'd disappeared from sight she made for her bedchamber. She didn't need any help from Mrs. James to pack her paltry belongings. At home she'd never given a second thought to her clothes other than the ghastly boots Mam insisted she wear. Now she dreamed of wearing the brightly colored clothes she'd seen on the women walking in the square and maybe a pretty dress to change into in the evening—something Finneas would like.

The thought brought her up with a shock and she stopped dead in the middle of the stairway, her eyes fixed on the enormous classical fresco above the landing. Perhaps at Wyck Hall she would need other dresses. Would she disgrace herself? At least the trip down to Cornwall offered no concern. It sounded like fun, and to ride again would be the greatest pleasure. She'd seen the ladies on their horses riding along the carriageway, going to the park in their beautiful outfits, feathered hats, and gloves, and she had none. Her three dresses and monstrous brown pelisse would simply have to do.

When a knock sounded on the door, Rose's dresses lay crumpled on the bed and her trunk open. Mrs. James poked her head around the door. "I'm here to help. Mr. Finneas has returned and I am to tell you he has managed to procure two seats on the West Country mail coach leaving this evening at eight o'clock."

"That's wonderful. I can pack my belongings. I've hardly any clothes."

"Which is a concern. You'll freeze to death."

Rose shrugged her shoulders. There wasn't much she could do about it. She had very little money. Pa had given her a few coins, but she doubted the holey dollars would even be accepted in London, never mind be sufficient to buy new clothes. She gave an involuntary shiver. How could this possibly be the beginning of summer?

"I think we can solve your immediate problem. The mistress no longer rides and we have several of her outfits here. She told me to dispense with them. I always hoped one day to see her back to her former health and I couldn't bring myself to part with them. Let me see what I can find."

"Won't she mind? I can't turn up at Wyck Hall wearing Lady Methenwyck's clothes."

"Trust me, she won't mind. She'd give the very clothes off her back if they would help someone. It'd be nice to see her here again. Maybe when the old man's time's up. He hasn't set foot in London for years now either." And with that Mrs. James trundled off.

Lady Methenwyck sounded like some paragon of virtue. How she'd like to ask Finneas all about her; perhaps this trip on the coach would give them time to talk.

Mrs. James reappeared and dumped an armful of clothes onto the bed. "This looks as though it might do the trick. Not the pinnacle of fashion anymore but nothing to be ashamed of." She held up a dark blue woolen riding habit—more pelisse really, and so much nicer than her dreadful brown one. "Needs a bit of a press. I'd hazard a guess it'd fit quite well. Quite slight is the mistress. Stand up."

Rose pushed off the bed. *Nothing to be ashamed of!* Fit for a governor's wife, almost military with the buttons and the white cravat. It looked more like something Mrs. Macarthur would wear. "It's beautiful. Are you sure . . . ?"

"Told you already. Can't having you freezing to death on the coach, and while we're at it, you need to do something about those boots."

Rose twisted her foot. *Those boots* might well be the cause of all her anguish. Her skin still crawled at the look she'd seen on Julian's face after their mad race back from Somerset House.

"Try these for size." Like a magician Mrs. James conjured a pair of blue half-boots, so soft and light, not like her clumping great clodhoppers. "They're walking boots, but I reckon they'll do the trick and keep those little toes warm."

"I'll try them on in a minute." She gazed longingly at the soft leather and the row of small buttons.

"Very well, we'll try the riding habit. No need to take off your dress." Rose stood stock-still while Mrs. James buttoned and fastened and pulled and twisted until she was encased in the long, fitted coat. "All that's missing is the hat." She turned back to the pile of clothes on the bed and produced a red felt hat festooned with the most delicious pure-white feather.

Rose couldn't keep the smile from her face as she turned this way and that, trying to catch sight of her reflection in the windows. If only Pa could see her now.

"Patience, patience, let me fetch the glass. Look a treat, you do."

Rose ran her hands over the soft wool, so warm, and the high collar would keep out the biting winds that had plagued her since she arrived. What would Finneas say?

"There you are now. What do you think?"

Rose had to pinch the skin on her arm. Could this truly be her? She looked like, well, like a lady.

"Think Mr. Finneas will be pretty happy with that. Asked me first thing this morning to have a hunt around and see what I could find. There's a couple of gowns too, warm-like. You're going to need them down in the West Country. Wind comes off that moor like the horsemen of the apocalypse even in the middle of summer. You'll need gloves as well. I'll be back in a moment. Try on those boots while I'm gone."

Waiting until Mrs. James had closed the door, she picked up the blue boots and sat down in the chair, her back to the door, and unlaced her boots as quickly as she could before Mrs. James returned. She pushed her feet into the soft leather and wriggled her toes. They fitted perfectly and were much more comfortable than anything she'd ever owned. Thank goodness Mam couldn't see her. She'd skin her alive if she knew she'd taken off her boots in daylight.

Chapter 15

Sydney, Australia
1908

Shaw made it off the last ferry and trudged up Blues Point Road. His attempts at the Births, Deaths & Marriages Registry had hit a blank. No one by the name of R Winton and no record of Winton. He'd spent hours in the dingy offices leafing his way through fifty-plus years of records, then discovered only individual churches held records prior to 1856. More than anything else he'd wanted to find some written proof R Winton was related to Charles. It would go partway to proving the book was authentic and hadn't been tampered with. Who the hell was she? *She?* Now Tamsin had him at it. Jumping to conclusions and making wild assumptions on the basis of handwriting simply wasn't good enough. He needed facts. Indisputable facts.

Twisting the key in the lock, he put his shoulder to the door and forced it open, stumbling over one of the mounds of boxes. He had to get some of them unpacked, at least make it easier to get into the place. He wandered into the kitchen and cleared an armful of books off the table and sat down, his thoughts circling around and around, wishing he'd brought the sketchbook home.

He spun around in the chair and stretched out his legs under the table. Pain ricocheted up his thigh. "Sod it!" He pushed up his trouser and examined the red line on his knee, then crawled under the table and shunted the offending tea chest across the floor. The metal edging had come loose.

Reaching for a knife, he levered off the lid, releasing a blast of mustiness, vanilla, and something that reminded him of almonds. He inhaled. It was almost floral, probably the old ink and disintegrating paper. Instantly he was back in Grandfather's library, the wooden steps hooked to the highest shelves running along on a pair of wheels, the neatly organized books under subject headings—everything ranging from anatomical works and botanical illustrations to various periods of history, the works of Shakespeare, and a collection of eighteenth-century novels; whatever had taken the old man's fancy.

He lifted the first few books from the chest and spread them onto the kitchen table, the dark green leather covers faded in places and the corners tattered. They looked like account ledgers. Tilting one, he ran his finger down the frayed spine, avoiding the loose pieces of cotton that held the book together—he could feel the indentations of some writing but stains sullied it. Holding it under the light, he smoothed the cover. *Cellar Book*, *West Wycombe*. Row after row of neatly entered names, dates, and amounts. Why would Grandfather be interested in this? From memory of his time in England, West Wycombe was on the way to London, about thirty miles away. Too far for a man whose entire life centered around Oxford.

The list of names read like some sort of eighteenth-century Who's Who: clerics, politicians, poets—the same names repeated time and again interspersed with pages of accounts.

He pushed them to one side and took out a pile of old papers. The sort of thing he imagined being pored over and debated in London coffee houses. No, not London coffee houses. Cornish.

The West Briton and Cornwall Advertiser. He turned the pages. Columns of announcements of births, deaths, and marriages. Shame he hadn't stumbled on something like that today—it might have saved him time.

Advertisements for horses for sale, work wanted, local events. He flicked through them, then stacked them under the ledgers to keep them flat before turning back to the box. Dictionaries, atlases, more reference books, some copies of Milton's poetry. His memory must have deserted him. Grandfather's library was meticulously organized. Perhaps the packers had just shoveled everything into the nearest box.

The thought reminded him of Mrs. Rushworth and the library at Will-O-Wyck. What he wouldn't give for a room like that. He'd fulfill his dream of leaving the law and setting up as an antiquarian book collector in a moment.

With a disgruntled sigh he wandered into the front room and threw himself down in the chair, the only piece of furniture in the room. He'd think about it tomorrow. He rubbed at his eyes. Too many birth and death certificates, too much spidery writing. He needed some sleep. Father expected him in the office tomorrow morning to recount the whole Rushworth saga. There was more to it than he'd been told; the old man was taking the whole case personally. He had a stake in the Rushworths' interests somewhere along the line, he'd put money on it.

Mr. Everdene lifted his head and eyed Shaw with a jaundiced look. "What time do you call this?"

"Good morning, Father." Cantankerous old fool. If it was going to be the prelude to yet another diatribe about keeping up appearances, he'd get up and leave. "If it's any consolation, I was working yesterday, following up on Kelly's estate."

"Ron Rushworth contacted me this morning. What's all this about a sketchbook? He wanted to know how matters were progressing."

"There were some old books in the house. Mrs. Rushworth seemed to think one in particular might be worth a bit. She wants to sell it. Thinks the proceeds will solve their immediate problems. It belonged to one of the early naturalists, Charles Winton. I decided to see if I could authenticate it."

"And?"

"I hit a blank. I can't even find out when or where he died. There was no compulsory registration of deaths in New South Wales until 1856. The book would be worth far more if I could establish the provenance. Find out something more about the man and his work." More importantly, find out who R Winton was, but that would just confuse the issue.

"Could have saved you some time if you'd bothered to ask."

Shaw sat up. He'd expected a bollocking for wasting time, and instead the wily old man was as good as helping. He squinted across the desk. What was he up to?

"Have a look at the old muster records."

"Muster records?"

His father gave one of his tedious sighs and shook his head. "I paid a fortune for your education; didn't they teach you any history? Knew you'd be better off in Australia than mucking around in the ivory towers of Oxford. Started with Phillip—he used the naval system. In the early days they used to keep track of the convicts. Then it expanded to a point where all non-military settlers were also required to muster. Under Macquarie's governorship they became annual events."

For once his father's doggerel held him captivated.

"The last muster in New South Wales was in 1825. First census in 1828. I'm not sure why you're bothering. What have you learned about Kelly? When did he die? When's his will dated?"

"I haven't got all those exact facts at my fingertips. Over ten years ago, his wife sometime well before that." Shaw ran his fingers through his hair. He needed to get his head in order. "The sketchbook might give us a clue to Kelly's next of kin. He or Mrs. Quinleaven must have acquired it from somewhere."

"And since books are your first love . . ."

He wasn't going down that path. Another argument about his plans to leave the law and set up on his own and he'd walk out and never set foot in the place again, and right now the old man was proving more useful than he'd ever been. "Where are these muster records kept?"

"Public Library of New South Wales. Where else?"

Of course. Perhaps Tamsin had thought of that by now—after all, she worked in the building.

"Ron Rushworth's keen to get the whole business sorted as soon as possible. We've got some investments hanging in the balance."

His guess about Father's involvement wasn't far off the mark. He'd suspected they'd been business partners for a while. Why else would he have been sent to deal with the matter?

"Off you go. Keep me informed. On second thought, check the shipping records. Winton might have left the country."

"He came out on the First Fleet. He was unmarried."

"Who told you that?"

"The librarian from the Public Library." As soon as the words left his lips he realized his mistake. Father was onto him.

"What's the Library got to do with this?"

"As I said, there's a slight hitch. Mrs. Quinleaven notified the Library of the existence of the sketchbook before she died and asked to have it appraised. She was considering making a donation."

"And the Library is on the trail too. Must be worth something. That'll please the Rushworths. Better than nothing. They'd presumed the whole lot would come to them. The parcel of land alone is worth a fortune if it's subdivided. What a mess. Go on. Off you go and see what you can find out about this Winton chap."

Approval for a course of action. Also unusual. "Right. I'll let you know what I find out."

"You do that."

Shaw bolted through the door and out into the sunshine. Next stop the Library—muster records first, then Tamsin.

After four hours plowing his way through the muster records, Shaw dusted off his hands, thanked the two cataloguers, and as good as danced up the steps to the foyer.

Mrs. Williams's face lit up. "Hello, Mr. Everdene. Back again so soon?"

"I'd like to have a word with Tamsin. Is she about?"

"She's downstairs poring over Winton's letters, matching signatures and trying to find some mention of an R Winton. Let me—"

"No, don't bother. I know the way." He took off at a gallop before Mrs. Williams had a chance to follow. The information he'd found was for Tamsin first. Not anyone else.

He pushed open the door to the workroom, reveling in the smell of antiquity and history and the sight of Tamsin, with her spectacles perched on the end of her nose, her unruly curls tamed into a braid that hung down her back.

She turned and smiled at him. "Shaw. How lovely!" Her face flushed and her lovely wide mouth broke into a smile. "I'm getting nowhere slowly and it's so frustrating. I need a distraction."

He'd be more than happy to oblige, and he had something that would put the light back into her beautiful eyes. She needed a break and he intended to provide.

"I've looked through most of the correspondence and I can't find anything after June 1818, a request from Winton to present to the Royal Society. That can't have happened. They would have made him a fellow in a heartbeat if he'd shown them his research. There's no mention of his personal life at all. No wife, no daughter, not even a son. I found a reference to Banks paying him a stipend—a paltry sum. And thanks for a set of sketchbooks and some materials. Paint and ink, I expect."

"Perhaps Banks had lost interest in Winton's work or he never followed through."

"I don't think so. At least I can't imagine why. The question of the platypus had the entire scientific world running around in circles."

"I found out something interesting in the muster records."

Her face lit up. "Why didn't I think of the muster records? I was so busy with the letters it didn't cross my mind. Tell me."

"Get your bag and lock up. I'll meet you upstairs."

"It's another hour until I finish."

"Mrs. Williams won't mind. I'll have a word with her." He wandered down the corridor, stopping every now and again to look more closely at one thing or the other. How he envied Tamsin working every day among all these antiquities. The law held no interest for him. It was the smell of polished wood, ink and old paper, dusty books and binding leather that made his blood thrum.

By the time Tamsin had tidied up her desk, locked the sketchbook back in the safe, retied her hair, pinched her cheeks, and shoveled the bulging pile of notes and the tin into her satchel, Shaw had disappeared and her heart rate had kicked up about ten notches. It was so good to see him so soon; not much more than twenty-four hours had passed since they'd examined the sketchbook. Without a doubt he'd be sweet-talking Mrs. Williams so she could get off early.

She belted around the corner and up the stairs and discovered him leaning across Mrs. Williams's desk, his broad shoulders straining his shirt and his jacket hooked over his shoulder, dangling from one finger. "Why don't you come with us, Mrs. Williams?"

"Oh, don't be silly. You don't want an old lady like me hanging around with you two."

Tamsin slammed her lips shut before she squawked something totally inappropriate. Neither of them had done or said anything to indicate they were any more than colleagues with a common interest. They weren't, she reminded herself.

"No. Off you go, I've had a busy enough day. I intend to have an early night."

Tamsin edged up to the desk. "You don't mind if I leave now, Mrs. Williams?"

"Enjoy yourselves. I'll see you tomorrow."

"I thought we'd walk through the Botanic Gardens to the Quay and find something to eat. I have a hankering for Chinese noodles and we're celebrating. Come on." Without waiting for an answer, Shaw took off across the foyer and headed for the doors.

Tamsin hefted her satchel onto one shoulder and ran a couple of steps to catch up with him.

"Let me carry that." He grabbed it and slung it over his shoulder, then slipped his arm through hers, his eyes sparkling. "I've got news."

"Tell me."

"Not until we're sitting down and I have your undivided attention."

As if he hadn't already. She tossed her head and tried for a pout, not something she was very good at. "Good news or bad?"

"The best."

Once they'd skirted the tram terminus, the bustling afternoon crowd around the Quay made it difficult to talk. Shaw grabbed at her arm and towed her through a tiny door into a dimly lit room and led her to a small table tucked into the corner. He dumped her bag beneath the table and squatted down on one of the rickety stools. The smell of frying spices from the huge pans made her mouth water, and after the mad hustle and bustle outside, even the banging and crashing and the hiss of the fat couldn't ruin the sensation that they were cocooned in their own private space.

Shaw eased a bottle of beer out of his bag and raised an eyebrow. "Yes or no?"

"Beer?" She'd never drunk beer before. The thought made her feel quite racy, thoroughly adventurous.

He took the lid off and poured it into two glasses that had seen better days, handed her one, and clinked his against hers. "Here's to Rose Winton."

"Rose! Rose Winton? You found her. How?"

"Drink up. It's a toast."

The bubbles fizzed against her lips, then transferred into her throat, making a potent mix with the excitement his words brought. *Rose Winton. R Winton.* She'd known all along that the signature was female, and now he'd confirmed it. "How did you find her?"

"I took my father's advice. The musters. Alphabetical arrangement, subdivided into male convicts, female convicts, freemen, and freewomen." He pulled a small legal pad from his jacket and fanned the pages until he found what he was looking for. "Taken between February 5 and March 5, 1811. Charles Winton, a freeman, listed as living with his housekeeper, an ex-convict, and a Rose Winton, a ten-year-old girl born in the colony."

"What about Rose's mother?"

"No mention of a mother or a marriage; no mention of marital status or religion at all."

A sense of satisfaction spread through her. She'd been right from the beginning. "Where were they living?"

Two large steaming bowls of soup appeared in front of them, vegetables and all sorts of bits floating on the top.

"Agnes Banks."

"Then it has to be her." Tamsin lost all interest in the soup and stared out through the narrow doorway at the twinkling lights of the Quay reflecting in the water. "It was the area where Macarthur had his land grant—the best land in the colony in the early days. The Aborigines used to burn along the river so it was all fertile grazing land. And there's that lagoon there, some native name. It's mentioned in one of Winton's letters." She squinted into the distance, trying to recall the name. "Yellow-Mundee. That's it. Winton told Banks the natives knew all about the platypus. It was only the arrogant English who thought they were exhibiting their ignorance of natural history, making up stories that defied the accepted laws of classification." Tamsin let out a huge sigh. "This is wonderful. I feel so much more connected with the sketchbook now we know Rose's name. I'm even more determined now to show that Charles Winton was the first person to make sufficient scientific observations and prove the platypus wasn't some Chinese sailor's idea of a hoax."

"Shh. You'll get us drummed out of here. Taste the soup; it's delicious."

"I feel a bond with Rose, as though I belong to a very special club." She took a sip of the delicious broth, then chased a small piece of bright red meat around the bowl.

"Is this a women-only club or can I join too?" His gray-green eyes twinkled at her in the half-light of the tiny, shabby restaurant, and her curl of excitement wound tighter. "Of course you can. You're a founding member—you found Rose. I'm going to see if I can find anything else about her."

"I do know a little more about her."

"There's more?" She punched him lightly on the top of his arm before sipping at the clear soup from the strange bowl-shaped spoon. "Tell me."

"Once I had a name I searched the shipping records, and a Rose Winton left Sydney in early December 1819 aboard the *Minerva*."

"She left Sydney." The spoon fell from her fingers and splashed into her soup. "Where did she go?"

"To England. London."

"London? Did Charles go with her? He must have accepted Sir Joseph Banks's invitation to present to the Royal Society."

"Winton's not listed on the passenger manifesto."

"That's strange. Why would she travel to England alone?"

"Maybe she wasn't alone. Maybe her mother went with her. Maybe she traveled with friends."

"There was nothing to show she had a companion?"

"No, nothing."

It was all very well having a job and living in a house by herself, but would she be brave enough to travel to England alone? "Why did she go? Did she come back?"

"I couldn't find any record of her returning." Shaw's face crumpled a little.

"I'm sorry. I'm just impatient. I know these things take time. Did you find anything out about the housekeeper from the muster records? They must have listed a name."

"That's where it gets a bit strange. A Jenifer Trevan."

"Jenifer Trevan?" Tamsin's skin tingled. "Jenifer Trevan?"

"What's the matter? You've gone as white as a sheet."

"How can you forget? The tin. Mrs. Quinleaven's Peek Frean tin—the piece of paper with the epitaph." She let out a huge sigh. "But it can't be the same person. You said an 1811 muster. That's over twenty years after she died."

She foraged in her satchel until her fingers clasped the tin, then pulled it out and eased the lid off. "See here." She unfolded the scrap of paper.

Shaw slapped his hand against his forehead. "I'd forgotten. Too caught up with everything." He lifted his eyes and gazed straight into her own and her heart skipped a beat. "Winton's housekeeper. I can't find anything in the earlier musters recording Jenifer giving birth to a child, daughter or otherwise. The only other records at that time would be church records, and if they didn't attend church, any birth wouldn't be recorded."

"Do we know anything else about this Jenifer Trevan?"

His lips twitched and she knew he had something else he wasn't telling her. He rested his elbows on the table, and for one second she thought that he would lean across the table and kiss her. Her face flushed and she batted the thought away.

"I found her in the convict records. She arrived here on the *Lady Juliana* . . ."

"The Floating Brothel?"

"The very one."

"We still don't understand the connection between Mrs. Quinleaven and the Wintons. I need to go back to Wollombi and see Mrs. Rushworth. Make sure there isn't anything else in the house."

"Mrs. Rushworth is back in Sydney."

The sizzle and hiss from the huge pans faded and stopped, the breeze from the open windows stilled, leaving nothing but the pounding of her blood as it pumped through her temples.

"Her husband contacted my father to see how we were going with the sketchbook."

His eyes skittered across to the window and she had the strangest sense he wasn't telling her the whole story.

Chapter 16

LONDON, ENGLAND
1820

The forecourt of the Gloucester Coffee House was a riot of activity. Three mail coaches, ostlers running back and forth harnessing horses, passengers clambering aboard coaches. Steam rose from the piles of straw littering the cobblestones and everywhere the overriding stench of horse manure permeated the damp mizzle.

Finneas grasped Rose's arm and steered her across the road. "That's the Exeter coach on the right."

The bright red wheels of the coach stood out in the lights; half a dozen people sat wedged onto the roof, and a passenger bundled up in a greatcoat had grabbed the spot next to the coachman. Thank heavens he'd managed to procure two of the four seats inside, otherwise they would have had to delay the trip.

Finneas turned to a scruffy boy lounging against the side of the inn, trying to look inconspicuous. "Pick up the trunk and carpetbag from the carriage over there, boy," he ordered, then led Rose to the side of the mail coach and opened the door.

The stench of alcohol and tobacco billowed out and the two portly gentlemen sprawled across the two seats eyed him with distaste;

obviously they'd hoped to be the sole occupants for the journey. "Make room for the lady, gentlemen."

With a deal of grumbling and rearranging, one of the two men moved across, leaving the seat facing backward vacant.

"Thank you." Where the hell was that boy?

"Where d'you want these?" The boy dumped the trunk down and tossed Rose's carpetbag at his feet.

"I'll take that." She grabbed at the carpetbag, not game to trust her precious specimen and sketchbook to the luggage racks. Clasping the bag close to her chest, she put her foot on the step, then turned back to him. "I pity the poor horses that have to pull this weight. There must be at least thirteen people, never mind all the baggage."

"They'll be fine. They change the horses every ten miles, once an hour on average. Sure you still want to go ahead?"

"Oh yes. I can't wait." Without a further backward glance, she skipped up the steps and, with a confident nod to the two men, settled herself into the far corner.

"I'll just see your trunk loaded and we're ready to go." He pulled the collar of his greatcoat up against the wind that whistled around his ears. What must Rose think of the English summer? Thank goodness Mrs. James had done such a good job raiding Caroline's wardrobe. Rose looked snug and comfortable with a pair of very fetching blue boots peeking out from beneath her matching riding habit.

With a nod to the boy, he flicked a penny into his hand and kicked the steps up before jumping into the coach. That way there'd be no additional passengers trying to wheedle their way inside.

"We'll be leaving soon. The best idea is to try and get comfortable and get a bit of sleep."

"I might be a bit too excited to sleep. I've never been on a coach like this before."

The two men opposite eyed her, making his hackles rise, then caught sight of the glare on his face and leaned back, their faces a picture of contrived innocence. With a loud shout, the coach pulled out and they were on their way.

Rose sat unnaturally quiet, and despite her assurances she wasn't tired, he could see her eyelids becoming heavier. Before long the swaying of the coach lulled her and her shoulder relaxed against him and she slept.

A few miles outside Andover the larger of the two men opposite straightened up and stretched his legs, sending Rose's carpetbag skittering across the floor. In less than a heartbeat her eyes flashed open and she reached down to rescue it, throwing a filthy look at the blockhead opposite. Served him right.

She leaned over and undid the clasp, lifting the creature from the bag and resting it on her lap, her hand smoothing the dark fur. Both men reared upward as though stung and stared first at the specimen and then at Rose before mumbling to each other behind their hands.

If the two obnoxious oafs didn't stop looking at Rose from under their heavily lidded eyes, he'd knock them out of the window. He moved a little closer to her, his thigh pressing against hers. Staking his claim. Making it pointedly clear they'd have him to deal with if they so much as raised their overweight buttocks from the seat.

The more florid of the two rummaged in his greatcoat pocket and brought out a piece of paper, which he carefully unfolded and passed to his companion. His finger stabbed at the center of the piece. "See the resemblance—no doubt about it."

Finneas didn't need to look to know what it was. He wanted to cover Rose's ears, turn her face from them. The color had risen to her cheeks and she'd closed her eyes in a vain attempt to block them out.

"Wonder if she's got her tail under that riding habit." The pipe-smoking fool jabbed at the paper and looked pointedly at the hem of her riding habit, which hid her neatly booted feet.

After a few moments the coach pulled to a halt. The driver appeared and threw open the door. "Andover. All out who's going."

The two men heaved themselves to their feet and tumbled down the steps toward the lights of the inn.

"With any luck that'll be the last we see of them."

Rose tucked the specimen back into the burlap sack and placed it reverently in the carpetbag and slipped the clasp. "I'm beginning to think you must be sick to death of me and all the fuss I have caused."

He'd never felt better in his life. This delightful fey girl had brought a ray of exotic sunshine into his life. She was hardly a traditional beauty with her unkempt hair and swarthy skin, but dressed in Caroline's cast-offs she could grace any country house party. And to add to it all she had a mind and knowledge of science that would rival most of the would-be physicians in London. "Not at all. Not one tiny little bit. I'm only sorry that your visit to the Royal Society wasn't better received."

"So am I. I feel dreadful about Julian. If only I'd been able to present Pa's work myself."

"Your work too, I believe. I had a closer look at the sketchbook."

"I don't think of it like that. I've just always worked with Pa. From the first moment I could walk I trailed around after him. I even had my own sketchbook, though the sight of my early drawings and diagrams make my toes curl with embarrassment."

She made his toes curl. The warmth of her body next to his on the narrow seat was enough to give a man an attack of chronic carditis.

After a little more than an hour the coach slewed to a halt again to change horses. There was a deal of shouting and the coach rocked, then the driver appeared next to the door arms akimbo and a fierce scowl on his face. "What's your problem?"

A plaintive wail broke the night air.

"Rose, sit tight." Finneas threw open the door and stepped out. "What's happening?"

The driver glared at the woman trying to clamber onto the roof with a wicker basket clutched in her arms.

"She can't ride up there. She'll fall and drop the baby." Finneas opened the door of the carriage and leaned inside. "Rose, would you mind dreadfully if we have some company? There's a woman with her baby. She can't travel up top—she'll freeze to death."

"You can't do that." The irate coach driver puffed up his chest.

"I most certainly can."

"If she can't pay for a seat, she doesn't get to ride inside. And there's passengers booked from here to Exeter."

"In that case I'll travel up top." Finneas turned from the driver to Rose. "The cost of seats is prohibitive for most." He passed the wicker basket with the child inside to Rose and handed the woman up. "Should the coach take a turn too fast or be involved in an accident, she and her babe could be flung off the vehicle or trapped underneath if it overturns, apart from the fact they'll freeze to death."

Rose reached out a hand and with a look of exhausted relief the woman staggered up the steps.

"I'll go into the inn and pick up something to eat and drink. Anything you'd like?"

"Hot chocolate perhaps?" She threw him such a delicious smile, his heart gave a thundering great heave as he rushed off to do her bidding.

By the time he returned with a steaming mug of chocolate, the two seats opposite were filled by a ratty-faced man and an oversized woman with an equally large hat. Rose had the baby on her lap, her carpetbag and the wicker basket stashed beneath the seat out of harm's way.

He passed the mug in through the window.

Rose pressed the hot chocolate into the woman's hand.

"I can't take that."

"Yes, you can. Drink up—it'll do you good. You're freezing."

Satisfied, Finneas secured the window and pulled up the collar of his greatcoat before taking delight in clambering across the driver to the roof of the coach, where he wedged himself between two trunks and a bale of wool. He'd be soaking wet when they reached the next stop, but it wouldn't kill him.

Sadly he was right, and by the time they'd crossed Salisbury Plains he was drenched. He climbed down from the roof and shook himself like a dog.

"Oh my goodness! Look at you! You can't stay out there. We can move over." Rose passed the baby to the woman and shuffled along the seat, making a small space.

He couldn't sit there; she'd be almost sitting in his lap.

She patted the seat. "Take your greatcoat off. It's warm in here; you'll dry in no time."

The other two passengers exchanged outraged glances. "Oh, don't be so selfish. Get in, Finneas, now."

He shrugged out of his coat, bundled it up, and stuffed it beneath the seat, then eased himself onto the edge of the seat and closed the door.

"There's plenty of room, shuffle back a bit." She turned her shoulders to give him more room.

What was a man to do? He moved back and instantly regretted his action. Through his damp clothes he could feel the heat of her body and it played havoc with his own. Hunching his shoulders, he clasped his hands tightly in his lap and shook.

"See, I knew you were cold. Sit back and enjoy the rest of the trip. Myriam and little Bob are getting off at Exeter."

She swept her hand over the baby's head. "You're not too uncomfortable, are you?"

"No, ma'am. No, not at all. Thank you, sir." The woman bobbed her head and clutched the baby tighter as the guard rapped the butt of his shotgun on the door to warn of their impending departure.

"Next stop Exeter."

The ratty-faced man shot to his feet. "Is this Sherbourne?" He belted his wife in the ribs with his elbow. "Hurry up. We're getting out here."

The guard pulled the door open. "Get a move on." The couple stumbled out into the darkness.

"Do you have a problem with bushrangers? I hadn't noticed the shotgun before." Rose twisted closer, too close, sending another convulsive tremor through him.

He couldn't stay there. Not now the opposite seat was vacant. He threw himself across the coach as it lurched off, sending him sprawling. "Bushrangers?"

"Mostly convicts who've escaped from the work gangs or the properties where they have been assigned."

"Oh. We call them highwaymen in England. They terrorize certain stretches of the roads. The shotgun protects the mail and us."

"We also call them bolters. They prefer to take their chances in the wild than put up with the deprivation and brutality of convict life."

"A hard life."

"Not so much for the women. My mam was assigned to Richard Barrington as housekeeper."

Myriam widened her eyes, no doubt amazed that this well-dressed lady would freely admit to a mother who was a convicted felon. Rose didn't seem the slightest bit concerned. He bit back a smile. Perhaps in the colony convict status didn't carry such a stigma. "And what do you know about your mother's life?"

"That she was convicted of theft. She was sent to Australia aboard a ship called the *Lady Juliana*, the first ship to arrive after the First Fleet, in 1789. She never really served her sentence, just worked as a housekeeper."

"And when her sentence was up?"

"She stayed with Pa and me." Her pretty brow creased in a frown as she studied the bag at her feet. He didn't ask any more questions, just let her thoughts settle. What a shock it must have been to discover she had a brother and that the father she'd known all her life was not in fact her father. It was worse than his own circumstances.

"Do you know how Julian came to live with the Methenwycks?"

He did, but was it his place to tell?

"You do. I can tell. You're chewing your lip—that's what you do when you're trying to decide what to say."

And how did she know that? He'd wondered if she'd noticed him watching her every move; it hadn't occurred to him she might be doing the same. Too many years observing, studying the behavior of the mallangong. The hallmark of a scientist: gathering data, observing, and applying the findings.

"You may as well tell me because otherwise I will have to ask Julian, and that will only make him angry."

And manipulative too, when it suited her. "Julian's father, your father, died at the Battle of Trafalgar. He was a naval surgeon." And here was the rub. "When he brought Julian back to England, he hoped his wife would accept him and bring him up as his heir."

The silence inside the carriage grew, expanded like a poisonous gas seeping into every crack and crevice.

"Barrington had a wife?" All color drained from her face and her lips took on a bluish tinge. He had no idea she hadn't known. He leaned forward and picked up her cold hand and rubbed it between his, warming her.

"Tell me the rest," she whispered.

"Barrington's wife refused to accept Julian, so he sent him to live in Cornwall with his sister, Caroline Methenwyck."

She pulled back her hand and sat fingering the blue wool of Caroline's riding habit. "And they took care of him?"

"Caroline was unable to bear children; Methenwyck wanted sons. It seemed the perfect solution. Julian is at least partly related by blood. He hopes one day to inherit."

"And then they took you in as their ward as well."

"The best thing that ever happened to me."

She gave him a shy smile as though she knew what he was thinking: if the Methenwycks hadn't taken him in, he never would have met Rose.

Her mind spiraled in ever-decreasing circles as she tried to piece together the parts of the puzzle Finneas had presented. Tried to make some logical sense of the information and remember what Mam had told her. "Mam said she wanted to return to England because of her granfer. He was old and sick. Barrington said he could help her. I think he duped her. Poor Mam." A great big tear trickled down her cheek and Finneas pressed a soft white handkerchief into her hands. "In a way I'm happy Richard Barrington deserted Mam, otherwise Charles Winton wouldn't be my father."

"I think you should be. He sounds like a delightful man."

"I believed I lived in paradise. I had the most perfect childhood anyone could wish for."

What she wouldn't give to see Pa smile again—that long, slow smile that spoke of his love. To see his eyes light up with pleasure when the mallangong played at sunset.

"I love him so much, Finneas." Her eyes filled with tears. "I can never love anyone else like that. When I was little I used to creep out of my bed and into his workroom, sleep under his desk like a puppy; then he'd scoop me in his big, strong arms and carry me to bed. When we sat by the river watching the mallangong play, we'd talk. He taught me everything, showed me everything there was to see from the tiniest beetle to the softest flannel flower. He called me the daughter of his heart. When I found out I wasn't his daughter, I was so angry, angry with my mother because of what she had done to me—taken my father from me. Taken the man I loved beyond all others and replaced him with a faceless man who didn't even know I existed.

"The day Pa was spurred I thought my life would end. The animal he loved above everything might have taken him from me and I was jealous. I sat by his bed, nursed his horribly ravaged body, and prayed like I'd never done before. When he asked me to come to England, it was a way to get Pa back, and now I've failed him." Sighing, she hunched into the corner, not crying; she had no tears left.

"He'll always be your father, Rose." He leaned forward and linked his fingers with hers, bringing her knuckles to his cheek. "And you have another opportunity to talk to Sir Joseph. I'm sure he will be responsive to your father's discoveries. After all, he corresponded with him for many years."

Finneas was right. She drew back her shoulders, unraveled her fingers from his, and stared out of the carriage window. "Mam's family came from the West Country."

"Do you know where?"

No, she didn't; just another part of Mam she knew nothing about. "I only know she boarded the ship in Plymouth." Why had she never thought to ask? She knew nothing, nothing at all. All about Pa and his work, all about his hopes and his dreams, nothing of Mam.

By the time the coach bounced and jostled over the cobblestone courtyard of the New London Inn at Exeter, the sun was low in the sky and Rose was beginning to believe every one of her bones had become totally disconnected. "I think my sinews may have become detached."

Finneas laughed. "I doubt it. Fibrous tissues are very resilient. The worst is over now—the Turnpike Trust has significantly improved the moorland road. We'll spend the night here and then it's a mere fifty miles to Jamaica Inn."

"Jamaica Inn. That sounds very exotic."

"The name of the inn derives from the Trelawney family, local landowners. Two members of the family served as governors of Jamaica fifty or sixty years back."

"And today they run an inn?"

"No, they don't." He laughed, making a flush rise to her face. He knew so much and what was she? A foolish girl who didn't even know her own mother.

"It's run by a family by the name of Penhaligon, and it's not far from Wyck Hall. We'll be there in time for a late lunch and then we'll pick up two horses and be home before nightfall. Now let's find ourselves something to eat and get a decent night's sleep."

Chapter 17

CORNWALL, ENGLAND
1820

"Mrs. Pascoe!" Finneas threw his arms around the rotund housekeeper. She'd been his lifesaver more times than he could remember with her secret jam drops and sympathy when he'd copped the raw side of Methenwyck's belt. "How are you?"

"And what are you doing here, my favorite boy? Are you well?" She pushed him away from her and examined him from head to toe, patting and prodding, making sure he was all in one piece.

"I'm very well. How is everyone?"

"Not much has changed. It's you I want to know about. Mr. Julian comes down more often and the master enjoys his company, even though he can't get out. Why don't I ever see you here?" She waggled a fat finger at him. "I know. I know. Nothing you like too much."

Nothing he liked or wanted to be a part of. Gentlemen's parties and the like.

"Not near as much work as it used to be now there's none of the hunting. But enough of my blather." Her gaze lit on Rose and her eyebrows danced. "And who's this pretty young lass? She has the look of the West Country about her."

"This is Julian's sister come to us from New South Wales." He brought Rose into the light.

"Oh my!" Mrs. Pascoe's face flushed bright red, then paled as tears sprang to her eyes. Her hand clawed at her chest and a ragged wheeze passed her bloodless lips.

Good God! The woman looked as if she might have an apoplexy. "Sit down, Mrs. Pascoe, come." He lowered her into a chair. "Rose, would you be so kind as to fetch my bag?" He tried to loosen her collar but she batted him away. "Mrs. Pascoe, please. Rose, open my bag and pass me the stethoscope."

"Stethoscope?"

He was taking too much for granted, imagining her a colleague, schooled in scientific jargon. "That wooden tube there. It amplifies the chest sounds." He waved his hand in the direction of his bag and within moments she'd placed the brown timber cylinder into his hand. "Mrs. Pascoe, I am going to put this to your chest and listen."

"Oh no you're not, young man. There's naught wrong with me chest. It's me heart that's twisted. Come here, lass."

She held out her quivering hand to Rose. "So you'd be young Jenifer's daughter, would you?" She smoothed her fingers over the back of Rose's hand and the color returned to her face.

"Yes, my mother is Jenifer Trevan."

"Same as Master Julian. And your father? Mr. Barrington?"

Rose almost shook her head. A look of conflict glided across her face, then she nodded. "Yes. However, I never met him. A man named Charles Winton is father to me, and has been all my life."

"And young Jenifer, how's she faring?"

Rose's face paled to a chalky hue. "Mam is well."

"You're the right image of her."

She offered a frail smile. "That's what Pa, Charles, always says; his two precious treasures brought to him by the piskies."

Finneas pressed a glass of water into Mrs. Pascoe's hand. She seemed none the worse for her momentary turn. "Drink this. Are you feeling more yourself now?"

"Aye, that I am. Took me by surprise, seeing young Rose here. Thought it was Jenifer back to work in me kitchen. Piskies, indeed."

"Mam worked here?"

"Best scullery maid I ever had. I'd have her back in the flick of a donkey's tail. Never believed her guilty. Why would she do a thing like that? Her granfer brought her up proper. Real nice man, he was. Broke his heart when they sentenced her to death. We buried him out yonder in the walled garden. He loved that spot."

Rose swayed and grabbed at the back of a chair. From what she'd said on the trip down, her mother's conviction didn't include a death sentence. But if Mrs. Pascoe spoke the truth, it would account for the fact Rose's mother hadn't accompanied her—transported for the term of her natural life, no doubt.

Mrs. Pascoe might have a heart of gold, but her mouth was bigger than a cavern.

"I'm going to show Rose to the guest room and perhaps, if you're feeling better, you could arrange a little supper for us."

"Of course I can. Beggin' your pardon, Master Finneas. Such a shock, so like dear Jenifer." With a deferential bob, Mrs. Pascoe bumbled out of the hallway, shaking her head and mumbling.

"I'm sure there must be some mistake." Rose's normal color hadn't returned to her face. "She must be wrong. Mam would have told me if she'd been sentenced to death. Maybe it slipped her mind with the shock of finding out that Julian was alive and in London."

That he doubted very strongly. No one forgot a death sentence, even if it was rescinded, and Mrs. Pascoe was rarely wrong.

"Everything was in turmoil. Those few weeks before I left home are all a blur now. I wonder if Pa has recovered." She swayed again and he reached out a hand to steady her and picked up her carpetbag. With the other arm around her shoulder, he led her up the stairs.

Strange that her thoughts should go to her father, not her mother. It was as though they had a greater bond, and Rose seemed to know nothing of her mother's earlier life. Perhaps Jenifer chose not to speak of it, knew she had no choice but to make a new life and put the past behind her. They said that many of the convicts who made good never thought to return.

"This is the guest room." He led her into the somber room furnished with heavy furniture, one of the rooms used by Julian's cronies when they visited. He'd have a word with Caroline tomorrow and see if they could arrange something a little less austere and forbidding.

"Thank you." She sank down on the side of the bed and sat staring at the huge dark timber wardrobe with a vacant look.

"I'll give you a proper tour of the house and garden tomorrow. Let's see what Mrs. Pascoe has scrounged up for us. We won't disturb Caroline or Lord Methenwyck tonight. They both retire early and you must be tired. It's been a long three days. Your trunk will arrive from the inn tomorrow. Where would you like me to put your carpetbag?"

"Anywhere." She covered her mouth with her hand and yawned. "I am tired."

On second thought, the last thing Rose needed was another dose of Mrs. Pascoe's reminiscences. "Then I'll bring a tray up to you."

"Really, I don't want to cause any problems."

How could she do that? He wanted nothing more than to cocoon her in a warm eiderdown and attend to her every need.

"How's Methenwyck?" Finneas loaded his plate with scrambled eggs and pork sausages. How he'd missed Mrs. Pascoe's breakfasts.

With his mouth watering he sat down at the dining room table and tucked in.

"Methenwyck becomes more intractable every day." Caroline let out a long sigh and broke off the corner of her toast. "No better."

"We knew that would be the case. He's lucky to be alive after the massive apoplexy he suffered. The doctor comes regularly, doesn't he?"

"Yes. But I never believe he's talking sense. He recommends bleeding and brandy."

"You are simply going to have to accept the fact that he'll never regain the use of his left side, and his speech will be permanently impaired. I told you that last year. Harsh words, I know, but there's nothing anyone can do but keep him comfortable. He's an old man now, well past his allotted three score and ten." And had no one to blame but himself and his abominable lifestyle.

Caroline's eyes hardened. "Sometimes I think it would be better if someone put him out of his misery. If he were a horse, he'd have been shot long ago."

"Don't be ridiculous. You know you don't mean that."

She shrugged her shoulders, her mouth set in a petulant pout. "He misses Julian dreadfully."

"He'll be here in a couple of days."

"Midsummer." Her face blanched. "Where's Mrs. Pascoe? I haven't seen her this morning. This toast is burned."

She was around somewhere—the piskies hadn't brought this delightful breakfast. "So she hasn't told you about our guest?"

Caroline lifted her head. She'd aged since the last time he'd visited. Sharp lines bracketed her mouth and her eyes had faded to a dull blue-gray. "A guest? No."

"Rose, Rose Winton. She had a terrible time in London. It seemed like the right thing to do. She's delightful."

"Who is she?"

Before he had the chance to reply, the door opened and Rose appeared in the doorway looking refreshed and very fetching in a butter-colored dress. He leaped to his feet. "Caroline, may I present your niece, Rose Winton."

Caroline's eyes bulged in a most alarming manner.

"Rose, your aunt, Lady Caroline Methenwyck."

"Pleased to meet you." Rose offered some sort of bob and stood with her hands clasped in front of her and her eyes downcast.

"Come and sit down." Finneas held out a chair. "There's hot chocolate, your favorite, and various other bits and pieces. You must be famished."

She sat down with no sign of her usual vivacity. When he placed a cup of chocolate in front of her, she offered a tentative smile, more a grimace really. The cup rattled in the saucer as she lifted it to her mouth.

He shot a glance at Caroline; the look on her face stopped him in his tracks. A look of softness, almost love. It was as though she couldn't pull her gaze from Rose, as though she was drinking in every contour of her face, the tilt of her heavy eyebrows, the polished walnut color of her eyes, her untamed curls caught loosely at the nape of her neck. The tip of Rose's tongue traced her pink lips as she removed the final traces of chocolate, then with a flush she picked up her napkin and dabbed her mouth. Oh, she was lovely.

"Lady Caroline." Rose gave a shy smile; surely that would break the ice. She had such an engaging smile. "Thank you so much for your hospitality." She toyed for a moment with the cutlery, then her expression firmed and she drew in a breath. "Mrs. Pascoe said my mother worked here as a scullery maid before she was transported."

A pulse pounded beneath the transparent skin of Caroline's temple.

"She never speaks of her life in Cornwall. Do you know what crime she was accused of?"

With a strangled gasp, Caroline pushed to her feet, her fingers tugging the tablecloth, spilling her tea.

"Caroline?"

"Excuse me. I have an appalling headache." And with that she left the room.

What in God's name was going on? First Mrs. Pascoe and now Caroline. "Take no notice. Caroline's upset with me because there is nothing I can do for Lord Methenwyck."

"Oh, I'm sorry. Has his condition worsened?"

He gestured to the large painted portrait hanging above the fireplace: the man's head cocked at an arrogant angle, a long, pointed nose and thin lips tilted in the semblance of a smile—more a sneer—that still had the ability to make his skin prickle. "Lord Methenwyck as a young man. Today you wouldn't recognize him. He's confined to his bed. As good as blind and totally debilitated by the apoplexy he suffered over twelve months ago."

"How dreadful. I spent sufficient time with Pa to understand just how frustrated he must be. Is there nothing you can do?"

"As I told Caroline, sadly nothing. Now, how are you feeling today? Recovered from our journey?"

"Yes, indeed. Though I have to admit I was ridiculously nervous meeting Lady Caroline."

"Lady Methenwyck," he corrected gently. No point in giving Caroline anything else to get upset about. Hopefully he'd get to the bottom of her strange reaction sooner rather than later. Meanwhile, he had more pressing matters at hand. "I thought I'd show you around today. Nothing too strenuous, and then tomorrow we'll take a ride out toward the coast and come back across the moors. They deserve a better look than we gave them yesterday."

"Should you not stay and attend to Lady Caro—Methenwyck? I don't want to take up all your time, nor add to your responsibilities. I am quite capable of entertaining myself."

"No, no. Caroline suffers from a recurrent throbbing headache, brought on by anxiety. She has never truly recovered from the difficulties she had in childbirth." He shouldn't be having this discussion with Rose; he kept forgetting that she wasn't one of his medical colleagues. "Are you certain you don't want anything further to eat? Perhaps you'd like just a gentle walk today after the rigors of the journey?"

"No, not at all. I enjoyed every moment of our journey. After the time in London it was lovely to see something of the countryside. In fact . . ." She looked up at him, her eyes dancing. "I'd love to ride on the moors again today, and perhaps I could take my sketchbook, if you wouldn't mind."

"An excellent idea, and I'll call into the inn and collect some pasties and cider, make something of a picnic. How does that sound?"

As they crested the hill Rose pulled to a halt, her eyes shining, and threw her arms wide. "Have you ever seen anything so beautiful in all your life?"

"A beauty that hides many a dark secret when the moon is high."

She blinked her big brown eyes and raised her eyebrows.

"Smugglers."

"Truly?"

"Or free traders, whichever you prefer."

"What do they smuggle?"

"French brandy. They bring it ashore at some of the smaller coves on the coastline and it's hauled by donkey cart up the winding paths."

"Don't they get caught? Isn't it illegal?"

"Oh yes. The law of the land strictly forbids smuggling, but everyone turns a blind eye, not wanting to feed the pocket of the assessors. They know the duty will never make it into the government coffers, just line the pockets of the local constabulary."

"At home it is the rum trade. It's as good as money—often better."

"I think I'd rather settle for French brandy."

"Look at that!" Rose raised her hand to her forehead, gazing intently into the distance. "The color of the water. It's almost silver." She slithered from her horse and rummaged in the saddlebag. "We have to stop."

"That is Dozmary Pool. The home of the Lady of the Lake. According to the legend, it is here that King Arthur received the sword Excalibur."

"I have to record this. To show Pa, to remind Mam. Tell her I've seen and experienced the country she knew. Bring back the past she's buried for so long. She'll like that."

He wasn't too certain. It seemed Jenifer Trevan had kept much of her past life close to her chest. "There's also another tale, but then, there always is in Cornwall."

She cocked her head to one side, the wind whipping her hair out of its pins.

"It's not so pretty."

"Tell me."

"There was a local magistrate with a particularly nasty record for brutality. His deeds caught up with him and he was damned to the bottomless Dozmary Pool, where he is tormented to this day; it is said his ghost can still be heard howling across the moor." He'd swear he saw a shiver cross her shoulders. "Scared?"

"No, I don't scare easily. I love stories. I grew up with the blackfellas' tales." She sank down onto a rock, nestled like a bird among the rough granite and heather, her hair streaming behind her as she stared out over the moors. Her eyes scanning, taking in every little bit of detail. He liked that, liked the way she noticed even the smallest detail. No doubt from years and years of working with her father. Trained from an early age.

"What's that mound over there?"

"One of the barrows—the moors are littered with them. Druid burial chambers. Some say there is hidden treasure beneath, but none has been found."

This time she did shiver and he took off his cloak and wrapped it around her shoulders. "It may be summer, but the wind can be bitter." He was a man of science, a man of rationality, but still his blood chilled up here where the ancients had buried their dead.

"At home it's never this cold. Either clear and sunny or torrential rain. Nothing in between. None of these scudding clouds. Look at the sky up there." Her pencil skimmed the page and the scene appeared before his eyes.

"And it can change in the blink of an eye. I shall await your pleasure and take in the view." He sat down and rested back on his arms, taking in the view, not of the moor he knew so well, but of her, the little frown of concentration, the way she licked the stub of her pencil, the sweep of her arm as she sketched the line of the horizon. He could think of no better way to spend a morning.

"What do you think?" Rose held the sketchbook aloft for his approval.

It was as though some magic eye had blinked and taken in the entire panorama, accurately representing it in only a matter of moments. No color, just pencil strokes, some crosshatched, others smudged with the ball of her thumb where the lead had left a gray stain. "It's wonderful. You must show it to Caroline when we return."

"I'm not sure how interested Lady Methenwyck would be. I think perhaps she dislikes me."

"No, no, she doesn't. As I said, she suffers from severe headaches; they come upon her without warning." Caroline had no reason to dislike Rose. "It's only an hour or so back to the house. Would you prefer to return for lunch, or shall I go to Jamaica Inn and procure a couple of their fine pasties and some cider as I promised?"

"Oh yes, please. I can't believe I'm so hungry." Her eyes strayed back to her sketchbook. "I'd like to draw a little more."

"You stay here. I shall return with food fit for a princess."

"A Cornish piskie, more like." Her laughter drifted away on the breeze and he dragged himself to his feet, loath to leave her but happy to prolong the time away from the stifling confines of Wyck Hall.

The dour atmosphere only served to remind him of the reasons he stayed in London. Julian had always been the one for Wyck Hall with his regular trips.

"I'll be back before you know it. Wait right here. I don't want to lose you on the moors."

Chapter 18

CORNWALL, ENGLAND
1820

Finneas didn't look or act a lot like a physician, except perhaps for his bag, which was always with him. Dressed in a buff-colored pair of breeches and rough woolen waistcoat, he seemed more like a profitable squatter as he galloped away.

By the time Rose lifted her hand to wave, he was no more than a dark shadow framed by the moor. In the distance she could see the chimneys of the inn standing against the blustery clouds. How much she'd missed the wide-open spaces, the solitude, and the sky. In London the very air itself cowed her and made her shoulders hunch, never mind the marauding crowds. She turned back to her drawing and sketched in the billowing clouds, coloring them with Pa's favored smudged shading to give the impression of their burgeoning weight.

She had no idea how long she'd sat sketching the wind-bent trees, the stone walls, and the view to the steely gray water of Dozmary Pool, but when an attack of pins and needles threatened, she tucked her pencil behind her ear and stood, stretching her legs and turning around and around, letting the rising wind whip her skirts.

Replacing her sketchbook and pencils in her saddlebag, she scanned the path toward the inn, pulling Finneas's cloak tight around her shoulders. She was cold, hadn't imagined the granite rock would be so chill in summer. It was more like an Australian winter.

There was no sign of Finneas, and to her right lay the soft mound of grass on the dome of the hill—one of the barrows Finneas had spoken of. Following her nose, she picked her way across a small stream, her hair dancing around her face in the wind.

A meandering path led between two high stones and into a small chamber. Casting a quick look over her shoulder, she ducked inside. The wind dropped and a solid silence wrapped around her, similar to the churchlike stillness of the caves she'd explored with Yindi and Bunji. Did the ancients decorate their caves as the blackfellas did? Perhaps there were drawings like the ones at home, pointing the way to good tucker—the kangaroo one way and the fish toward the river. This place had the same brooding weight, as though the past guardians watched and waited.

The old stones were rough under her palms as she felt her way inside, beneath a heavy rock lintel balanced on two eroded pillars, and into a small chamber. The air was stale and sweet, as though some animal had crawled inside and died. With her hands pressed against the wall, she stood stock-still while her eyes adjusted to the semidarkness.

She ran her fingers over the indentations in the rock, wishing she had a lantern. At that moment the sun chose to appear from behind the clouds and a shaft of light spilled into the small cavern. She followed the beam to the wall, a flat, smooth rock with ingrained marks. She stepped closer, her mind refusing to believe what her eyes beheld.

HERE LIES JENIFER TREVAN, LOVING
GRANDDAUGHTER OF GRANFER TOMAS TREVAN
MAY 24, 1772–FEBRUARY 2, 1788

Rose traced her fingers over the etched words, the lump in her throat growing bigger by the moment, tightening until she could hear her throat rasp as she tried to suck air into her starved lungs.

Jenifer Trevan.

She traced her fingers over each roughly hewn letter. Granfer Tomas Trevan. *Granfer.* The word Mam used. He died after she'd arrived in New South Wales. She'd overheard Mam and Pa by the fire while she lay in her trundle bed. Mam sobbing her very heart out because she'd had to leave Granfer but never talking about Wyck Hall. She'd never mentioned the place, yet Mrs. Pascoe had said Mam was a scullery maid here and Granfer was buried in the walled garden.

And the dates? Her heart twisted like a wrung-out rag. *February 1788.* Mam was no more dead than she was. First Pa was not Pa and now . . . was Mam who she said she was? The sun slipped away again and she stumbled out into the light, sweat coating her forehead and her pulse pounding. A hard hand came down on her arm and spun her around, and a shriek of pure terror escaped her lips.

"What are you doing here? There's a storm coming." Finneas's thunderous face glared down at her. Gone were the soft brown eyes, the welcoming smile. In their place was anger so fierce and so intense it stole her breath.

He clamped his arms tight around her and dragged her between the entrance stones, onto the rough path, away from the knoll.

"Let me go. You're hurting me."

"I told you to wait for me there, until I got back." He pointed to the horses grazing the tufts of heather next to the stone where she'd sat and sketched.

"I finished my drawing." She sounded like a child explaining how the time had slipped away and she'd forgotten her chores.

"I thought you'd roamed, got lost. The weather on the moors can change in a moment." His voice still held a panicked edge, but his breathing had slowed. Why was he so angry?

"I found something in the barrow. I want to show you. I think Mam came here. Her name was on the wall."

His eyes flashed again and his face turned to a grim mask, at one with the granite beneath their feet. "Don't be ridiculous. Your imagination is running away from you. I played here as a child. I know every inch of the place. It's the moors; they have that effect on people. Make them imagine strange happenings. It's time we got back. Caroline will be worried that we're not home."

Not half as worried as she was. When she got back, she intended to ask some questions. Find out what exactly they knew about the scratchings in the barrow. Finneas, well, Finneas could go to hell if he was going to behave like some enraged bull because she'd chosen to take a walk.

Before long the roof of Wyck Hall came into view and still Finneas hadn't broken the stern silence between them. He'd sat chewing on his lips and letting out disgruntled huffs for the entire ride. Not that she'd tried to talk to him. All she could see were the words dug into the wall of the barrow and the dates. May 24—Mam's birthday right enough, but she hadn't died in 1788. Mam's lies about Pa and her past swooped around her head and roosted on her shoulders, weighing her down.

Mam lied about Richard Barrington, lied about Julian; how many more lies had she told? Had she made that inscription knowing she'd be leaving Cornwall? Was leaving a death to her? And why would she scratch her name and the date of her death into the wall of an ancient burial barrow? Nothing made any sense. Rose's head throbbed and her heart ached with confusion.

When they entered the courtyard, Finneas dismounted in one fluid leap and strode into the house, banging the door behind him. She slipped from the saddle, her legs barely able to support her weight, and stumbled through the nearest door and found herself in Mrs. Pascoe's kitchen.

"You all right, dearie? You look as though you've seen a ghost." Mrs. Pascoe's hands came down and eased her into a chair. "You're freezing cold. Here, move closer to the fire."

She sat like a corpse while Mrs. Pascoe unbuttoned Finneas's cloak and pulled off her gloves, chafing her cold, blue hands in her work-worn palms. "Let me get you a cup of tea; we'll put a splash of brandy in it. That'll bring the color back to your cheeks. Now, where's Master Finneas? I heard him come in. Banging around like I don't know what. More like that brother of his than himself." Mrs. Pascoe's chattering washed over her, her mind still stuck on the words she'd seen carved in the wall. *Here lies Jenifer Trevan.*

What if Jenifer Trevan was buried there and the mother she knew was not her mam, just like Pa was not her pa?

A row of pilchards lined the table awaiting the knife, the smell making her stomach roil; she hated fish, and this was the worst she'd ever smelled. Mrs. Pascoe put a steaming cup of tea on the table next to her. She picked it up and inhaled the steam, the brandy fumes hitting the back of her throat. She pushed it away.

"Nay, drink it. Drink it now." Mrs. Pascoe held the cup to her lips. "Sip. Go on. Sip it. There's a good girl."

The mellow scent of nutmeg and mixed spices and warmth blossomed as the brandy hit her throat.

"And another, that's a girl. That's better."

She grasped the cup and took it in her hands, wrapping her fingers around the warmth as the brandy made her blood flow and the room came back into focus. "Mrs. Pascoe."

"There, there, dearie. That's brought the color back to those pretty cheeks. Don't talk. Let the brandy do its work. Good strong French brandy, that is. Old Bill from up Trevithick way stopped by with a couple of flagons. Don't be telling the mistress, but it's good stuff to have. Specially for moments like this."

Mrs. Pascoe could be right. Rose took another sip. "How well did you know my mother?"

"Young Jenifer." The pitiful murmur slipped out between her lips. "Good as a daughter to me."

"How did she die?"

"My Jenifer? Die? She didn't die. Not as far as I know. Not unless you've kept something from us. You be the living, breathing image of her."

She took another sip of the brandy; it washed away the ugly taste in her mouth and loosened her tongue, gave her courage. If Finneas wouldn't speak of it, then she'd have to ask. "I went into the burial barrow on the moor."

"That'd account for the look of you. You don't want to go poking around in them barrows—they're no place for a young girl, no place for anyone."

"My mam went there."

Did she imagine it or did Mrs. Pascoe's eyes slide toward the door? "What makes you say that?"

"I found an inscription, scratchings, really, on the wall. It said, 'Here lies Jenifer Trevan, loving granddaughter of Granfer Tomas Trevan.' Her date of birth and the date of her death." Her voice choked on the final words.

Mrs. Pascoe fixed her gaze on the smeared window and rubbed at the thick glass with the heel of her hand, then cleared her throat. "Feeling a bit better, are you now? Color's come back to your face. You go and get yourself into some warmer clothes. I'll busy meself. Master Julian will be home tonight. It's Midsummer Eve. Always home for Midsummer, he is."

Rose swirled the rest of the brandy-laced tea in her mouth. No one wanted to speak about the barrow. She'd seen the writing, seen it with her own eyes. Why wouldn't they tell her? Finneas, then Mrs. Pascoe. Maybe Lady Methenwyck would offer some answers.

Once she reached her bedchamber she unbuttoned her riding habit and lay down on the bed. She searched the edges of her mind. She'd forgotten something. Something important.

"Always record your evidence. It's the only way."

That's what Pa said. Proof. She needed to validate her findings. Something she could hold up in front of their eyes and demand answers for. She'd return to the barrow and copy the scratchings, draw them. Once she had tangible evidence, they couldn't brush her aside like some unimportant scrap of dust.

If she left now, she'd be back before dinner. It couldn't take long, even on foot; if she ran she'd cover the distance in less than an hour. She reefed off the pretty blue boots, grimaced, and pulled on her old clodhoppers. She'd be more comfortable and faster. Then she grabbed the lantern and the little tinderbox beside the bed and jammed her pencil and a piece of paper into her pocket.

Ignoring the strains of Finneas's raised voice and Lady Methenwyck's incoherent murmurings, she slipped out of the door and into the courtyard.

"Julian hasn't arrived yet?" Finneas paced the carpet in front of the fireplace.

"To the best of my knowledge, no, unless he's with Methenwyck."

"He isn't and I checked the stables. No matter how much you dislike talking about the past, it is time."

"The past is just that, past. There is nothing to discuss."

He hunkered down in front of her and she shuffled farther back in the seat. "Caroline, I know you find it difficult, but the time has come. I found Rose in the barrow."

Her pasty face turned even paler and she groped in her sleeve for her handkerchief and sat picking at the initials embroidered in pale pink silk in the corner.

"I'm not well."

"No, you're not, and for that I am sorry. However, I don't feel it is a malaise of the body, more of the heart."

"You shouldn't have brought her here." She turned her head and stared out of the window. "And why the barrow? Everyone knows the stories."

"I didn't take her to the barrow. I left her sketching Dozmary Pool while I went to the inn to fetch lunch. It took longer than I expected. I got waylaid by old Bill, and when I returned she'd vanished. I found her stumbling out of the barrow, looking as though she'd seen a ghost."

"She had."

He had the most overwhelming need to shake Caroline until her bones rattled. Ever since he could remember she'd had a fear of the barrow and the tales surrounding it. As a child he'd challenged her, slipped into the cavernous cave at twilight. Played games with the local boys, counting while they ran in circles around the burial stone, scaring each other to death. She'd had him beaten black and blue—that had cured him, but the rumors persisted. The village girls who never returned. Never any tangible proof, no evidence that could prove they were anything but unsubstantiated rumblings. "A ghost, an apparition?"

"A ghost of the past. Her mother."

What was she talking about? He picked up Caroline's cold hand and rested his thumb against the hammering pulse in her wrist, then chafed her hand. "Her mother, Jenifer Trevan, is alive and well and living in New South Wales, or she was when Rose left. You know that."

"Only too well. But for me she would not be." She twisted her handkerchief in her hands, and with her head bent pulled another thread from the embroidered initials.

"She was transported for theft. I don't understand. What did Rose find in the barrow?"

Caroline let out a long sigh. "Jenifer was trapped in the barrow one night. There is an inscription. She wrote her own epitaph on the wall of the small chamber."

"Epitaph?"

She nodded her head. "You know as well as I do of the hunting parties."

The traditional hunting parties once held at Wyck Hall. Methenwyck's cronies would arrive from London for rollicking gatherings to celebrate the start of each new season: the wild rides across the moor, the drunken revelries, the all-night celebrations. "They're still happening?"

"They're long over. Only Julian is true to the old ways."

Julian, the heir apparent who'd fashioned himself in the mold of Methenwyck to assure his inheritance. Never quite certain he'd receive what he saw as his due.

"Rose's mother, Jenifer, worked here as a scullery maid. Her grandfather had one of the grace-and-favor cottages. The walled garden was his work. He had the touch—anything from daffodils to roses would blossom. So did Jenifer. She could cure anything with her herbs and potions. But for her I wouldn't have survived the loss of so many children."

Finneas rocked back on his heels, dropped Caroline's cold hand, gritting his teeth to keep his patience. He'd stayed away too long, too involved in his studies to take the time to visit and care for the woman who had given him shelter, made him what he was today. Age sat uncomfortably on her haggard face, lines etched deep that he'd failed to notice, a pallor to her skin. "Tell me what happened to Rose's mother."

Caroline dragged back her concentration, shook off the faraway look in her eyes. "She took shelter in the barrow."

He wanted to prod her further, shake her, make her speak faster. He glanced out of the window at the lengthening shadows; the sky had darkened, almost as though Caroline had summoned the storm to illustrate her turmoil. "She was trapped, thought her turn had come, so she wrote her own epitaph."

So it wasn't a figment of Rose's imagination; she had seen her mother's name. And he'd been so taken up with his need to keep her safe that he hadn't let her speak. "It's true? You've seen it?"

Caroline closed her eyes, laid her head back against the chair. "Just once, long ago. The words are only visible when the sun is high."

"And Jenifer didn't die."

"No. When daylight came, she found a way out through one of the old tunnels. Three weeks later she was accused of theft and transported."

And that's what Rose found? Why hadn't he gone to look himself? Why had he dragged her away? "You owe Rose an explanation. And so do I."

"Where is she?"

Unable to find the small bell Caroline kept on the side table, Finneas strode to the door and called out, "Mrs. Pascoe, would you come here, please?"

He drummed his foot as he waited by the door, his thoughts swirling. What must Rose be feeling? Quite one thing to visit the grave of your family, quite another to find an epitaph of someone you believed to be alive.

With a lot of heaving and puffing, Mrs. Pascoe's flushed face appeared at the top of the stairs.

"Mrs. Pascoe, would you please bring some tea, perhaps a little brandy, too, for Lady Methenwyck, and ask Rose to join us?"

Sighing and shuffling, Mrs. Pascoe disappeared and he turned back to Caroline, the gruesome tales of his childhood sounding in his ears. "There's never been any proof of the rumors about the girls who disappeared."

"You know about them?"

"Of course. The village boys used to tell tales about the evil spirits that lurked there and carried girls away. Never boys." His laugh died in his throat at the sight of Caroline's blanched face.

"What could be keeping Rose?" He flung open the door to see Mrs. Pascoe bent double, spluttering furiously. "Mrs. Pascoe, sit down. please. I'll give you something for that cough."

She waved her hand in front of her face, paused for a moment, then the wheezing and snuffling began all over again. Respiratory infections were the plague of the moors.

"Not here. She's gone."

"Gone where?"

"There be a storm coming."

"Finneas, close the door and come here." Caroline's voice, far stronger than he'd heard for many a year, made him turn.

"Julian is here. He said he had matters to attend to and not to mention his arrival."

A cold shudder traced Finneas's neck. Rose alone on the moor, the weather closing in, the light fading. "Thank you, Mrs. Pascoe." He closed the door on the housekeeper and turned to Caroline, who stood with her face pressed to the window, fists clenched.

"Go now. Do not waste any time. Go this minute and find Julian."

"I'm not worried about Julian. He can look after himself." Probably had some girl in the village he liked to visit. "Rose is out there somewhere. The storm's way past brewing; it's about to hit. I must find Rose."

"Go and find Julian. Now. And don't let him out of your sight."

"Caroline, what are you talking about?"

"Just do as I say. Find Julian before history repeats itself."

"History?"

"You have no time to lose."

"It is Rose I'm concerned about."

"Find Julian and bring him home. No matter what it takes. Bring him home before it is too late. Tomorrow is Midsummer Eve."

Chapter 19

Sydney, Australia
1908

Shaw stifled a yawn and tried to concentrate.

"How are matters proceeding? I've been doing a bit of research myself. It seems that there might be another avenue we haven't pursued."

No point in asking any questions. Father would get around to it in his own good time and then Shaw would go home and sort out a couple of boxes. He'd rather hoped he'd be spending the evening with Tamsin, but the moment they'd left the Chinese place, she'd jumped aboard the first ferry and left him on the wharf like a plate of cold noodles. Hadn't given him an opportunity to arrange another meeting.

"Aren't you even remotely interested in what I have to say?"

"Yes, of course." He hadn't expected anyone to be in the offices when he'd dropped in to pick up the paperwork Father had left for him.

"Will-O-Wyck, the property in the Hunter." Shaw sat up a little straighter in his chair. "It seems it was granted in 1826. One of the first and one of the biggest, pretty much everything between Wollombi and the village of Broke, with the exception of the Paynes' family holdings. Close to a thousand acres of prime land and it's never been subdivided. The grazing lease came up for renewal a few years ago, and Ron Rushworth got wind of it."

Kelly owned more than the house and the small parcel of land around it. He might have been a recluse, but he was a rich one. Shaw narrowed his eyes. The unmistakable sheen of sweat on Father's forehead and the constant scratching as he rubbed his hands together signaled there was more to this than Shaw was party to. By comparison to the land value, the sketchbook was worth nothing. "What exactly is our relationship with the Rushworths?"

With a splutter Father laid his hands flat on the desktop. "A business one. As you know, Ron Rushworth has been buying up large parcels of land on the north shore, building blocks. That's what people want these days. A bit more space, a modern house, outside the city. Improved transport and the like. And the possibility of this bridge."

"And you've been facilitating these purchases."

"Made an investment or two. If the stupid woman had done what she was asked and approached her mother six months ago, we wouldn't be in this position."

That's why he'd been sent off to Wollombi with Mrs. Rushworth: to keep Father out of the dealings. It was all about money. "And you borrowed money to finance the purchase of land on Rushworth's behalf."

"That's about it."

Now he got the picture. "And Rushworth doesn't have the wherewithal to meet the payments."

"That, coupled with some heavy losses on the share market."

"He was banking on his wife inheriting the property. The extensive property."

With a curt nod, Father rocked back in his chair. "The old lady lasted a lot longer than anyone expected. It'd be to your advantage to follow up on this. Not going to look good if Everdene, Roach, and Smythe default on a loan. Ron Rushworth's convinced they can make some claim on the property via squatters' rights and circumvent Kelly's will. In the meantime we need the money from the sketchbook."

Shaw exhaled slowly. They were clutching at straws. What he wouldn't give to walk out of here and never come back. "To whom was the original grant made?"

"One Finneas Methenwyck."

A bunch of campanologists took up residence in Shaw's head. He had seen the name somewhere, written, not spoken. Recently. "I've got to be going. I'll see what I can find out about this Methenwyck fellow." *Methenwyck*. If he'd seen the name written, then chances were it was either in some of the records he'd been trawling through looking for Rose Winton or in one of the books and papers he'd unpacked at home. The Library would be well and truly closed by now, so that would have to wait until tomorrow.

He left the office, jumped aboard the next ferry, ran along the road, and by the time he reached Blues Point Road he could hardly put one foot in front of the other. He flung open the door and stumbled down into the kitchen. The lamp hissed and spat. Not tonight. He needed decent light tonight; he envisaged some long hours ahead.

His jacket landed on the table with a thud and he grabbed a bottle of beer out of the ice chest, and then, easing past the piles of timber he'd stacked against the wall, he slumped down on the single chair in the middle of the room and closed his eyes. One day every wall in the tiny house would be covered with bookshelves and he'd know where everything was.

Concentrate.

Methenwyck.

Handwritten manuscript or print? Book cover.

Something. Anything to narrow his search.

Images of Tamsin bent over the sketchbook kept drifting into his mind. Her hair slipping out of the pins no matter how hard she tried to restrain it, her teeth worrying her bottom lip when she concentrated, the look on her face when he'd opened the tin, like a child at Christmas. He groaned and stood up, taking a long gulp from the beer bottle.

Methenwyck. It was handwritten, faded. On a page full of lines and columns.

He rubbed his hands over his face. What was his father up to? Squatters' rights. The whole thing was becoming more and more contrived. How much money had he sunk in these investments? He could smell a rat and he didn't like it. He didn't want to be involved, and he certainly didn't want to have to tell Tamsin that Mrs. Rushworth intended to sell the sketchbook. Why hadn't he come clean in the first place?

Methenwyck. Methenwyck.

He pushed aside the pile of books he still hadn't looked at. It wouldn't be there. Then his eyes lit on the smaller pile tucked on the seat of the chair. Larger books, foolscap, thin. The ones he'd dumped last night. He picked them up and sat back down in the chair, the pile on his lap, and opened the cover. *Paul Whitehead, Steward. Medmenham Abbey.* It sounded like something out of a penny dreadful. A Gothic thriller. He turned the pages. Just columns of numbers and figures, dates, provisions, something to do with alcohol, and lists of names.

Find the name. *Methenwyck, Methenwyck.* He ran his finger down the spidery writing, more dates and more names, then others. He scrubbed at his eyes and squinted down at the faded print.

Methenwyck.

He opened the ledger wide on the table and stared down, blinked to make sure his eyes weren't deceiving him. It was there. *Methenwyck*. There could be a hundred Methenwycks in England, any number who might have taken passage to Australia.

An insistent rapping on the door brought him from his reverie.

Dumping the armful of books on the table, he eased his way to the front door and threw it open. "Tamsin."

Wishful thinking.

"That could possibly be a compliment bearing in mind the difference in our ages."

"Mrs. Rushworth." What was she doing here? "Have the solicitors had an answer to their advertisements?" In some strange way he hoped they had, then at least he wouldn't have to deal with the woman's irritating demands.

"No, they haven't. And that is why I am here." She took a step closer and peered around him. "Are you going to invite me in?"

That was the last thing he wanted to do. "I'm not really set up for guests. Perhaps we could meet tomorrow at the offices?" Besides, he had no idea whether Father had told the Rushworths of his title deed search.

"Don't be so ridiculous." Before he had the chance to reply, she barged past him and marched down the narrow hallway.

He skittered after her, steadying boxes as her shoulder thumped against first one stack and then another. "Straight ahead. The kitchen, I'm afraid." At least that way there'd be enough space for her to sit. He brushed past her and pushed the pile of books into the center of the table. "Sit down."

She perched on the edge of the battered bentwood chair, her fingers rubbing at a groove in the scarred tabletop.

"How can I help you?"

"I won't beat around the bush. Have you found a buyer yet?"

He gazed up at the peeling ceiling. "No, I haven't. I'm still trying to establish the provenance. It could make an enormous difference to the price." Especially if Tamsin was correct about the importance of Winton's research. "And there is a question over the will."

"Don't be ridiculous. The sketchbook belonged to my mother. No matter who inherits Will-O-Wyck, the sketchbook is part of my mother's personal possessions. No one else knows about it and no one has made a claim to it. We've been over this before. I want the sketchbook, now."

"It's not here."

Her eyes bulged. "Where is it?"

"It's safe under lock and key at the Library."

"You had no right to give the book to the Library. It belongs to me, my mother's possession. I shouldn't have let your father talk me into dealing with you. Get it back."

"As I said before, there is little or no point in putting it on the market until the provenance is established. I have made some headway in establishing authenticity. I—"

"Provenance be damned. I want it—need it—sold now. To the highest bidder. No one can prove it didn't belong to my mother." She reached out her fingers, clawing at his shirtsleeve. "I am sure you are aware of our financial issues. Your father also stands to lose if the quarterly loan repayment is not met. Selling the sketchbook for a slightly lower amount will ultimately reap a higher financial reward."

"This would be far better discussed in the office. I have said I will collect the sketchbook at the beginning of the week. The Library has every right to evaluate it, especially after your mother's letter."

"Where is this letter? I presume you've sighted it."

No, he hadn't. He'd taken Tamsin's word for it.

"Shaw, please." She lifted her gaze to him and he noticed the telltale sign of tears pooling.

He couldn't stand tears.

She gave a delicate sniff and dabbed at the corners of her eyes. "No one needs to know that the sketchbook was part of Kelly's estate. We can say my mother wasn't in her right mind when she wrote the letter, that she'd forgotten she'd given me the book. Isn't possession meant to be nine-tenths of the law?"

Oh no. He wasn't going down that path. He was trying to establish his reputation, not destroy it.

"When the time comes to dispose of the library at Will-O-Wyck, you might like first refusal." She dangled the bait in front of his nose like a seasoned fly fisherman, and he was tempted, sorely tempted. "I know there are several more books that you expressed an interest in. Perhaps we can come to some arrangement. Payment doesn't only have to be in the form of a commission."

For a split second he wavered. She was right; there were more than several books he'd give his eyeteeth to own, but they weren't hers to give. Might never be. Nor was the sketchbook, and besides, now he'd discovered more about Rose Winton, he wanted to solve the mystery of Winton's disappearance from the world of science and why he had never been given credit for his discoveries.

"I can't do that." He turned back to face her. "I've told the Library they can keep the book until next week."

She rolled her eyes and picked at the binding on the book on the table in front of her. "What are these? In fact, what are all these books?" She waved a gloved hand in the air. "The house is full of them."

"It's my grandfather's library. Shipped out from England."

"And these?" She thumbed through the pages of the top ledger and he leaped forward and snatched it from her, unwilling to share his half-baked theories. He had to get her out of here.

"Are you looking for something specific?" She glanced at the floor where the random piles of boxes lay. "Perhaps I can help."

No. Not even as a last resort.

"I sent my driver away; he'll return shortly. I may as well do something useful. Perhaps I can convince you of my sincerity."

"I was just having a look at some old ledgers." He lifted the Cellar Book and a yellowed newspaper slid onto the table.

She reached for it.

His hand came down on top of it, but she tugged it toward her. Terrified the page would tear, he let go.

"How quaint. 1820. *The West Briton and Cornwall Advertiser.* Did your grandfather come from Cornwall?"

"No, not as far as I know. Grandfather lived just outside Oxford. I intended to go to university there but it never came about." Because his bloody father had summoned him back to Australia to make sure he followed in his footsteps instead of reading classics as he and Grandfather had intended.

She shook her head. "I remember visiting Oxford—like something out of the Dark Ages, all those damp, cold buildings and hushed voices." She gave a melodramatic groan. "I don't think I ever visited Cornwall. Wasn't that where King Arthur kept his Knights of the Round Table and the Lady of the Lake? I always particularly loved that story."

The Lady of the Lake. Dozmary Pool. Cornwall. The drawing folded in the back of the sketchbook. Every single one of the hairs on the back of his neck stood to attention.

"What time is it?"

He pulled his watch from his pocket. "Eight thirty." Hopefully time for her to leave. His mind was rushing in a series of circuits and bumps like one of those newfangled air machines. He needed to make notes, write things down, order his thoughts. Too many frail tendrils were tantalizing him.

Mrs. Rushworth let out a sigh and stretched out her legs in front of her. “And you’re not prepared to discuss the sale of the sketchbook until the will is resolved? I can’t convince you to change your mind?”

“No.”

“In that case, perhaps you could offer me a cup of tea while I wait for my driver.” She turned in the chair and studied the disgusting sink packed with random cups and empty beer bottles. “You do have the facilities?”

“Yes, of course. I’m sorry.” He reached for the teapot and set it on the table. “Sugar?” He turned to find Mrs. Rushworth with her elbows on the table, staring intently at the old newspaper. “Mrs. Rushworth?”

She lifted her head. “This is more than quaint.” Her finger stabbed at the center of the page. “ ‘Calamitous Fire. Yesterday morning a fire broke out at Wyck Hall.’ That’s a coincidence, isn’t it? Wyck Hall and Will-O-Wyck. Where does the word come from?”

The hairs on the back of his neck rose again. *Will-O-Wyck. Methen-wyck. Wyck Hall.* Too much of a coincidence.

“What does ‘wyck’ mean? I didn’t pay much attention to the name of the house when I arrived in Wollombi.”

More interested in the inheritance she believed had landed in her lap. “Haven’t got a clue. Wick of a candle?” He grabbed at the paper and pulled it toward him.

“Surely you have a dictionary among all these books. Look it up.”

“In a moment, in a moment.” His eyes raced across the page.

> . . . the home of Lord Methenwyck that we fear has been productive of the most disastrous effects. The constables of Bodmin, Camborne, and all the neighboring parishes were called upon to protect the property, and by their exertions and those of the other persons present, it was hoped the principal front would be saved. The wind, however,

afterward changed, and when our informant left, great fears were entertained that the building would be entirely consumed. The origin of the fire was not known, and the damage is likely to be immense.

He stretched out his arm and sent the teapot flying. "I'll sort it out later." Thank God he hadn't spilled tea across the paper.

A knock sounded on the door.

"That's my driver." Mrs. Rushworth stood. "Think about what I said. The library at Will-O-Wyck could house a gold mine." She raised her eyebrows in question. "I'll come with you when you collect the sketchbook."

The library and the tea forgotten, he escorted Mrs. Rushworth to the door and waited while she drove off, then returned to the kitchen. Dozmary Pool, the additional picture in the back of the sketchbook. That tied it to Cornwall. No, it was a long shot. The drawing was tucked inside the back cover of the sketchbook; it could have been put there at any time.

A faint light illuminated the windows when he picked up the last of the *Cornwall Advertisers*. He flipped through the pages until his eyes locked on the headline:

FIRE AT WYCK HALL. THE FOLLOWING IS A MORE PARTICULAR ACCOUNT OF THIS DISASTROUS EVENT THAN THE SHORTNESS OF THE TIME ALLOWED US TO LAY BEFORE OUR READERS LAST WEEK.

His eyes raced across the page, his heart rate keeping pace with his mounting excitement . . . *flames spread, and speedily consumed the whole house . . . Lord Methenwyck and his heir, Julian, perished. Lady Caroline*

Methenwyck . . . taken the afternoon mail coach . . . with her guest, a Miss Rose Winton, visiting from New South Wales.

He placed a piece of paper on the page where he'd found the article, almost as though he was frightened it might disappear, that it had been a figment of his overtired imagination.

Lowering the paper to the table, he stared down at the headline. Of all people, Mrs. Rushworth had found what he was looking for!

Chapter 20

Sydney, Australia
1908

The hands on the clock clicked and Tamsin groaned. She'd achieved nothing all day, absolutely nothing. She'd spent the entire time working her way backward and forward through the sketchbook and Winton's correspondence as if she could in some way absorb Rose's story from the pages. Why had she gone to London? Had she taken the sketchbook with her? Why hadn't Winton gone with her?

"Tamsin, I'm locking up. Time you went home." Mrs. Williams stuck her head around the door. "Get some fresh air. You look as pale as a ghost."

"I'm just leaving." She threw her notebook and pencil into her bag and lifted the books from her desk. Perhaps the answer lay in the tin. Jenifer Trevan, the epitaph, the dates all wrong because she was listed on the muster twenty years after she had died. Why had she been sent to Australia? What crime had she committed? Shaw hadn't told her that. Where was the tin? Not on the desk. Perhaps it was still in her satchel.

No, nothing. "Come along."

"Just coming, Mrs. Williams." When had she last had it? Not today. It must have been the first day she hadn't pulled the daguerreotype out and looked at it. "Damn! Damn! Damn!"

"Are you all right, Tamsin?" Mrs. Williams threw open the door.

"Yes, I'm fine. I'm sorry, I seem to have lost my tin."

"Oh. The biscuit people. When did you last have it?"

"Yesterday." Oh no! She'd shown Shaw Jenifer Trevan's name, to remind him. "Last night, when I was with Shaw. I might have left it in the café." Would they have kept it? Thrown it away? "I have to go." She pushed past Mrs. Williams, took the stairs two at a time, and flew out into the street.

By the time she reached the Quay, she was bellowing like a steam engine and she slumped against the lamppost outside the café, trying to get enough air into her lungs to go inside and ask. She pushed open the door and glanced around, hoping against hope Shaw would be sitting there. The table was empty. She'd half expected—no, not half expected, hoped—he'd turn up at the Library today, but she hadn't seen hide nor hair of him. The old man turned from his flaming pans and nodded at her over his shoulder. She made her way to the counter. "Yes, missy?"

"I was wondering if you found an old tin last night."

"Old tin?"

"We were sitting at the table over there." She pointed into the corner.

His eyes lit up. "Ah! With Shaw. No, no tin. No Shaw."

Resisting the urge to stamp her feet and scream, she nodded her thanks and made her way outside. She couldn't remember having it in her hand when she left. Maybe Shaw had picked it up. Her panic eased a little. That'd be it. She'd been so absorbed by his news they'd hardly spoken a word on the way to the ferry. She'd jumped aboard and he'd disappeared into the sunset.

She slipped onto the wharf just as the ropes were being thrown from the ferry. "Wait for me."

"Better be quick."

She jumped across the expanding gap of water and landed with a thud.

"You've done that before."

"Just a couple of times." She handed over her fare and sat on one of the seats outside, enjoying the breeze in her hair. Mrs. Williams was right, not enough fresh air.

As soon as they docked, she started to walk across the park and then stopped; instead of going home, she headed down Blues Point Road looking for Shaw's car. What had he said? *"Number 121."* It could only be about five minutes out of her way, and she wouldn't sleep without knowing what had happened to the tin. Besides, she'd quite like to see him.

She grabbed at her hair and tried to rectify the mess the wind had made, then gave up. It wasn't a social call, just a quick knock on the door and . . . maybe he'd ask her in for tea; she wasn't sure she'd accept beer. Her head had felt strangely fuzzy when she'd woken this morning, more likely due to the fact she'd barely slept than anything else, her mind on Mother and Father and life before the Islands for some strange reason.

She couldn't fault them for their missionary zeal, but their parenting was another matter. Once she'd reached the age of ten, they'd as good as washed their hands of her. Bundled her onto a ship with some other passengers returning to Australia who, following their instructions, had deposited her at the Sydney Ladies Academy under the guidance of the two Misses Green. And she'd never seen them again.

All their promises about returning, taking her out of school, had never eventuated, and with the news of their death two years later, she'd become a permanent fixture, remaining at school year in, year out. That became a double-edged sword: seen by the other girls as privileged, seen by the Misses Green as a nuisance, she spent her entire time betwixt and between.

By the time she reached eighteen she had more than overstayed her welcome, and with their assistance had enrolled in the Women's College at Sydney University, intent on furthering her education, fulfilling Mother's dream to see her daughter as one of the new breed of women—a doctor.

She'd hated it. Couldn't summon the courage to stick it out. The moment she reached twenty-one and came into her inheritance, she'd left, employed Mrs. Birkenhead, and moved into the family home in Miller Street, but the place held nothing but faded memories. She felt like an interloper, too scared to face the past, too pathetic to fulfill her destiny. She couldn't walk into the surgery where Father had run his practice, couldn't look at his desk and shelves of medical books, all a constant reminder of her failure. Heavens, she hadn't even found the courage to stick to university. It wasn't until she'd been summoned by the bank that she'd realized she hadn't a bottomless purse—just the house and a parcel of worthless shares. It was time she put her foot down and called the tune. The prospect of nursing or missionary school didn't appeal. She'd rather be a nun. Mrs. Williams had saved her life when she'd championed her employment. And here she was, totally immersed in the most fascinating adventure. Perhaps she did have something to thank her parents for.

She stopped, looked up, and discovered she was standing outside a tiny little workman's cottage, the gate hanging off one hinge and the paint peeling from the door.

Her hands grew clammy. What was she doing? Should she knock?

Who lived in a place like this yet had the money to drive a motor car? What she wouldn't give to be able to see inside. She lifted her hand and rapped her knuckles on the door. After an eternity it swung open a crack and there he was.

Same old Shaw. Same corduroy trousers and shirt he'd had on last time she'd seen him, the sleeves rolled up, revealing his brown forearms.

"Hello, Tamsin. What are you doing here?" He forced the door farther open with his hip.

She heard him swallow, then he pulled the door wide and ushered her into the narrow hallway crammed with boxes. Trapped in the small space, she felt her heartbeat race. Ridiculous. This was Shaw. They had a common goal. She'd traveled with him from Wollombi to Sydney. Spent hours in his company. She squeezed her way along, turning sideways to edge past the rows and rows of tea chests stacked one on top of the other.

"I wasn't expecting company." That was more than obvious. His face looked drawn and haggard as though he needed a decent night's sleep. "Come and have a cup of tea."

"I won't stay. I was on my way home. I can't find my tin. I wondered if you'd picked it up at the café last night."

"Hmm, yes." He scratched his head and gave a distracted glance at the table. "Yes, I did. It's in here somewhere." He slid a pile of old ledgers across the tabletop, releasing a plume of dust and a scurry of silverfish and cockroaches. "It's in my jacket pocket."

"I was talking to someone at the Library about the daguerreotype. They seem to think there might be records in George Goodman's studio. It's still in George Street. Have you got it?"

"It's here somewhere, I know it is." He tossed aside an interesting pile of yellowing pamphlets, then turned them over and slapped one of the books down on top. "Load of old rubbish. Here it is."

Her hand reached for the tin but he held it close to his chest and pulled off the lid. "Let's take another look at the daguerreotype."

The paper crackled as he unwrapped it and tipped it from the red cardboard frame into his hand. He held it up to the lamp sitting on the table. "Who do you think they are?"

"I don't know. I like to think it's Charles Winton and maybe Rose and her children."

"Winton would be too old. He was born in 1764. He'd be over eighty if Goodman took it. She's pretty, like you."

She flashed him a look from under her lashes and her face reddened. How she wished he'd stop making comments like that. She didn't know how to react, whether he was serious or just sweet-talking her the way he did Mrs. Williams.

Impossible to tell. Tamsin let her hair fall across her face to hide the blush in her cheeks.

He shook his head and took back the daguerreotype. "It's badly scratched. Maybe it's Mrs. Quinleaven? I'll put it back."

His long fingers carefully refitted the frame and folded the tissue paper and tucked the little parcel into the tin.

She turned to face him, every muscle in her body tight, and held out her hand. "May I have it?"

After a long pause he sighed. "Tamsin, I need to talk to you. Let's go and sit down."

She followed him back down the hallway and into the front room dominated by a sagging leather armchair and books. Nothing but books. No shelves. Just piles and piles of books against every wall, three and four deep.

She swallowed the lump in her throat. "I didn't know you collected books."

"I don't. That is, I want to. These are my grandfather's. I hope to go into business one day."

"Into business? Doing what?"

"Antiquarian books. Buying and selling."

A wave of nausea washed over her and she plonked down onto the edge of the chair.

"You look pale. Let me get you a glass of water."

Tamsin sank back into the collapsing chair. Her mind wouldn't stop swirling. If it wasn't for the fact he had her tin, she'd be out of the door so fast. Buying and selling old books? Did he intend to sell the sketchbook? She tried to backtrack through the conversations they'd had. It seemed like hundreds of hours. Surely she was jumping to conclusions. And then the odd phrase or two popped into her head. His fascination with the sketchbook, asking how much it would be worth. What did he want it for? For his own collection or to sell to someone who'd keep it hidden away in their private collection behind some locked gate and high fence so no one else could see it? Winton's sketchbook belonged in the public domain for everyone to enjoy.

After an eternity Shaw returned. He'd put on his jacket and had a glass of water in his hands. She was a fool.

Relying on too many years in the posh school with the Misses Green, she rose to her feet and smoothed her jacket. "My tin, please?" She raised one eyebrow, wishing she looked less windblown, more businesslike.

Shaw exhaled and sank down into the chair she had just vacated, the tin still in his hand. Maybe there was something in all those assertive women articles she'd been reading because now he had to look up at her. Resisting the temptation to place her hands on her hips and demand to know his intentions, she waited, sipping the water as it brought her internal and external temperature into some sort of harmony.

"I haven't been entirely honest with you." A grim smile ghosted across his face.

Too right he hadn't. She pressed her lips together, refusing to offer him any solace. Wanting to see him smooth-talk his way out of this.

"This collection"—he waved his hand around the room—"and all the others outside in the boxes arrived from England. They belonged to my grandfather."

He'd have to try a little harder than that. He'd told her that already.

She swallowed the *and* hovering on her lips and took another sip of water.

"Mrs. Rushworth intends to sell the sketchbook."

And then it hit her. "She asked *you* to sell the sketchbook, when we were in Wollombi." She dumped the glass down on the side table and stared at him. Right from the very beginning she'd known something was not quite right, and she'd chosen to ignore her suspicions. "And you thought if the Library authenticated the sketchbook, it would increase its value." Too taken with the man. Blindsided by his charm.

Two spots of red flared on his cheeks.

And that made her temper snap. Guilty as charged. It was his duplicity that disgusted her. He'd intended right from that very first day to sell the sketchbook. He'd used her, used her contacts to find out the provenance, and she'd gone along with it like a lamb to the slaughter. "It is a national treasure and belongs to the Library." She couldn't sacrifice the sketchbook, or her principles. It meant even more to her now that they had discovered Rose Winton.

The thought that Mrs. Rushworth might have already claimed the sketchbook—or worse still, that Shaw had found a buyer—tiptoed down her back. And no matter what Shaw said, she couldn't get past the fact that he'd used her. Courted her—funny how these old-fashioned words kept slipping into her mind—not because he liked her but because he wanted information from her. It was mortifying. How could she have been so naive?

"Tamsin, please. Let me explain. I have something more to tell you."

"You have nothing to say that I want to hear. Give me my tin. The contents belong with the sketchbook. In the Library." She held out her hand, palm open. "Give it to me!"

"I told Mrs. Rushworth that I didn't condone selling the sketchbook until the solicitors had verified her claim to ownership."

"You shouldn't even have considered agreeing with Mrs. Rushworth to sell the sketchbook. Mrs. Quinleaven wanted to donate it. You lied. Lied to me and used me. Give me the tin."

"Technically it doesn't belong to you."

"Mrs. Rushworth gave it to me." She snatched the tin from his hands and rammed it into her satchel.

Cursing men, money, and greed, she stormed down the hallway, slamming the door behind her, hoping against hope that the stacks of books would topple and bury him.

———

Now that Tamsin had gone thundering off in high dudgeon without giving him the opportunity to show her the article about the fire and tell her about the land deeds, he couldn't concentrate. He'd had every intention of telling her his plans for approaching the Mitchell people. There was little or no point in going after her until she had calmed down and he had something more concrete to offer. The sketchbook was locked out of harm's way in the safe at the Library. There was nothing Mrs. Rushworth could do to get her hands on it, and anyway, a buyer wouldn't appear overnight.

He turned away and stared at the filthy window into the darkened street, trying to block the picture of Tamsin's face when she'd accused him of acting behind her back. He owed it to her to unravel the story, then at least the Library would have the opportunity to present a decent case, though he didn't like their chances if Father had his way.

West Wycombe, Medmenham Abbey, Methenwyck, Wyck Hall, Cornwall.

Was there a link? How many Methenwycks were there in the world? And what was Rose Winton doing down in Cornwall? The report of the fire placed her there and so did the drawing of Dozmary Pool. Had she taken the sketchbook to England? How on earth had it fallen into Mrs. Quinleaven's possession?

He grabbed the pile of ledgers across the table and opened them. Grandfather had obviously had some interest in Cornwall and Medmenham Abbey. Shaw returned to the tea chest and pulled all of the books out and piled them onto the table. The only way this could be sorted out was systematically. His mind was in such a muddle, full of names and places, like a spiderweb. What he needed was a piece of paper and a pencil.

With the yellow solicitor's pad in front of him and a freshly sharpened pencil, he wrote Rose Winton's name in the middle of the first sheet and drew a circle around it. Then on the right-hand side of the paper he wrote the names Finneas, Julian, and Methenwyck, and then he paused and his heartbeat raced as he added Charles Winton and his housekeeper, Jenifer Trevan.

Now what? He swiped the pad aside. One step at a time. Perhaps Mrs. Rushworth's claim was valid. Maybe Mrs. Quinleaven had inherited the book; maybe she was related to Rose Winton. He scrawled her name on the pad. No matter what the solicitors in Cessnock came up with in regard to Kelly's estate, Mrs. Rushworth would be entitled to her mother's possessions.

He had to make some basic assumptions. The first was that Rose Winton was at some time in possession of her father's sketchbook and had visited Cornwall. How did that lead back to a land grant in the Hunter?

Chapter 21

CORNWALL, ENGLAND
1820

No matter what Caroline said, Finneas had no intention of searching for Julian. Rose was his only concern. Julian could go to hell in a rowboat for all he cared. Only Rose mattered, and something told him she would have returned to the barrow.

She was enough like him, determined to accurately record what she'd seen. He groaned aloud. He was as bad as the jackasses at the Royal Society. He'd failed to listen.

He urged the poor horse onward. He could have traveled as fast on foot, the terrain was so rough; however, if he found Rose—no, *when* he found Rose—she'd be thankful for a ride. It was a long walk for anyone, even a girl who'd spent half her life roaming the countryside with her father and the natives she spoke of.

A break in the clouds showed the barrow looming ahead. A sense of dread weighted his chest, along with it the memories of the rumors. Even as a child he'd shunned the stories, wanted proof. Always proof. There'd never been any. If he hadn't dismissed Rose's discovery, would she be back at the house, warm and tucked up in front of the fire, her dark curls bouncing when she laughed?

Sod it! He dug his heels into the horse's flanks and urged it around the last bend before the barrow. With his hands cupped he called her name. "Rose! Rose!"

An owl hooted its reply.

He slid from the horse, wishing he'd thought to bring a lantern as he stumbled over the loose shale on the entry path between the two standing stones where the last vestiges of light disappeared.

The darkness was so black. He closed his eyes and opened them again, hoping some pinprick of light might lead the way. With the palm of his hand flat against the wall, he edged farther inside, then stopped, inhaling the air. He recognized the smell, no different from the cadavers he dissected, the coppery tang of blood. "Rose!"

Nothing but silence.

He strained his ears, trying to pick up the faintest sound.

His foot caught and he stumbled. Face-first, hands outstretched. He clenched his fists, felt metal cut into his skin. Pulling himself up into a sitting position, he lifted the object into his lap, feeling its shape. A lantern. Dear God, let him never lose his sight. A pang of remorse shot through him as he imagined Methenwyck's plight, lying day after day, unable to see even the sunrise. Forcing his heart rate to settle, he reached his fingers into his inside pocket for his small tinderbox. With it safely balanced on the dirt floor, he struck the flint and held the spill to the wick. The sulfur flared and the candle ignited.

Cupping his hand around the frail flicker of light, he waited for it to build, then eased to his feet, the lantern held aloft. The air was tinged with the smell of fish oil, the scent of blood—his own or Rose's? Good God, where was she? He eased his way farther into the barrow, the lantern held high.

The sight of a large stone standing in the center of the cavern brought back his morbid childhood fears. He counted his strides. Five, four, three, two—

Light spilled across the stone.

The stain of blood. He ran his index finger through it. Still damp. "Rose!"

He searched wildly. Tripped in the darkness. Stumbled to his knees, hands groping. A bundle of black cloth. A hand, palm up, fingers open. Working his way under the cloak, he encountered a warm, soft body. "Rose!"

With a rush of relief he turned her slowly, checking for injuries. Her back, her head. His fingers raced across her face. Alive. The flutter of a pulse in her neck. Slipping his arm under her shoulders he raised her, pulled her to his chest, cradling her against his body. In the half-light his eyes raced across the shadowy outline of her face, his fingers searching through her hair feeling for lacerations. Nothing.

Easing to his feet he carried her to the stone, almost lowered her down, then his vision clouded. Not where blood lay. Reaching out, he grasped the lantern in one hand and edged out into the night.

A blast of wet, cold air hit him as he stepped out of the barrow. Rose stirred, groaned, and opened her eyes. Even in the frail light the flash of terror in her eyes hit him. She struggled against him.

"Rose, it's me. Finneas."

Still she struggled, threatening to topple them both. He lowered her to her feet, keeping one arm tight around her body. She shrugged him free. And stood, arms clasped tight around her body, rocking. "Finneas?" Frowning, she wiped her hand over her face, pushing back her damp hair.

"Come, let me get you home."

"Home?" Her eyes grew even larger and she shook her head. "Not Wyck Hall. No." Fear scored her face and the shivering began in earnest.

Shock. He must keep her warm, get her out of the weather. "It won't take long. I have a horse. We can be back in no time and Mrs. Pascoe will have a warm drink. You need rest."

Whatever had happened? He wanted to shake her, punch questions at her. The air smelled fresh now, none of the macabre taint of the barrow. He'd smelled blood, seen the stain across the altar stone, but she hadn't a mark on her.

"Not Wyck Hall." She grabbed her skirt and took off down the path.

He belted after her. Even though his strides were longer, it took him moments to reach her, grab her around the waist, lift her to prevent her running. She squirmed and squealed like a stuck pig until he as good as dropped her onto her feet. The air escaped from her mouth in a rush. He lifted his hands to her shoulders. "You're safe. It's over." Whatever *it* was. "If not Wyck Hall, then the inn. It's closer."

She nodded her head. "The inn."

"Come then." He held out his hand, palm up, like a man approaching a terrified animal, waiting for it to take the scent, know there was no danger. After an eternity she took his outstretched hand. "Take my cloak. You're cold." She did as he bade and allowed him to lead her down the path toward the horse. The rain had stopped and a pale moon hung in the sky; at least now there was some light. His horse stood patiently waiting and he picked up the reins. "Let me help you up."

"I'll walk."

"No. You'll ride." Not prepared to argue any longer and fearful that she would collapse as the tension wore from her system, he scooped her up and deposited her on the saddle. Then before she had time to think, he leaped up behind her, encircling her with his arms as he grabbed the reins.

After a few moments she relaxed back against him, the fight seeping out of her, and the tears began.

Thankfully a light still showed in the windows of the inn. He suspected it probably burned all night, welcoming the wagons loaded with illegal French brandy. Tonight he'd welcome a large slug, as would Rose.

Once they'd entered the courtyard, he slipped from the horse and pulled Rose down. Her legs crumpled and he lifted her into his arms and made for the door. Loath to put her down, he kicked the door three times in succession, heavy and loud. The Judas window opened.

"Master Finneas!" The door swung open. "What's all this? Come in. Come in."

Heads lifted as he carried Rose into the taproom toward the fire.

"Move yourself for the lady." Old Bill booted a half-sleeping form out of the chair closest to the fire and Finneas lowered Rose into it.

The shaking had worsened and her face was colorless, her lips carrying the telltale bluish tinge of cyanosis. "Brandy."

"Here." A mug found its way into his hand.

"What's all this about, then? Not like you to be in trouble with a woman. Thought that was your brother's game."

Finneas shook his head, elbowed Bill Penhaligon out of the way, and held the pewter mug to Rose's mouth. The tip of her tongue moistened her lip and then she took a sip and coughed, sitting bolt upright, making the hood fall back from her head. She pushed the mug away as color seeped into her cheeks.

An audible gasp filled the room, then a heavy silence.

"'Tis young Jenifer."

"'T'aint. Never be."

Would it never end? Finneas tossed back the remainder of the brandy and held the mug out for more. "Her name is Rose. And you're close. She's Jenifer's daughter."

Chapter 22

CORNWALL, ENGLAND
1820

Rose blinked the room into focus and squinted through the haze of smoke and candle glow. Wizened faces, wrinkled brows, sweaty bodies, and above all, curiosity. She felt like a specimen under glass, no better than the poor mallangong the Royal Society had rejected.

"You say she's young Jenifer's daughter?"

"She's got the look of old Tomas about her."

"And Jenifer's eyes. Never forget those. Bold."

Finneas held the mug out again and she took it, gripping both hands tight around it to still the shaking. Lifting it to her lips, she took a sip, and another. Perhaps this liking for brandy was something she got from Mam.

"Her name is Rose Winton." Finneas stood with one hand reassuringly on the back of the dilapidated stuffed chair she sat in.

"So young Jenifer got herself married." The one they called Bill nodded and folded his arms with satisfaction. "Plenty who would have liked that job. Thought I might have a chance."

"You're old enough to be Jenifer's grandfather." A thin, lanky man with a beard smelling strangely of earth and dirt moved closer and peered into her face. "Always thought I'd have the pleasure."

Rose swallowed the last of the brandy and put the mug down on the table. She couldn't sit here and let them discuss Mam or her like they were Macarthur's fine Spanish merinos ready for breeding. And what about Finneas? Why was he just standing there letting them stare and point?

"And what're you doing here, lass?" The man with the brandy flagon squatted at her feet and filled up the mug. She shook her head. If she had any more the room would spin and the warm glow would toast her alive. She looked up at Finneas, hoping he would save her. As she'd warmed up, the memories had come crowding back. All she could see was the poor girl.

"Finneas." She struggled up out of the deep chair. "I have to talk to you. Now. Privately."

"Who's a lucky lad, then?"

Finneas lurched as someone dug him in the ribs. He nodded his head. "Do you have a private room we could use, Bill?"

"Wiv or wivout a bed?"

The color flew to her cheeks as raucous laughter filled the smoky room.

"Without will do just fine, preferably with a fire, unless you're ready to return to Wyck Hall, Rose."

She shook her head. Julian might be there. She knew now without a doubt she hadn't dreamed it. It was Julian she'd seen hovering over that poor dead girl. The thought chilled her blood; she never wanted to see him again.

She'd visit the barrow in her nightmares for the rest of her days, of that she had no doubt. She'd thought she'd die without having told

Finneas how much she appreciated his help and cared for him, without having achieved Pa's dreams, without fulfilling the trust he'd placed in her, without knowing Mam's story.

"Use the snug. There's a fire in there and the missus has taken to her bed."

"Thank you." Finneas held out his hand to her. "Come with me." He must have known the way because no one gave him any directions. She had to duck her head as they left the room and went down a darkened passageway. Darkness had never held any fear for her before, but now she clutched Finneas's hand and his fingers clasped hers in a reassuring squeeze. "It's just down here. Mind your head."

He pushed open the door on his right and led her into a small parlor. Two chairs sat on either side of a roaring fire and a sweet smell filled the room. "This is where Bill and his wife hide out when they've had enough of their customers." The room was warm and the chairs inviting. "Sit down and I'll get you something to drink. Are you hungry?"

"No." And she never wanted to touch another drop of brandy. "A cup of tea. I would love a cup of tea."

"I'll be right back."

A flutter of panic rose in her chest as the door closed behind him, but she leaned forward and spread out her palms to the fire and let the tranquility of the cozy room calm her. A pang of homesickness hit her. After the splendor of Grosvenor Square and the ancient majesty of Wyck Hall, this felt more like home than anywhere since she'd left New South Wales.

The warmth from the fire seeped into her blood and she slipped the cloak from her shoulders and rested back in the chair, her eyes drifting shut. And then it all returned.

Julian. The swirling black cape. The smell of blood and the girl. The girl sprawled on the stone slab. A hand landed on her shoulder. And her scream bubbled up and exploded, filling the tiny room with her anguish.

"Rose, Rose. Shh. It's all right, I'm here."

She tipped her head back and saw Finneas's concerned face hovering over her, his caring brown eyes nothing like the cold, hard obsidian chips of her brother. A long, quivering sigh eased between her lips.

"We have to talk. You have to tell me. I should have listened before."

She didn't want to talk. Wanted to bury all she'd seen deep within her, lock the door, and barricade it tight.

Finneas's warm fingers massaged her shoulder and she leaned back into his exquisite touch, half pain and half pleasure. Relief and so, so soothing.

"One step at a time. Tell me what you found in the barrow when we rode out on the moors this morning."

She tried to order her thoughts. This morning seemed a lifetime ago. Sitting and drawing the picture of Dozmary Pool. "I finished my picture and went to the barrow. There's a small chamber to the left. The sunlight comes in through the broken wall. I was looking at the walls. At home the blackfellas make their drawings on cave walls. I thought I might find some. Instead, I found an inscription." The words were etched in her mind as deeply as any carving, but she couldn't bring herself to utter them, as though by giving them voice she'd prove them true. "It had my mam's name and her birth date—and another date, February 2."

"Candlemas." Finneas's voice was hardly more than a whisper.

"Candlemas?" She'd never heard the word before.

"It's one of the dates on the old calendar. A celebration of sorts. Go on."

"That's all, really. I thought perhaps Mam wasn't Mam, that she'd died and someone else had taken her name." It sounded so foolish now spoken aloud in the warmth of this cozy little room with Finneas's comforting hand resting on her shoulder. "She lied to me about Pa, about Julian— Oh God, Julian."

"What about Julian?" Finneas's hand fell and he leaped to his feet, standing in front of her, peering down at her, all compassion wiped from his face.

"Nothing. I . . ." She couldn't say it. Julian was Finneas's brother and she was going to have to tell him that she saw Julian standing over the body of a dead girl. The shivering returned.

Finneas dropped to his knees in front of her. "I'm sorry I scared you." He picked up her hand and rubbed his thumb across her knuckles. "Tell me."

"I went back to the barrow. I wanted to record the inscription. To show it to you. I didn't think you believed me. I didn't do it. I have to do it before I forget." She rummaged in the pocket of the cloak.

"Leave it now. Tell me. We'll record it later. You won't forget."

No. She'd never forget.

"It was almost dark . . ." She couldn't do it. Couldn't put the horror into words. But she had to. "I saw a light, thought perhaps it was the brandy smugglers you'd talked about. It wasn't."

———

Anger and concern vied for pride of place. He had to force her to tell him, force the words from her before they grew in her mind, and selfishly, to validate his fears, suspicions that he'd never voiced, pushed away for lack of evidence.

"A man in a swirling black cape." Her voice quivered, barely above a whisper.

"And?" It couldn't have been Methenwyck. He could hardly lift himself from his bed, never mind make the journey to the barrow; his lack of sight alone would prevent him. Julian had taken his place, was responsible for the missing village girls.

"On the stone, on the stone . . ." She raised her hand to dash away her tears, then she lifted her head, the same look he'd seen when she faced the Royal Society: steely determination. She dragged in a steadying gulp of air. "There was a girl, naked, on the stone slab."

"There was no one else . . ." He'd seen no evidence of a body. Was she imagining it? Someone, Mrs. Pascoe perhaps, had filled her head with the local rumors.

"I saw her with my own eyes. I touched her. She was dead." Rose's voice strengthened. "No pulse. Her skin was cold to the touch."

His index finger and thumb rubbed together as he remembered the smell of death and the dark pool on the altar stone.

"Once again you don't believe me." She tossed back her corkscrew curls, her eyes blazing. "I don't invent things. I am an observer. I've been trained to watch and record the details. Pa taught me."

She was right. No hysterical woman. No passing flight of fancy. A trained scientist. Something he kept forgetting to take into account.

"He greeted me, told me I was welcome."

"Who was it?"

"I didn't recognize the voice; it was muffled by his cowl. Then he reached out and touched me." Her hand went to her neck. "When I saw his eyes, I recognized him." Her face paled. "It was Julian. He had a drop of blood here." She touched the corner of her lips. "He licked it away. I tried to run, but he brought me down. He put his arm around my neck and hugged me to him."

Compressed carotid artery. How would Julian know to do that? An inheritance gift from Methenwyck, perhaps. The bastard. "The next thing you were there, lifting me." She held her palms up in a gesture of defeat. "You know the rest."

He touched the delicate skin of her neck; there was no sign of bruising. How long had she lost consciousness? He tried to work out the time. How much time had Julian had to clean up his filthy work, and what had he intended to do with Rose? It didn't bear thinking about.

And Caroline knew. That's why she'd said, "Find Julian." Not Rose. He ran his hand over Rose's hair, smoothed it back from her face, then tucked his cloak tighter around her legs. "Try to rest. It will be different in the morning."

"Please don't leave me. I don't think I could bear to . . ." Her voice petered out.

"We both need some rest. Close your eyes."

He sat watching the rise and fall of her chest as her lashes fell like dark moons against the pallor of her cheeks, the movement of her eyes settling, her muscles relaxing, until she slept.

More than anything else he wanted to return to Wyck Hall, challenge Julian, and confront Methenwyck. Caroline held the key. She knew more than she admitted. What he'd seen as anxiety and frailness was no such thing. It was fear and some form of guilt. She'd picked her words carefully, oh so carefully. He drummed his fingers on the arm of the chair and Rose mumbled something and turned slightly.

He cast his mind back to his childhood, the pranks, enacted for generations, rites of passage. And the girls who were rumored to have vanished from the village, always at the change of season. He could no longer write it off as the unsubstantiated rumbles of a village that still marked the old calendar with May Day dances, Beltane fires, and harvest festivals. He'd wanted proof and now he had it. The rumors were in fact truth.

Easing himself out of the chair, he stepped lightly to the door and opened it a fraction. The noise from the taproom wafted down the hallway. He closed the door behind him and made his way toward the sounds, catching the words. *Trevan, old Tomas, Jenifer.* He slipped into the taproom and reached out a hand to Bill, inclined his head to the door.

"I need your help, Bill. I've left Rose asleep in the snug by the fire. I don't want her disturbed. Can your wife stay with her in case she wakes? I have business. I'll be back before daybreak." He reached into his pocket for some coins.

Bill stilled his hand. "Not necessary. Old times' sake. We owe it to the Trevans. Many a folk he fixed with those herbs of his, and young Jenifer too. She was a good girl. Never thought she'd stole nothing."

Finneas nodded. "Thank you. I'll be back as soon as I can." He headed for the stables.

His horse gave him a belligerent look as he slipped the bridle over its head and threw the saddle onto its back. "I know. I know. Too much for one night, but this can't wait."

With the moon full he gave the horse his head and took the track from the inn. The West Country mail coach slowed as their paths met and the driver lifted his hand in recognition, probably relieved he wasn't a lone highwayman out to try his luck, and then Finneas cut across the moor.

It couldn't have been much past ten when he arrived back at Wyck Hall, though all the lights were doused except for the kitchen. He left his horse in the stables and made his way through the scullery door.

Mrs. Pascoe sat at the table, a cup of tea in front of her, legs stretched out and her skirt up around her knees. She leaped up the moment she saw him. "Master Finneas! The mistress is waiting for you. Refused to go to bed until you got back. And where's young Rose? She's not . . ." Her face blanched.

"I'll go to Caroline immediately. She's in her sitting room?"

"No, downstairs. By the fire. Told me to douse the lamps. Sitting in the dark, she is."

"And Julian? Is he back?"

She gave a dismissive shrug, her mouth tilting down at the corners. "Not as I know, but that's as may be."

Caroline first. Rose was safe. Julian never set foot in the inn; that was way below his dignity. And even if he did, Finneas would like to see him get past Bill and his bunch of free traders. He pushed open the door and closed it behind him.

"Finneas, is that you?"

Caroline shot upright in the chair and onto her feet in one swift movement. How could he have believed she was sick? He had every intention of discovering the truth, even if it took all night.

"Have you spoken to Julian?" he asked.

"No. He returned and went straight up to see Methenwyck. What of Rose?"

"Rose is safe."

"Where is she?"

"She's . . ." He started and then stopped. If walls had ears, then houses held secrets, and he would not jeopardize Rose's safety. Not now. Not ever.

"Sit down, Caroline. It's time. I need to know the truth."

"The truth?" She sank back down onto the sofa, her hands wringing her ever-present handkerchief until it resembled a hangman's noose.

"Rose went to the barrow. Julian was there."

Every vestige of color drained from her face. "What happened?"

"That's what you are going to tell me. She's your niece, for God's sake, your own flesh and blood."

"As is Julian. My brother's child."

"They are both your brother's children. Tell me about Jenifer. What happened to her?"

"I can't. I've never spoken of it." She threw a panicked look over her shoulder. "Methenwyck." The name spilled from her lips like poison.

"What happened to Jenifer?"

"Nothing." Her hands tore at her handkerchief.

"What was her crime?

"She was innocent." Caroline lifted her hand and the square-cut emerald she always wore caught the light. "I am responsible. Mrs. Pascoe and I, we slipped the Methenwyck rose, wrapped in my handkerchief, into her grandfather's food parcel and told the constabulary she'd stolen it. I never believed they would sentence her to death."

"To death?"

"At Bodmin Court."

"But she's alive. In New South Wales. Rose is her daughter. Julian, her son."

"She was reprieved, her sentence transmuted to life. Never to return."

"Stop. Stop right there. You have to tell this to Rose. Not to me. She has to hear it. Why would you do that?"

"There was a good enough reason. Rose and Julian wouldn't exist but for my actions. I saved Jenifer."

"And sentenced her to a life of shame and lies."

She dropped her head, tears streaming down her face. "You don't understand."

"But I will, and so will Rose. Come with me. I'll take you to her."

"I can't. I can't leave here. I haven't, not since I was sure. Not since I knew for certain what he'd done. What will happen to Methenwyck? He's an old man, sick. Surely you as a physician should show some compassion."

Compassion! He had no compassion for Methenwyck. Not now. Not anymore. He owed him nothing—Caroline perhaps, not Methenwyck. That slate was wiped clean. And as for Julian . . . he would get nowhere near Rose again. He never should have brought Rose here. Never should have subjected her to the horrors she'd endured. He should have stayed with her in London, helped her achieve her aim. He slammed his palm against his forehead. "Methenwyck will come to no harm. Julian will see to that."

"It's late, dark, well past midnight. I am too frail."

Anything less frail he'd yet to see. Too disturbed, perhaps. "In that case we will wait until first light. I shall fetch you a blanket." He didn't trust her. Didn't trust her not to put Methenwyck and Julian first as she had always done, and he had no intention of confronting them until Rose was out of harm's way and back in London.

He returned with a blanket and draped it over Caroline's legs, locked the door, then stoked the fire and settled down to wait.

Much to his surprise, Mrs. Pascoe woke him stirring the fire and settling a pot of tea at his right hand. "No idea why you saw fit to lock the door. Had to use the servants' entry." She cocked her head to the small door behind the heavy curtains framing the portrait of Methenwyck.

So much for his precautions last night. Caroline might well have sneaked out and spoken with Methenwyck or Julian, but he doubted it. She still lay on the sofa, her head back against the cushions and her eyes closed. Whether she'd slept he had no idea, but she appeared drained. Perhaps he'd been a little less than kind when he'd dismissed her remarks about frailty. She was, after all, approaching old age. "Thank you, Mrs. Pascoe. I'll take care of the tea. Would you be kind enough to ask one of the stable hands to harness the buggy, please?"

"And where would you be going? 'Tis barely light."

"Just do as I ask."

The poor woman stood dumbfounded for a moment, then turned tail and scuttled back through the door behind the curtain. He poured a cup of tea, added several teaspoons of sugar, and took it to Caroline. Her eyes flashed open immediately. "Where are we going?"

"To see Rose."

"What time is it?" She struggled into a sitting position and took the tea.

"Early. I promised Rose I wouldn't leave, and I intend to be back before she wakes."

"In that case, perhaps . . ." She sipped at the tea and grimaced.

"No, Caroline. You are coming with me. Drink up and we'll be off."

Chapter 23

Sydney, Australia
1908

No matter which way Tamsin considered the situation, she couldn't see a way out. Mrs. Rushworth would sell the sketchbook. No one could prove it didn't belong to Mrs. Quinleaven. If only she'd had the opportunity to speak to her before she'd died. And more to the point, while she was in Wollombi, why hadn't she asked more questions? Mrs. Adcock surely would have had something to offer. She had on every other topic.

She crossed the foyer and pushed open the door to the tearoom. "Mrs. Williams? There you are. We have to return the sketchbook on Monday morning."

Mrs. Williams looked up. "Can't you talk her into donating it? After all, it was her mother's dying wish. Surely it wouldn't raise sufficient money to make a difference to her lifestyle. I would have thought the social prestige would be worth more."

"I'm almost a hundred percent certain I'd have no hope of convincing her. Especially now I know about Mr. Everdene's little game."

"Shaw?" Mrs. Williams's piercing currant eyes pinpointed her.

Damn, how had she managed to let that slip? She had intended to keep it to herself. Her face flushed the color of a beet every time she thought about the way he'd manipulated her.

"Shaw?" Mrs. Williams repeated, leaning across the table.

"Mr. Shaw Everdene is not only a solicitor; he's an antiquarian book collector. He has a house bursting at the seams with old tomes. And he intends to go into business. And Mrs. Rushworth wants him to sell the sketchbook."

"A bibliophile. Fascinating."

"I'm sorry?"

"Someone who loves books. Every one of us at the Library could be called bibliophiles. Mitchell certainly was."

"I know what a bibliophile is. I don't understand how a love of books can translate into a way to make money. Mitchell donated his collection."

"Tamsin, there are times when you can be thoroughly naive. You know very well people value books for many reasons, because of their contents or their physical characteristics; therefore there's bound to be a market for unusual and unique books—even in medieval times it was a lucrative business. It's becoming quite the thing with so many of the larger estates being sold off and with the upswing in interest in Australian history."

"But he lied to me."

"Are you sure that's the case? He seems like such a nice man."

"Why else would he keep harping on about the book's value? It was his intention all along and he simply used me, us, the Library, as a way to guarantee the authenticity."

"We can compare the paper and the ink to other manuscripts of a similar date, match the handwriting with Winton's letters . . . Other than that, unless they've discovered some method to scientifically test and date the paper and paint, there's not much more we can do, simply make an educated guess and pass it over to the people at the Mitchell for their opinion. Personally, I have no doubt."

In that case the only thing she could do was to have one more stab at finding out how it came into Mrs. Quinleaven's possession. Prove without a doubt the rightful owner. "That's it. I've made up my mind. I'm going back to Wollombi. I should have done it before. Ask around and see if I can find out any more about Mrs. Quinleaven. How she came by the book. You've still got her letter, haven't you? If I can prove the sketchbook belonged to Mr. Kelly and that his intention was to donate it, perhaps the solicitors will support the case." Solicitors! Ha! Not if they were as crooked as Shaw Everdene. But it was worth a try. "There was something Mrs. Rushworth said that's been ringing bells in my head."

"What was that?"

"Actually, it was more what she didn't say. She didn't want to talk about her mother, said they were estranged. I think that's one of the reasons I want to make sure the sketchbook goes where it belongs. I feel in some peculiar way Mrs. Rushworth doesn't deserve it. Doesn't value it. Why would she if it reminds her of a mother she didn't like?" Her chest seemed hollow—she knew how easy it was to hold a grudge against a mother, even a father, especially if you felt deserted.

"I'll leave this morning if you can do without me; I can be there before dark. The Family Hotel is very comfortable. Do you mind giving me Mrs. Quinleaven's letter?"

Two hours later Tamsin was weaving her way, with a change of clothes in her satchel and the letter from Mrs. Quinleaven tucked inside her notebook, through the crowds at St. Leonards station to pick up the Northern-line train. It wouldn't be as fast as the Brisbane Express, but she'd make it well before nightfall, and it would give her time to think everything through, although it would be nowhere near as much fun as driving with Shaw. Damn him. She'd die rather than admit it, but she'd fallen for him hook, line, and sinker, with his attentiveness and their *common interests*.

Blah! She kicked out with her booted foot against the seat opposite and glared out of the window at the mighty Hawkesbury, wishing she could throw all the questions and inconsistencies into the deep water and start afresh.

By the time the shadows lengthened, she was back in Wollombi. Arriving in the town sent a surge of delight through her. Just climbing out of the mail coach and seeing the familiar buildings made her feel more at home than anywhere she'd lived before.

She crossed the road and walked down to the Family Hotel at a brisk pace.

"Well, fancy seeing you again."

"Hello, Mrs. Adcock. I was wondering if you had a room for the night."

"That we do. Been mighty quiet around here. Good to see your smiling face again. Take your bag up to your room. I'll be in the front parlor. Would you be wanting something to eat?"

"I'd love something. I missed out on lunch because I was on the train."

"Got a nice piece of pork pie. How does that sound?"

Tamsin's stomach rumbled in response as she trundled up the stairs to her room. She took the daguerreotype from the tin and pushed it into the pocket of her skirt, and by the time she was downstairs, Mrs. Adcock had the table set and a mouthwatering slice of pork pie and chutney waiting. There was a lot to be said for country living.

"Sit yourself down, and if you don't mind, I'll be joining you. Due for a break before the locals arrive."

Tamsin slipped onto the bench seat and thanked her lucky stars. Just what she wanted and without having to ask.

"Hot and strong with one sugar, if I remember right."

Hopefully there'd be a lot more she could remember. "Thank you. Yes."

"Now, where's that nice young man of yours? Thought you two seemed like a match made in heaven racing off in that lovely motor car."

Thankful for the excuse the mouthful of pork pie offered, Tamsin didn't respond. Shaw Everdene could be in Timbuktu for all she cared—as far away from her and Winton's sketchbook as she could keep him. He wasn't getting his money-grubbing little hands on it. Over her dead body.

"And what brings you back here? Not that we're unhappy to see you. Did you find out all about the drawing book, then? My Bert carried on like you two had some sort of pact with the devil and now he can't stop talking about them T Fords. Reckons there's a chap in Maitland who puts them together, just up the road apiece, and he didn't even know. Got some lunatic idea about buying a delivery van."

Tamsin licked the crumbs of pastry from the corners of her mouth and picked up her cup and inhaled. Somewhere along the line she'd come to prefer this strong sweet tea to the more perfumed blend Mrs. Williams offered. "I was wondering if you could tell me a little more about Mrs. Quinleaven and have a look at this." She pulled the wrapped daguerreotype out of her pocket and laid it on the table.

Mrs. Adcock cast her eye over the small parcel, then fussed around with her pinny, picked up her cup, and took another sip before giving a loud sigh. "I'm not one to gossip, as you very well know, so it'd have to be between you and me like."

"Absolutely," Tamsin fired back. "You'd be helping the country, you know. It's really important that early Australian works are recognized, especially since Federation."

That made Mrs. Adcock sit up straighter. Tamsin schooled the smile tweaking the corner of her lips.

"I wondered if you'd take a look at this and see if you recognize anyone." Tamsin unwrapped the tiny daguerreotype.

Mrs. Adcock watched her every move, her head tipped to one side like an inquisitive magpie. "Oh, it's one of them old pictures." Mrs. Adcock held out her hand.

With a strange reluctance Tamsin handed it across the table. "Try not to touch the glass because it's quite damaged. Just hold it on the frame."

Mrs. Adcock tipped it from side to side, trying to get the light in the right place. A few silent seconds ticked past.

"Look at them dresses—I'm glad we aren't expected to get around in stuff like that and the whalebone corsets we used to wear. Had one meself when I married Mr. Adcock, sucked me in a right treat." She put the daguerreotype down on the table with a bang and Tamsin snatched it back while Mrs. Adcock spread her hands on her ample hips. "Believe it or not, in those days I was a sylphlike thing. Me waist was just nineteen inches once they pulled those stays tight—mind you, I couldn't breathe, not even enough puff to do me wedding dance. Just as well because Mr. Adcock, he's no dancer, two left feet, and my shoes, they were like slippers, not like those boots of yours."

Tamsin tucked her feet under her chair. "Do you think this might be Mrs. Quinleaven?" She held the daguerreotype up to the light from the window in an attempt to guide the conversation away from Mrs. Adcock's nuptial reminiscences.

"Can't really tell. That's a long time ago. Mind you, she'd have been pushing seventy when she died. That's what I meant about my wedding dress. We all change, don't we?"

"Yes, I suppose we do." Now what? She'd harbored some vain hope that Mrs. Adcock would say, *Oh yes, that's Mrs. Quinleaven's mother with her two daughters and her husband . . .* Chance would be a fine thing.

"And it's pretty scratched too. Wouldn't even know that those two were girls but for their clothes; faces are as good as gone." Mrs. Adcock screwed up her nose, took back the daguerreotype, and twisted it to the light. "Looks as though it could be round here. Same trees. The weeping trees down by the brook just this side of Cunneens Bridge. There's that nice cleared spot people like to use for picnics, where the old church used to be. Why don't you ask Gayadin?"

"The old lady in the cemetery?"

"She's lived round here all her life, still got the old cottage on the brook—down the road and take the path just before the bridge. Everyone tried to get her to move because of the floods, but she won't hear a word of it. Just hoicks everything out and lets it dry, sweeps out the mud, and starts again."

"That's a wonderful idea." Out of the window the sun was disappearing behind the hills. "It's probably getting a bit late now."

"You'll be all right so long as you don't hang around. And Gayadin's often up at the cemetery this time of the evening." Mrs. Adcock held out the daguerreotype. "Not sure how good her eyesight is these days, but you never know."

Tamsin slipped the picture into her skirt pocket and bolted for the door. The light was fading and she didn't fancy the cemetery after dark. Throwing a thank-you over her shoulder, she ran up the road. Nothing had changed since her last visit; in fact, she doubted much had changed since the cemetery had opened its gates except for an increase in the number of headstones. She slipped inside and turned to her left, making straight for Mrs. Quinleaven's grave. Already someone—she doubted it would have been Mrs. Rushworth—had erected a simple headstone to match Kelly's. Just her name, Emily Quinleaven, and her dates. A bunch of flowers lay across the grave; not today's, maybe yesterday's. It would depend how often Gayadin visited.

With a sigh she scanned the rest of the cemetery looking for Gayadin's stooped figure, and when a hand touched her arm, the blood rushed from her head and her feet almost went from under her.

"You back."

Tamsin rested the palm of her hand flat against her chest, hoping to slow the thunderous thumping of her heart. Mrs. Adcock's warnings had affected her more than she imagined. "Hello, Gayadin. Shall I put the flowers down for you?" She took the posy from Gayadin's grasp and knelt down, picking up the dead flowers and laying the fresh ones neatly across the dry earth, then she straightened up. "I wondered if I could show you something. Maybe you can tell me about it." She pulled the daguerreotype from her pocket and unwrapped it.

Gayadin's arthritic fingers closed compulsively around the two-inch square of glass and Tamsin wanted to tug it away, frightened it might shatter. Gayadin took a very brief look at it, then smoothed the pad of her thumb over the glass, tears pooling in her eyes. "We blackfellas don't hold with pictures of people past. We remember our stories. Don't need pictures. Don't need writing it down." She handed the daguerreotype back. "This here—this my story." She tapped her finger against her forehead.

Tamsin's hopes plummeted. Gayadin hadn't even bothered to study the image.

"That's me there with Jane and Mam and Pa."

Who was Jane? Not Mrs. Quinleaven. She was Emily. It hadn't crossed her mind that the old Aboriginal woman might be related to the Kelly household. It would account for why she tended the graves.

Tamsin racked her brain. "So is this Mrs. Quinleaven?" It couldn't be—the clothes alone pegged the era, never mind the style and date of the daguerreotype. It had to have been taken in the late 1840s.

"Nah! That's not her—that's Jane and Mam and Pa. I told you. Not Mrs. Quinleaven. This here's her." She sank down onto the grass and patted the dirt that had already begun to settle.

"That's why I stay down by the brook, with the mallangong girl. I can't leave. Don't know what'll happen after me. No one left after me." She sniffed and handed back the daguerreotype before wiping her nose on the sleeve of her tattered jacket.

"My Yukri. She there when the English Rose came. We blackfellas, we called her the mallangong girl. Her story is mine—her mam, a beautiful young duck, tricked by the water rat and the mallangong girl was born. That there the mallangong girl." She pointed at the picture in Tamsin's hand. "Long time ago now. Floodwater took my Jane just like it takes the mallangong." Gayadin sniffed and shook her head.

Tamsin's brain whirled as she tried to make sense of the old woman's words. She looked again at the daguerreotype, but the light had faded and only ghostly shadows glowed beneath the scratched glass.

"Tomorrow I show you mallangong girl. Come my place."

Tomorrow.

Tamsin hardly slept a wink; she tossed and turned as the moon rose and sank, and then finally, when the first gray streaks of dawn lit the sky, she slipped from her bed and got dressed, pulling her jacket tight and buttoning it against the early morning chill. As a last-minute thought she opened the tin and pulled out the daguerreotype. She'd take it with her. If Gayadin forgot what she'd told her last night, it might help her remember, though the old woman seemed to have a tight grasp on the story. *Her story*. She tucked the daguerreotype into her pocket, then tiptoed down the stairs and let herself out of the parlor door.

"Down the road and take the path just before the bridge." Mrs. Adcock's words hummed through her mind as she strode along the road. Not as far as the driveway to Mrs. Quinleaven's house. A path branched off to the right, then followed a small track along the edge of the brook.

Gayadin was waiting for her, her clawed fingers pulling a tattered shawl tight around her shoulders. "Down here. Not so bad. Can't keep it all tidy no more."

The damp grass clung to her skirt, soaking her stockings as she followed Gayadin down through what might have been an old gate.

"Is this where you live?"

Gayadin stopped and pointed ahead to a vacant patch of grass, unkempt, full of tiny purple and pink orchids, kangaroo grass, and the purple vine of the native lilac crowding the ground, the wattles' almond scent filling the air.

"The old church here. Not up there." She frowned and waved her hand in the direction of the town. "Meant to be here. Not moved up there." She pursed her lips and let out a sigh of frustration.

Something caught in Tamsin's throat and the same prickle of fingers walked her spine as they had when she'd first seen the sketchbook. "We leave 'em here. They like it here. Where the mallangong play. Close by their house." She pointed over the brook and Tamsin craned her head. Through the yellow puffs on the wattles she could make out the three chimneys standing proud.

"They like that. Mallangong girl where she like to be, with her family."

Tamsin pushed through the tall grass until she reached a cleared patch, neatly trimmed, and four small, weathered headstones. She knelt down on the damp ground and ran her fingers over the etched words: *Charles Winton, Father of My Heart 1764–1840.*

She'd found him!

Charles Winton. And he'd lived all that time. Not died when the correspondence with Banks ended, all those long years after the dates in his sketchbook. Why had he stopped working? What had brought him to this place so far from Agnes Banks?

Crawling on her hands and knees, her heart pumping, she reached for the next: *Jenifer Trevan 1772–1842, Loving Granddaughter of Granfer Tomas Trevan.* Jenifer Trevan, the epitaph on the piece of cartridge paper in the tin. She hadn't died in 1788. Far from it.

"Mallangong girl's mam."

Tamsin turned to Gayadin, tears pouring down her cheeks.

"No crying. She happy now. Her girl, she came back. See here?"

Gayadin moved to the next headstone. "And this one here, the mallangong girl."

Tears blurred her eyes as she turned to the next two headstones.

Rose Methenwyck 1800–1865 and *Finneas Methenwyck 1794–1860.* "He doctor. He good, very clever man. He look after my people when the smallpox come."

Her heart picked up a beat or two. "Gayadin. Tell me—in the picture. That's Rose and her husband, Finneas, and you and Jane."

"You right. My Jane. We sisters. Not blood sisters." She rested her gnarled hand on her scrawny chest. "Heart sisters."

Now the blood was pumping so fast she could hardly see straight. "Who did Jane marry?"

"Why, Mr. Kelly. I told you that. My Jane, the floodwaters took her. She got no resting place."

Jane Kelly. Jane Methenwyck. Rose and Finneas's daughter. Tamsin plopped down on the ground. It couldn't be the case. She was jumping to conclusions. Five years in the strict environment of the Library had taught her not to do that. And there was still Mrs. Quinleaven. "Gayadin, tell me about Mrs. Quinleaven."

The old woman shrugged her shoulders, making her shawl slip down her arms. "She come after my Jane. Sad, sad lady. Her husband up and gone. Mr. Kelly, he don't want me there. Says I remind him too much of his Jane. That when I come here." She gestured to the little cottage tucked on the banks of the river. "Mrs. Quinleaven his housekeeper, many, many years, and his friend. They talk and talk, read them books in that study."

"But they didn't marry?"

"No. Friends, not lovers. Mr. Kelly, he just love my Jane. We all love my Jane. You don't listen to that gossiping. Just friends."

And who would believe that in a small town? No one. A widow and his housekeeper under one roof. She could just see Mrs. Rushworth having to live down her mother's indiscretion. Which brought her straight back to the sketchbook. Perhaps Mrs. Quinleaven had made a promise to Mr. Kelly to see the sketchbook where it belonged. Perhaps he recognized the importance of it; maybe he'd made a promise to Jane. Damn Shaw Everdene and Mrs. Rushworth. And why, oh why, hadn't Mr. Kelly put anything in writing—something that would stand up in court, some legal document?

"You got that picture?"

The man was a solicitor, for goodness' sake. Why was there nothing in his will? "I beg your pardon?"

"You got that picture of my Jane?"

Tamsin burrowed in her pocket and pulled out the daguerreotype, unwrapped it, and handed it to Gayadin.

"You got her look." Gayadin didn't look at the picture, just held it out in front of her like a mirror.

"Whose look?"

"Mallangong girl. Rose."

Tamsin pulled her spectacles from her pocket and rammed them onto her nose and then snatched the daguerreotype from Gayadin's fingers. The woman had light hair, messy, curly, as though it wouldn't do what it was told, but fair. Hers was black as black.

"She's got your nose. Pointy. Way you hold it up like you smelling the air."

She lifted her head, realized what she was doing, and dropped it again to look at the picture.

"And your eyes."

Maybe. Maybe not. There was no way to tell from the daguerreotype. Rose had very heavy eyebrows. Tamsin knew all about those. Spent hours turning them into something that resembled the high, curved arches all the girls favored now in a vain attempt to look modern. But the expression on the woman's face spoke of laughter and contentment. Maybe her hair was gray, not fair. "Were they happy?"

"We all happy, even after Mam and Pa gone, very happy till the flood come."

A great wave of exhaustion turned Tamsin's bones to jelly and she sank down into the grass, her back resting against Rose's headstone. The stone was rough but not cold, almost warm. The sun had risen and the mist had cleared. Tears burned her throat.

"Tell me your story, Gayadin. Right from the beginning, please."

The old woman lowered herself to the ground with a groan, picked a series of long strands of grass, and laid them in her lap, her fingers moving unexpectedly fast as she plaited the strands together as though trying to remember, trying to get her thoughts in order.

"I told you. That sneaky water rat, he mated with beautiful duck and the mallangong girl, she born."

She didn't want some legend; she wanted fact. Who else was there to tell her? Patience. She had to be patient. "And Rose was the mallangong girl."

Gayadin grunted. "Yukri, she there, she help. The water rat, he took Rose's brother, Julian, across the water. Then the mallangong girl came. Everyone love her, just like my Jane. Jenifer sad, always sad for her boy, but Rose, she had her pa."

"Who was the mallangong girl's father?"

"Why, the water rat. You not listening?"

"But she's Rose Winton."

"Father of my heart. See, it says it there." She stabbed at Charles Winton's headstone. "She daughter of his heart, not his blood. Same like Jane and me. Heart sisters, not blood sisters. You going to listen more now?"

Tamsin nodded. She still didn't understand it all, needed time to put it together. What she wouldn't give for a piece of paper. She'd start with Jenifer Trevan.

"My mam and pa, they showed Mr. Charles the mallangong Yellow-Mundee speared. He sent it across the water to the King and made pictures, lots of pictures for the King. They showed him where the mallangong live, where she make her house, where she keep her babies. Then the old man mallangong came. He angry. He get Charles real bad. He sick, so sick."

"He was spurred?"

"Yep. Then mallangong girl, she takes his book to the King, but he don't want it. She comes back; she brings the doctor." Gayadin turned and lifted her head toward Finneas's headstone. "He good man—he saved me from the white man's disease." She fingered the smallpox pits covering her face. "We came, all of us, to his new place. Here."

Her hand swept in an arch. "Too long now. My man, he and the doctor work hard. He whitefella. Lovely whitefella. He dead too, and my babies. Only me now."

Tamsin took the plaited grass strand Gayadin held out.

"All tied up now. You know. Now you take care of them. They your family."

How she'd like that to be.

"You take off that boot. I show you."

"What?"

"Take off that boot."

"No!" She wasn't taking off her boot, not for Gayadin, not for anyone. She hated her feet, never looked at them unless she had to.

"You take it off. Show me."

Heat filled her face. How did the old woman know? She unlaced her right boot and slipped out her foot, then slowly, very slowly, slid down her soggy stocking.

Gayadin's cold hand clasped her foot and pulled the stocking free. "See here, the web here." She parted Tamsin's second toe and her third and ran her finger over the stretched webbed skin that she hated so much. "The beautiful duck's foot. My Jane, she had it, and her mam, Rose. That's why we called her mallangong girl."

Chapter 24

CORNWALL, ENGLAND
1820

A great gulp of icy air shocked Rose to wakefulness, her jaw still locked tight and her head cocked to one side, ears pricked for footsteps, for chanting. She inhaled, searching for the scent of decay, cold stale air, and the coppery tang of blood. She snapped her eyes open, leaving the nightmare behind her, wiping away the tendrils of fear that seized her in their relentless grasp.

Where was Finneas? He had promised he'd stay. She pushed back the cloak covering her. The metal hinges keened as the door swung open and he was there; in two strides he covered the space between them and clasped her in his arms.

"You promised me you wouldn't leave."

"You haven't been alone and I'm here now." He readjusted the cloak over her lap. "I've brought someone to speak to you."

Her heart stopped when a figure stepped into the room and threw back her hood.

Lady Methenwyck!

She blinked her eyes clear, hand pressed to her breast, willing her heart to pump.

"Sit down." Finneas indicated the chair opposite her and bent to throw some more logs on the fire while an old woman shuffled in with a tray of cups and a pot of tea.

"Thank you, Mrs. Penhaligon."

She put the tray down on the table, almost tripping over her skirts in an attempt to curtsy to Caroline. "And thank you for caring for Rose."

Caring for her? He had left her in the care of this old woman. How long had he been gone? "What time is it?"

"It's morning. Mrs. Penhaligon stayed with you while you slept." He threw back the heavy curtains, allowing the frail morning light to filter into the room.

She'd slept all night. It must have been the brandy. And what was Lady Methenwyck doing here? "I don't understand."

"You will. Sit tight." Finneas sat down on the arm of her chair and took her hand in his, warm and soothing. "Caroline, it's time."

Lady Methenwyck uttered a pitiful moan. "I would tell this to Jenifer, but I cannot, so you must take my words to her, and my apologies. I thought I was acting for the best."

Whatever was she talking about? She opened her mouth and Finneas squeezed her hand, silencing her.

"Your mother, Jenifer, was a scullery maid at Wyck Hall, and a very good one. Everyone loved her, especially as she had inherited her grandfather's proficiency and she took care of the herb garden. She had a skill with healing, with tinctures and poultices."

Rose felt her heart settle, some kind of validation. This was Mam as she knew her. Not some surrogate, as the scratchings in the barrow had led her to fear. Jenifer *was* Mam.

"I had tried for many years to provide Lord Methenwyck with an heir, but I couldn't hold a child. Each time I became sicker; but for Jenifer's herbs I would have died more times than I care to remember. I think perhaps I did a little with every child I lost. She came to my aid time and time again.

"On the night before Candlemas, with thirteen guests, their horses, and servants to attend to, poor Mrs. Pascoe and the staff were run off their feet. It was very late when Jenifer left to go home. As she crossed the moor, a storm came up. She took shelter in the barrow."

A cold tremor whisked its way across Rose's flesh. Her feet had known the path, not because she'd walked it before, but because Mam had. Some kind of knowledge passed down to her.

"She witnessed something . . ."

Goose bumps flecked Rose's skin. She didn't need to hear what came next; she knew, with a deep abiding certainty, that it wasn't only the path she'd shared with Mam. She pushed Finneas's hand away and sat up a little straighter in the chair, her heart galloping just as it had when she'd followed the flickering light into the barrow.

"Thirty years ago Lord Methenwyck was still an active man with certain appetites." A sting of color rose to Caroline's cheeks and she twisted her handkerchief. "I could not fulfill his needs." She cleared her throat. "A primitive, carnal need I could never satisfy. When Jenifer stumbled into the barrow, he marked her for his pleasure."

The bitter taste of bile filled Rose's mouth and a picture of Mam spread-eagled like the girl on the stone filled her vision, hair cascading like a waterfall, skin lilac in the guttering candlelight.

"He locked her in the small room off the central chamber and left her. She didn't expect to survive."

Rose clutched at Finneas's jacket sleeve, searching for some comfort in the rough wool. Mam expected to die. *February 2, 1788.*

"Continue, Caroline." Finneas sounded so harsh, his back ramrod straight, his fists bunched.

Lady Methenwyck lifted her face, dabbed her eyes with her crumpled handkerchief, and uttered a mournful sigh. "When Jenifer didn't turn up for work the next day, Mrs. Pascoe and I feared the worst. We found her, against all odds, alive. I told her to flee, offered her money. She wouldn't leave her granfer. He was too sick to move. I insisted she should stay away from Wyck Hall. Not to come back. I had to keep her from Lord Methenwyck. He would have taken her as he took the others." A strangled sob slipped between Lady Methenwyck's lips and she sank back in the chair.

Finneas leaped to his feet. "Took the others?"

With a nod of her head, Lady Methenwyck acknowledged the awful truth. "Yes, like the others. Sacrificed to his evil whims."

"Why did no one stop him? Why didn't you?"

She shrugged her shoulders. "He is my husband."

"What did you do?" Rose spat the words. She didn't want to know why. Not now, not yet. She wanted to know what had happened to Mam. Test the misbeliefs that had shaped her life, hear the story Mam had never spoken.

"I had to save Jenifer—no matter what she wanted, I had to get her away. She'd saved my life, and I owed her her own. I'd turned a blind eye in the past. I couldn't make that mistake again."

Finneas sank back onto the arm of her chair. "Was my mother one of those girls?" He didn't give her the opportunity to respond. "That's why you took me in, from the Poor House, in a vain attempt to atone for your husband's sins."

Rose clutched at Finneas's hand; his fingers tightened.

"I put the Methenwyck rose into a handkerchief in a parcel of food Mrs. Pascoe regularly gave Jenifer for her granfer. Once she had left, I sent for the constabulary saying she had stolen the ring. They arrested her and took her to Bodmin. I mistakenly believed she would be sentenced to transportation, far better than to be sacrificed to Lord Methenwyck's perversions. But he does not like to be thwarted. He gave evidence, and she was sentenced to hang."

"Thwarted, be damned! The Methenwyck rose is priceless. You must have known she'd hang."

This woman had sentenced Mam to death as surely as if she'd put the noose around her neck. Rose's nails bit into the palms of her hands. She wanted nothing more than to beat her within an inch of her life. "Did she hang?" She had to know, had to know if this Jenifer was her mam or yet another deception that would upend her reality.

"No."

The air whistled out between Rose's lips as she waited for Lady Methenwyck to continue.

"Her sentence was transmuted along with hundreds of others when King George recovered from a bout of madness. However, she was transported for the term of her natural life, not for the seven years I'd imagined." The woman at least had the grace to lower her gaze. "It was the only way I could get her away from Methenwyck. Don't you understand? It was Candlemas."

"The hunting parties." Finneas leaped to his feet. "The rumors were true, only not the hogwash about ghosts and the ancients returning to claim their sacrifices. It was Methenwyck. And you protected him."

"What else could I do? Bring shame on the family? And it wasn't only Methenwyck. His friends and the people who went out with him were powerful men of government, of business. Men who were in a position to manipulate the courts, cover up the deaths, indulge their passions. Jenifer would have died."

"And yet you stayed here with him, a murdering degenerate."

"What else could I do? A woman alone . . ." Her voice trailed off. "Jenifer saved my life, not once, not twice, more times than I care to remember. Every time he beat me, every time I lost my baby." Caroline's hands covered her barren belly in a futile gesture of protection.

"And you never thought to admit this. Have Jenifer's name cleared. You let her live her life in exile, carrying the knowledge she was unfairly sentenced."

Lady Methenwyck raised her head, her eyes sharp pinpricks in the dimly lit room. "She at least had a life to live. But for my ill-conceived actions, she would have become just another sacrifice."

Something akin to a growl slipped from Finneas's lips. "Couldn't you have done something for her, anything to make her life easier?"

Caroline squared her shoulders. "I did. I wrote to my brother, Richard."

"My father." The words slipped out, reminding Rose that this woman, this woman whose story made her flesh crawl, was also her aunt.

"Richard had traveled with the First Fleet to New South Wales. I wrote to him asking him to look out for Jenifer. Told him she was from Cornwall."

"And he took her to his bed, despite the fact he was a married man." Finneas shook his head.

"Life in the early days of the colony was different. No one knew what lay in store."

Finneas's groan silenced Lady Methenwyck, and the dawning realization made Rose's heart race. Julian, her brother, was no different from Lord Methenwyck. The glittering drop of blood in the corner of his mouth, the greed in his eyes when he'd stared at her.

She could have become the girl on the stone, as easily as Mam might have, as Finneas's mother had.

Rose stared at the hunched woman wringing and twisting the sodden handkerchief in her hands, hardly the picture of a woman who'd played God. Who'd cut out Mam's heart yet at the same time saved her from a certain death.

"I've spent a lifetime attempting to atone for my husband's sins. I was young when I married him. I imagined myself in love. He cut such a dashing figure astride his gray stallion. He wanted sons, and I wanted nothing more than to provide them for him.

"I failed, and for that he could never forgive me." She raised her hands in some sort of futile gesture. "Time and time again, always at the same time of year, girls would vanish. Every Sabbat. Candlemas, Midsummer, the spring and autumn equinoxes. I feared for you, Rose. So like my poor Jenifer."

"But Methenwyck is confined to his bed, as good as blind, unable to move . . ." Finneas's voice trailed off. He ran his fingers through his hair, closed his eyes as he finally accepted the reality. "So Julian became heir not only to the lands and title but also to Methenwyck's diabolical perversions."

"At first I didn't realize, didn't understand why he would seem to recover, seem more alert; then I put it down to Julian's appearance . . . until the day I tied the two together."

"And knew that Julian had stepped into his father's boots."

"Not his father. His true father—your father, Rose—my brother, was a good man."

Rose raised an eyebrow. How could this woman excuse these men? "A good man would not bribe a woman with promises he couldn't keep, then take her child from her."

"A good man who fell in love, made a mistake, and thought he could have everything. It wasn't so unusual in those days for a married man to take a woman from the lower classes while he was away. Many men in higher positions than Richard did just that. Men whose English wives were more accommodating than Richard's."

"So my mother's sentencing was a hoax." She used the word with care. It brought back thoughts of Pa. She'd set out for England determined to upend the misconceptions about the mallangong; instead, she'd stumbled upon a deliberately fabricated falsehood, more intricate than anything the Royal Society could lay at Pa's feet.

Finneas gazed down at Rose. He'd expected her to be a sobbing mess—instead, a fierce light shone in her eyes, as though she now saw her way clear. Despite her ordeal in the barrow and Caroline's dreadful confession, she seemed to have recovered.

"I intend to return to London and have my mother's name cleared. If necessary, I shall enlist Sir Joseph's assistance."

Caroline choked back a sob. "You can't do that. What will happen to Methenwyck and Julian?"

"I don't honestly know, nor do I care."

He had to hand it to the girl—she lacked nothing, especially not courage. "We could, of course, facilitate the whole proceedings if you accompanied Rose to London," he said to Caroline.

"To London?"

"Yes, to London. Rose cannot return to Wyck Hall. Surely you agree with me."

"I do. Yes, I do, but . . ."

"Caroline, it would give you the opportunity to present your case in the most favorable light and secure an Absolute Pardon for Jenifer. It's for the best and the very least you can do. I shall go and have a word with Bill and find out the next available seats on the mail coach."

Leaving Caroline and Rose in the snug, he strolled down the hallway to the taproom. He wanted seats this afternoon, if not sooner. The quicker Rose was out of Julian's reach, the happier he'd be. Once they'd left for London he'd return to Wyck Hall and take Julian and Methenwyck to task. They would stand trial. He might not be able to bring back his mother or the girls who had perished, but their incarceration would be a fitting retribution, and if nothing else it would ensure Rose's and Caroline's safety.

"Bill, any idea if there are seats on this afternoon's mail coach?"

"Give us a tick. Got a list here somewhere." He rummaged under the counter and pulled out a dog-eared piece of paper. "No one getting on 'ere, and four leaving. There're carriage seats. Going back to London, are you?"

"Seems like the best idea. Book all four for me, please. We require privacy."

"Done."

"And would you ask Mrs. Penhaligon if we could impose on her good nature and avail ourselves of some of her delicious pasties, some tea, and some cider? Thank you."

With a determined step he returned to the snug, where he could have cut the atmosphere with a scalpel. Both Caroline and Rose were staring into space, lost in their thoughts. Rose chewing her lip as she always did when she was worried, Caroline wringing her sodden handkerchief.

"I have booked four seats on this afternoon's mail coach. Does that suit?"

Rose nodded, then a frown marred the smooth skin of her forehead. "It does, but I have to ask you to do one thing for me."

Only one thing. He could think of many things he would ask her in a similar situation. "And what is that?"

"My carpetbag. The mallangong and the sketchbook. I will need them before I see Sir Joseph and they are at Wyck Hall."

She'd played right into his hands. Given him the perfect opportunity. "In that case I shall return to Wyck Hall and collect them. I shall bring your trunk and my bag as well. Caroline, you have everything you need?"

She nodded absently. "I have clothes in London. You'll miss the coach. It leaves in two hours."

"I shall take the next coach, be right behind you. Take rooms at the New London Inn at Exeter, and I'll join you there." After he'd confronted Methenwyck and Julian. If it was the last thing he did, he'd ensure these appalling revelries were brought to an end and the two of them faced justice. Rose had made no mention of anyone other than Julian. Perhaps the days of the hunting parties were over and only Methenwyck and his heir clung to the old traditions. "Now let's see if we can find something to eat before I see you onto the coach."

He stood up and opened the door just in time to help Mrs. Penhaligon into the room with a tray laden with her mouthwatering pasties.

"Here you are, Mr. Finneas, and I brought a copy of the *Cornwall Advertiser* with me. Thought you might like something to read to pass the time. Take it with you on the coach if you like."

"Would you like me to serve you, Caroline, Rose?"

"Just tea for me." Caroline waved her hand at him. "But without the ladle of sugar this time."

Rose stood and walked to his side. "Are you sure this is a good idea? No harm would come if we waited until tomorrow's coach. I don't want to go back to Wyck Hall, but I'm happy to stay here. I can't possibly leave Pa's sketchbook."

"Everything will be fine. Trust me, I shall take great care of your possessions. You remember the New London Inn, don't you? We stopped there on our way here." He put two pasties on a plate and handed it to her. "Why don't you sit here at the table?" He slid the tray across the table and the headline on the newspaper screamed at him:

BRITISH NATURALIST, BOTANIST, AND
PATRON OF THE NATURAL SCIENCES
SIR JOSEPH BANKS DEAD.

A strangled gasp whistled between his lips and he folded the paper in half. This was the last thing Rose needed today.

He wasn't quick enough. She was onto him faster than the shot he'd like to put in Julian's head.

"Give it to me." She slumped down in the chair and pushed away the plate of pasties, her eyes scanning the small, smudged print.

"What is it?" Caroline peeled herself out of the chair and peered over her shoulder. "I see. That's going to impede your plans somewhat." He'd swear he saw a glimmer of relief in her eyes. "Perhaps returning to London is not the most appropriate course of action."

"Of course it is." Rose stood. "I'm not giving up now, not even if I have to crawl on my hands and knees to the King himself. I will get Pa's work recognized and I will have Mam's name cleared." Her eyes flashed, no longer the lovely warm walnut color but the obsidian black of her brother's.

"I'm not certain this is the best option, Finneas."

"Caroline, you gave your word. Are you going to renege on it? Don't you think you owe Rose, and Jenifer, your support?" She'd be on that coach if he had to tie her up and carry her.

"I hear you, Finneas." With a sigh Caroline sank into the chair again. "You can trust me."

Could he? He hoped so.

Julian threw Finneas a lazy glance from his spot in front of the fire, legs stretched out as though he hadn't a care in the world. The old man lay propped in his bed, a fanatical light flickering in his clouded eyes.

Finneas stood, every muscle tensed, back to the door, preventing Julian from leaving. "I want to speak to you."

"The floor is yours." Julian gestured expansively.

"I found Rose in the barrow."

"Ah, my little sister . . . Been wandering, has she? Dangerous place to be, that barrow. You know the local rumors."

"And I also know they are based in fact. What were you thinking of?"

"Me? What's it to do with me? I haven't been anywhere near the place—ask Mrs. Pascoe; she served us dinner. Ask Father."

Methenwyck inclined his head, his chin lolling against his chest. Julian rose, walked to the bed, and lifted the old man and brought a glass to his lips. A curiously caring gesture.

Grasping the chance, Finneas searched the room, his eyes alighting on the puddled cloak beneath the heavy curtains. He stepped forward and grabbed it from the floor. The stale smell of blood billowed as he shook it out. "This, look at this." His fingers grasped the dried bloodstain tarnishing the heavy wool and thrust it under Julian's nose.

"A spot of blood. Shot a deer on the way here. With no hunting parties anymore, the animals are like vermin. Perhaps we should go out tonight and see what we can bag, just like old times."

"I've never had anything to do with the hunting parties, as you well know." Hated them, in fact; hated the way the poor defenseless animals were run down, loathed the thought there might be more to the rumors he'd refused to acknowledge. He was no better than Caroline, turning a blind eye, ignoring the truth. "It's not deer you hunted but girls, poor defenseless girls snatched from their homes, their families."

"For God's sake, man. Don't give me that holier-than-thou look. You knew what was going on and have for as long as I have. That you chose not to follow the old ways is your decision, but it is not for you to criticize. They're just girls. No one cares; no one misses them."

"Good sport." Methenwyck lisped his approval, his usual pallor replaced by a flush of blood to his cheeks.

"You perverted, murdering bastards." He wanted nothing more than to take the old man by the throat and choke the last remaining gleam of life from his withered body and then beat Julian into a senseless pulp. Not kill him. Oh no. He wanted him to stand in front of a jury and take the full weight of the law, as Jenifer had done. "First you take my mother, then the woman I love." His words brought him up short. *The woman I love*. Yes, he did love Rose, but sentiments like that didn't belong in front of these two depraved excuses for men. He would not sully Rose by letting her name pass his lips in their presence.

"A pretty turn of events. Isn't that some form of incest, falling in love with your sister?"

Finneas didn't dignify Julian's ludicrous remark with a response. "Caroline has returned to London. She intends to clear Jenifer Trevan's name and explain her responsibility in Jenifer's entrapment and the reasons for it."

"For goodness' sake, a woman cannot give evidence against her husband. Everyone knows that."

"But she can against her ward."

Snarling with fury, Julian leaped forward. "I'll see you in hell."

A strangled gargle came from the bed and Finneas turned to see Methenwyck blue-faced and gasping. All compassion leached from him, and for a moment he stood while the old man's eyes bulged. So easy to let him die, rid the earth of this vile man, but he wanted him alive, to be shamed for the evil he'd perpetrated.

Finneas raced forward, slipped his hands under the old man's armpits, and heaved him up, then leaned him forward and thumped him on the back. Methenwyck's eyes glazed, then with a monstrous shudder he sucked in a mouthful of air through his withered lips.

"Perhaps you should ride to Bodmin and call the constabulary to arrest Lord Methenwyck. I'm sure they'd be tripping over themselves to accommodate your nonsense."

Finneas lowered the old man back onto his pillows and took stock. He hadn't given much thought to what he would say or how he would deal with the pair of them. God would have his revenge on Methenwyck soon enough, or maybe he already had—condemned him to life in a body that was no more than a shell, unable to care for himself.

A cold blast of air from the window brought Finneas back from his reverie. Julian sat back in the chair, a twisted smirk on his face as he swirled his brandy, and the old man lay, eyes closed, as though exhausted. What he wouldn't give for a bolt of lightning to strike them both down.

Methenwyck wasn't going anywhere, and he doubted Julian would leave him; he had too much to lose. He snatched up Julian's cloak and strode toward the door. He'd promised Rose he'd get her carpetbag and sketchbook. It would give him a moment to clear his head and think.

"Run out of vitriol, little brother? Too much the carer, too much the healer?" Julian stood and sauntered toward him, blocking his path to the door. "Perhaps I should teach you the old ways, more than you'd ever learn from those cadavers you enjoy."

Finneas didn't remember raising his fist, nor how the blood appeared, pouring from Julian's face in a torrent. He waited until his brother slumped to the floor, then stepped over his prostrate form and strode from the room.

Chapter 25

Wollombi, New South Wales
1908

"Gayadin, do you think your Jane was my grandmother?" Tamsin tested the words. *My grandmother*. She'd never called anyone grandmother, or grandfather, come to that.

"I know, not think. In your eyes, in your voice, I hear my Jane. You mallangong girl too." She pointed to Tamsin's foot and Tamsin uncurled her toes and looked again. "Jane's baby—she not mallangong girl. She a water rat—she run away across the sea, say poor Mr. Kelly let the flood take my Jane."

Maybe genetic traits skipped a generation or two. Mother hadn't inherited funny feet. The memory made her cold. How she hated her feet. Always trying to hide them, especially at school; always terrified the girls would see them, tease her, make her feel even more different. Those times were best forgotten. "When did Mr. Kelly die?"

"By and by. Mrs. Quinleaven, she alone long time."

Sitting here beside the brook with the birds flitting across the water and the dragonflies hovering, she was more at peace than she'd been for a long time. She could almost feel Rose's arms tight around her, holding her close. Something she'd never known from Mother, or Father. How she wanted to be hugged tight, to know she wasn't alone. Why didn't she know more about her family? Why had Mother and Father shunned them? They'd buried themselves in their missionary work, taking care of others instead of their closest family. Had Mr. Kelly ever known he had a granddaughter?

"So what you going to do? That house." Gayadin tipped her head across the brook. "That house be yours by rights. Not that rushing woman."

Tamsin sat up as the implication hit her. Never mind the house. If she was Mr. Kelly's granddaughter, would the sketchbook belong to her?

Heavens above—the perfect way to foil Shaw Everdene and Mrs. Rushworth. Serve them right. Both of them. She slipped on her boots and retied the laces, then stood up. "Gayadin, I've got to go."

"Where you go? You stay here. Look after your family."

"I'm going to go and see what I can do to save the sketchbook."

"What sketchbook?" Gayadin held out the daguerreotype and Tamsin wrapped it up and slipped it into her pocket.

"I've got Charles and Rose Winton's mallangong drawings. They're in Sydney."

Gayadin nodded her head and heaved herself to her feet. "They always drawing and painting with them little boxes."

She'd like to give the daguerreotype to Gayadin as a thank-you, but right now it was one of the few tangible pieces of evidence she had—if you could call it that. In all honesty, who was going to believe an old Aboriginal woman? Although she could see no truth in Mrs. Adcock's words that Gayadin lived between two worlds. She might be old, but there was nothing wrong with her memory . . . she hoped.

"I'm going to go into Cessnock to see about Mr. Kelly's will. Thank you for showing me; thank you for telling me."

"You good girl. You come back quick. Old Gayadin not got much time."

Her words brought Tamsin up short. She hadn't much time either. She had to have the matter resolved before Shaw reclaimed the sketchbook from the Library.

Fired with determination, Tamsin took off down the path. She had no idea how she'd get to Cessnock—the post wagon met the Cessnock train and then went back, but at what time?

Before she'd even made it through the door of the Family Hotel, Mrs. Adcock nabbed her. "Well. Did you find Gayadin? Did she know who was in the picture?"

"Yes, she did."

"Tell me."

"Mrs. Adcock, I'm in a bit of a hurry. I need to get into Cessnock and see the solicitors. Is there anyone I can get a lift with?"

Mrs. Adcock's eyes lit up. "And aren't you the lucky one. Bill's just having a bit of morning tea and he'll be heading back."

"Bill?"

"Bill does the post run. He'll give you a lift—let's go and ask him. Then you'll have time to tell me all about it while he finishes his scones and tea."

Tamsin clambered out of the wagon right outside Kelly, Baker, and Lovedale. She had exactly an hour, no more, no less, or she'd miss her lift back. The bell above the door jangled as she pushed it open and she found herself face-to-face with an older woman with gray hair pulled back into a severe bun.

"I'd like to speak to Mr. Baker or Mr. Lovedale, please."

"Do you have an appointment?"

"No, I don't."

The woman sniffed and began to shake her head.

"It's a matter of urgency. It relates to the will of the late Mr. Kelly of Wollombi."

"Your name?"

"Alleyn, Tamsin Alleyn."

Her eyebrows rose and her mouth pursed as she stood up. "I'll see what I can do. Appointments are necessary."

"Thank you very much." Tamsin lowered herself onto the wooden chair pushed up against the wall, her feet jiggling, quite unable to sit still no matter how hard she tried. When she walked out of the door, she might well have the answer to the ownership of the sketchbook and a whole lot more. A fast pulse beat in her temple and her mouth was dry as dust. She couldn't, mustn't think about it. She'd be disappointed if Gayadin was wrong, and no matter what the old woman said, the facts had to be proved.

After an eternity the door opened and the gray-haired woman came back out followed by a small rotund man, his watch chain stretched across his ample stomach. "Miss Alleyn, come this way, please." He held out his arm and directed her into a sparsely decorated office, leaving the door open. "Please sit down. My name's Lovedale."

"Thank you for seeing me."

"I believe you have something you wish to discuss about the will of the late Mr. Kelly. I presume you saw our advertisement in the *Maitland Mercury*, or perhaps the Sydney papers."

Her mouth framed the word *no* and she changed her mind. She couldn't imagine Gayadin having much success explaining her story to this man. "Yes, yes, I did."

"You do realize any claim will have to be accompanied by written evidence such as birth, death, or marriage certificates."

"Yes, I do."

"And you have those documents."

"No, not at present." And it was highly unlikely she'd ever be able to produce them. She had no recollection of anything like that when the house was packed up. Mother and Father probably carried their paperwork with them when they traveled. Maybe the Misses Green could help. Or even the Missionary Society.

Mr. Lovedale let out a sigh. "Perhaps when you have the documents you would like to call back."

In for a penny. "I believe Mr. Kelly was my grandfather." There, she'd said it. Now what?

"I see. That's a very close relationship."

"My mother, Mavis Alleyn, was Mr. Kelly's daughter."

He pursed his lips, might have whistled given half the chance. "May I suggest you bring your mother into the office when you return with the necessary documents."

"Both my mother and father are deceased."

"In that case you'll have copies of their death certificates."

"No, I don't. I was orphaned when I was twelve. Over ten years ago. My parents were missionaries, and they were killed in the Islands. I don't have any family papers."

Whether it was the use of the word *orphan* or the sudden wave of exhaustion that hit her, so strongly that she was forced to rest her hands on her side of the desk, she had no idea.

Mr. Lovedale's eyes softened. "As you may know, Frederick Kelly was the founder of our little business. It still carries his name. He was very kind to me when I was a struggling clerk, after my own father died. I see it as a duty to ensure that his will is honored, hence my somewhat defensive stance. Advertisements in newspapers tend to bring out a series of fortune hunters. Perhaps you would be good enough to recount your story and I will do everything in my power to see if we can find the necessary evidence to support your claim."

Twenty minutes later Tamsin stood outside Mr. Lovedale's office, her thoughts swirling. She'd told the story of the sketchbook and the subsequent search for Rose Winton and had given him Mrs. Quinleaven's letter to the Library, although he hadn't appeared particularly interested. However, something she'd said along the line had hit a chord and Mr. Lovedale had produced a notebook and started firing questions at her, demanding dates, addresses, and so many names her head was spinning.

And then he'd asked the unthinkable. He'd called the gray-haired woman into the room and introduced her as his wife, who hadn't batted an eyelid when he'd asked Tamsin to remove her boots. Tamsin thought she'd die of embarrassment, until Mrs. Lovedale had clasped her hand and nodded. Mr. Lovedale refused to offer any explanation, just insisted she remove her boots. When she'd done it, he'd nodded and explained that simple syndactyly was passed down the generations. And that's when she'd realized Gayadin was right.

Who could have known that the toes that she'd seen as an affliction for so long would be the very thing that would save the sketchbook? Not just the sketchbook but Mr. Kelly's entire estate.

Bill was true to his word, and when she arrived at the corner where he'd dropped her, he was sitting behind the wheel of a Model T van, looking very pleased. "Got a run to do. Thought you might enjoy the ride."

She climbed inside and settled onto the wooden seat. Nowhere near as comfortable as her previous experience, but beggars couldn't be choosers, and she wasn't going to be begging Shaw Everdene for another ride in his car, or anything else for that matter.

An hour later Bill dropped her off and she raced up the stairs, praying the Telegraph Office hadn't closed. She fell through the door and was greeted by an apple-cheeked woman with a huge smile.

"What can I do for you, lovey?"

"I'd like to send a telegram to Sydney."

"Forms are over there. Fill it in and I'll get it off before we close."

She turned to the little shelf and wrote a quick message to Mrs. Williams.

> *staying in Wollombi stop might have found owner of sketchbook stop do not return to Everdene stop Tamsin*

There was no *might* about it, at least not in her mind; however, it seemed a bit presumptuous to claim anything until the matter was sorted out. Mr. Lovedale had said he was "cautiously optimistic" and suggested she stay in Wollombi for a few more days while he "made some inquiries" and hopefully found some "hard evidence." Mrs. Lovedale showed no such restraint. She'd caught her in the tightest, most rib-cracking hug she'd ever encountered and dropped a kiss on her cheek. Neither of them had made mention of Mrs. Rushworth, just referred to "the other claimant," giving her the distinct impression that Mrs. Rushworth hadn't endeared herself to them.

Shaw couldn't avoid the inevitable any longer. His father and Mrs. Rushworth had to be faced. He peered into the mirror dangling over the kitchen sink and scraped the razor across his chin. He'd managed only a few hours' sleep collapsed over the kitchen table when he couldn't keep his eyes open a moment longer. Sadly, he needed to have another word with Mrs. Rushworth and see what she could tell him about her mother's background. She must know something that she wasn't giving up. How Mrs. Quinleaven had met Kelly would be a great start. What he wouldn't give for some machine that could pull all the answers up at the flick of a switch.

With a sigh he knotted his tie and shrugged into his jacket before making his way down to the ferry. Someone was in his corner because in under an hour he was outside Everdene, Roach, and Smythe in George Street. He buttoned his jacket, hoping to detract his father's usual comments about his appearance, then entered the building.

"Morning, sir." The bulldog doorman guarding the entrance ushered him inside. "Mr. Everdene's expecting you. Asked me to tell you to go in as soon as you arrived."

He took the stairs two at a time, trying not to lose any momentum; the very air in the building sucked the life out of him. He knocked and entered without waiting for a response.

Father looked up and nodded tersely, then returned to the piece of paper he was studying.

"Good morning, Father." He pulled up a chair and sat down on the opposite side of the desk and waited.

"We've come to a decision."

We? No point in asking the question. He knew this trick. If he jumped in, he'd put his foot in it.

"The Library doesn't have a leg to stand on. I want you to go with Mrs. Rushworth to collect the sketchbook. There is no reason for them to keep it any longer. She's meeting you there."

"It's not due to be collected until Monday." He'd promised Tamsin they could have it until then.

"What difference does a day or two make? According to Mrs. Rushworth, when she rang the Library they said they'd come to the conclusion it's authentic."

"Who told her that?"

Father gave a dismissive wave of his hand. "Some old biddy, a Mrs. Williams, I think. Quite why we are expected to deal with these underlings, I have no idea."

Neither "old biddy" nor "underling" suited Mrs. Williams particularly well; however, it wasn't an argument worth having.

"Mrs. Rushworth wants the book in her possession and on the open market."

Mrs. Rushworth or his father? Something snapped. He was sick of it, sick to death of this God-given right Father believed he had to ride roughshod over anyone who stood in his way. "I gave my word that the sketchbook would remain in the Library until Monday."

"Pah! A couple of days here or there isn't going to make any difference."

"But legally Mrs. Rushworth hasn't—"

"Don't give me that rubbish. She's signed a statutory declaration to say that her mother gave her the sketchbook several years ago, to ensure it remained in the family."

How had Mrs. Rushworth come up with that gem? Was she intending to claim a link to Charles Winton?

"Mrs. Rushworth is entitled to her mother's possessions. The rest can wait."

He clamped his mouth firmly closed. If his research was accurate, the sketchbook belonged to Rose Methenwyck's family.

"Now, what arrangements for the sale have you made?"

"I have to follow up on a couple of leads." None that had anything to do with the sale of the book, but Father didn't need to know that. Perhaps he could stretch it out by another day or two.

"Why? If this is to do with the ownership of the sketchbook, I wouldn't waste your time—and certainly not the company's resources."

"I won't be wasting your money. It will be my own." Though God alone knew where he'd get it. Curiosity could be an expensive vice. "I thought with your copious connections and contacts you could help me." Flattery. It should work. It always had in the past.

His father leaned back in his chair and interlaced his fingers across his expansive girth. "Contacts. Worldwide. Yes. Reputation is all that matters in this day and age."

"The sketchbook contained a pencil drawing of Dozmary Pool in Cornwall. You wouldn't by any chance know of a company of solicitors I could contact in Cornwall, would you? Cambourne or Bodmin, to be precise." And the clincher. "It could well affect the final value."

"Perhaps I misjudged you. You have been following through. Very good, very good. Give me a moment." He rummaged in the bottom drawer of his desk and pulled out a notebook, somewhat the worse for wear. "When we were in England, your grandfather asked me to collect some paperwork. Took a very pleasant few days touring around while he enrolled you in school."

That Shaw remembered—the horror of those first few days in boarding school, the odd boy with the strange accent and skin that was far too dark after spending his first thirteen years under an Australian sun. He forced the memory aside.

"Here we are. And as luck would have it, the solicitors are in Bodmin. Thought I remembered the name." He scribbled something down, tore the sheet from his pad, and slid it across the desktop.

Shaw folded and pocketed the piece of paper without a word.

"Now off you go. Don't want to keep the clients waiting. Mrs. Rushworth will be at the Library"—he looked up at the clock on the wall—"on the hour."

"I'm not going back on my word." Tamsin thought little enough of him already. If he went barging in there and demanded the sketchbook before the date they'd agreed, she'd never speak to him again, and that was something he didn't want to happen. In the last few days he'd come to realize how much he'd enjoyed her company, enjoyed working with her, and in his heart of hearts he agreed with her: the sketchbook should be on public display.

"Don't give me that claptrap."

"I firmly believe putting the sketchbook on the open market is a grave mistake." He'd lose his golden key into the world of bibliophiles, and the chance at the library at Will-O-Wyck, but there'd be other books and morality was more important than money. It had taken him a while to come to that conclusion, and sitting here in front of his father, knowing that the man was motivated by greed, firmed his decision.

"Let me be the judge of that." Father lumbered to his feet and stomped to the door, throwing it open. "Big mistake asking a boy to do a man's job."

Tamsin couldn't tolerate Mrs. Adcock's inquisitive stares a moment longer, so she downed her cup of tea and took off without any breakfast. There was a large possibility that she might be arrested for breaking and entering, but she couldn't help it. She had to go and have another look at Will-O-Wyck.

She trudged up the road, framing her defense in case she was caught. If worse came to worst, she at least knew a solicitor who might bail her out.

Shunning the driveway, she cut through the trees and walked along the bank of the brook on the opposite side to Gayadin's cottage. She didn't want to speak to her. Not until she knew. As she rounded the bend, she saw Gayadin bending down pulling at the weeds surrounding the gravestones. Maybe that would be her job one day.

Feeling more like a thief than anything else, she tiptoed across the lawn where she'd seen all the people taking tea after Mrs. Quinleaven's funeral and then bolted the last few yards and landed on the verandah, panting from a strange mixture of excitement and sheer terror.

She'd never done anything remotely illegal in her life. Miss Goody Two-Shoes, the Misses Green's perfect student. The thought made her smile; she'd waited long enough to break the rules. She dropped down on the steps to catch her breath.

Not a sound came from the house; the door was firmly closed and the windows shuttered. How on earth would she get inside? Perhaps there was a kitchen out at the back, a servants' entry. Once her heartbeat returned to normal, she edged along the verandah down one side of the house, past more shuttered windows, through the heavy silence.

As she'd expected, she found the kitchen around the back, a separate stone building joined by a covered walkway to the house. The door hung wide open. She slipped inside. The tabletop was covered with crockery, all washed and stacked in neat piles. No heat was coming from the wood-fired stove and the ice chest was dry. One cupboard held a mishmash of glasses, no food—not even a tin of the Peek Frean biscuits Mrs. Quinleaven favored. Mrs. Rushworth must have cleared up, ready for the sale.

Pulling the door closed behind her, she gazed around and made a split-second decision. She flung her shoulder at the back door, the entry to the house. It groaned and swung open, and she stood inside blinking furiously, trying to get her eyes to adjust to the dim light. To her left a staircase led to the upper level, and ahead of her stretched a long hallway with closed doors. The very hallway Shaw Everdene had led her down from the front door the first day she'd seen the sketchbook, when she'd believed he was the answer to all her prayers. The toad.

She pushed open the first door on her right, the dining room. The brass work lamp sat in the center of the table. Four chairs were tucked underneath, but the huge cedar sideboard was gone. Crossing the hallway, she peered into the room opposite. It was completely empty—no rugs, no chairs, nothing except the fireplace, which was as clean as the rest of the floor.

Mrs. Quinleaven had died only two weeks ago and already it was as though no one had lived there. Closing the door behind her, she bypassed the third room and made her way into the library at the front of the house. The massive desk was no longer there, and all that remained was a series of tea chests stacked almost as high as the top of the shelves lining the walls. Taking care not to topple the stack, she peered at the side of them and her heart stopped. Every single one carried the same stenciled address.

Shaw Everdene
121 Blues Point Road, North Sydney

"Double-crossing, two-faced, conniving bastard." The words ripped out of her mouth, breaking the dusty silence. It wasn't just the sketchbook. He intended to sell the entire library. The rat! All those books at his house must be part of this collection. And he'd tried to tell her it was his grandfather's library he'd inherited from England. Thank goodness the sketchbook was in Mrs. Williams's safekeeping.

Slamming the door behind her, Tamsin stomped down the corridor and threw open all the doors. Dust sheets covered what remained of the furniture and every room carried the sense of desertion and loneliness.

The library and the kitchen appeared to be the only rooms used. Mrs. Quinleaven must have slept somewhere. Closing the last door, she made her way up the stairs and stopped on the small landing. Above her were four doors.

The one at the top of the stairs was ajar and she pushed it open. The dusty scent of roses and talcum powder greeted her. This must have been Mrs. Quinleaven's room. A hand mirror and two brushes sat neatly atop the dressing table next to a small scent bottle. Otto of Roses. She picked it up and brought the bottle to her nose, as if by inhaling the perfume she could in some way get closer to Mrs. Quinleaven. How she wished she'd arrived in time. The bedside table was empty except for a mottled-glass, bronze-based lamp sitting on a lace doily.

The large wardrobe pushed into the corner contained a coat and several cotton dresses, a pair of slippers incongruous next to a pair of sturdy walking boots, and a couple of utilitarian felt hats on the shelf above.

After she'd closed the door, she peeked into the other three rooms. Two covered with dust sheets like the rooms downstairs and one with the sheets neatly folded and piled on the floor, the wardrobe and dressing chest empty and the single brass bed made up. She flopped down on the bed and a waft of sickly sweet jasmine filled the air. No doubt Mrs. Rushworth had slept here.

Walking back onto the landing, she paused once more outside Mrs. Quinleaven's bedroom. She had no idea what she'd hoped or expected to find in the house. If there was anything in here, it wasn't advertising its presence.

She pushed the door open again and inhaled. Beneath the rose petals and talcum powder she could smell something else, something that reminded her of her parents . . . hospitals, carbolic, and rubbing alcohol. Sniffing, she walked around the room, stopping when she reached the bedside cupboard. She dropped down onto her knees, lifted the latch, and peered inside. No shelves of pills or bags of stockings, just one large lump. Something wrapped in a pillowcase. She reached inside and pulled it out, then slipped down onto the floor, her back resting against the bed.

Balancing the bag on her lap, she ran her hands over the outline. It felt like an old toy, a teddy bear, perhaps. Screwing up her eyes, she pushed her hand inside.

Her scream ripped through the musty air.

Throwing the pillowcase aside, she danced to her feet, shaking her hand, expecting to see a rat dangling from one of her fingers, its teeth impaled in the soft flesh at the pad.

Slowly her heart rate settled and she kicked the bag over, letting out a hysterical giggle as the upended pillowcase delivered its contents. Someone's old stuffed toy, a keepsake; perhaps Mrs. Rushworth's, and Mrs. Quinleaven had kept it to remind her of the daughter who'd once loved her.

She crouched down for a closer look, cursing her appalling eyesight. Rummaging in her skirt pocket for her spectacles, she rocked back on her heels. A leathery bill protruded from the bag along with two short stubby paws with sharp claws.

A platypus. A taxidermied specimen, no less!

She pulled it fully out of the bag and settled it on her lap, her hands moving over the moth-eaten fur. One of the back legs dangled—the stitching loose, some sort of long thread of yellowed catgut. The nose-twitching odor of carbolic and rubbing alcohol was overpowering.

She pushed her hand into the crevice above the torn leg, her fingers wrapping around some soft stuffing. She tugged gently. A little piece pulled out, then more and more, easier as the packed material loosened until it fell free. With both hands she shook it out, a smile tugging the corners of her lips as her fingers clasped a worn and patched chemise, a smattering of handmade lace across the neckline.

Had it once belonged to Rose? Was she holding her great-grandmother's chemise in her hands?

What was the creature doing here? It was very old, a crude attempt at taxidermy, nothing like the impressive birds and animals so many people valued, placed in their front rooms under glass domes for all the world to wonder at.

Without a doubt the room belonged to Mrs. Quinleaven. Why had she hidden it here, beside her bed? Surely it belonged with the sketchbook and would have had pride of place in the Library. Unless she'd deliberately squirreled it away. Kept it from prying eyes. Mrs. Rushworth's steely blue gaze sprang to mind. She kept insisting she and her mother were estranged, but supposing, just supposing she knew of the sketchbook, knew of its potential value, and poor Mrs. Quinleaven's letter had been one last and vain attempt to save it from her daughter's greed.

Stuffing the platypus and the tattered chemise back into the bag, she trailed down the stairs. The sense she'd found another piece of the puzzle weighed heavily, the same certainty she'd felt when she'd held the tin in her hands.

By the time she reached the town, the sun was high and her blouse had stuck to her skin where she'd clasped the platypus to her chest. What she needed was a glass of Mrs. Adcock's lemonade and a quiet sit-down. Time to think away from prying eyes.

"Miss Alleyn! There you are." Mrs. Adcock stood on the verandah of the hotel waving something above her head. "You've got a telegram."

Quickening her pace, Tamsin took a shortcut across the grass and headed diagonally across the road. A telegram! Perhaps Mr. Lovedale had found some hard evidence already.

"Thank you." Tamsin held out her hand and Mrs. Adcock stepped up next to her and dangled the folded buff-colored paper tantalizingly out of reach.

"What's it say?"

"I have no idea. Perhaps you'd let me read it." She snatched the telegram and turned her back on the nosy parker.

Mrs. Adcock gave a loud sniff. "What have you got there? Smells terrible."

"Just something I found." Tamsin clutched the telegram tight and bolted up the stairs to her room. If it was from Mr. Lovedale and contained bad news, she had no intention of sharing it. She flopped down on the bed and unfolded it.

regret to inform sketchbook claimed by Rushworth solicitors stop Mrs. Williams

"Oh!" Rushworth solicitors? That was Everdene, Roach, and Smythe. Damn Shaw. He couldn't take it. Couldn't sell it. Not now.

"Not bad news, I hope." Mrs. Adcock appeared at the door and took three steps toward the bed. Tamsin screwed the telegram into a ball and thrust it in her pocket and shunted the platypus under the bed with her boot.

"Do you have a telephone?"

"Chance would be a fine thing. None of those newfangled devices around here."

Then she'd have to go into Cessnock again and speak with Mr. Lovedale. Surely he could do something. "Is Mr. Adcock going into Cessnock, or is there a post run?" What she wouldn't give for her own motor car. Gallivanting around hither and yon without having to spend hours wasting time getting from one place to the next. Ha! That would put Shaw Everdene in his place.

"Not this afternoon, and Bill's not here. Got some sort of a problem with his new toy. Took off to Maitland first thing this morning."

"Has the Telegraph Office got a telephone?"

"Miss High 'n' Mighty? No. Best she can do is a telegram. Probably closed up shop by now. Can only say no, can't she? I'll come with you." Mrs. Adcock started to untie her pinny.

And then everything would be around town in two seconds flat. No. She didn't want that. "Thanks for the offer, but I'm sure you're very busy. I'll go by myself. There's no harm in asking, as you say." She didn't remember the lady in the Telegraph Office being anything but charming. Surely if it was an emergency . . . She'd give it a try.

Tamsin took off before Mrs. Adcock had the chance to follow, and when she pushed open the Telegraph Office door, she was greeted with a welcoming smile.

"I was wondering if you could help me. I need to send an urgent message to Kelly, Baker, and Lovedale in Cessnock. Is it too late?"

"I was just closing up. Not sure if it'll be delivered today."

Tamsin's heart sank. This was ridiculous. Stuck out here in the middle of nowhere. So much for the delights of peace and quiet—now all she wanted was to be back in Sydney with everything in easy reach and telephones on hand.

"Best idea would be to send it to the Telegraph Office in Cessnock and ask for a special delivery. My niece works there. I can get her to relay a message. Would that do?"

"I really need to discuss something with Mr. Lovedale. Is there any way we could ask him to contact us here?"

"Leave it with me. I'll see what I can do. Pop out onto the back verandah—there's a nice seat out there in the shade. Keep the gossips at bay. Rest and settle yourself. I'll let you know. And by the way, my name's Harriet, Harriet Michaels—that's where the High and Mighty comes from, my initials."

"And I'm Tamsin Alleyn." Throwing the lovely lady a grateful smile, she slipped out of the door and settled down in the shade.

After an interminable wait, Miss High and Mighty, who definitely wasn't, stuck her head out of the door. "I've got Mrs. Lovedale at the Telegraph Office. Mr. Lovedale's out on business."

The image of Mrs. Lovedale's reassuring smile when she'd sat next to her in the office and removed her boot flitted through her mind and she leaped up. Perfect. Perhaps even better than Mr. Lovedale. Sometimes woman-to-woman could be so much simpler. She sat down at the desk and wrote out her message.

Harriet moved discreetly into the back room, leaving her alone.

Now that the time had come, she wasn't sure exactly how important the news was. Could they do anything to stop Shaw and Mrs. Rushworth?

sketchbook taken from library stop must prevent sale please help stop Tamsin

During the interminable minutes while Miss Michaels sent the telegram and they waited for a reply, Tamsin chewed her fingernails almost to the bone. Miss Michaels sat by the telegraph, her fingers drumming on the desk, and then the tapping began.

will relay message ASAP stop wait at telegraph office stop Mrs. Lovedale

The air sucked out of Tamsin's lungs and she shot to her feet and started pacing the small room. She might go insane.

Miss Michaels appeared at her shoulder with a glass of water. "You look as though you could do with this. Feel free to wait here if you'd like to."

"Thank you, I would. I'm at a bit of a loss."

"It would be about the sketchbook, would it?"

She knew about it. Was there anything that remained private in this town? Tamsin nodded.

"Poor Emily, she had quite a bee in her bonnet. Time just caught up with her and she was so certain she'd finally found a home for it."

All Tamsin could hear was the air rasping in and out of her mouth. "You knew Emily Quinleaven?"

"Of course. Everyone knew Emily. We shared a bit of an interest, so she talked to me about her mission. She was determined she'd fulfill her promise."

"Her promise?" She sounded like a parrot.

"Her promise to Mr. Kelly. It always means so much more when it's a promise made in the last moments of life, doesn't it? When I heard you were in town, and from the Library, I thought at least her backup plan had come good."

"Do you know what this promise was?"

"Of course. I thought everyone did. That's why Mr. Kelly arranged for her to stay in the house—to give her time, you see. They'd been trying for years to find his daughter. Mr. Kelly always thought she'd left because she'd disapproved of his friendship with Emily, even though their relationship was nothing like that. Just the rumor mill. Carried a candle for his wife till the very end, did Mr. Kelly."

Gayadin's words echoed in her mind. *"Friends, not lovers. Mr. Kelly, he just love my Jane."*

"And Mrs. Quinleaven didn't find Mr. Kelly's daughter?"

"Such a shame, it was. She married some missionary and they took off overseas and Mr. Kelly never heard from her again. Couldn't find hide nor hair of her. So Emily decided she'd go backward, try and trace the family tree, see what she could come up with. That's when we became friends. I've still got her tin of notes here. To be honest, I wasn't sure what to do with them, thought there'd be something in her will and maybe her daughter would come asking, but she didn't come anywhere near me. Half of us wouldn't have had an opportunity to pay our last respects if she'd had her way."

"Her daughter doesn't want the sketchbook to be donated to the Library."

"But that's what Emily wanted, since she couldn't find Mr. Kelly's daughter. It's what Mr. Kelly wanted."

"Would you mind showing Emily's notes to me?"

"Reckon I could do that. Hang on a tick. I'll go and find them."

Tamsin dropped her head into her hands, tears pooling in her eyes. She'd only ever thought of Mother as Dr. Alleyn's wife, Mavis, not Mavis, daughter of Frederick Kelly. There must be thousands of Kellys in Australia; it was such a common name, and she'd never made any mention of Wollombi.

"Here you go, love."

Tamsin lifted her head. Miss Michaels stood in front of her with a tin in her hands, a replica of the Peek Frean tin sitting in her bag back at the hotel, except a little newer.

"These were Emily's favorite biscuits. She'd go through them like a house on fire. Still, it made for good storage, keeps things nice and dry." Harriet pulled off the lid and grunted with satisfaction. "Looks like everything's there, all the information we tracked down and letters from the churches and the like."

As Tamsin held out her shaking hand, the telegraph started clattering again.

"Excuse me a minute, expect that's your reply—so busy nattering I as good as forgot."

Tamsin worked her way through a pile of notes recording the time and place of birth and death, marriage dates. Names, so many names. Some she recognized, some she didn't. Charles Winton, Jenifer Trevan, Rose and Finneas Methenwyck, Jane Methenwyck. All the hard evidence Mr. Lovedale could ever want.

"Tamsin, Tamsin. Mr. Lovedale must be in the Telegraph Office. The message just says 'Lovedale here.'"

With her mind reeling, Tamsin settled the tin on the chair and stumbled to the desk. "I think perhaps you have given me everything Mr. Lovedale is looking for. Please send him a telegram saying 'Have all evidence required except copy of my birth certificate.'"

How impossibly simple. She turned the pieces of paper over and over, her eyes darting back and forth to the crude family tree. She traced the wavering pencil lines with her finger, and there under Mother's and Father's names, an empty box where her name belonged.

"Miss Alleyn, I have your reply."

Miss Michaels placed the paper on the desk in front of her. Tamsin crossed her fingers before she read the neatly printed words.

> *must sight all documents to confirm stop will contact Rushworth solicitors stop family traits indisputable stop tomorrow 9am Will-O-Wyck stop Lovedale*

Chapter 26

Sydney, Australia
1908

Shaw bounded through the doors and tipped his hat to the doorman. For once Father had turned up trumps and the solicitors in Bodmin got back to him in record time. He patted the three telegrams already in his pocket, to ensure they were still there, and took the back stairs two at a time. There was no doubt about it: Rose Winton and Rose Methenwyck were one and the same and the sketchbook belonged to her family.

When he reached the first landing, he slammed to a halt.

"It is daylight robbery. I will do no such thing."

Mrs. Rushworth's stringent tone filled the dark space and curiosity got the better of him. He hadn't even bothered to go to the Library, certain Mrs. Williams could hold her own and would refuse to hand over the sketchbook to the woman she'd heard so much about, unless . . . He stopped in his tracks, swiveled, and knocked on Father's office door and without waiting for a response walked straight in.

Mrs. Rushworth stood with her back to the door, leaning over the desk, a veritable cloud of jasmine-scented fury emanating from her as she tugged at the sketchbook Father had clasped in his big, sweaty hands. Shaw strode forward and snatched it.

They both flopped down in their respective chairs and eyed him with looks akin to two children caught scrapping behind the toilets.

He placed the book gently back on the table, picked up the linen bag, and slid it inside. "The sketchbook won't be any good to anyone unless you show it some respect." Whatever was it doing here? He wasn't due at the Library for another two hours. He couldn't imagine Mrs. Williams, or Tamsin, for that matter, handing the book over to Mrs. Rushworth before the due time without a fight. His trust in Mrs. Williams's capabilities was seriously misplaced.

Two bright spots of color flared on Mrs. Rushworth's cheeks. She straightened her hat and studied him through narrowed eyes. "It belongs to me. I have every right to have it in my possession."

"Do you want to explain what is going on?" Shaw pulled up a chair and sat at the side of the desk with the sketchbook on his lap.

With a harrumph, his father tugged down his waistcoat and rested his pudgy hands on the desktop. "I accompanied Mrs. Rushworth to the Library and collected the sketchbook, since you refused."

That wasn't all. His father's eyes gave him away as they slid to one side.

"And?"

"We have an interested party."

"The sketchbook belonged to my mother. I have signed a statutory declaration to that effect. I have every right to sell it, and I intend to challenge the will and make claim on the property. My husband will be in contact." Mrs. Rushworth stood and smoothed her skirt. "And bear in mind that any failure to recoup the funds will impinge heavily on the standing of Everdene, Roach, and Smythe."

The *tip-tap* of her shoes across the timber floor echoed until the slam of the door filled the heavy silence.

His father rested his elbows on the desk and dropped his head. "My hands are tied."

Shaw rocked back in the chair. "Suppose you fill me in." There was no point in bringing up the Methenwycks until he knew what he was up against.

"Nothing to fill in, really. Kelly, Baker, and Lovedale contacted me to say they have found Kelly's next of kin and that the property and all contents will pass to her."

"Her?"

"A Tamsin Alleyn, Kelly's granddaughter. They've tracked her down."

Shaw's heartbeat stuttered to a halt. Tamsin was Kelly's next of kin? How had that come about?

"Mrs. Rushworth can still make a claim against the sketchbook. We should still pursue the buyer."

"Stop right there." Shaw found himself on his feet, hands resting on the desk, eyeballing the old man. "If Tamsin Alleyn is Kelly's next of kin, the sketchbook belongs to her. How can you go ahead with the sale?"

"Mrs. Rushworth is entitled to her mother's personal possessions. Just not the property or the shares."

"That's ridiculous. There's nothing to indicate the sketchbook belonged to Mrs. Quinleaven."

"It's well worth Mrs. Rushworth contesting, and I'm leaving it in your hands. The last thing I need is for my involvement in this development to come to light. I want you to enlist the services of another company. They can handle the sale of the sketchbook—the monies from that will tide Ron Rushworth over, while you follow through on the will."

"I will do no such thing." He couldn't believe what his father was suggesting. "If Tamsin is the rightful heir to the Kelly property, then

I will not stand in her way, and selling the sketchbook under those circumstances is tantamount to daylight robbery."

"Oh, get down off your high horse. It's the only way out. If you're going to be a part of this business, then you'll do as instructed."

It was as though someone had thrown him a lifeline. "In that case, Father, this is where you and I part company. I resign." The words were out of his mouth before he had a chance to think.

"Yes, yes. Off you go, boy. Take the rest of the day and have a look around that cottage of yours, and while you're at it, have a last run in that motor car."

It wouldn't take the rest of the day to think about it. It wouldn't take any time.

It wasn't until he was standing in George Street that he realized he had the sketchbook tucked under his arm. He stopped and looked up at the sign: Everdene, Roach, and Smythe. The doorman swung the door open. "Mr. Everdene?"

"Nothing. Thank you. I'll be on my way." He bounded down the street, his feet barely touching the ground, and within a matter of minutes he was standing outside the Library.

The moment he pushed open the doors, Mrs. Williams appeared at his side. "Oh, Shaw, you've got it, thank goodness. I felt so absolutely dreadful when your father and Mrs. Rushworth insisted on collecting the sketchbook. She had a statutory declaration. There was nothing I could do. Was there some mistake?"

"Yes. Yes, there was. I was wondering if I could have a word with Tamsin. I'd like this locked in the safe. Is it all right if I go down?"

A frown crossed Mrs. Williams's face. "She's not here."

"Not here? Where is she?"

"In Wollombi."

He'd been so busy chasing the Methenwycks he'd somehow managed to miss a vital piece of information. He still couldn't get his head around the idea that Tamsin could be Kelly's heir. How had she found out? And he thought he'd solved the mystery of Rose Winton. He handed the sketchbook to Mrs. Williams. "I'll leave this in your capable hands. It is to stay under lock and key, and don't let anyone tell you otherwise."

"Tamsin will be so pleased. I'll send her a telegram and let her know as soon as I finish work."

"Don't worry. I'll tell her when I see her." Without waiting for a reply, he shot down the steps and took the path through the Botanic Gardens to the Quay. With an overnight stop in Wisemans Ferry, he could be in Cessnock tomorrow morning. He needed to have a word with this Lovedale chap before he spoke to Tamsin and got her hopes up. The Rose Winton / Rose Methenwyck connection had to be sorted out. Cessnock by tomorrow, then on to Wollombi, and he didn't have to worry about fronting up at Everdene, Roach, and Smythe ever again.

Wollombi, New South Wales
1908

"I'm happy to inform you, my dear, that I have located a copy of your birth certificate." Mr. Lovedale smiled benignly at Tamsin. "Obviously I will have to check these documents and complete the paperwork. Nevertheless, I'm privileged to inform you that, as Frederick Kelly's granddaughter, you stand to inherit the entire estate known as Will-O-Wyck and a substantial portfolio of shares."

Good heavens. She hadn't thought very much about the property, never mind a portfolio of shares . . . she hadn't much faith in those. "Did you have any luck with the sketchbook?" It was all she cared about.

"Ah yes. Everything is under control. We'll get an injunction to prevent the sale until Kelly's will is finalized. It might be a little difficult. Mrs. Rushworth is, of course, entitled to her mother's personal possessions. Basically, anything that can be proved to belong to her, not part of the estate."

"But I have a family tree here in front of me, a direct line back to Jenifer Trevan, Rose's mother."

"We have a good case, and of course the family trait that you display, that's indisputable."

Tamsin wriggled her toes and laughed.

"I expect you'd like a good look around the house." He pulled a bunch of keys from his pocket and jiggled them.

A flush of color filled her cheeks. She might not mention that she'd already done that, jumped the gun. "I'd like that, Mr. Lovedale. Thank you."

"Come along, then. There's someone who's been waiting a long time for this moment." He glanced skyward and tipped his hat.

Several days later Tamsin sat on the sandstone bench staring out across the brook and kicked off her boots. The sun had begun its slide below the surrounding hills, bathing the garden in a golden glow. Mr. Lovedale had appeared totally convinced she would inherit her grandfather's estate, and when he pressed the keys into her hands and insisted it was all aboveboard and that she should take the time to get to know the property, she had finally believed him. It seemed extravagant paying for lodging when there was a perfectly good house crying out for some attention.

Mrs. Adcock had loaded her up with enough lemonade to fill the brook, and after lunch every day called to check on her, armed with pork pies, fruitcake, sandwiches, and soup. It still felt rather odd, as though she were a visitor looking after the house, but staying had given her a sense of belonging that she'd never known.

Yet somehow she still felt incomplete, as though something was missing.

And that brought her mind back to Shaw Everdene. She hadn't seen or heard from him since she'd stormed out of his house. The books in their packing cases in the study addressed to him were a constant reminder of his duplicity.

There was little she could do about it. In a perfect world she'd like to share with him the full story of Emily Quinleaven. How she'd worked for years to solve the puzzle for Grandfather Kelly. If it hadn't been for her persistence and determination, her cobwebbed notes and the daguerreotype in the tin, no one would be any the wiser. She'd still love to know the story behind the handkerchief, though.

There was nothing intrinsically wrong with Shaw's ambitions; in a way she admired what he wanted to do. Rescuing long-forgotten books, becoming an expert in the field.

Sighing, she shifted on the sandstone bench and lifted her head at the sound of a slight splash. And there she was, the female platypus encouraging her little ones from the burrow in the sandy bank. She tiptoed closer, absorbed by the antics of the fully furred juveniles as they braved the water for the first time.

"She's brought them out."

She jumped as the whispered words grazed her ear and the warmth of his breath trailed across the back of her neck. "Mr. Everdene. I didn't hear your motor car."

"I parked at the end of the driveway. I wasn't certain . . ." He paused, his gray-green eyes downcast. "May I sit down?"

She returned to the bench and he lowered himself down next to her, stretching out his long legs. Shaw, dressed in corduroy trousers and one of those soft shirts he favored. He hadn't shaved for a few days.

It suited him, made him look more carefree, more like the man she'd first come to know.

"I heard you'd handed Mrs. Rushworth's case over to your father."

"I had something more important to do."

"Another job?" She had the most absurd impulse to stroke his cheek.

He glanced at her and smiled. "You could say that."

"Oh, well. That's good." Something the size of a bogong moth batted against the wall of her stomach. "Can I ask you something?"

He didn't look at her, just nodded.

"Why didn't you tell me from the very beginning Mrs. Rushworth was determined to sell the sketchbook? Why conceal the truth?"

He gave a long sigh. "I didn't set out to conceal the truth. I didn't think she'd have a leg to stand on."

Unable to sit still, she wandered back to the edge of the brook and sat down on the bank, searching for any sight of the platypus, but they'd vanished, along with her ludicrous feelings for Shaw. He was pacing. He might have something on his mind, but it was going to have to be good, otherwise she'd be asking him to leave very soon. She still wasn't sure he deserved the opportunity to explain.

He threw himself down next to her, raking his fingers through his hair. "I made a mistake. I was wrong. I was so determined to prove myself, my ability to be something other than a replica of my father, that I was swayed by the prospect of establishing my reputation as a bibliophile and I lost sight of what was important."

Tamsin paddled her feet in the water, kicking up the cool water and tracking the fall of the drops. "Yes, you did. Winton's sketchbook belongs to the people of Australia. All of them, not just someone with more money than sense."

"Lovedale is convinced you're Kelly's heir. He wouldn't give a specific reason, just said he had indisputable evidence."

She kicked another splash of water into the air, then lifted her feet and wriggled her toes. He continued staring out across the brook, not the least interested in her toes. Come to think of it, she wasn't quite sure why they'd caused her so much concern. "It seems there is a family trait. My grandmother and my great-grandmother had it. Mr. Kelly told Lovedale about it just before he died. Said it was the surest way to know any claimants were who they purported to be. Simple syndactyly between my second and third toe." She waved her right foot in the air and showed him the webbing between her toes.

"And you didn't know?"

"That it was a family trait? No. I don't think my mother suffered the same affliction. Apparently it can skip a generation."

"It's not an affliction, just a quirk of nature."

"That's not what I was led to believe as a child. Mother said it was the mark of the devil."

"What a load of archaic nonsense."

After a long time Tamsin tipped back her head and gazed into the gray-green of his eyes. "I'd love to know the full story behind Rose's trip to England and how she met Finneas."

"I might be able to help there. I've been in Cessnock doing some poking around. Mr. Lovedale gave me the use of one of his offices. Can we go up to the house?"

"I suppose so." She picked up her boots and the shadow of a smile crossed his face, but the light had almost gone and it was difficult to know whether she'd imagined it or not. "What is it?"

"Nothing."

"Something. Tell me." She stepped up onto the verandah and opened the fly-screen door. "Would you like a drink? I've got some glasses, and Mrs. Adcock set me up with enough lemonade to last a lifetime."

"I can't think of anything I'd like more, except perhaps to sit out here rather than inside."

"We'll have to. I'm a bit short on furniture. The daughter of the previous tenant as good as stripped the house."

He threw her a wry smile.

"I'll be back in a minute." She skipped down the hallway, butterflies circling around in her insides like the Ferris wheel she'd ridden on at the Royal Easter Show. It was so good to see him, but he'd hardly apologized. More tried to excuse his behavior. She pulled the bottle of lemonade from the bucket in the shade on the back verandah and gave the glasses a quick rinse. Perhaps she should apologize for jumping to conclusions. No, she didn't owe him an apology.

She couldn't get back outside fast enough—her heart was doing the most ridiculous skips and bumps and hops. What did she want? She had to sort this out once and for all. She stopped, her shoulder against the screen door. Shaw Everdene was what had been missing for the past few days. She hadn't realized his absence had made her feel incomplete, as though she'd lost something.

He'd pulled the table out from the wall so the light from the hallway shone directly on the surface and placed the chairs opposite each other. She poured out some lemonade and passed him a glass.

"Cheers." He raised his glass. "To the Wintons and the Methenwycks."

"And the Methenwycks?"

It wasn't until she put her glass down on the table that she noticed the brown envelope in the center of the table. "What's that?"

"Oh, that?" Shaw shrugged his shoulders. "Something I've been working on and I thought it might interest you."

She frowned at him and sat down at the table, lifting the brown envelope and hefting it in her hand. It was heavy but not a book, maybe some papers.

"Go on, open it."

For some unaccountable reason her fingers shook as she unraveled the piece of string and opened the split pin securing the envelope. "Do I need gloves?"

"No, sadly not."

No gloves, nothing old. She pulled out a sheaf of papers. "Originals?"

"Some and some." He took another sip of his lemonade.

"Then I need gloves, a magnifying glass, and an ivory rule."

He sketched an ironic smile. "The papers belong to me."

She could tell he was coiled tighter than a spring no matter how much he tried to disguise it. She pulled out her spectacles and angled the sheaf of papers toward the fading light. *The West Briton and Cornwall Advertiser.* The words blurred and her hands began to shake in earnest.

> The following is a more particular account of this disastrous event than the shortness of the time allowed us to lay before our readers last week.
>
> About half past five o'clock in the morning of Thursday the 19th inst., an alarming and, in the event, destructive fire broke out in the mansion of Wyck Hall, the seat of Lord Methenwyck. A female servant, one Mrs. Pascoe, first discovered it. On awakening she found her room full of smoke, and on looking out of the window perceived fire issuing from below. She instantly alarmed Master Julian, Lord Methenwyck's ward, but such was the rapidity of the progress of the flames, that all attempts to extinguish the fire were in vain. The flames spread and speedily consumed the whole house.
>
> It has now been ascertained beyond all doubt that the fire originated from a fallen candle, which ignited the curtains

> and consumed Lord Methenwyck's bedchamber before the alarm was raised.
>
> It is our solemn and melancholy duty to inform our readers that Lord Methenwyck and his heir, Julian, perished. Lady Caroline Methenwyck fortunately was not on the premises, as she had taken the afternoon mail coach with her guest, a Miss Rose Winton, visiting from New South Wales.
>
> Finneas Methenwyck's whereabouts are unaccounted for, and there are fears that he may also have perished in the fire. Members of the Bodmin constabulary are keen to interview him.

Tamsin forced down the lump in her throat. *Finneas Methenwyck.* Rose's husband. "Where did you find this?"

"In my grandfather's papers. It seems he had an interest in the monks of Medmenham Abbey."

"Who are they?"

"Have a look at the rest of the papers and then I'll explain."

She put the newspaper face down on the table and pulled the last remaining papers from the envelope.

On the top was a drawing, a cartoon. A man running down a street—London, she'd guess from the houses and the streetlamps. His long black legs and coattails flying and an angry group of men chasing him. Tucked under one arm was something that looked remarkably like a mermaid—flowing black curly hair, almost as untamed as her own, trailing to the ground, and a fishlike tail curving around his upper leg, and dangling from the fingers of his right hand—her heart almost ceased beating—was a platypus. "What is this?"

"A satirical print, a lampoon, a very popular way of making social comment. The magazine *Punch* is the master these days. Read what is written underneath."

Tamsin unrolled the remainder of the sheet of paper, hardly able to believe her eyes. "'*Nullius in Verba*.' The motto of the Royal Society."

"I think we can safely assume that Rose took the sketchbook to England."

"Following up on Winton's request to present his findings. I wonder why he didn't go himself."

Shaw shrugged. "One of the many things we'll never know."

"Who is the man?"

"No idea. A few theories, but if this is anything to go by, Rose didn't succeed with the Royal Society."

"So she brought the sketchbook back to Australia, and Winton's research was never acknowledged."

"That and the fact Banks died in June 1820, only a matter of days after the lampoon was published."

"And Rose and Finneas Methenwyck came to Australia."

"In December 1820, aboard the *Neptune*. Rose Winton may have left Australia, but Mrs. Finneas Methenwyck returned with her husband. That's why I missed it in the shipping records. They left almost immediately after the fire."

"How on earth did you find all this out?"

The corners of his mouth turned up, making the dimples she'd missed so much appear. "One of the few advantages of working for my father. That devious and rather nasty job I had provided me with a lot of contacts. Combine it with calling in some long overdue favors, my grandfather's passion for the history of Oxford and the surrounding area, plus Lovedale's help and a bit of a vivid imagination, and I think I've filled in the blanks." He drained his glass and put it down on the table. "A series of telegrams have been going back and forth to a company of solicitors in Bodmin. They've done some serious digging. A lot relies on local hearsay, nothing written down, so no proof. So many questions and we'll never really know all the answers."

"Is there anything left of Wyck Hall?"

"Not a lot. No one ever lived there again. Only a couple of old chimneys. A walled garden with a gravestone, which reminds me . . . a little bit of information that I stumbled across in my research. Your name."

"Tamsin or Alleyn?"

"Tamsin. I remember you saying you believed it belonged to a Cornish witch."

The man had a memory like an elephant. She'd always thought her strange name had been some deliberate ploy on her parents' part to label her as different.

"It's Cornish, the female form of Tomas."

"Tomas! Granfer Tomas Trevan. Jenifer's granfer."

"Whose tombstone still stands in the walled garden at Wyck Hall. I'd hazard a guess that's why. You'll never really know."

There were lots of things she'd never really know, but there were plenty she did, and she'd embrace them with open arms.

"And now to the not-so-pleasant side of the story. Apparently Methenwyck had a penchant for young girls. In his youth he attended the meetings at Medmenham Abbey, popularly known as the Hellfire Club. Have you heard of it?"

"Who hasn't? Though I was never very sure how much was truth and how much fiction. A club for high-society rakes established in the eighteenth century—the meeting place of men of quality, politicians and the like. I think something to do with Brooks's. How on earth did you find all this out?"

"Luck more than judgment. When Father checked the land title and mentioned the Methenwyck name, it rang a bell with me. I'd been unpacking Grandfather's books. Among them I found a ledger, a Cellar Book, which recorded the accounts and attendance of some of the meetings held at Medmenham Abbey. Methenwyck's name was listed. And then in the most amazing quirk of fate, it was Mrs. Rushworth who sealed it. She stumbled on an account of Wyck Hall burning down in an old newspaper Grandfather had tucked into the ledger when she came and tried to bribe me with the library here."

So that was how the boxes came to have his name stenciled on them.

"That's what led me to Cornwall. Around the same time as the club was disbanded, Methenwyck inherited Wyck Hall from an uncle and he left London. About the only thing he took with him was his penchant for the club's mock ceremonies and pagan rites. He created his own club and used to hold rituals in one of the ancient barrows on Bodmin Moor—combined them with hunting parties to celebrate various dates on the old calendar. Nobody thought too much about it, the aristocracy doing what they did, until someone noticed the spate of young girls mysteriously disappearing. Caroline Methenwyck—"

"Caroline . . . Caroline Methenwyck. *CM*. The handkerchief with the faded initials, the embroidery picked and pulled."

"*Lady* Caroline Methenwyck. She and Methenwyck never produced any children. They took her brother's son, Julian Barrington, as their ward."

"Barrington. The man Jenifer was assigned to when she first arrived in Australia."

"His son, yes."

Before her eyes she could see the pieces coming together, the links in the chain snapping shut, inextricably joining the past and the future.

"Born in Australia."

"Jenifer's child. I think it is fair to assume that."

"Rose's brother. And he inherited Wyck Hall?"

"No, remember the report of the fire? He died at the same time as Lord Methenwyck. Back to the rumors, then. Locals say Finneas was responsible for the fire and that's why he fled the country, married

Rose, and came to Australia. It's another of those things we'll never know."

"So many questions, their answers buried in the past. Did Finneas inherit the title?"

"I wondered that. I checked in Debrett's and the Methenwycks weren't titled. That was just another hoax in a long line, an affectation Methenwyck perpetrated. I suspect it sprang from his other title: Lord High Master of the Wyck Barrow. And Julian, Jenifer's son, thought to follow in his footsteps and cement his inheritance."

"What happened to Caroline?"

"She lived in the family's London home and died not long after the fire."

Tamsin flicked through the papers until she reached the last one. Smaller, old—not a copy.

"And what's this?" She looked up at him and then looked down, too impatient to wait. "It's a pardon."

"Not just a pardon but an Absolute Pardon. It means Jenifer Trevan's sentence was completely remitted."

A smile crossed her lips. "So she was free to return to Cornwall."

"It would seem so."

"Granfer's girl. How dreadful being sent away from everything and everyone you knew and loved for a crime you didn't commit."

"And that's the last bit of the puzzle. There's no proof, but local rumor has it that one of Lady Methenwyck's favorite scullery maids caught Lord Methenwyck's eye and she knew she would be the next girl to disappear. So rather than see her die on his sacrificial altar, Lady Methenwyck set the girl up. Planted the Methenwyck rose, a bloody great carved emerald, on her and she was accused of stealing it."

"But in those days she would have hanged."

"Mad King George saved her. To celebrate his return to sanity in May 1789, her sentence, and that of all other condemned women, was respited. Instead, they were transported 'to parts beyond the sea.'"

"On the *Lady Juliana*. That's how she ended up in Australia." Tamsin delved into her pocket and gazed down at the daguerreotype in her hand, running her thumb over the surface. "Do you think they were happy?"

"I think Rose learned to accept all life threw at her and to forgive, and that's the most important thing. Maybe she'd decided there were things more important than ambition."

Perhaps that was the apology she was waiting for.

"Now, can I tell you the real reason I'm here?"

"You didn't come to tell me this?"

Something shifted; only someone who truly cared would have gone to all this trouble.

"I came to give you this." He put a small, square box on the table and opened it. A rose-gold ring, the pinkish color highlighting a carved emerald, sat nestled on a stained cushion of threadbare satin.

She swallowed, her hands shaking, and picked up the box. "Is this the ring that Jenifer was accused of stealing?"

"Lovedale assures me it is. He asked me to give it to you. Kelly had it in his safe deposit box, perhaps the very reason he was so determined to find the person who should inherit. It's where your story began."

"Come with me. I'll show you where my story began." Tamsin stood and held out her hand. He grasped it tight, gave a squeeze, and stepped up beside her.

"Where are we going?"

"My turn. Wait and see."

The long, dry grass brushed at her skirt and little puffs of dust rose around her feet. It was as though she were walking on air. When they reached the stepping stones across the brook, she dropped Shaw's hand and lifted her skirt above her calves. "This way. It's not too tricky; just be careful because the stones can be slippery." Or so she'd discovered in the past days. She'd come every afternoon to see Gayadin and help her clear the area around the headstones and the path leading to her tumbledown cottage.

As she suspected, the old woman was waiting, sitting with her back resting against Rose's headstone, plaiting the long strands of grass.

"I've brought someone to meet you. Gayadin, this is Shaw, Shaw Everdene. Shaw, this is Gayadin. She knew my grandmother and my great-grandmother. They were friends of hers."

"We all friends." Gayadin dropped her eyes to her plaiting, but a gentle smile played on her face.

There was no need to show Shaw the headstones. He spotted them in an instant and walked slowly around, reading the inscriptions and running the palm of his hand over the engraving. Finally he let out a long, long sigh. "And to think that very evening we sat and watched the platypus we were so close to the truth."

"As I said, this is where my story began, and this is where it will end."

"You lucky you got so many stories. Make sure they don't get lost."

"That won't happen, Gayadin. I promise you that." Tamsin wiped away the solitary tear trickling down her cheek.

Shaw's hand clasped her fingers, held them tight and warm.

"Can you imagine how Rose must have felt? Shunned by the Royal Society, then discovering her mother's sentence was nothing but malicious deceptions, a string of deliberately fabricated falsehoods masquerading as the truth."

He pulled her into his arms and held her tight. "There'll be no more falsehoods, no more lies. That's my promise to you."

Epilogue

Wollombi, New South Wales
1912

"What have you got there?"

Tamsin shaded her eyes to better appreciate her daughter's gap-toothed smile as she sat on her father's shoulders, arms stretched wide.

"An invitation."

Shaw hoisted the girl over his head, then settled her on the ground, patting her coal-black curls as she tottered into her mother's embrace. She swung her up onto the sandstone bench next to her. "Sit quietly and maybe they'll come."

The little girl slapped her chubby forefinger over her lips. "Shh! Mallangong time."

"Is there room for me?"

"Always. Make room for Pa, Rose."

The little girl shuffled closer, eyes riveted on the water in front of her.

Tamsin handed the invitation to Shaw. He scanned the words and his eyebrows disappeared into the thick thatch of hair dangling over his eyes. "Are you going?"

"Of course. I feel a little bit of a fraud, though. Charles Winton was no relation of mine."

"But Rose was, and Charles was the father of her heart."

"True. I suppose that makes him the great-great-grandfather of my heart."

"You can hardly refuse an invitation like this."

"Read it to me."

"You must know it word for word. You've been sitting out here looking at it for the last hour."

"I do, but I'd like to hear it again."

> The Royal Society of New South Wales requests the attendance of Mrs. Tamsin Everdene at the Admission Day Ceremony on the fourth day of July, 1912, to accept on behalf of Charles Winton a Posthumous Honorary Fellowship for his substantial contribution to furthering the natural knowledge of *Ornithorhynchus anatinus*.

Historical Note

In 1835, the *Penny Magazine of the Society for the Diffusion of Useful Knowledge* ran a front-page article about the platypus. It stated, "Among the strange and interesting productions of that little explored country, Australia, not one is so anomalous, so wonderful, such a stumbling block to the naturalist, as the Ornithorhynchus platypus or as it is termed by the colonialists the water mole. Its first discovery created the utmost surprise; nor has the feeling much abated." Almost two hundred years later, this still holds true. From the Dreamtime stories to the comparison of human and platypus genomes, the platypus continues to fascinate.

I chose to use *platypus* for both the singular and plural noun, but it is still an ongoing debate. Some dictionaries state the accepted plural as *platypuses*, then add, particularly in scientific and conservation contexts, *platypus*.

Should you wish to discover more, I thoroughly recommend Ann Moyal's book *Platypus: The Extraordinary Story of How a Curious Creature Baffled the World*.

The great platypus debate began in 1799, when Governor John Hunter watched an Aborigine spear a "small Amphibious Animal of the Mole Kind" and sent the skin, preserved in a keg of spirits, to the Literary and Philosophical Society of Newcastle-upon-Tyne.

However, it was one line in an old journal that sparked my story. It suggested Sir Joseph Banks had already received a strange pelt from an "unknown source" in the antipodes before Hunter's discovery. I have no idea whether this is true. And if it was, why would Sir Joseph have kept quiet?

And so, my story began. Although you may recognize some of the characters and settings, this is a work of fiction. Charles Winton did not exist, nor did any of the other major players in *The Naturalist's Daughter*, except in my imagination.

Acknowledgements

I'd like to begin by acknowledging the Traditional Owners of the lands on which this story takes place and pay my respects to Elders both past and present.

Thanks to so many people. Firstly, my publisher, Jo Mackay, and all the fabulous team at HQ. Jo and Annabel, your belief and support in this book has been both flattering and heartwarming. I must also thank both Alex Craig and Julie Breihan for their expert and insightful editing. I'm still not quite sure how they managed to get their heads around that timeline! And in the US, my thanks to Amanda Bostic and every member of the Harper Muse team. It has been a pleasure and a privilege to work with every one of you.

As always, my love and thanks to my team of long-suffering writing friends, without whom my books would never see the light of day. I owe you all more than I can ever repay. And, most especially, Charles—the most patient and long-suffering plot wrangler in the business!

Discussion Questions

1. Historical fiction books often give us insight into the past. What information was new or surprising to you as you read this book?
2. Tamsin goes on quite the hunt for the sketchbook's origins and learns a lot about her own heritage in the process. Have you researched your heritage or family tree? What was that like for you?
3. Tamsin didn't want to be a doctor, as her mother had dreamed for her, and Shaw didn't want to be a lawyer, as his father expected. Have you ever felt pressure to fulfill a role you didn't want? What happened?
4. Rose is ridiculed at the Royal Society meeting and essentially run out of the room. How might you have reacted if you were in Rose's shoes?
5. Were you surprised by the revelation of Julian's (and Lord Methynwyck's) depravity? What did you think about that plot twist?
6. What do you make of Caroline Methynwyck and the motivation behind her actions? Do you have any sympathy for her? Why or why not?

7. How do you think the fire in the Methynwyck home started? What do you think happened?
8. Tea Cooper's books often touch on women's issues of the day, such as the obstacles women faced in their work toward equality with men. What issues came up in this book?

About the Author

Tea Cooper is an established Australian author of historical fiction. In a past life she was a teacher, a journalist, and a farmer. These days she haunts museums and indulges her passion for storytelling. She is the internationally bestselling author of several novels, including *The Naturalist's Daughter*; the *USA TODAY* bestselling *The Woman in the Green Dress*; *The Girl in the Painting*; *The Cartographer's Secret*, winner of the prestigious Daphne du Maurier Award; and *The Fossil Hunter.*

---

teacooperauthor.com
Instagram: @tea_cooper
Facebook: @TeaCooper
Pinterest: @teacooperauthor